THE MAY BRIDE

THE
MAY BRIDE

A NOVEL *of* TUDOR ENGLAND

SUZANNAH DUNN

PEGASUS BOOKS
NEW YORK LONDON

THE MAY BRIDE

Pegasus Books LLC
80 Broad Street, 5th Floor
New York, NY 10004

ISBN: 978-1-60598-630-2

10 9 8 7 8 6 5 4 3 2 1

Printed in the United States of America
Distributed by W. W. Norton & Company, Inc.

Contents

MILK MOON

I

Twice my life has turned on the step of a girl through a doorway; first when I was fifteen and my new, first-ever sister-in-law came walking into Wolf Hall. The May trees were holding blossom as thick and thorough as snowfall when Katherine crossed our threshold as the twenty-one-year-old bride of my twenty-one-year-old brother. Two days on the road, but she was as fresh as a daisy in her buttercup silk. Thirty miles from her home to ours: the furthest she'd ever ventured and, to me, unthinkably far. An heiress in her own right in a minor way, she came stepping up to be daughter-in-law of a knight and wife of the Seymour heir. When she dipped her head beneath the lintel and then looked up at us, the bones at her throat opened like fingers in a gesture of greeting, and although she buttoned her lips, modesty itself, her smile swept regardless into her honey-coloured eyes. My brother's hand was at – not quite in – the small of her back.

I didn't stand a chance: looking back over thirteen years, that's what I see. In the very first instant, I was won over, and of course I was: I was fifteen and had been nowhere and done nothing, whereas Katherine was twenty-one and yellow-silk-clad and just married to the golden boy. Only a few years later, I'd be blaming myself for not having somehow *seen* . . . but seen *what*, really? What – really, honestly – was there to see, when she walked into Hall? She was just a girl, a lovely, light-stepping girl, smiling that smile of hers, and, back then, as giddy with goodwill as the rest of us.

A lifetime ago it might've been, that afternoon when we Seymours gathered to welcome Edward's May bride. We'd done our utmost, spending days cleaning and tidying the house, then taking the entire morning to dress, but as we stood there to receive the newly-weds, I fretted that our best still wasn't good enough. Edward was bringing home his bride and, quite possibly, we were letting him down. And if Katherine had expected us to be like her groom, she'd be disappointed, because, it occurred to me, we Seymours were nothing special: Edward, yes, but the rest of us were respectable and dependable and that was all we were. It was the first time I'd ever thought like that about my family; until then, for me, we just *were*. Now, thinking back, remembering us assembled there, I find myself marvelling at our innocent happiness, that it could ever have been possible.

So, there she was, Katherine, coming long-boned and loose-limbed towards us, and, in her wake, Edward: clever, cautious Edward. At twenty-one, he could've had several more years before being expected to marry but – typically decisive – he'd already chosen, and he'd chosen her, and of course he had: *just look at her*. I stood spellbound, drinking down the vision of her. She was at least as tall as him, and moved ahead of him with animal grace.

If I put myself in her shoes, coming across Hall towards us, the Seymour I find hardest to recognise is me. In no respect do I easily recognise my fifteen-year-old self, but least of all physically. Odd to think that back then I was a scrap of a thing; in those

4

days, I was quite often wearing my younger sister Elizabeth's hand-me-downs.

My new sister-in-law's first sight of me would have been obscured in part by Dottie, my nine-year-old sister, who was bobbing excitedly despite Elizabeth's jabbing at her back in a poor attempt to keep her in line. Dottie's delight was what Katherine saw first of us: her jiggling on the spot and her occasional Elizabeth-dealt lurch. I might have jiggled, too, I suppose, had I not been so ill at ease in my new kirtle. My mother had at last deemed me, at fifteen, to be of an age for a kirtle and gown; but Elizabeth, too, annoyingly – Elizabeth, a whole year younger than me! – just for my mother's convenience.

Beside Dottie was Margie, her junior by a year but, in contrast, admirably composed. Margie's eyes would have been trained on Katherine in naked appraisal: Margie's cool, grey, widely spaced eyes. No such circumspection from Antony – at seven, the baby of our family – who would've seen someone new to be subjected to his questions and challenges: How far can you hop? Would it be better to be blind or deaf? Behind me were my two older brothers: Harry and Thomas. Sandy-haired Harry's lack of physical resemblance to Edward must have struck Katherine but she'd have seen, too, how deeper ran the difference between them, Harry's being such an easy-going smile. Actually, Harry was raring to be off to Barbara's, thinking only of her and their own forthcoming nuptials. Thomas was just as keen to turn and go, but less cheerfully. He begrudged each and every success of Edward's, which, to him, was what Katherine was.

No wonder I was the one to fall so readily for Katherine. Look at me there: within our family, I was peculiarly alone, the eldest girl, my three older brothers so much more worldly than me but the children – Dottie, Margie, Antony – so much younger. True, Elizabeth was in the middle with me, but, being younger, she had it easy, shouldering none of my responsibilities, and anyway we never got along, and still don't.

As my mother bustled forward to greet her new daughter-in-law, I cringed to see her as Katherine might: bulky, flustered, frowzily dressed. We Seymours didn't stand on ceremony, had no airs and graces, which Katherine seemed to understand, responding fulsomely by clasping both of my mother's hands in her own. What a natural she was, this girl whom my brother had so cleverly and carefully chosen. How did my mother feel when Katherine's hands closed around her own? She herself had once been the bride to cross Wolf Hall's threshold – she'd been the one with the money and connections, though, and even several years, too, on her husband – and one day, in turn, this new daughter-in-law was to take her place as matriarch of the Seymour family.

And my father? Where was he? How odd that I can't locate him there in my mind's eye. In view of what later happened, it's as if he's taken cover. But he was never one to step forward if he could hang back, and he probably just stayed behind us, as gaunt and shadowed as my mother was flushed and dimply. For my parents, Katherine was the answer to all the prayers of their married life that their heir would marry well: her arrival was an end in itself. For me, I knew in my gut that her step across the threshold was the beginning of something, although at the time I couldn't have known it as anything but a change for the good.

If anyone was going to spoil the occasion, it would be Thomas and, duly, only a little later, at supper, he made his move. We'd endured a reading from Father James and some polite conversation about Katherine's parents' health when Thomas unwrapped his roll from its linen, asking, 'Anyone want this?' but by which time it was in the air on its way to his sister-in-law. She caught it before she knew: there it was in the palm of her raised hand, which stayed raised as she looked to the little ones for applause. Antony couldn't stop himself – 'Yeeesss!' – and a squeal escaped

6

Dottie despite her fingertips pressed to her lips. Katherine's own delayed exhalation was as exuberant as a laugh. I was still trying to take in what I'd seen; the Seymours didn't lob bread rolls, or indeed anything else, at guests. Not that Katherine was, strictly speaking, a guest.

'Thomas!' It was all my mother could do to utter his name, my father rushing to back her up, 'Thomas!', and then Margie having to have her say, 'Thomas!', which had my mother turning on her, 'Margery!' Down the table, Father James murmured an oath. Elizabeth was tutting louder than should have been physically possible, and sweet-natured Harry was rubbing his face as if to erase what he'd had to see.

And Thomas? Well, he affected a suitably sheepish look, but only just, the smirk still detectable. He'd had an instinct about Katherine and had taken a gamble which, in his view, paid off when she'd shown herself to be game. And if truth be told, I doubt anyone around that table was all that displeased to have seen it.

Anyone except Edward, that is, who, beside his new wife on the bench, had been perilously close to the trajectory of that roll. He looked levelly at Thomas and, although restrained, his tone was all the more deadly for it: 'Apologise.'

Thomas must have anticipated it, Edward being Edward in any case but now, too, being Katherine's knight in shining armour, yet, incredibly, he still managed to bridle: a jut of the chin and a slouch that was as close to a swagger as he could manage on a bench.

Katherine interjected, conciliatory, or tried to – 'Really, Edward, it's—' but he cut across her to demand of his brother: 'Apologise.' Directed at Thomas, that all too palpable disgust was actually, I sensed, for every one of us: for admiring his wife's catch and for being slow to take Thomas properly to task. And thus reprimanded, we were all subdued; Katherine, too, judging from the bowing of her head and her surreptitious discarding of that briefly fêted roll, which lay friendless near the middle of the table. What else could she have done, though, but catch it? I wanted to whisper down the table to her, Not you, he's not angry with you. But, actually, he probably was. Thomas had thrown it and even though Katherine couldn't have done otherwise, she'd caught it, which, in Edward's eyes, made them partners in crime.

And worse, Thomas was now going to stand up to Edward, to pick a fight. If any of us had been hoping that Edward's getting married would improve Thomas's attitude to him, we were disappointed. I closed my eyes as if that would also close my ears, but then came the surprise: Thomas launching himself into his apology, disarmingly direct, faultlessly sincere, utterly charming, 'I'm really sorry, Katherine; that was unforgivable of me.'

Forgive him, though, she did – 'No, really' – and with a merry little laugh. So, then, incredibly, it was Edward, for making too much of it, who looked the fool.

Nevertheless, the evening recovered to end well, and I should have slept soundly that night in the knowledge that my brother had made a brilliant choice of bride. But I was quite unable to settle. In the bed that I shared with my three sisters, I lay awake for a long time because when my new sister-in-law had walked through our doorway, I'd had my eyes opened to something. Unwittingly, she'd as good as broken the news to me. I had been growing up believing that, one day, in some years' time, that would be me: the bride. In so much as I ever gave it any thought – scrap of a thing as, back then, I still was – that, I felt, was what would be happening. However unlikely a prospect it had seemed to me, there had always been a fair bit of time still ahead and somehow – I'd had faith – it would happen. There I would be, one day, grown up, and a wife.

That night, though, as I tried and failed to sleep, I began to suspect that it wouldn't be happening for me as it had just happened for her: a bride adored, family dazzled. I was nothing like her: by comparison I was plain and dull, but that wasn't news and didn't even particularly bother me, being just the way it was; the revelation was that it mattered. I'd been brought up believing that it was enough for me to be diligent and dependable. What was clear that night, though, was that if I weren't adorable and dazzling, then no one like Edward would ever be ushering me into his family home. And that, too, I realised on that night: I wanted someone like Edward, or as much like Edward as someone like me could expect. I'd glimpsed our newly-weds strolling after supper in the flower garden; she in front of him, walking backwards, laughing as she spoke, while he hung on her every word. No one – I knew it, I just knew it – was ever going to love me as he loved her, and, that night, I keenly felt the loss of it.

Lying there in that suffocating darkness, I wondered what, really, I'd been thinking. I *hadn't*, I realised, which was precisely the problem: I *hadn't* been thinking. I'd grown up taking my mother at her word that it was enough for me to be mild-mannered, hard-working and sensible: enough to enable a girl to marry well, or well enough for someone like me. But what I'd seen when Katherine had walked into Hall, and then when she'd caught that bread roll, was that she wasn't sensible in the least, and look who'd married *her*.

Panic gripped me: the best I could hope for, it seemed to me during that interminable darkness, was a several-times widower, a man prepared to settle for a good housekeeper and stepmother to his children. I saw my future that night and it looked to be a fate worse than death. A husband with gout, as I saw it, and a houseful of hard-done-by children. Worse, though – far worse – would be to fail to marry at all, because then there'd be no chance of babies of my own. No kidskin babies of my own; no hay-scented babies with hair that's a joke on them (*call that hair?*); no babies with bizarrely big chuckles and poorly aimed, splay-fingered, too-vigorous clapping.

9

I'd been old enough when Dottie, Margie and Antony had been born to be able to relish their babyhoods. I'd stood over the crib marvelling how sleep claimed them, how they lay abandoned to it, how it burned in them like a fever but then suddenly they'd open their eyes and they were free: *what's next?* I'd loved how they presided over a room, subjecting us to scrutiny as if they were king or queen, although Antony's shy delight in our company had had him act more like an honoured guest. Even at seven he lacked the newly found composure of his sisters: gloriously gangly, made of angles, he looked like a scribble. On the rare occasions when he seemed to be still, he was, if you looked closely, swaying or drumming his heels, the life in him close to the surface like a pulse in a tender spot. However vigilant I was – and it was me back then whose job it was to take care of him – his hair and nails were always too long and his clothes too small. His body was faintly preposterous on him, like sticky buds on his back.

Who knows how well our newcomer slept on the other side of my wall, that night, but I barely slept at all. It was a long night, for me, that first of Katherine's beneath our roof, when I faced the prospect that I might never be anything much to anyone nor sleep anywhere else. Quite possibly, I realised, I would be staying for ever at Wolf Hall, tolerated and trying my best to make myself useful while everyone around me either grew up and left or grew old and died. And if so, there would be no end of nights exactly like that one until I was carried from the bed to be lowered into the chapel floor. No end to it: the surreptitious settling of my room's floorboards in their particular, precisely executed steps, and, above, in the roof, scattered mouse-rattle. Beyond the shutters, there would always be the jeering of the sheep; and beyond the door, my father's dogs left to their own devices, the whispering of their nails on flagstones as they dared to nose around the unpeopled stairwell.

2

Such a bad night made the following morning's prayers a trial, and my attention kept drifting across chapel to my new sister-in-law in the idle hope of catching a glimpse of the mischief I'd seen in her eyes the day before. No luck: those eyes were closed, and her head bowed. She was the very picture of devotion, which put Edward to shame because for all his earnest efforts elsewhere, in chapel he could never quite hide an impatience. To one side of me, Elizabeth picked at a hangnail; to the other, Thomas yawned repeatedly, and his breath smelled of ale.

After prayers, Edward rode off with my father to Eaton on business, leaving his bride to look expectantly to her new mother-in-law: what could she do to help? My mother was thrown; she had failed to anticipate this; having focused on the wedding and Katherine's arrival at our house. She had looked no further ahead. She hadn't had a daughter-in-law before, didn't know what to do with one.

'Oh, Katherine . . .' She played for time, cast around. 'It's a lovely day; why don't you . . .' and she indicated the door, the garden beyond it.

Katherine made a show of being amused – the very idea! – and shook her head as if what my mother had said was the obvious joke to be made before the pair of them could get down to the business of being women together in the house. Leaving them to it, I embarked on the stairs. My mother was already in her apron and it would be easiest for her to take her new daughter-in-law along with her to the kitchen, to assist Bax, our cook, but then I heard her saying, 'Why don't you lend Jane a hand?'

Inwardly, I reeled: this shouldn't be falling to me; and today of all days, after the night I'd had, I didn't feel like doing my mother any favours. I hadn't had a sister-in-law before: I had no idea how much of 'a hand' I should expect from her, nor from which tasks I should shield her. Crucially, I had no idea what to say to her. Twenty-one to my fifteen, and such a natural by comparison with clueless me; she was a daunting prospect.

And worse: what came first every day was the dirty work. My first job of the day was to clean and tidy our room – mine and my sisters' – which, I recalled in a fluster, had been left in considerable disarray. No one had as much as emptied the pot. I'd woken late and listless, and, anyway, we hadn't been expecting a visitor to our room, had we. Not only did I not want my perfect new sister-in-law to see our squalor, but there was also my shameful ineptitude with my sisters. I was supposed to supervise them – they were supposed to help me – but I was pitifully useless in the face of Elizabeth's truculence, Dottie's distractedness, Margie's sense of superiority, and the sad truth was that I tended to give up on them, let them get away with it and do most of the work myself. It was quicker that way, and easier, more peaceful.

Katherine couldn't be deflected, though, and up those stairs she came. But that morning, up in our room, she more than proved her worth, toiling efficiently alongside me and enthusing the girls so that everything was put straight in no time. The pot was emptied by Elizabeth, wonder of wonders, who further excelled herself by vigorously sweeping the floor and even going so far as to shake the carpet from the window. The rest of us contented ourselves with less heroic tasks: replenishing the water jugs, spreading the bedding for airing, sorting the laundry and carrying some of it outside to Lil and Moll, who were taking advantage of the good weather to do some washing.

When Katherine drew me aside at the door and whispered, 'Which one's which?' I paused to consider how to pitch the answer. My mother would've gone for a tactful, respectful, 'Moll's the more experienced,' something Moll never let us forget, which Elizabeth would've translated as 'old' although actually Moll was nowhere near as old as my mother (older than Lil, though, who was, by comparison, a girl, the pair of them being opposites in every way). I'd once heard Thomas describe Moll as 'girthly', and for the briefest moment I was tempted before opting for something less offensive but as indisputable: 'Moll's the one doing all the talking.'

Katherine herself didn't talk much while she worked, humming tunelessly instead, which should have been irritating but, surprisingly, was cheering. Whenever she did speak up, it was to express what seemed to be genuine pleasure in the various aspects and simple contents of our room: the view from the window, the embroidered coverlet on our bed, the little walnut stool in the corner, even the pungency of the flea-repelling wormwood scattered under our bed. She herself was a breath of fresh air: that was how I felt about her that first morning. Her company made light work of the drudgery, and, really, how better to endear herself to me? Me, of all of the Seymours. I'd had no sense before then of having been biding my time at Wolf Hall, but that morning, whenever I glimpsed her across my room, I'd think, What took you so long?

When we'd worked our way through the house – sweeping and shaking carpets and curtains, wiping and polishing, collecting and replacing candle-stubs – we ended up in the long gallery, along which she skipped with arms outstretched as if to brush her fingertips along the panelling at either side in celebration of the length and breadth of it. Exhilarating though it was to watch her take off across those floorboards, I knew even by then that she didn't have to skip into a room to light it up. She went into any room looking for the pleasures it could offer her, simple though they might well be, which for me was an eye-opener, because I'd only ever gone into rooms looking for what needed to be done. It didn't occur to me then that such *joie de vivre* might bring its own dangers.

When the house was in order, Elizabeth took Margie to help her set the places for dinner and got rid of Dottie by sending her to pick posies for the tables (that old trick), so Katherine and I returned to the laundry pile for a proper sifting because, if the weather were to hold, Lil and Moll might progress to bleaching and we should give them enough to keep them busy. And that was when we had our first proper conversation, just the two of us. Setting to the task, I mentioned that the girls' laundry was my job while my mother did my father's and the boys', but then worried I'd said too much because perhaps Katherine would want to be the one, now, responsible for Edward's; after all, he was no longer one of the boys, but her husband. How to backtrack, though, I worried, without drawing attention to the prospect of his underclothes in her hands, her intimate scrutiny of them for blemishes and unravellings? Luckily for me, she didn't seem to have heard; she was still considering the girls' laundry.

'I had it easy,' she said, frowning at the pile, 'with there only being the two of us, my sister and me.'

It was unimaginable to me, so small a family.

'I'm the younger,' she told me, although of course I already knew it, but there was a twinkle to the way she said it, as if to suggest that, in being the younger, she'd been getting away with something. 'The naughty one.'

That I doubted; she was merely having fun: Edward would never have married someone who was 'naughty'.

'Nancy was always such a goody-goody,' and this accusation of hers was voiced just as pleasantly. At that, though, I was a little uneasy, because I could be said to be a 'goody-goody' in our household. Had I been said to be a goody-goody? Had Edward said it to her? He probably hadn't actually said 'goody-goody', because surely the same could be said of him.

'Except she never really was,' Katherine cheerfully contradicted herself, 'because no one ever really is, are they? What she was good at was never getting caught.' And this was said admiringly before she glanced at the door and lowered her voice to admit, 'It was always me who was still – you know – making the face when my father turned around. There was Nancy, all butter-wouldn't-melt . . . and then there was me . . .'

She said it as if I'd sympathise, as if I'd spent my own childhood making faces behind my own father's back, whereas I didn't recall ever having done such a thing and probably wouldn't even have known what face to make. Not that he'd have minded, probably, if I had, and that was if he'd even noticed, which he almost certainly wouldn't have. But then again, who knew what I'd have been like if I'd had a sister like her? If she'd have been at Wolf Hall to egg me on, I felt, perhaps I would indeed have done it. She'd had her sister to encourage her, even if that sister did then leave her in the lurch; whereas Elizabeth had never lowered herself so much as to catch my eye.

'I was never quick enough,' she lamented merrily, 'or I just didn't think or something – oh, I don't know, I don't know – but whenever my father turned around, it was always just me who was making that face.'

And her laugh came as her smile had done the day before, escaping from her, running away with her, and this time it snatched up my own and took it with it as I imagined her at eight years old, gawky and spindly, haplessly overstepping the mark, her own silliness having gone on for a moment too long, leaving her cruelly uncovered and having to hope for mercy. At eight, I recalled, Edward had had to step up to be the eldest son, when John – a year older – had died. So, Edward would have been serious-minded even at eight, or especially at eight. But then we Seymours in general were a stoic lot. My new sister-in-law, though, seemed utterly unlike that, and my heart opened to her.

'Nancy's clever,' Katherine was saying, approvingly but rue-fully, the implication being that in this, they differed. Again, I was sure she was merely making fun of herself. 'She can read and write really well, whereas me: oh, it makes no sense to me, I'm useless – it just dances around in front of my eyes.' Eyes which she now flicked skywards in exasperation. 'I "don't concentrate".' The precise annunciation made clear she was quoting. 'But . . .' She shrugged jauntily: Who cares?

Then, as an afterthought, 'Did you have a tutor?'

'Father James.' I resisted adding 'for all the good it did me'. I'd liked to have said that words danced in front of my eyes, but, sadly, nothing so lively; they lay on the page and I crawled my way through them. Edward had gone to university at Oxford but the rest of us had learned whatever we'd managed to learn from Father James.

Katherine sighed, which I took to mean that although Father James's tuition might not have been much, nor much fun, it was more than she'd had. Well, perhaps if not bookish, I decided, then my brother would have chosen for a wife someone who was naturally astute. Thinking back, what amazes me is that I assumed Edward would be as sensible as in other spheres of his life when it came to matters of the heart.

3

Strange, too, that I didn't recognise Edward's ambitiousness for what it was. Then again, how could I have? I'd never come across ambition, not really. My father took his duties very seriously, but that's not the same. And Thomas? Well, back then, Thomas was a fledgling; but, anyway, the nature of his aspirations – for material gain, personal advantage – has always been quite distinct from Edward's. As is everyone's at court, it seems to me, with the possible exception of Cromwell's. Cromwell and Edward: perhaps, then, Edward's is a new kind of ambition, and perhaps I couldn't have recognised it back at Wolf Hall, even if I'd known to look. Come to think of it, perhaps he didn't, at that stage, even quite recognise it himself. In retrospect, it's clear that his new wife didn't.

What I did know was that he was hardworking and exceptionally able, and by the time I was fifteen I'd picked up enough from eavesdropping to know he was keen to improve the lives of our tenants and all the men and women on whom my father had to pass judgement in his capacity as a Justice of the Peace. Edward has always been able to see clearly where there are changes that can be made; he has an instinct for what can and can't be done. And if anything can be done, he's almost certainly the one to do it, the one with the capabilities and the resolve. That's Edward's particular gift, I think: not only to know what can and can't be done, but to know exactly what he's capable and incapable of. It's that practical bent that makes him lethal.

Perhaps we aren't so dissimilar after all.

If I was oblivious to how ambitious he was, I did realise that he was quite unlike everyone else at home. He wasn't often around during my childhood, what with his years in Oxford and then his assisting my father in the running of family business; and then, around the time that he married, he began to be away at court, with the help of our distant cousin Francis Bryan, whenever occasion could be found. All of which meant that whenever he came back to us, he was invigoratingly different from everyone else. None of my father's dithering, Harry's loping and mooching, Thomas's swagger; none of my father's vagueness, Harry's undisguised lack of interest, Thomas's verbal sparring. And because being home was a novelty for him, he was able to be interested in us, to give measured responses even to Antony's various madnesses and Elizabeth's endless gripes.

Back when I was fifteen and he was twenty-one, I'd have simply said that my eldest brother was wonderful: it was as simple as that, for me. Not that I'd have said it to his face, but, then, I didn't say much at all to him, didn't dare, was hopelessly shy of him. Good job, too, because he'd have failed to appreciate it, partly on principle – hero-worship being unhealthy – but also because he would, I think, have been genuinely perplexed. Judging from the habitual worried frown and the diligence with which he undertook his various duties, I suspect he considered himself barely to measure up as the eldest Seymour son.

I didn't care what he'd read in books at Oxford, nor was I properly conscious, then, of how unusual were his ideas about the lives of ordinary people. Books and new ideas, no: it was his worldliness that impressed me, his having been places and seen things. Not that he bragged, as Thomas did: Thomas only had to go to horrid old Salisbury for the day for us to suffer months of hearing how amazing it was.

Not from Edward himself but from my mother did I know that at thirteen he'd waded from a run-aground ship to the French shore behind our king's bedraggled eighteen-year-old sister. Edward was one of three pages at her marriage to the old French king and he saw her laughing as she held her soaked gown up around her knees because she guessed (correctly) that the marriage – the king – wouldn't last long and she'd soon be free.

Then, a year before he himself had married, he'd accompanied my father to join the hundreds of knights and nobles welcoming the Spanish Emperor to England. He had stayed at inns in Canterbury, Sittingbourne and Greenwich before riding into London behind the silk- and ermine-clad Archbishop Wolsey and his hundreds of servants liveried in crimson velvet. There in London he had watched pageants, and at Greenwich, jousts. All this he'd done. When he arrived back home, we crowded around him in the parlour and he opened his hand to reveal, in his palm, something pebble-sized and dun-coloured.

'What's that?' asked Elizabeth, curl-nosed.

'An acorn,' he'd said, unperturbed by the less than rapturous reception. 'Or, rather, it isn't: it's a piece of wood that's been turned to make an acorn, and there were two-and-a-half thousand of them. Two-and-a-half thousand, that's what Mr Gibson said, and for just five minutes on stage.'

Did he think that good or bad? I couldn't tell.

'Who's Mr Gibson?' Margie, keen as ever to establish the facts.

The gentleman, Edward said, who was in charge of all the court entertainments. So, Edward knew such a man; he'd actually conversed with him. But he told us so little of life at court, whether because he didn't want to turn our heads or because he was unimpressed, I still don't know. Perhaps both. He didn't tell us about the woodland scene to which that acorn had belonged: the wood-turned and fabric-sewn hawthorns, oaks, maples, hazels and ferns; the papier-mâché beasts and birds; the centrepiece, a castle holding a silk-flower-garlanded, crowd-pleasing maiden. It was my father who described all that for us, just as he described the joust, of which that scene was merely one of many interludes. It was from my father that we learned of the king and queen's gold-canopied stand and the king's newly minted silver armour, and the hundreds of horses, grooms and footmen, players and heralds dressed in white velvet and gold damask. I can see, now, how odd it must've been for Edward, back in those days, having seen all that he'd seen, to have to come home to us: we Seymours with our clothes darned and handed down, our food plain and predictable, our horses tired and our opinions – if we had them, and if we expressed them – poorly informed.

Yet he was still a country boy at heart, because he'd gone ahead and married a local girl. He could have waited to marry until he fell for a girl at court, which was probably what my parents expected and what Francis Bryan, his mentor, had hoped. At twenty-one, Edward had yet to make his way. Well, he'd be making his way with a wife already at his side, I thought at the time, and how could Katherine fail to be an asset? On that first day of hers at Wolf Hall, sitting across that laundry pile from her, I pondered how it might have happened between the two of them.

Our families went way back but were separated by two days' ride. Katherine had visited us once, I'd been told, when she was nine; I'd been three and had no memory of it. Ten years later, our father and Edward had made the journey to her Horton home on business, and then Edward had found reason to go again, alone, and again and again. I imagined Katherine's goody-goody sister had been too busy at virginals practice to entertain him, so

Katherine had been the one to sit with him, in the company of her father, enquiring about his journey and, perhaps, the family to whom he'd be returning. She might have told him something of life on the Horton estate, which he'd have drunk down because he was an interested listener, his serious-mindedness never taking him away from the world but deeper into it.

Then perhaps, one late afternoon, the pair of them ventured into the garden, stopping only at the edge in the haze of dusk and beyond the earshot of anyone at a window. Precisely calibrated; what they could get away with. Just a little too far from the house and a little too late in the day. Nothing spoken of it, but nevertheless the pair of them complicit. That might have been all it was, but it would have been enough; it might have been the start. That's what I dreamt up for them, when I was fifteen, and I suspect I wasn't far wrong; I suspect there was never anything very complicated about it.

And why should there have been? That's what we Seymours would have thought, at the time. Why not follow one's heart in matters of the heart? It all looked set to be perfect. How ideal his bride seemed, that first evening, as she settled to her embroidery in the parlour, stitching steadily and absorbed by the rhythm of it. I was stitching, too, whereas my mother was one for cards at the end of the day, turning determined and devious, pitting herself against Elizabeth, who was, of course, more than a match for her. Dottie and Margie were playing shovelboard, which, although they played noisily, was preferable to Dottie's plodding practice on the virginals. Antony was learning chess under Thomas's tutelage, so that evening, like many others during that spring and summer, was punctuated by exclamations of dismay at moves good or bad or puzzling. Harry was over at Barbara's. Edward was looking through paperwork, briefly, with my father, whose long eyelids were creeping longer, and then played his lute, head cocked as if listening for an element not easily discernible.

Father James muscled in among the dogs at the fireside, ostensibly reading but actually dozing.

It was an evening like any other for us, that first evening of Katherine's, except that we younger Seymours, who still embroidered solely in black, had rarely seen the likes of the vivid silks in our sister-in-law's folded wallet. I glimpsed a creamy quince, a dusky raspberry, a blaring cornflower blue, and the zingy sweet green of wild garlic.

Margie raised it: 'Where d'you get those?'

'London.'

'London?' Dottie was round-eyed. 'You went to London?'

'My father's steward did.'

Margie frowned, sceptical. 'And he knows how to buy silks?'

Katherine widened her eyes, amused. 'I had him well trained.'

Our own steward would never have gone off into shops to buy us any silks – not that any of us had ever dared ask.

Margie put it to no one in particular, 'Which is your favourite colour?' and suddenly we were all up for the challenge of choosing but frozen in the face of it, afraid to commit. Well, all of us except Elizabeth. 'The green,' she said, unbothered, as if it should get up and thank her for having chosen it.

My mother nodded at the slip in Katherine's lap. 'That's a lovely piece of work, Katherine.' The colours shone in the fireglow, in shapes that formed buds and petals, fruits and vines.

She shrugged off the compliment. 'It's for an altar cloth.'

Piled on top of her sewing box were more slips: a pair of stocky, golden little bodies, one with a fuller head of hair than the other, and a cheerfully red-baubled tree.

She said, 'You're welcome to have it for chapel here, or perhaps it could go to St Mary's.' Our local church in Great Bedwyn.

'Oh—' my mother was concerned, anxious to do the right thing. It would be improper to expropriate it, was what she would've been thinking, wrong to assume that it would come to us rather than the church at Horton just because its maker had. 'I'm sure we can send it down to Horton when it's done.'

Katherine merely looked bemused. 'But this is where I am now.'

It took only until the second evening for us to get a glimpse of Katherine's own true colours. The evening started well enough: she had Margie learning to make thread buttons for a new shirt for Edward ('That's nice tight work, Margie'), and Dottie embarked upon a tidying-up, if in name only, of her sewing box. My mother and I were working on our own stitching, and Elizabeth, having none of it, was playing cards with Antony. Freed from tutoring Antony in chess, Thomas could indulge in some moody strumming of his lute, to which my father – eyes closed after a wide-travelled day – was listening, or half-listening, or perhaps just appearing to listen. Harry had taken the visiting warrener to the henhouse to ask his opinion of a new, supposedly fox-proof fence, while Edward was absorbed in a ledger, having moved a stool beneath one of the windows to make use of what remained of the natural light. And so there we were, the Seymour family at home of a late spring evening and Katherine might always have been one of us.

It was Father James who, inadvertently, caused the debacle. He began snoring, but we Seymours were so accustomed to it as barely to notice. A couple of exasperated glances were exchanged at the first few vigorous snorts, but otherwise we simply knuckled down, as always, to endure it. When he'd started up, my mother had been quick, I'd noticed, with an apologetic smile for her new daughter-in-law, or perhaps more of a wince, to make clear that this was, unfortunately, nothing unusual and to be tolerated, as if Father James were simply one of the dogs among whom he lounged at the fireside. Only Elizabeth had begged to differ, tutting extravagantly and rolling her eyes: How embarrassing. The children were too busy to notice, and, anyway, to them, I suppose, all adults were eccentric or distasteful. Katherine had given my mother a smile in kind, keen to be obliging.

Not too many snores later, though, she made her own small sound. She'd pricked her finger, I assumed, glancing up from my own work, but finding that she was focused on the cloth in her lap, not reeling as she would have done from a needle-prick. The needle was suspended: she'd halted mid-stitch. Father James snuffled loudly again and a gasp escaped Katherine even as she drew in on herself to quell it, which was when I realised with a mixture of horror and delight that she was laughing: she was laughing at our priest. No one else seemed to have noticed the lapse, perhaps because we were so well practised of an evening at closing our ears. There they were, all around me, the Seymours at play as usual, or as much at play as they ever were. Edward, Thomas and the little girls were absorbed in their various activities. Elizabeth was peering at her cards and cursing under her breath, making a drama of the hand she'd been dealt, and, wisely, Antony was scrutinising her for any evidence of cheating. A slackening of my father's features suggested he'd fallen asleep. Anyway, Katherine's indiscretion, against Father James's protracted nasal calamity, had been no louder than a sniff.

A second glance around showed me that I was wrong: her helplessness hadn't entirely escaped notice because my mother was repeating that smile but with emphasis, to indicate that she understood, that she was being understanding. I knew rather better than to trust to that, but poor Katherine rose to it, her long, supple backbone unfolding her so that she was looking – respectfully and gratefully – into my mother's eyes. Unfortunately, such an unguarded stance rendered her vulnerable and, in the same instant, Father James emitted a particularly bestial grunt, which had her felled, doubling over, fingertips of both hands pressed hard to her lips to suppress a moan. And somehow, this time, I was swept along with her, a sensation both mortifying and delicious, so that there we were, the two of us, laughing despite ourselves, laughing into that silent room.

If I dared look up, my mother's disappointment, I knew, I just knew, would be staring me in the face, but for once I couldn't take the prospect of it seriously, could only think of it as a kind of mask, a doleful, pitiful mask. It wasn't Father James who was funny, I felt, or not really, not our poor old, tired Father James; it was us, we Seymours, because how absurd and incredible that we had ever sat around primly pretending not to hear him.

I couldn't hear him again, I knew; I simply couldn't bear to hear a single snore more. But I'd have to, and very soon. Nor should I catch a glimpse of Katherine, but there was no avoiding her because there she was, in the corner of my eye, shoulders comically quaking. I closed my eyes but heard her fractured, unsuccessfully held breath and then my own breath needed stilling because if any air got into me, any at all, I'd burst. I was on the brink of disaster; I had to be unseeing, unhearing, unbreathing, and the strain of it had icy sweat springing at the roots of my hair. Even though I resolved with every fibre of my being to hear nothing more from Father James, I knew that a snore was on its way, up close, and there'd be nowhere for me to hide. And Katherine, with her bowed head and narrowed shoulders: meekly though she sat there, obliging though she was trying to be, there was no disguising her thrill at her own glaring failure.

Misguidedly, she tried to mitigate it: 'Sorry, I'm sorry,' barely articulating it, rushing it out on a breath before that breath could become a laugh, but this desperate apology only served to alert everyone and then the worst was happening, in that everyone had turned to her. Only my mother spared her, smiling down over her needlework, contriving to look untroubled and giving us all the lead to follow: we were to look away, we were to leave her in peace. But the girls gawped, and Antony hooted a laugh despite not quite knowing why. My father opened his eyes to give his daughter-in-law a fond but surprised smile. Thomas flicked her a glance as if merely to confirm something he'd known all along. And as for Edward: I didn't have to see his face to know that he'd have mustered a puzzled half-smile while he attempted to fathom what was going on, belatedly aware that his wife was indisposed and that he should probably be coming to her assistance.

Edward's attention was enough to prompt another unspooling of Katherine's spine, and, sitting tall – an impressive trans-formation – she now looked ahead, looked carefully nowhere. Particularly not, I sensed, at me, an omission that I found exhil-arating. Her face was flushed, not blotchy as I knew mine would be, as if she'd been indulging in pleasurable physical activity, and a tendril of hair was loose from her hood. Her intentions were admirable, but as soon as Father James snored again she was beyond herself; me, too, along with her. Her whimpered apology was quite fabulously insincere, testing my mother's patience and unsettling Edward, and she looked to me, her eyes luminous with tears of laughter.

'Air,' she pleaded, and together we scrambled to the door, her shoving me aside to be first through it, then clattered through Hall into the courtyard where we could at last give full vent.

'Their faces!' she shrieked, astounded and jubilant, 'Their faces!'

Those Seymour-quiet faces, she meant: their polite concern. Well, for fifteen long years I'd been one of them, I'd suffered being one of them, but then there I was, outside with my new sister-in-law, my saviour, under the milk moon, drinking down that sparkling evening air and noisier even than the swifts.

4

Even by that second evening, then, it had begun, my turning from my own family in favour of my new sister-in-law, my falling into step with her. My mother had probably put Katherine's outburst down to nervousness, but I doubt she cut me any such slack. Not that I much cared, emboldened as I was by having an ally, which was how, in a matter of mere days, I'd come to see Katherine. She was a better kind of sister, I felt, than my real ones.

In general, my mother appeared pleased with her new daughter-in-law, who knew how to handle her, had the knack of dealing with her. Unlike me, Katherine was able to listen to my mother's chatter and seem interested. But I'd already endured fifteen years of it and was facing the prospect of many more when Katherine had gone, as she and Edward were residing with us only until they decided where to make their own home. My mother didn't so much converse as think aloud about household matters or merely relay news of neighbours and relatives (someone's illness, someone else's difficult pregnancy). I had no idea how Katherine managed to listen so intently, or at least give the impression of doing so. In every other way, too, she was what my mother would have wanted, making light of work around the house and making the treasured eldest son happy, or so it then seemed.

My mother continued to keep her distance from her, though, but that left Katherine and me to work together, which suited me fine. Since my sister-in-law's arrival, I was no longer just my mother's helper or the girls' supervisor, and I looked forward to each new day. Perhaps, I felt, the reason for my mother's reticence with Katherine was that although Katherine was a married lady, she had yet to become a family lady: she'd stepped up from her girlhood but not yet stepped properly into the world that was my mother's, to run a household and rear children. Katherine inhabited my world at least as much as she inhabited my mother's, although I had to remind myself that her presence in mine was a mere visitation, in that she'd soon be moving on.

At that time of year, my mother's domain was the dairy-house: she was an expert cheesemaker and didn't need anyone's help. She should have been teaching the technique to Elizabeth and me – it was something, in time, that we'd need to know – but never seemed able to bring herself to risk any of our sheep's milk. It had rankled with me before Katherine arrived, but from then on I wasn't much bothered. Although I wasn't making cheese, I was in charge of the daily cleaning of the dairy-house, which was exacting in its own way, spotlessness being crucial to the success of each batch. Elizabeth, Dottie and Margie were forbidden to go anywhere near.

It was my job: 'Jane's thorough,' my mother used to say, 'Jane can be trusted.' She did make noises to suggest that Katherine wasn't expected to get down on her hands and knees with scrubbing brushes, but she must've known that her daughter-in-law was joining me there. I did try to put Katherine off, simply because I felt I should, but she wouldn't have it; 'I'm fine,' she'd say, and, 'Let me,' and I chose to see it as her wanting my company, which might well have been true – but at least as true, upon reflection, was that she liked to be busy.

My mother jealously guarded her still room, too, but in that case the role of assistant was most definitely the preferable one. As her assistants, Katherine and I spent a lot of time, that summer, in the gardens, collecting the herbs and flowers – rose petals, lavender heads, sage leaves, sprigs of thyme – from which she distilled the various deceptively clear, headily fragrant waters for cooking, medicines and washing.

When we weren't picking herbs and flowers, we were har-vesting fruits and vegetables, all of which suited Katherine fine because she loved the sunshine. Honey-coloured, she didn't burn. I did, but she'd usher me into the arbour for some shade while she carried on; I'd sit there doing whatever I could to be useful, pod-ding peas, perhaps, while we continued our conversation. Until she'd come to Wolf Hall, I'd only had my mother's wittering to suffer, or Elizabeth's complaints and demands, or the little ones' sillinesses, which was why, to me, Katherine's chatter seemed wide-ranging and unpredictable.

Once, I remember, she rose in a tangle of gown from onion-harvesting to wonder aloud, 'What if we girls wore doublets and hose? What would that be like? We'd be—' and she frowned to contemplate it, 'Well, we'd be all legs, wouldn't we.' And, buttoning down her smile, she confided, 'I tell you, Janey, I thank God every minute of every day that no one sees my knees.' Was she serious? I had no idea. Could her knees be quite so bad? Could any knees be quite so bad? It's hard to believe, now, but such talk was unconventional – daring, even – for the Seymour household. No one in my family talked about hose – repaired them, yes, endlessly, but never mentioned them – nor the look of legs. Well, Thomas probably did, but never in my earshot.

On another occasion: 'Is God really watching us all the time, d'you think? I mean, really all the time? Even when we're doing this?' She pulled a face to show her frank opinion of such divine time-wasting, and, provocatively, with her eyes heavenwards, tipped a handful of our newly picked peas into her mouth. We Seymours weren't overly observant, but none of us would've dared question how God spent His time, nor filched any of the household's peas.

And once, when the chapel bell began ringing for prayers, she glanced up from the strawberry patch to ask me, 'Have you ever heard that bell ring when you've known – known for absolute certain – that there's no one there?' I didn't think I had. 'Oh, well, I have,' she said, as I'd known she would. 'Back at home,' she clarified, 'Our bell back at home. Once. In the middle of the night.' Her coppery eyes were round with intrigue. 'And I lay there thinking, Please make it stop, please, please stop it, but at the same time thinking, Let it go on and on and on.'

'It was probably bats.' I hated to sound boring but the fact was that it was almost certainly bats.

She shook her head. 'It was a regular tolling.'

'Didn't anyone else hear it?'

She shrugged. 'They never said, but they wouldn't, would they.'

She was superstitious about birds, too. When I first saw her recoil from a hopping blackbird, hand to heart, I assumed she'd been startled, but then she said in all seriousness, with a shudder, 'Souls of the dead, doing their penance.'

It was an old belief, I knew, the kind that Moll would hold. I said nothing, but I did wonder how Edward would react if he heard something like that from her.

For Antony, our new family member was heaven-sent: a kindred spirit. He regaled her with the preposterous questions that preoccupied him, confronting her by hopping from foot to foot, fervent and insistent, almost indignant at the enormity of the topics that – he was convinced – required examination: Which would you rather have as a pet, a leopard or an elephant? Would you rather drown or burn to death?

She tried very hard not to laugh at her own helplessness, cornered, and at Antony's fierceness. Her sidelong glances in my direction would have the same effect on me, although when I'd had to endure his interrogations alone, I'd tended to find them exasperating. Adore him though I did, I found him hard work, although I've since come to regret ever having rolled my eyes, ever having sighed and looked into the middle distance. Katherine had never had a baby sibling, so, for her, Antony's tenacity was novel. Who knew, though, why he ever bothered to fire his precious questions at her, because, to his mind, he already had the answers; he was bursting with them and he'd unleash them on her as soon as she'd offered her own.

'But a leopard would ...'

'But, but, but ... But then you'd ... And what if ...? And I'd ...'

And so whatever she'd ventured in reply was immediately dismissed and she was put firmly back in her place, which only delighted her further.

On St John's eve, Antony was bothering us when we were helping with preparations in the kitchen. Katherine and I only helped with cooking for special occasions, but there were a fair few special occasions that summer because my mother was keen to show her off. Harry's Barbara's family was to be joining us for the feast of St John. The kitchen was quiet, it being a fast day, and Bax was always well organised in advance of a feast so that he could take a brief fortifying break before the busy day itself. Katherine had set Margie making little marzipan hedgehogs, using slivered almonds for their spikes and raisins for their eyes and snouts, and Margie had embraced her responsibilities: that after-

31

noon, she was Confectioner Extraordinaire, and we, making mere gingerbread medallions, were beneath her.

Antony had extracted a promise that he could stamp out our rounds, and while he waited for us to mix and roll the mixture, he took the opportunity to pass on some of his wisdom regarding dragons ('They're not all huge, you know; some of them are not much bigger than dogs'). Dragons led him to St George, and, jovially, he reported, 'Thomas says that when that maiden was cut free from the stake, she was probably just fussing about her hair,' before honouring us with his impression of a preening girl.

'Antony,' I warned; it was reflex, taking him to task for disrespect of a biblical story. It was what my mother would have done, so I did it, because, like it or not, I was still, back then, very much my mother's daughter.

He took offence with enthusiasm. 'What? I didn't say it; Thomas did.'

'But you don't have to repeat it.'

After a brief sulk, he muttered, pointedly, 'Saint Antony put his sister in a nunnery.'

Katherine was delighted by the transparency of the threat. 'Yes, but that was so he could go off and be a monk.'

Antony was thrilled again. 'He was the first-ever monk,' he crowed, 'and the best-ever monk! Out in the middle of the desert, fighting off all those wild beasts that were really the Devil in disguise — the lions and wolves, the snakes and the scorpions . . .'

'I think,' she glanced at me to check, 'he just laughed at them, actually. Isn't that right?' she asked me. 'Isn't that the story?'

As far as I remembered, it was.

Antony protested, 'But that's still really brave! I mean, would you laugh at a lion?'

'Probably not,' she admitted. 'Not unless it told me a joke.'

He raced on, 'Saint Katherine was going to get bashed to death, tied up on a wheel and bashed—'

'Talk of the Devil,' she said, and I glanced up to see Thomas coming in.

'Where's the bread for the dogs?' he demanded. 'Where does Bax keep it?'

We didn't know.

Belatedly, he remembered himself: even if it was acceptable that he should address his own siblings in this way – which, frankly, it wasn't – there was no excuse for such a brusque manner with his new sister-in-law. He mustered a smile for her and said, 'Katherine,' by way of apology and greeting, then inclined his head towards the gingerbread mixture. 'Getting your hands dirty, I see.'

'But keeping my nose clean.'

He dabbed an index finger into a scattering of flour and onto the tip of her nose. 'That's what you think,' and then he was gone, presumably in search of Bax.

Antony looked appreciatively after him; Margie's expression, as she glanced up with reluctance from a hedgehog, was momentarily glazed but turned to one of disgust. Katherine's mordant stare at me across the bench made me laugh.

'They are so alike, aren't they?' she said. 'Edward and Thomas.' But seeing she had me baffled, she clarified, 'In looks, I mean.'

Oh, well, yes, perhaps, although I hadn't really ever thought about it. I'd grown up with them and didn't look at them as she did, as an outsider. And they were so utterly different in temperament that the possibility of there being any similarity whatsoever between them had never crossed my mind. In reply, I muttered something non-committal.

'Both so like your father,' she enthused, kneading the gingerbread dough. 'Good-looking man, your father.'

Really? My father was my father, as far as I was concerned: good-looking simply didn't apply. In his mid-forties, he was greying, but once upon a time he must have been black-haired, and of course his eyes were as dark as they'd ever been. He was still as lithe, too, as a boy. Kneading my own dough, I recalled the story of my parents' courtship, which they'd sometimes tell as a comic turn when we were young. Katherine wouldn't have heard it. We children used to beg to hear it, but by the time Katherine arrived, most of us had outgrown it: it had had its day; we were bored by it and it was becoming embarrassing.

The story was that my father had fallen for my mother when he'd first set eyes on her and had vowed to win her heart, but he'd had his work cut out for him because she was Margery Wentworth, descendant of the Plantagenets, of Hotspur himself, and was in the service of the Countess of Surrey. Yes, Margery Wentworth was someone, in the old days: impeccably connected, well regarded and accomplished. Twenty-three, too.

And what was her suitor, at that time? Nothing much, compared. A lad of eighteen. 'So I made a pest of myself,' he used to tell us, with characteristic kindness even for his own young self. It had been hard for me to imagine: he'd become such a diffident man; sweet natured, but happiest withdrawing into the company of his dogs, the old dogs who'd retired from hunting to the fireside. 'I had to make a pest of myself or she wasn't going to so much as look at me,' he'd told us, and, at that, my mother would roll her eyes, cheerfully long suffering. He'd even written poems for her, apparently.

Elizabeth would usually ask my mother, 'Didn't he annoy you? Didn't you just want to get rid of him?' Once, though, she'd asked, 'Was he handsome?' and my mother, caught by surprise, had replied before she knew it, 'He was, actually.'

To which my father had said, 'Your mother was a real beauty,' adding, hurriedly, 'still is, of course.'

She wasn't, though, not really, not by then, or not that I could see. She had a pleasant enough face, as round as our father's was angular, but ten pregnancies had taken their toll and by her late forties she was a large, ungainly lady with no inclination to dress up or to fuss in any way over her appearance: by the time I was fifteen, those days were long gone. Indeed, I couldn't recall mention of her ever having been back to court after she'd married.

Antony drew Katherine's attention to the flour on her nose, 'You need to wipe that off.'

But she stuck that daubed nose in the air, enjoying it, and challenged, 'Why should I? He can.' Thomas, she meant. 'He put it there.'

And so it was Edward who ended up wiping her clean, that evening at the chapel door. He did so absently, with a fond half-smile, as if flour-splattering was a foible of hers, new to him, and no doubt thinking it to have been innocently acquired.

Often during those first days of Katherine's at Wolf Hall, I'd feel something like pride at how familiar most of us were able to be with her and she in turn could be with us. Thomas could be Thomas, for instance, tiresome though he was, and she'd take it in good spirit. But that was only when I gave it any thought at all, which usually I didn't. Edward should've been the one giving consideration to how she was settling in, but for him, I suspect, she was done and dusted, in that he'd married her: it was done, he'd married her. Edward has never been someone to look back. Which, paradoxically, meant that in the case of his wife, he didn't see what was coming.

Who did, though? Katherine didn't put a foot wrong, and our St John's feast allowed her to show just how good she was not only with us, but with everyone else. I dreaded social occasions, clueless as to what to say to anyone, but that evening I stuck by her side and she did enough socialising for us both. She danced beautifully, too, not so much because of her technique as her lightness of step and her bearing: that long, slender, effortlessly straight back of hers. Me, I was born a clodhopper; even back when I was slight, I was heavy on my feet. Not only was Katherine a good dancer, but she was even a good spectator; from the sidelines she'd be first to be clapping a rhythm, unabashed, urging the others on, and at the end she'd applaud – Oh, well done, Dottie! – so that we all had to follow, bringing dimples to Dottie's anxious little face.

She retired early, though, that evening, only a little later than the children. Sidling up behind Edward, who was in conversation with Barbara's father, she encircled his waist with her arms so that he had to extricate himself before he could turn to her. I didn't overhear what she said, but evidently she was making her excuses, and she did look tired: lilac shadows beneath her eyes. Wine wouldn't have been the reason, because she didn't much drink; that evening she'd declined all offers of wine with a wrinkle of her nose, even the lovely, syrupy, spicy hippocras.

Warm milk was what she wanted; that was what I discovered shortly afterwards, going into the kitchen to replenish a bowl of almonds. There she was, holding a pan over a brazier, and she smiled that smile of hers when she asked me, 'Want some?'

I didn't – milk was for children – but I rather liked that she did. She was a creature of whim, I felt, and unafraid to go and get what she wanted. I'd seen something of that when she'd made her excuses, back in Hall; all evening, she'd seemed so keen to please, but then, when she'd had enough, she hadn't hung around for the sake of appearances. I was impressed. Back then I was easily impressed.

Two days later, some little gingerbread medallions left over from our St John's feast were muslin-wrapped and ribbon-tied in Katherine's hand as she waited to leave with Edward to visit one of our tenant families. The father of the family had been injured a week earlier in a fall from a cart, and was still unable even to sit up. Initially, Edward had taken the barber-surgeon to him, and also a lot of my mother's salves and syrups; now he was visiting again to take provisions to the family and find out what else he might be able to do. My mother had packed baskets with bread, one of her cheeses, potted meat, a bird pie, peas and beans. I happened to be standing alongside my brother and sister-in-law in the doorway because I was calling across the courtyard for Antony to come in and give his boots and, I hoped, everyone else's a polish. I'd already called three or four times. Beside me, Edward asked, 'What's that?' and the sharpness in his query had me look around at him, but it was his wife he'd addressed: he was peering at the pretty little package in her hand.

She paid no heed to the note of challenge. 'It's what's left of those gingerbreads,' she told him cheerily, and even dangled the package as if to entice him.

I beckoned exaggeratedly for Antony, who was trying and failing to persuade Mort, our cat, to accompany him.

Edward's brief laugh was dismissive, incredulous, exasperated, perhaps even ridiculing. Katherine didn't let it pass: 'What?' Without looking round at her, I imagined her head cocked to prise an honest answer from him.

'Well,' he seemed hardly able to bring himself to have to say it, so obvious it was to him, 'it's not gingerbread they need, is it.'

He was right, of course, but then he was always right as far as I was concerned. The handful of muslin glowed ribbon-soft in the corner of my eye and I saw it, now, for what it was: a frivolity. That family needed sustenance; what they needed was my mother's basketloads of food.

'Isn't it?' Katherine spoke pleasantly, but I sensed her standing taller and I was surprised: no one ever stood up to Edward; Thomas would goad him, yes, but that was just for the sake of it. I was listening hard even as I called again for Antony and, patience depleted, turned to leave him to follow me, Mort or no Mort.

'It's bread they need,' Edward was saying emphatically but kindly, as if explaining to a child.

'And they're getting bread,' was Katherine's mild reply, and actually there was no arguing with that, either. They were getting the staples, plenty of them – I was having to step around all the baskets – and the gift of biscuits was extra. And so that, suddenly, was how I saw it: why not gingerbread?

Antony began yelling for me and I turned to find him bounding towards me, having given up on the cat.

Edward was being unreasonable, I realised; he was right, but still he was being unreasonable.

He knew it, too, because now he was trying to shrug off his disdain, adopting in its place an airy, unconvincing resignation: Oh, all right, bring along your little treats. Marvellously, though, she didn't allow him get away with it. She insisted on his full attention as Antony bolted past. 'Edward . . .' His name spoken softly as if she was letting him on something. 'There are children in that family.'

He didn't argue, or not as I heard as I hurried off with Antony. A final glimpse revealed my eldest brother to be standing humbled, looking away over the courtyard, keeping his face averted from his wife.

So he could be right but at the same time unreasonable, and how liberating it was for me to realise it. Katherine was good for him, I decided, she was really good for him. He needed her: there were still things for him to learn, and he could learn them from her.

What I might have seen, though, just as easily, were two people who would never, even remotely, see eye to eye.

5

Edward left it almost a month from the wedding before he allowed work to take him away overnight from his new wife and, that evening, she didn't join us – me, my mother and my sisters – in the parlour after prayers. Beyond the windows the cooling air was deep with birdsong. My father had gone with his old dogs for their last walk of the day, accompanied by Father James, and Harry and Thomas were hawking, taking advantage of the meltingly long dusk. Antony was with them for a while, but then suddenly he was back, bursting in on us, piping, 'Where's Katherine? I need to ask her something.'

Roused, my mother blinked heavily and realised, 'You need to go to bed, Antony.'

Yes, though, where *was* she?

My mother looked to Elizabeth – 'Elizabeth ...' – who returned an insolently big-eyed stare, a parody of incomprehension, *Not my job*. She was right: it was always me who put Antony to bed. My mother countered, 'Jane's going to go and find Katherine, check she's all right.'

Was I?

'I'll go.' Margie laid aside her needlework.

39

My mother sighed. 'No, Margie.'

Margie stood up to inform me, 'I'll go *with* you.'

'Margie, *no*.' My mother told her to finish up her stitching and pack it away; time for bed for her, too.

Margie's frown made abundantly clear her disappointment, but I rather hoped she'd put up more of a fight because although it was fine for me to be with Katherine during the daytime, she had probably retired to her room – hers and Edward's, even if on this occasion he wasn't in it – and I felt uncomfortable at the prospect of following her there, uninvited.

'Jane . . .' my mother prompted.

As I climbed the steps to their door, my reluctant footsteps rebounded on me and my heart made its disquiet felt. I knocked warily, knowing that such a knock was ridiculous: either I intended to be heard or I didn't. No response, but I felt I couldn't knock again – that'd be too much. Instead, I called to her, doing my level best to sound reassuring rather than interrogatory. My anxiety, though, was unfounded, because her reply was cheerful and welcoming: 'Come on in!'

I knew the room, of course – intimately, even, because my mother and I had furnished it. A couple of days before Katherine's arrival, my mother and I had wrestled with the heavy bed-hangings that had once been my grandparents' – a design of seed-rich pomegranates swelling and splitting to reveal rubied hearts – and for several months beforehand my mother had been embroidering the coverlet and pillows with butterflies in mid-shy.

When the door opened, though, that evening when Katherine was alone in there, I saw how different those fruits and butterflies were from when they had been ours. They had a life now; around her, they'd come alive, the fruits no longer just a weight of thread as they'd been in my arms, and the butterflies so much more than regular little stitches in my mother's lap. It was only as we'd intended, of course, that all this be properly hers. Those fruits and butterflies looked as Katherine did, in that room: glamorous, gleaming. There she was, in the middle of it all, reclined on her bed in her nightdress, and, actually, she wasn't alone. Mort, who should've been making better use of his time, in the granary for starters, was pressing himself alongside her, his spine undulating beneath the rhythmic sweep of her hand. Her hair was loose over her shoulders and I was surprised by how wavy it was. She was propped up on a lot of cushions, many more than my mother and I had left there for the newly-weds. They must have come squashed in the two chests that had accompanied her on the two-day journey from Horton.

I was taken aback, didn't know what to make of what I saw because no one at Wolf Hall ever reclined on beds. No Seymour would go voluntarily to bed, and certainly wouldn't make something of it when there. Our beds were functional, were there to take the strain when we could no longer stand on our own two feet. We were only ever brought to bed by weariness or sickness; our beds were where we gave up on each day, and, in the end, life. But Katherine didn't look weary or sick — quite the contrary. And, anyway, beds for me back then meant hard work: they needed to be kept free of mites and bugs and fleas (oh how I itched to get Mort off there), to be laundered, aired and the mattresses beaten, and then to be dressed, equipped with covers and hangings enough to shut out the night-time chill. Perhaps my mother had started something with those beautiful butterflies: perhaps it was she, I felt, who had inadvertently encouraged her daughter-in-law differently.

Moreover, the whole room was aglow. It was midsummer and darkness was still a couple of hours away, but Katherine had candles burning, lots of them, little ones on the hearth on what looked to be a piece of slate. They were beeswax, too, not tallow; no fatty smoke but instead a subtle, slightly spicy aroma. Where had she found beeswax candles? Not in our chandlery cupboard, that was for sure; we had them, yes, but only a few, for special occasions, and not these little ones. Katherine's candles twinkled like stars in the dark cavern of the fireplace.

'Come in,' she said, which was when I realised I hadn't: I'd halted on the threshold, the doorway gaping around me. So I did as she said, pulling the door closed behind me, and she patted the bed to indicate that I should sit there, Mort complaining at the momentary absence of her hand with a questing lift of his head.

Again I hesitated. The newly-weds' bed, where, as I pictured it, the pair of them would lie side by side like statues on a tomb, well dressed, peaceful and facing resolutely heavenwards even in their sleep. I perched on the edge and she didn't take issue with it, didn't encourage me any closer. My feet stayed square on the floor, not relinquishing it. I felt I should explain myself: 'My mother sent me.'

She shrugged this off, and for a while neither of us spoke. I was thinking of the others downstairs, how odd and how good it was to have left them there. Katherine's stroking of Mort continued apace; the mattress seemed to bow with each sweep of her hand, although of course in actuality it didn't. Nevertheless, it lulled me and I shut my eyes, inhaling the beeswax fragrance, chasing it with my concentration, teasing it from the air before it escaped from the open window. Outside, the dusk was swift-happy, the bats yet to swoop in on it. Eventually, I offered a heartfelt, 'It's lovely in here,' because the loveliness was palpable and as such, I felt, should be acknowledged. Again, though, a shrug from Katherine, as if the loveliness was by the by, was natural to her, something that she couldn't help.

This, then, was how my brother now ended the days when he was home. What, I wondered, did he make of it? Very occasionally, over the years, he had mentioned to us the fabulous decor of the king's great halls and great watching chambers, and of Francis Bryan's lavish London house: gilded ceilings and walls, and jewel-like windows; thick Turkish carpets, and solid gold platters enamelled with roses. What was here in his room was a very different kind of loveliness: the stars spluttering in pools of wax; the sparkle-threaded, scratchy wadding of cushions; the cosseted cat. Perhaps, though, it occurred to me, he hadn't actually ever seen it; perhaps she had been saving it as a comfort for herself when he was gone.

She sighed contentedly. 'You know, Janey, this was what I dreamt of,' and the warmth and in her voice told me that, in her view, she'd been right to dream of it, she'd been more than vindicated. It had been a good dream to have, said the wonder in her voice, but the reality was even better.

We Seymours didn't have dreams. Well, Thomas did, that was obvious, but despite no one in our household saying as much, I knew it was seen as his failing: impetuous and embarrassing. We Seymours didn't acknowledge dreams; we were practical people. Plans, yes, plans were acceptable, or even laudable: Edward had plans; plans were calculated and achievable, or certainly Edward's were. Dreams, though, were somehow improper, we didn't lavish dreams on ourselves. With considerable ease, though, Katherine was owning up to doing just that.

I didn't know how to respond, didn't even know if I should respond. I wanted to, though: she was confiding in me and I was keen to honour that, as well as to prompt more. Her gaze was at the window, on the chalky sky – she was expecting nothing from me – and I was grateful for that because I didn't yet know what it was that she was telling me. Of what, exactly, had she dreamt? So, I stayed listening and duly it came: 'Being married to a such a gorgeous man.'

Did I want to hear that? Because that, surely, was for him alone, *Oh, you gorgeous man, you.* Even 'man' unnerved me, although of course I knew very well that Edward was no longer a boy – indeed he was a *married* man – but as a boy was how I'd always known him. And anyway, no one in our family ever passed comment on anyone else's physical attributes. It had always been impressed on us that what mattered was what was on the inside. True, there was the story of my mother having been beautiful and my father handsome, but it was exactly that: a story, family lore, for fun. It was something of which we couldn't know the truth and wouldn't wish to. The truth of it – or otherwise – was irrelevant. But to proclaim Edward as gorgeous ... well, he was, but, again, wasn't it somehow indecent to say so?

'And he's so good with people, isn't he,' she said, awed and humbled, looking at me now, although this wasn't a real question. She was looking for affirmation and I had no qualms in giving it. Edward had time for everyone, from Marcus, our kitchen boy, to our neighbour, Mr Dorell, who was forever poaching in the forest, and Lady Wroughton, whom not even our mother could stand. Good, even, with itinerant wool-winders and wandering minstrels. Edward was hardworking on everyone's behalf, scrupulously fair and respectful, and everyone knew it. Thomas might make fun of him, but that was because he knew that, in truth, his eldest brother couldn't be faulted.

'People really like him, don't they?'

Actually, I wasn't sure that 'like' was quite the right word. People trusted him, that was what I would have said. It was Thomas they'd be more likely to choose to have a drink with, to play cards with; Thomas would give them a better time if a good time was what they were after.

'He's so kind.'

Again, I didn't know that it was kindness as such; I didn't know if it was as simple as that.

I said, 'He thinks things could be fairer.'

She half-laughed at that: 'Everything could always be fairer, couldn't it,' as if it were pointless to wish for it, and I felt a twinge of unease that perhaps she didn't understand him as well or take him as seriously as she should. But then again, what did I know? Perhaps that didn't matter; perhaps, even, in the early days of a marriage, that was how it should be. Perhaps it was quite touching, or one day would be, to look back and see how little, at the beginning of their life together, she'd understood him.

'Anyway, that was always my dream,' she concluded, sleepily pleased with herself, 'to marry a wonderful man.'

Even back when I'd assumed that a husband would eventually come my way, how had I envisaged such a man? As being like Edward, albeit a lesser version to befit me. Not that I'd ever come across anyone who'd even approximated him and that was the disadvantage, I knew, of having a brother such as him; such boys were few and far between.

'To make a home,' Katherine was saying, 'and have a family with a wonderful man — isn't that every girl's dream?'

She looked for me to agree, but while marrying a wonderful man was better than not marrying a wonderful man or marrying a man who wasn't wonderful, I wasn't sure that it was what I'd have called a dream. Could it be said to be a dream? I experienced a flutter of panic because, yes, marrying and having a family was what was supposed to happen, even if I'd come to doubt that it'd happen for me; it was what would happen, I felt, for anyone who had just enough luck; it was what life was, or should be ... But dreams: weren't they something else?

Being queen, for instance, wasn't that something every girl dreamed of?

So, I said it, tentatively, testing it out on her: 'I used to dream of being queen.'

Katherine laughed a little at that, enjoying the absurdity of it — 'Well, that job's taken' — and I was flustered to have been taken at my word, even in jest, because of course I didn't dream of replacing our actual queen, so I clarified, 'Just *a* queen,' which

45

was no clarification at all, really. Which other queen could I possibly be?

'*Queen* ... ' She was repeating it, doubtful, and then she warned me, 'You wouldn't be sitting here, like this, if you were a queen.'

Wouldn't I?

'Well, you'd be——' She had to stop and think about it. 'You'd be on show somewhere, wouldn't you. Attending some ... entertainment,' the word said derisively: in her opinion, nothing of the kind. 'You'd have to be on your best behaviour, all the time. Surrounded by your ladies. Courtiers, ambassadors,' and suddenly it was indeed an awful prospect, that the pair of us couldn't be alone in her room, taking our time together over the ending of a summer's day. Because, quite simply, there could be nothing better, I realised: the slow-spun light, the laciness of what was left of it, the febrile birdsong spread on the air, and the sweetness of the milkshed. Outside, I knew, would be the first star of the evening, bold in the blue. If I were to go to the window, I'd come up against its bright-eyed watchfulness. And then the first breath of stars on the surface of the sky. Inside, with the simmering down of the day, the mustiness of old wood – floorboards and panelling – was coming to the fore, a muted but resonant note. The bed-hangings had held on to the day's warmth but were beginning to release it, as would a night-scented flower. Our waiting for it was bringing it all about, I felt, the evening was playing to us. I wouldn't have given it up for the world.

I felt I should try to explain: 'I think I just wanted not to have to do the cleaning,' although that, too, was only a small part of it. I could have gone on to say that I would have loved a bed to myself, a whole bed to myself, free of Elizabeth's bulk, Dottie's laboured breathing and Margie's feet. I could have said that I dreamed of sitting down to melting, juice-rich venison on every meat-eating day and sturgeon on every fasting day; of spooning

46

caramelised orange slices from a syrup of spiced wine, and pocketing sugared almonds inside my cheek. An end to long winters of stockfish and mutton, and powdery baked apples. And I wondered about the sensation against my skin of a cloth woven from gold that had been made thin enough to thread. And stockings made of silk instead of wool. And how it would be to sit back in chairs, instead of having to balance on stools and benches or slump against floor-cushions. Sailing through London, too – not only going to London, but being swept through it in a silk-draped, velvet-plush barge, serenaded by musicians. Imagine that.

And there was more, but back then it was beyond me to explain and I knew it: I knew to say nothing because I wouldn't have been able to make myself understood; I didn't quite even understand it myself. When I dreamed of being a queen, what I'd dream of was being merciful. Full of mercy: brimful and bountiful with that best and most precious of qualities. As a queen, I knew, I'd be merciful not because I was a good person but simply because I was queen: there I would be, above and beyond everyone else, singular, and my very business would be mercy. The king might dabble, he might take an interest and sometimes try his hand, but he'd be occupied with affairs of state. As queen, mercy would be mine to give: mine by right, whether or not I wanted it; invested in me, to be bestowed. My subjects would come to me in their desperation and I wouldn't have to know or understand them: nothing so complicated. I'd pass no judgement, but simply change everything for them: dissolve the past and conjure up a different future.

Katherine had linked her hands behind her head and was reciting a litany of our household duties: '... cleaning and cooking and sewing, gardening, larder-stocking and egg-collecting, pickling and bottling, malt-sprouting and brewing, butter-churning ...' but although she did so with a put-upon air, we both knew that she didn't really mind the tasks. She was efficient around the house, and had thus earned the right to a gripe. I didn't much mind the work, either, because what else would I have been doing with my time? Katherine said, 'If you want to avoid all that, Janey-jay-jay, you just need to marry a very, very rich man. He doesn't have to be a king.'

I made myself smile to show that I was taking her advice in the spirit that it was intended.

'Problem solved, then,' I said. 'I'll make sure to marry a very, very rich man.'

A satisfied little smile from her. 'Make sure you do.'

From then onwards, we retreated together to her room whenever Edward was away. 'Coming?' she'd ask me after evening prayers when our time was our own, and she'd ask it merrily and unself-consciously, as if there were no question that I'd be joining her. And oh how right she was. Gladly I set myself adrift from my family. As for her, I don't think it occurred to her that she was expected to sit downstairs; she was simply doing what she wanted to do, creature of whim that she was, and didn't consider that she might be missed. Not arrogance or disregard on her part, I don't think; if anything, the contrary: in her view, she simply wasn't that important. The Seymours had always sat together in the parlour of an evening, was how she'd have regarded it, and they were sitting there still, so what could be the problem?

As for me, my family didn't exist when we were in her room; we two alone existed, we sisters of a kind, of a special kind, a perfect kind. I could say that I fell under her spell, but, really, honestly, Katherine didn't have the wit to cast spells. It was all of my own doing, my giving myself over to her, and there was nothing complicated to it, just the joy of lolling around talking about nothing: the day's events, such as they'd been; the household's various characters, of whom we knew little. 'Did you see the look that Lil gave Bax when . . . ?' 'Marcus has an odd way, doesn't he, of . . . ' 'D'you think Father James has ever been in love?'

She'd pass me her jar of comfits, and even now I associate those evenings with the beguiling resistance of a sugar coating and the shock of its fracture, however much anticipated, before the wince-inducing crunch into the seed, the flooding of my mouth with flavour. Where did they come from? I did ask, but all I got was the shrug, 'Oh—' As if the acquisition of comfits was simply something else that – like so much else – just happened to her. She encouraged me to indulge in them, although once, early on, peering down into the much-diminished contents, I did object, 'But—' *But then they'll be gone.*

'Oh—' and my quibble was dismissed with an airy wave, was of no concern and, sure enough, the supply was regularly replenished, the source remaining a mystery to me but not one to tax me greatly, because what mattered, ultimately, was that they were there in that jar, and they always were.

And Katherine was, in general, a girl who had things, little things, all the more eye-catching for being ephemeral. She had lace ribbon: her plaits were tied with it beneath her hood, whereas we Seymours used strips of old fabric. I'd never seen lace before I picked up those ribbons of hers, I didn't know what it was: snow-white, intricately petalled, much of my fingertips remaining visible through it. Made of very little, barely holding itself together, yet clearly tough. Bone lace, she called it, made on bone bobbins. '*I* didn't make it,' she laughed when I looked up at her in wonder.

Who did, then?

'Oh, *I* don't know,' as if that were quite beside the point. 'Comes from Italy or the Low Countries or somewhere.'

She had a handheld mirror, an oval of shiny steel like a fragment of armour set into a wooden frame. Until then, I'd never seen a mirror, nor knew anyone who had one. Myself, I didn't hanker for one, having no wish to capture my own face, but I was impressed by Katherine's having one. Her comb, too: nothing like the grimaces that were ours, bared and ready to savage our hair, hers was exquisite, its handle carved with sinuous stems and leaves to match the mirror's frame. It wasn't as if she was vain, though, I never saw her give the slightest regard to how she looked. But then, she didn't need to.

Little luxuries, they were – those pieces of lace, the mirror and comb nestled in their own red velvet pouch, a pot of rose-scented beeswax hand cream – but somehow all the more captivating for that. The same was true of the freshly picked flowers in that room; just a few, but always there in a small clay jug that was her own, which she must have thought to bring with her for that very purpose. I didn't envy her the actual objects; what I envied her was being able to allow herself such luxuries.

Recently I've accrued clothes and jewellery that I couldn't even have imagined in my days back at Wolf Hall, but I'm glad to be merely their safe-keeper, their custodian; they haven't been given to Jane Seymour, these fabulous gifts from the king and others seeking favour, but to England's queen-in-waiting. Back at Wolf Hall, I never even had anywhere to keep anything. Katherine's room, then, was something to envy – she didn't have to share with Elizabeth, Dottie and Margie – although perhaps not so much for the physical space as the time alone that it gave us. Before she came to Wolf Hall, I'd never had time of my own. My daydreaming I'd done as I'd worked. My evenings I'd given over to family duties, minding the children and listening politely to a laboured recital of Dottie's or to Thomas's musical musings, to Father James's readings or the conversation of our guests. Why would I have made time for myself? I'd had no one with whom to share it.

Well, all that changed once Katherine arrived. Up in her room during those evenings, it was my freedom from Elizabeth that was particularly heady for me. I wonder, now, what Elizabeth made of Katherine's favouring of me, because my sister never made any secret of considering me deadly dull. She could have wheedled for a share of the friendship, but why would she have bothered? Katherine was of no use to her; Elizabeth had ascertained that Katherine held no sway in the household. And Katherine? Why no interest, from her, in Elizabeth? Of we two sisters, so close in age, Elizabeth was the one never at a loss for something pithy to say. But then, Katherine loved an easy life – I can see it now – and I was the one who was no trouble, I was easy company. At the time, I would have hated to think it of myself, but it stood me in good stead when the king came looking for the quietest of company and I was so much better practised than any other lady.

Back then, the future was a long way off, an impossibly long way off, and in Katherine's room on those long summer evenings, we'd reflect on our day and speculate no further than an upcoming feast. There was no more mention of marriage for me, nor – it occurs to me now – of babies for her: no talk such as the adults downstairs would have probably imagined us to be having, and probably wanted us to have. And absolutely no one, least of all me, would have guessed that my dream would be the one eventually to come true.

6

Edward had had a month's grace after the wedding but then his proper return to work took him away ever more often, and for longer, commonly several days at a time. My father was stiffer in the saddle, so tended to stay local, busy enough with his sheriff's duties, his role as a JP and as warden of Savernake Forest, whereas Edward rode beyond Wiltshire into Dorset and Somerset and even occasionally as far as Bristol. From then on, his homecomings were less predictable and his new wife could no longer be listening for him as she once had at the end of each day: listening for him speaking to Mr Wallensis, our stable master, or Ralph, our stable lad, or – indoors – to my father, reporting back to him, or if it had been one of those days when they'd worked together, mulling it over with him.

When Edward had come home every evening, what had often been audible first of his return was not his own voice at all but someone else's, yet somehow it was clear to us that it was he who was being addressed, perhaps from the attentiveness in the tone, the sound of someone on his or her toes. An Edward-distinctive shutting of a door was also easily discernible: nothing careless in it, no trace of a slam but nevertheless resolutely done. Detecting him, Katherine would lift her head, the better to catch the clues, and then, satisfied that it was indeed him, she'd resume her task, confident that he'd be coming for her. But when he was gone for days and no one knew which evening he'd get home, he'd be suddenly upon us: a door opening and his voice pitched in greeting. And then Katherine was on less sure ground. Rising, she'd almost trip over herself, and that slight loss of composure of hers would in turn wrong-foot him so that, stepping backwards, he'd gather himself with a hasty clasp of his hands, which then left the pair of them standing facing each other, somehow at a loss. They were still so new to each other and, in my innocence, I found it touching, even comical, to see their shyness of each other. I was secretly proud, too, that she was more comfortable in my company than his.

Thomas, too, spotted the newly-weds' lack of ease with each other, and he couldn't resist exploiting it; he'd grab any opportunity to get one over Edward, and Edward's self-consciousness in the presence of his wife made him easy prey. One evening Katherine and I had gone into the garden after chapel and were sitting in the arbour when Edward came to find us. He'd been away at court, at Francis Bryan's invitation, for the first time since the wedding. I was about to leave him and Katherine to become reacquainted but suddenly Thomas was there, too. He'd got wind of Edward's return and tracked him down.

'You're back,' Thomas announced cheerily, as he always did: it was as much greeting as he ever gave his elder brother.

'I am,' Edward confirmed, dryly, careful not to open a conversation, hoping to send him on his way, and I felt sharply for my eldest brother: Thomas's looming there in the opening in the yew hedge was wearying even for me, and I hadn't been on the road for a couple of days. Edward would have had a splash-down and brush-up before he'd come looking for us, but he had an insect bite on one eyelid and his cheekbones were risen like bruises. Thomas shouldered past me and made himself at home on the bench, thighs spread and elbows on knees, chin in his hands. Katherine caught my eye, looking faintly amused: *All legs*, I recalled her saying.

Thomas asked, 'And how was our good man Francis?' It was an innocuous enough enquiry, so Edward was obliged to answer; and because Francis hadn't visited us since his own marriage the previous summer to Philippa Spice, I paused to hear what he said.

Fine, Edward told us, and he'd done well in the tiltyard against his new young brother-in-law, Nick Carew. Nick Carew was the best jouster at court, even I knew that, just as I knew, as did Edward, how Thomas would have loved to have seen that joust for himself. Only Edward, though, had received Francis's invitations so far. They made an unlikely pair, Edward and Francis, similar in age but little else. Edward was no jouster, to say the least. Nevertheless, Francis seemed to have recognised Edward's qualities and was busy furthering his interests, which, as a Gentleman of the Privy Chamber and Esquire of the Body, he was ideally placed to do.

I retreated onto the path, hoping that Thomas would follow my lead, but, jovially, he asked Edward, 'Will the king be making a prince of the little Fitzroy?'

What Fitzroy? I stopped in my tracks. Royal bastards belonged to the olden days, didn't they? That was my understanding, back then. Our king had married Spanish Catherine for love; that was the story I'd grown up with. The king's first action, at eighteen, against the advice of his councillors had been to marry his elder brother's widow, to rescue her from obscurity and poverty. Everyone knew it. Everyone said theirs was the ideal marriage. The king was larger than life, whereas the queen – five years his senior – was wise and serene, and they adored each other, were devoted to each other and made the perfect pair. That was the story. So why on earth, then, I puzzled, would there have been a mistress? I couldn't leave, because I had to hear what Edward would say. Thomas's claim was quite something; I couldn't walk off as if it were nothing. Keeping my eyes lowered, I stayed listening. My guess was that Thomas was somehow mistaken and Edward would enlighten him.

Nothing, though, from Edward, and curiosity had me sneak a glance to see that he didn't appreciate this ambush from Thomas nor, probably, the topic itself, and certainly not its airing in present company. Judging from his discomfort, though, there was something to what Thomas had said. But what, exactly? And how had Thomas known? But then, it struck me, perhaps everyone knew. Everyone except me. Katherine, too? I looked to her, to find her glancing back and forth between my brothers in obvious delight at the prospect of a spat. Surely she knew better than that.

Edward spoke, albeit barely. 'No idea.'

No denial, then, of the existence of the king's illegitimate son. Katherine transferred her wide-eyed gaze to me: *Well, well, well.* It was news to her, then, but welcome — a generous helping of tasty gossip — and she looked keen for more. Me, too, I admit, even though I was mindful of Edward's reticence, and pitied him: the two of us hanging on his every word, and Thomas needling him. Thomas wouldn't let up: once he had Edward on the defensive, he'd be merciless.

'Yes,' Thomas came back at him, 'but what are people saying?'

He'd asked it lightly, a perfectly reasonable question, which made it difficult for Edward to object. Edward should have told him to shut up and go away but, tempted though he must've been, in the company of ladies he wouldn't do that.

He took refuge, instead, in a stiff rebuttal – 'I've heard nothing' – which was a miscalculation because Thomas could act incredulous, head cocked – *Really?* – to cast doubt on Edward's much-vaunted new connections.

Katherine hooted a laugh at Edward's walking into that particular trap.

Edward revised, acidly, 'Because there's nothing to hear.'

Still under the woefully thin mantle of bonhomie, Thomas objected. 'Oh, come on! Someone, surely, must be looking into the possibility of it.'

If Edward denied it, he'd look either ignorant or churlish, but if he joined Thomas in speculation, he'd be gossiping.

Thomas pushed on. 'Because how old is the queen now?'

At this, Katherine flew playfully into the fray. 'Thomas! A gentleman never asks a lady's age.'

Thomas liked that, but Edward looked daggers at his wife – *Don't encourage him* – and the savagery of his glare took me aback. Katherine was unrepentant, though, barely registering his disapproval, and I marvelled at how she brushed it off, stayed untouched by it. Bolstered, perhaps, by Thomas's company.

Thomas persisted: 'She must be – what? – late thirties?'

Edward said nothing, which served as confirmation. And the fact spoke for itself: there was a low and rapidly decreasing chance of a male heir. I tried to think: how old had my mother been when she'd had the last baby, little John, who hadn't lived? She'd been forty, I remembered, when Antony was born. My mother, though, had had a long history of having children, of having sons, which the queen conspicuously lacked.

I doubt I'd ever considered the queen's age until then; perhaps I'd been regarding her as somehow above and beyond having an age. I'm not sure, even, that I'd been aware of the anxiety about the lack of an heir, but in any case I'd have understood, back then, that whatever happened or didn't happen, even for a king and queen, was God's will. Certainly it didn't seem right, to me, for Thomas to air the issue. Why, I wondered, didn't Edward put him in his place? He was acting as if that were beneath him.

And inevitably, Thomas took it too far, leaning forward to

spell it out to Edward: 'So, the king himself acknowledges that little boy, but you don't,' his tone light, but tauntingly so.

Edward stood, abruptly: 'I just don't think it's helpful.' Tight-lipped, he reined himself in, refusing to give Thomas the satisfaction.

Quickly, Katherine rose beside him, as if remembering her place. By contrast, Thomas's own rise from the bench was deliberately laboured. 'All I'm saying,' he sighed, as if disappointed to be alone in being man enough to face up to it, 'is that I'm sure the princess will make a good marriage somewhere, but for us here in England . . . Well, *something* has to *happen*, doesn't it?'

But Edward was already stalking towards the house, leaving his wife a step or two behind, as if it were she just as much as his brother whom he wanted to escape.

Katherine seemed happy enough to play up to Thomas when Edward was there, but she was a lot less sure of him when he wasn't, which, unfortunately, in turn only further provoked Thomas. One afternoon, not long after that altercation in the arbour, Katherine and I and Elizabeth and Lil were sewing (or in Elizabeth's case, purporting to sew) in the day room, when Thomas dashed in on us with a button to be stitched back on to his jacket.

Elizabeth wasn't having it. 'Ask Ma!'

But our mother was in the kitchen, and anyway the job would be done in no time, so I did it then and there, while my brother craned from the window, fretting at having left his new, difficult horse with Ralph at the stables. Just as I was tying off, Lil, who was patching her apron, pricked herself with her needle and exclaimed, cradling her hand, steadying herself after the shock.

Katherine said to her, 'You'll get kissed in that apron.' Then, faced with our collective incomprehension, explained as if reciting from memory, 'Prick your finger when you're making a dress – or apron, I suppose – and you'll get kissed in it.' She looked pleased with herself as the bearer of good news.

Thomas swung round from the window. 'Kissed?' He glanced at Lil's finger, head inclined, playing at giving it some consideration. 'A prick . . . a bit of blood . . .' And before we knew it, he'd lunged, snatched up her hand and drawn the bloodied fingertip into his mouth. Releasing it, he asked her, 'Better, now?'

She was mortified, sitting rigid, the offending hand hidden in the clasp of the other, her always troubled complexion turning florid.

'Oh, don't worry about Lil,' Thomas announced to the room as he whisked the jacket from me, 'she already gets kissed plenty, both in and out of dresses.' And with a word of thanks thrown in my direction, he was gone.

Even if I didn't fully understand what I'd witnessed, I knew it was bad and in the stunned silence looked to Katherine for one of her dismissive retorts. But her head was bowed over her stitching and it was clear to me that although I didn't understand why, all her usual confidence had deserted her.

Most of us, though, my sister-in-law simply bowled over, that first summer. Even old Father James. One glorious June afternoon, we came across him in the garden, crouched on an adjacent path, fixated on a poppy, and Katherine strode up behind him to peer down over his shoulder before exclaiming, 'Father! You can *draw*!' I worried she'd made too much of it – she sounded amazed that he should have any talent at all – but, fortunately, he didn't take it that way, beaming as he rushed to downplay his skill, 'Oh, no, really, it's just a scribble . . .'

She closed in on him, crouching beside him and roping me in, too: 'Janey-jay! Just look at this! Isn't this lovely?'

The sketch was indeed lovely, but that came as no surprise – Father James had always sketched. Feeling awkward alongside the pair of them – Katherine ebullient and Father James demurring – I mumbled something about a sketch that he'd recently made of Elizabeth, how good it was.

He tried to be dismissive of that, too, but what I'd said had my sister-in-law draw back onto her heels. 'Really?' and I watched it occur to her: 'Could you sketch me, d'you think, Father?' The artlessness of the request was rather touching; I'd never have offered myself up to be sketched. But, then, of course, I wasn't pretty as she was.

Events were moving fast for poor old Father James. 'Oh, well . . . ' But I could see that he was already along for the ride, he'd already begun considering her as a possible subject; the idea had been sown and he couldn't help himself. But only when she asked him, 'Where shall I sit?' did I realise that she intended the sketch to be done that very minute. The sketch of the poppy that she'd so admired but which had yet to be finished; that, it seemed, would have to be set aside.

Father James had to think quickly, casting around – 'Um, well . . . ' – before indicating the arbour. 'I suppose you could just—'

And she did; she swept to the bench. But what about Father James? Where would he go? It looked as if he'd have to kneel in front of her, so I said I'd fetch a stool.

When I returned, they were deep in conversation, Katherine asking all the right questions about where and how Father James had learned to draw, and which subjects he favoured. Flattered by attention of which he'd almost certainly never known the like, he was rallying his reedy old man's voice to give fulsome answers. Placing the stool at his disposal, I drew back – the arbour would be Katherine's alone for the duration – but then didn't quite know where to put myself, and ended up having to hang around Father James as he worked, uncomfortably aware that I might be cramping him.

'How's it looking?' Katherine would call to me from time to

time, and I'd report back favourably, doing my pathetic best to sound knowledgeable of the process ('The outline's done now').

But then, once, when Father James glanced down at the sketch, her gaze darted to mine and I saw something different in it: mischief. She was finding it funny, this situation. Until then, I'd assumed she was taking it seriously: too seriously, really. That glance, though, revealed her as amused to be posing there in that arbour with Father James at her feet; and of course she was, because it was indeed funny. When he looked back up at her, though, he found her as composed as ever, picture perfect.

As soon as his attention had returned to the drawing, she was lightning quick with her two front teeth on her lower lip and a twitch of her nose, but then, in the nick of time, expressionless again, as if it hadn't happened. But it *had*, and, as her audience, suppressing a laugh, I was complicit. It'd been nothing much, that flash of a bunny face, but inside me welled a deliciously excruciating unease because I had a strong suspicion that she hadn't finished, that this was only the start. And indeed, when he looked down again, she waggled her eyebrows at me. That was all it was, two ridiculous hitches of her eyebrows, but the point was that it was at Father James's expense: his earnestness mocked, his innocence.

At the next opportunity, her eyelids drooped until her eyes were three-quarters closed and then the tip of her tongue protruded in what I recognised as an impression of a dozing cat. Of course it was very silly, but, still, it was too much: *Stop it*, I begged her under my breath, *stop it, stop it,* even as I was willing her on to worse.

'Nearly done?'

It was unclear which of us she was asking, but there was no mistaking the implication that the sketch should be nearly done, which had Father James suddenly flustered. 'Oh, well, er . . .'

And that was when I felt bad for him. The sketch had seemed like a good idea at the time, but minutes later Katherine was bored. There was no malice in it, and she was properly eager to see what he'd achieved; she made much of her delight with it, assured him she'd treasure it, but still, she'd had enough. She had been playing with him, I saw, but suddenly she'd finished with him. I did see it, and I didn't like it, but how I wish I'd better heeded it.

7

For all her apparent breeziness, Katherine was already in trouble. Not that any of us knew it. They both were. I suspect I did once see something of it, but back then, couldn't make anything of it. From the long gallery, one afternoon, I'd glimpsed the pair of them in the garden, pacing side by side but slowly, barely moving. From the bowed heads I guessed something to be under discussion, if only tentatively. Then she halted, which halted him, and she reached for him, her hand on his shoulder as if to stop him, although he showed no intention of going. Beseeching, too, that hand; with the gentlest touch, she turned him to her. She was the one who was talking, but guardedly; none of her usual liveliness.

I knew I should look away but I, too, was held there, way up above them. What I was seeing, even if I didn't know it at the time, was the distance between them. A distance, however small, and despite her attempt to bridge it. She squeezed his shoulder in a gesture of reassurance. He was refusing to look at her, he was resolutely downcast, but her gaze tucked itself beneath his, and then she gathered him to her: her hands – both – on the back of his head, his neck, to guide him to her. He surrendered, but reluctantly, didn't reciprocate, didn't reach for her, his arms remaining at his sides, but nevertheless his forehead came to rest on hers.

Late one midsummer night, it was to my shoulder that her hand came, to fetch me from sleep. My eyes opened to hers and there she was, my sister-in-law, beside the bed, watching me come awake and half-smiling as if I were late for something, as if by falling asleep I'd been a little remiss. She held no light, had no need of one: we were a mere sliver short of the flower moon, and its radiance was oddly definite and dense everywhere in the room. The shutters and bed-hangings were open to let drift the considerable heat that had built up during the day, but I lay stranded, sweating, in nightclothes and bedclothes. Something must be wrong, I knew, despite that smile of hers, because why else would she be waking me? Beneath the weight of my sisters' sleep, I hardly dared breathe. 'What?' I mouthed, my throat silted with sleep, but she dismissed my concern with a shake of her head, whispering, 'Come to the brook.'

What?

'The brook.'

I had no idea what she meant. Had she left something there?

'To the water,' she urged, and then I got it – *water* – and suddenly nothing else in the world mattered but free-flowing fresh water, the slash of it through the dense heat onto my skin. Carefully, I slid up from the bedclothes, only to realise that there could be no lovely cold water because the day was done and the brook had retreated into the night. Two separate worlds, we were: we Seymours wrapped in our beds and dreams, and the brook, down among distant trees, wriggling belly up in the moonlight and the gleam of animal eyes. And anyway, 'Where's Edward?' Because shouldn't she be with him? Night time was when they were a pair again; wherever else he had had to be for the day, they were a pair in bed when darkness fell.

'Asleep,' and a trace of impatience in it: stuffy Edward, more fool him.

Again, I pictured their bed as a tomb; but this time Edward alone on it, marble, untroubled, trusting. Somehow, Katherine had got loose.

'Come on,' she urged. 'It's like daylight out there.' Far too good to miss, and so then I was the laggard, stubbornly unmoved by its wonders. Her urgency did ignite a spark beneath my breast-bone, but I knew we couldn't leave the house – this locked, dog-guarded house – to go traipsing away over pastureland. Anyone could be out there, poaching, trying their luck, arrow-happy. Nor should I leave the girls untended in here: as eldest, I was guardian of their safe sleep; they'd been entrusted to me. Dottie's face, across the pillow from mine, set against the heat. Margie's feet, between Dottie and me, eerily still, as if listening.

True, though, it was intolerably hot. And anyway, I was awake.

Was this, then, something that she used to do, I wondered, down in Dorset? Was it something that she knew how to do? – move undetected through a dark house, come by keys and then brave whatever was out there before getting herself back unmissed into bed? Could she do all that? Standing expectantly at my bedside, she certainly gave that impression, and I was cap-tivated. Never once in my life that I could recall had I stepped out of line. If I did go with her, I reasoned, we wouldn't be long, because it wasn't far, just beyond the gardens. And anyway, as long as we were careful, who would know? And Elizabeth, snor-ing down at the other end of the bed, was only a year my junior: she should be almost as capable of looking after the girls as I was.

Katherine was right: the water was there, down among the trees, a mere string of steps away; there it was, God-given, being water, busy doing its absolute best to be cold, and so it could only be right to use it, wrong to waste it. Anyway, I sensed that she'd be going, regardless, and I knew I shouldn't let her go alone.

The warm floorboards received my bare soles and so I was on my way.

'I knew you'd be awake,' she whispered appreciatively, tip-toeing ahead of me to the door, although we both knew that she'd woken me. That was to be the story, though, that we told each other: that we were equals in this endeavour. She had a way of doing that, I'd learn in time, of magicking up complicity; she had a knack for it. She pulled open the door, a scent billowing from her; the scent of her but more so, unfettered by daytime dress.

'You're in your nightdress,' I said, meaning that perhaps we should be getting dressed.

'It's night,' was her simple answer as she started her descent of the stairs, and I heard her smile in it. Not that our state of undress would matter, because, I felt, we probably wouldn't venture far. Any minute now, I feared, someone would hear us – the dogs, if no one else – and then the escapade would be out of our hands and we'd be back safely in our beds in no time. We could say that we'd merely been on our way to get some air, to stand in a doorway or at one of the bigger windows downstairs. There need be no mention of any trip to the brook.

Ahead of me, she was already at the foot of the stairs and an eddy of shadows told me that she was placating the dogs, offering them her hand. I heard her soothing whispers, even if I couldn't distinguish the actual words, amid the surprisingly delicate tapping of the dogs' nails on the flagstones. Reaching her, though, I found that it was only George and he was unalarmed because – of course, of course – he'd recognised our footfalls. He was merely intrigued, being nosy: he'd come to investigate and to discover if he might be of any help.

I took over settling him while Katherine went to find the keys then sifted through the bunch, trying a few before coming across the correct one, its grinding in the lock having me cringing in anticipation of someone waking, and realising how badly I wanted us to get away with the escapade. When the door opened, there was the outside world looking steadily back at us. The night was mostly sky, poised in all its finery and hung with the overly large moon. I was drawn behind Katherine onto the path, the graininess of the brick under my soles bringing me up sharp. The night seemed to lay itself down before us and suddenly it was absurd that anyone could ever contemplate keeping to the house. Before then, I'd been shut up indoors and simply hadn't known. She had, though: Katherine had known, and, thank God, she'd shown me.

The dark air had a physical presence: we had to press ourselves through it. The fragrance was earthy with the smell of foliage but somehow also the opposite, there being a sweetness to it like something on the turn. A creature darted away into a bush, furtive: a rip, then a whispering of leaves in its wake. We were trespassers in this night-time world. As I strode after Katherine, my nightdress clamoured around my knees and shins. Shadows were everywhere, sleek, their clarity unnerving. Her own shadow ahead of me slid below her like a fish just beneath the water's surface, quicksilver but blunt-nosed, disturbingly insensate. Above it, though, her steps were jaunty, tossing anklebones as if they were handfuls of pebbles. I was awed by her purposefulness – she was so very full of life – and had the sudden, dizzying notion that she might be carrying a baby; the start of a baby like a pearl inside her. It seemed to me, then, that nothing had happened at Wolf Hall for as long as I could remember, but now, marvellously, any- thing could happen.

I had to concentrate to keep up with her, and we were at the water before I knew it: there was the brook, a skein amid the trees, rippling as if drawing its fingertips along its own surface.

She didn't break her stride but hastened, those merry footsteps tumbling over one another. Grabbing a fistful of nightgown, she extended her other arm in search of her balance, coaxing it into play as she waded into the water, onto the little stones on its bed. I winced to think of their grudging shift beneath the soles of her feet. She halted abruptly, as if snared, and looked back at me, exhilaration spilling from her. 'Come on!' and it soared like bird-call.

She tottered backwards, making something of surrendering to the depths even though the water would only cover her ankles, and gasping at the cold, which was like a trick played on her again and again, the delight of it failing to diminish. For me, dipping my toes, the chilliness came both as a shock and no surprise at all, as if I'd been let in on a secret that I found I had known all along. Emboldened and beguiled, I held my breath as the brook gloved both my feet. The sensation was delicious: why did we ever spend any time anywhere else? I'd never be able to thank her enough for waking me and bringing me with her.

Laughing, she hauled her nightdress up around her knees; shins revealed, she had a raw look to her, skinned, and I looked away to spare her. Bending double, she stirred the stream with her free hand, arcs sweeping her from side to side so that she might've been in search of something that playfully eluded her. Then she released her handful of nightdress; it floated around and away from her. I swallowed my warning cry because she didn't need alerting, she'd clearly done it on purpose: she was wallow-ing in it, seemed to be relishing the drag of its dead weight. Both her hands were down in the water now, and she exclaimed at the cold, thrilled to be tormented, before dropping to her heels, then forward onto her knees so that she was properly in the stream, her nightdress sodden to the hips. She looked up wide-eyed to me for congratulations, but actually I could think only of her walk, drenched, back to the house and her arrival dripping on the threshold. Where was she going to hang that nightdress to dry so that it didn't give us away?

'Come on in!' She looked both aghast and amused that I hadn't joined her.

Kicking up a couple of splashes to show that I could pursue pleasures of my own, albeit small ones, I broached it: 'You're soaked, now,' hating that I sounded peevish.

'I'll dry off,' she countered over the clattering of water from her cupped, raised hands.

She wouldn't, though. Not unless she took off that nightdress. Should I go back to the house to fetch her a dry one? Back to the house, then back here again: two stretches of darkness to be braved alone. 'Edward'll know where you've been.' What should have been simple, a mere paddle, had gone too far. We had a drenched nightdress on our hands and a dry one to dig from the depths of one of the chests in her – his – room. No longer would she be able simply to slip back into the house and into bed beside him, but either she hadn't grasped that or she didn't care. I didn't want to be a killjoy; I'd been such a dutiful, timid sort before Katherine had come to Wolf Hall but I'd hoped I'd left that conventional girl behind. Suddenly weary, I turned from my sister-in-law, waded a few steps away. Perhaps I should just leave her to it, see how she liked that. Only the one dark stretch, for me, back to the house. That, at a push, I could probably face.

'Edward *won't* know!' She was laughing not only at the very idea but at me, too, for entertaining it, for fussing. 'And anyway, so what if he does?'

Her bravado drew me back around, curious, because did she really not know of Edward's deep distrust of impulsive behaviour? And sneaking from the house to the brook in the small hours was surely that. And he'd blame me for it, I feared, as much as he'd blame her, because as a Seymour I should have known better.

There she was, though, kneeling, comfortable and unconcerned, patting the water's surface, unmistakably pleased with herself. Perhaps I was wrong, then, perhaps Edward made an exception for her. Because what did I know? Perhaps the exception was what she was, for him, and he loved her for it; perhaps it was even what he loved her for. Perhaps when she turned up, later, at the bedside, shivery and overexcited, he'd murmur, 'Oh, you, what on earth have you been up to? Come on, get in and let me warm you up.'

'Can you swim?'

Her change of tone threw me, and, anyway, 'In *this*?' The slightest flex of my foot broke the surface.

Her laugh was devoid of edge now, warm and appreciative instead. 'Well, anywhere.'

This was silly, though, because where else had I ever been? 'No.' Where – how – would I ever have learned? 'Can you?'

'Yes.'

Suspicious, that pause before her answer. 'How did you learn?' She didn't have brothers, who could've taught her.

She was sweeping her hands in arcs again, so the shrug was done with her mouth. 'Dunno. Just did.'

That I definitely didn't believe. If she'd learned to swim, she'd recall the circumstances.

'I could teach you if you like.' Her offer seemed genuine – shyly voiced, her gaze steady and guileless – so then I didn't know what to believe.

'In *this*?' The brook was the only water for miles around.

She smiled as if her offer had been a joke between us, which perhaps it had. 'Everyone should learn. I mean, you don't want to drown, do you?'

I gave her a look, which she dismissed with a roll of her eyes.

'Wherever you end up going,' she said, and there was a hitch to my heartbeat as I absorbed the ring of the words. Was she humouring me? She didn't give that impression. Did she really think I'd have a life away from Wolf Hall? Could I perhaps confide to her my fear that I'd never marry? Possibly I could – possibly I could manage to get it voiced in this faraway darkness. But what if she laughed it off? That'd be even worse than keeping it to myself: to have it laughed at, to be left with it. The moment was fast passing. Could I do it? Could I say it? In a couple more heartbeats, the opportunity would have vanished.

So I did it, made myself do it: leapt in, but careful to make nothing much of it. 'Oh, I doubt I'll be going anywhere,' as if so long reconciled to my future failure as to be bored by the prospect of it. The suggestion, too, that my impending spinsterhood might be regarded as a quirk; harmless, even amusing.

'You'll get married,' she said, rising, done with the water, letting it fall as she emerged. 'Everyone does.' At the time, I was so relieved to hear it that I didn't register what I should have, and it's only all these years later, free from the anxieties and preoccupations of my fifteen-year-old self, that I detect the defeat in her words.

8

What should have been the first clear sign of trouble between my brother and sister-in-law, I was only too ready to put down to the physically arduous circumstances of a particular evening, and I doubt I was alone in that. It happened on the first of August.

July had sweltered until the heat itself seemed weary, going through the motions so that the long days had something to them of a child's wide-eyed stare of exhaustion, incapable even of giving up, and then, come our Lammas celebration, the mid-evening air was hotter outdoors than in Hall. Stepping through the doorway, what I took in of the trestle tables in the gardens wasn't the banquet on offer but the tablecloths, the heaviness of all that linen. Myself, I was as lightly dressed as possible but, despite a ribbon-made caul rather than a hood or a cotton coif, my hair was damp with perspiration. Even my eyelids were sticky with it.

On those long tables were bowls and platters of fruits which should've been refreshing but were defeated: strawberries going slimy in rosewater syrup, raspberries bleeding into custard pastries. We girls had spent a week picking and preparing those fruits, but then Bax's burning, salty meat had been the success of the afternoon. The air had been slathered with the rich aroma of roasting, and all through the day the lining of my mouth had puckered at the prospect of it. We'd all eaten our fill in Hall before stepping outside to the banquet of sore-looking straw-berries and raspberries. Standing there on the terrace, I was parched, but the sickly floral scent given off by the jugs of honey-mead was distinctly unappetising. There was some wine – our mother having done her trick of adding damson syrup to eke out and pep up the dregs of our annual Christmas delivery – but I headed for the jugs that contained ale, much of which had had to be bought in when we'd realised that however hard we worked, we'd never be able to brew enough to quench everybody's thirst.

The children, our own Seymour children and those of our guests, had run on ahead and had kept running to end up just beyond the gardens, where they melded into the shadows. Over there, the flurries of activity were punctuated by periods of notable stillness: a code tapped onto the dusk, but one that I couldn't decipher. Wondering if I should go and check on them, thinking Margie and Antony should soon be getting ready for bed, I remained on the terrace, beyond caring, staring blindly in their general direction with a suspicion that they were getting one over on me. Even the old dogs, usually so keen to poke their noses in, had failed to make it over there. I envied them their drastic sprawling in the relative cool of the grass, but pitied them their laboured breathing, the spasms of their ribcages.

Katherine and I stood in the thrum of dragonflies, watching the evening go by. Despite the valiant efforts of the trio of musicians to earn their fee, it was far too hot for dancing. Gamely, though, they kept grinding on, two of them sawing at the strings of their viols and the third subjecting those of his harp to spiteful-looking plucks. As for us, after all our hard work, Lammas was at last here, the evening under way so that it took on a life of its own and had us bowing to it, casting us aside, making mere bystanders of us. Well, so be it. It seemed to me that we'd been waiting for this evening for quite a while, perhaps for longer than we'd known, and it was a relief that it was finally here.

The Dormers were our principal guests. Beside us, my mother and Mrs Dormer were in full flow on their usual favoured topics: the shortcomings of particular servants ('... had to make it very clear ...'); achievements of various sons ('... really very pleased ...'); their own ill health ('... stiff, first thing ...') and that of relatives and acquaintances ('... tremendous swelling ...'). Katherine and I were nominally in attendance but not expected to contribute and, anyway, I doubt we could have got a word in edgeways. Our own happily desultory exchange was the undertow to theirs; we spoke of nothing much, this and that. She showed me a blister, I remember, kicked up a heel, eased down the back of her shoe and there it was, a nasty little nub, tight-lipped white.

Across the terrace, my father and Edward stood with Mr Dormer, and, although I couldn't hear, I knew what would be under discussion: incidences of poaching and disputes over land-ownership; the trustworthiness or otherwise of various labourers, artisans and suppliers; the impending appointment of a Justice of the Peace for Somerset. Edward looked inattentive, which was unusual for him. Katherine noticed it too. 'Just how bored,' she laughed, 'does Edward look?'

'Well, it's business, isn't it.' I sympathised; Edward never allowed himself to go off duty. 'What he's doing, over there, is keeping on good terms with the neighbours.'

She said nothing to that, whispering instead, 'You and me, we should be down at the brook,' as if this were something we did at the drop of a hat, when actually we'd only done it the once. We both laughed guiltily, or at least self-consciously, and I guessed she, too, was thinking of everyone else stuck at the house on their best behaviour in arduous circumstances while we frolicked at the brook, half-undressed under the alders, giving ourselves to the immediate, physical pleasures of the water.

Then she surprised me with, 'Not bad, is he, the Dormer boy.'

Will Dormer? He and Thomas were in the garden, sprawled across the bench in the arbour, and the deepening dusk made it hard to distinguish between them. Similar build, similar sprawl. Friends of old, they hadn't seen each other for a while, and this was their chance to get reacquainted. When the Dormers had turned up in the courtyard, I'd been struck how Will had changed since he'd last visited us a year ago; his face, in particular, was no longer boyish but bone-heavy, especially his jaw. It was as if he were wearing a crudely made mask of his own face. Perplexed, I'd been narrowing my eyes, all afternoon, to try to see through it. 'Not bad'? Well, I really didn't know how to respond to that; didn't even quite know how to go about thinking about it. Didn't know if I should. He was Thomas's friend: that was what he was. That was all he was. He was Thomas's friend: he was just . . . there. Except, of course, when he hadn't been.

Katherine was asking, 'Any plans for him?'

I dredged up what I could recall: 'He's at Oxford, for now, but—'

She laughed: 'No!' I'd misunderstood. With exaggerated patience, she elucidated: 'For you and him.'

What? I whirled to her. *What?* But that was ridiculous! Completely ridiculous. Was she mocking me? 'No!'

Will Dormer never so much as looked at me and, actually, even if he did, I realised, I'd resent it. Because I didn't like him. The realisation came as a physical jolt; I really didn't like Will Dormer. What was shocking was that I'd not considered myself to have any feelings whatsoever for him – didn't care enough – yet here was a feeling, loud and clear, if damning.

But was there something wrong with me? Everyone else

seemed to like him. And now so did Katherine. Everyone seemed to regard him as genial, affable: Will Dormer, good bloke. Indeed, that was how he was careful to present himself, and it was exactly that, I realised, that I mistrusted, the way he'd come ambling over as if he were shucking off welcoming claps to the back, as if embarrassed by the abundance of goodwill that surrounded him. *I'm just a bloke, just a good bloke.* But his eyes were dead: couldn't Katherine see that? *Look at the eyes.*

Whereas Thomas, well, Thomas might be full of himself, but there was life in his eyes. He burned with it. And although he could be exasperating and obstructive, and thoughtless and reckless, although he could be all those things, just occasionally he'd desist from making life difficult for everyone and then it was clear, even if he wished to pretend otherwise, that he had a heart. It was definitely true of Thomas back then, no longer the case, perhaps, a couple of years later, after what happened, but back then, I'm certain it was the truth.

Will Dormer, though? No. No heart, and could Katherine really not see that? Katherine, who'd fallen in love with Edward; Edward, who was everything that Will Dormer wasn't. It made no sense to me that she of all people failed to see it; it even sort of scared me that she didn't.

Unfortunately, the boys had sensed our attention on them and were rising to it.

'He's coming over,' Katherine hissed excitedly.

'Ladies!' Thomas heralded their approach.

Katherine laughed. 'Gentlemen!'

Will Dormer honoured her with one of his calculatedly bashful smiles and Thomas cocked his head towards the table of ale jugs.

'We need a top-up,' he explained, before adding, in passing, to his sister-in-law, 'Your husband's been hitting the wine hard.'

'Has he?' She was surprised, and me, too, because Edward

never drank to excess. We both looked over to see that Edward was dishevelled, a little more so than might've been expected of any of us under the circumstances, but especially of him. There was the inattentiveness, too, accompanied by a distinctly downcast air. Had he misjudged? — had one too many cups to try to slake his thirst? Easily done, I supposed, on such an evening, but surely not by Edward. Edward never made mistakes.

Thomas grinned. 'He certainly has. Problem is, he doesn't know how to handle it,' the implication being that, by contrast, he and Will did. 'He'll be no use to you tonight.'

Rather than giving him the withering stare he deserved, Katherine merely looked blank. 'I'd better—'

'Leave him,' said Thomas, as he and Will strode off towards the table of jugs.

Their exchange had drawn Edward's bleary attention, I noticed, but when Thomas moved away, Edward's eyes stayed with his wife, an intense, questing gaze, as if he were trying hard to remember something about her. My father turned, the better to include him in the conversation with Mr Dormer, but to his obvious surprise saw at once that his eldest son was a lost cause and hastily covered for him by returning to Mr Dormer with uncharacteristic vigour, as if in a debate. Left to his own devices, Edward looked down again, morosely, into his cup.

I was worried. 'Edward's always so careful,' I said. 'I've never seen him even the slightest bit drunk.' Thomas, yes, of course, endlessly, and Harry was merry on occasion, but never Edward.

Katherine affected antagonism and boredom, rolling her eyes: *Let him stew.*

Edward looked poorly, though. He needed help. Any worse and he'd be attracting Dormer-attention, and when he sobered up, he'd be mortified. He'd made a mistake — somehow, incredible though it was, he'd made a mistake — and he needed saving from himself.

'Should—?' Should we do something? What, I didn't know, but surely Katherine would know.

She declined to meet my eye. 'Leave him.'

Thomas's words coming from her, but with added pique. Edward was showing her up, letting her down, and she was going to make him pay, that was what her belligerence made clear. She was the wronged wife, suddenly, and I was awed into silence because what did I know of being a wife of any kind? It left me distinctly uneasy, though.

Perhaps a quarter of an hour passed, during which time he didn't refill his cup and I hoped he'd realised he was in trouble and was sobering up. While Katherine and I were busy helping Lil to refill the jugs, I kept him in the corner of my eye. He'd managed to excuse himself from my father and Mr Dormer's company, retreating to a bench against the wall of the house, which kept him out of trouble for a while but then came a problem when he tried to get back up: he lurched like a wounded beast and plonked back down, the bench banging the wall. I prayed that no one else had noticed, but Katherine tutted with exasperation, despairing of him, muttering viciously, 'What's the *matter* with him?'

Well, it was all too horribly clear what was the matter with him. Suddenly she was gone from my side, simply slipping over there to him, and so, belatedly, I felt, it was going to be all right. She'd made her point but, at last, was going to do her wifely duty, was going to help him.

She stood over him, bending down but with her hands clasped in front of her skirts like a counterbalance; attending to him but, I saw, keeping her distance, which he didn't like, making far too much of reciprocating, of returning her attention, looking up into her face with a slow, inaccurate swing of his heavy head. This sullen, rude Edward wasn't the Edward I knew, and my heart went into freefall. Katherine's presence was only antagonising him.

Instinctively, Katherine began to glance around, presumably to look for help, before checking herself, probably fearful of drawing unwelcome attention. I doubted she'd got away with it, though, Mrs Dormer's curiosity regarding all matters Seymour being best described as athletic. Katherine looked so alone, over there. It'd been Edward who'd been hopelessly isolated, a moment ago, frowning down into his cup, but now that was at least as true of his wife. I should do something – but what?

Then Katherine straightened, Edward rearing back to keep his eyes on hers, and again there was insolence in the reeling, a challenge in it. I saw – didn't hear – that he said something to her, an utterance which, on impact, had her take a step back. Her own response was similarly minimal, just a word or two: 'Stop it,' perhaps, or, 'Don't.'

I was biting my lip, I realised, and my palms were slick with sweat. She did now glance properly around, right around, but the glance slid past my parents, who were belatedly and shamefacedly making themselves available, pausing their respective conversations and turning in her direction but nevertheless obviously reluctant to be called upon. Katherine couldn't bring herself to look to them; it was to me, instead, that she looked. There was nothing in the look, none of the self-righteousness of the wronged wife; there was just the fact of it, and I found it all the more powerful for that. She was at a loss, utterly at a loss, and it was to me that she looked for help.

Meanwhile, Edward seemed to be regretting whatever it was that he'd said to her, lowering his face into his hands and rubbing his eyes as if trying to bring himself to his senses. Well, it was too late for that. An ominous air had descended on the terrace to which only Thomas and Will Dormer paid no mind, Thomas teasing Lil for some alleged clumsiness and Will Dormer egging him on. I flushed with fury for Thomas: was he really oblivious, or did he just not care? Was he pleased, even?

If no one else was going to make the move to help, I realised, I'd have to do it. Despite having no idea of what actually I might do, I made myself take the first step and then there I was, headed for my brother and sister-in-law, making sure to saunter as if dropping by for a chat. In truth, my blood was chaotic inside me. I had the sense of stepping into the middle of a situation from which I wouldn't easily be able to extricate myself, had the sense of it closing over my head, but I knew I could no longer stand by. Some unpleasantness had developed between my brother and his wife, and perfectly understandable though it might be, the result of one cup of wine too many on this hottest of nights, it was happening in front of everyone, so it had to stop.

When I reached the pair of them, Katherine took a breath as if to speak, but nothing came and she merely stood there, in a kind of standing back. Abandoning the pretence of the casual chat, I did what she'd so far resisted doing: crouched down in front of Edward so that our eyes were level.

'Edward?'

I'd probably never before been so close to him. He was stubbled – the barber had visited, that morning, but already he was stubbled – and his breath was wine-dank.

'Jane . . . ' he sighed, full of feeling, although which particular feeling, I didn't know. 'Jane . . . '

It felt improper to be so close to him and in receipt of such heartfelt expression. Katherine shifted, and in that scratch of her soles on dirt-dry stone I heard her barely contained desperation to be elsewhere. In the same instant, I recognised what it was that had resounded in Edward's sigh: despair. So, from Katherine, desperation, and from Edward, despair: that was when I had an inkling that this was something more than one cup too many. But I didn't have time to think about it, because Edward's eyes, which I'd taken to be red from exhaustion, turned glossy with tears and all that concerned me was how best to get him away from everyone.

Careful to sound sympathetic, I whispered, 'You're not well,' while trying to think how we could most easily get him to his bed. Under any other circumstances, it would be Edward to whom I'd look for ideas. Thomas could provide physical assistance, if he could be made to help; Harry hadn't been around for a while, but Thomas was there on the terrace and he'd be strong enough to take Edward's weight. No less importantly, he could carry off any fracas with aplomb, his mere presence somehow persuading everyone that everything, however awry, was in fact just fine, even hilarious. His refusal to come to Edward's aid, though, was uncomfortably obvious, and, even as I silently raged at him, I knew there was no point forcing him because that'd only end up looking worse.

It didn't occur to me to turn to my parents; for them, I was feeling only an increasingly familiar exasperation. My mother, always ready enough with that disappointed expression of hers but never actually voicing what was on her mind; and my father being kind, but in retreat from family life.

'You're not well,' I repeated to Edward, intending it as reassurance: That's all it is, you're not well. 'You need to sleep this off. Can you come with me?'

'Oh, Jane . . .' The groan was an appeal, but for what? He was appealing to me not as his little sister, but as someone who might understand something of what he was going through, although actually I didn't. Gently, I took his arm, gauging how cooperative he might be, before looking to Katherine to take his other arm. She didn't hesitate and he offered no resistance, probably glad to be going.

All the way back into the house, he gave us no trouble; on the contrary, did his best for us, concentrating on each and every step. One of the dogs – dear old Bear – chose to escort us, which rather dignified our retreat. Indoors, the stairs presented a challenge but, by ordering Bear to stay at the bottom and then taking it slowly, we managed. Only at their door, and despite a pleading look from Katherine, did I extricate myself from the pair of them, by which time all I felt was relief. I'd had a job to do and I'd done it: that was all I could think at the time, and I was more than ready to turn away and put it behind me.

9

I don't think anything quite like that did happen again, although I suppose I might have been too busy to notice because August, more than any other month, demanded the utmost of us from dawn to sundown. We girls were harvesting from the gardens and orchard, pulling up bulbs and roots, picking herbs and pods, fruits and berries, teasing currants intact from bushes and whacking walnuts from branches, and then preparing our gains to last us the rest of the year. We'd spread our spoils on sacking in the sun or hang it in bunches to dry, or slice or strain it for stewing and cramming into jars. We layered it with spices and packed it with sugar or drenched it in verjuice, then tamped it down and left it to seal in the heat of the hearth.

Elizabeth couldn't pick strawberries – the leaves gave her a rash – but more than made up for it by wielding a big stick at the walnut trees while the children scurried to gather the fallen nuts and Katherine pushed a needle tip into each case to judge for ripeness. I did the pickling: it was left to me because, in my mother's view, I could be relied upon to make the least mess of that messiest of jobs. Walnuts were undoubtedly the worst, but the red fruits and blackcurrants were by no means easy and we spent the month swaddled in aprons which, laid over bushes to dry in the evenings, were suggestive of the scene of a catastrophe. Those aprons provided no protection for our hands, of course, and every nail bed was dark-stained, every fissure and fingertip whorl vivid.

Our work in the kitchen had to fit around Bax's roasting of half an ox or steer every day for the workers in the fields, and my mother baking the bread to go with it. The supposedly cooling fly-deterrent fern fronds hung at the kitchen window were annoyingly ineffective, but we knew there were worse places to be. The brewhouse, for one: even from across the courtyard we could hear the swearing of the brewer at his scald-scarred sidekick, the two of them stuck in the heat there together for the month to brew the whole hogshead of ale that was downed daily by the harvesters. And the mouthy brewer wasn't the only reason that a step outside provided less than a breath of fresh air: Moll and Lil were doing a lot of bleaching, so the courtyard was crowded with urine-filled barrels.

The Seymour men were over at the household farm, Suddene, every day of that month, rolling up their sleeves and getting down to harvest alongside our villagers. Bax's roast was taken into the field in the late morning, but at the end of the working day everyone trooped up to Wolf Hall for supper. Sometimes the labourers' children brought bundles of kindling to exchange for biscuits but they were just as likely to present scrapes, bruises and sprains for my mother to treat, to say nothing that year of sunburn.

Edward did his fair share of the physical labour at Suddene, but was also overseeing the workforce. Inevitably, under the circumstances, there were perceived injustices, and, occasionally, tempers would flare and he and the reeve would have to step in to calm the situation and try to resolve the dispute. As well as being responsible for their welfare, he also paid the work-ers' wages, so, in the evenings, he'd stay up, frowning over ledgers, keeping records and making calculations, long after Katherine had gone to bed. They barely saw each other that month.

Two feasts were celebrated in August, Assumption and St Bart's, but, being so busy, we made minimal efforts for them and issued no invitations, although Harry's Barbara joined us. Assumption Day was when Katherine and Barbara first met, because before then Barbara had spent a couple of months laid low by a cough and congestion. Barbara was a pretty, petite blonde who never said much – or not in Seymour company – but that evening the prospective Seymour daughter-in-law basked in Katherine's solicitous attention. Which was understandable, because Barbara was a likeable enough girl. I couldn't claim to know her very well, but she was comfortable company. Thomas's nickname for her – behind her back, behind Harry's – was Boring Barbara, but, well, as Katherine caustically remarked to me, 'You wonder, don't you, who'll ever be interesting enough for our Master Thomas.'

Edward didn't get drunk on those evenings, but then, he'd never make a mistake twice. He and his wife stayed close, often holding hands, and even now I can picture them strolling around together, Katherine's arm swinging with Edward on the end of it. He'd be working his thumb back and forth over the base of hers in what I took to be a soothing gesture, absently done, although, come to think of it, Edward was never less than mindful. At the time, I saw those joined hands slung between the two of them as an intimacy, but I suppose I could just as easily have seen them as a dead weight.

And then, before we knew it, we were into September, nearing the end of the farming year and about to knuckle down to a new one. The year was turning, moving on from the wedding, so that Katherine was becoming just another Seymour, just as it should have been. The wool-winders were about to descend on Wolf Hall, but they were migrants, skilled workers, able to look after themselves, and so we girls could stay busy in the orchard and along the hedgerows. Sometimes, Thomas would oblige by climbing up into the trees to pick for us, from where he'd taunt us with how far he could see – 'Hey, it's really good up here!' – and Katherine would yell back that he should get a move on, 'Because *some* of us have work to do.'

We certainly did, because in place of the bright-eyed summer berries came autumn's big, thick-skinned, fibrous fruits with their pips and cores. Whatever we couldn't preserve, we stored, which is where Antony made himself particularly useful, the apple loft being his domain because of his enthusiasm for spiders ('The bigger, the better!').

The days were still warm for the time of year although no longer in the mornings and evenings, which tended to catch me unawares. The morning air had a sharpness at which, inexplicably, my stomach tightened; and at the end of an afternoon I'd step outside and, before I was quite ready for it, there was dusk. From the first of the month, we were back to using candles. Autumn was coming creeping in and despite my vigilance it kept springing its unsettling little surprises: the dawn later and dusk earlier, the air colder and flowers gone. It seemed reproachful, to me, as if in its view we'd got beyond ourselves and had forgotten its existence so that it had to make itself felt.

Then, mid-September, something happened to change everything, to knock our little world akilter, and never again were we the Seymours that we'd been, generations of us dependable and respectable. Had the messenger not ridden up on that afternoon or any other, would we still all be there? All of us, at Wolf Hall, just older, ever older, with our children. Margie and Antony, even, with children. That unlived life taunts me like a tatter of dream. How would it have been, to have lived it? The life I was born to, my birthright, my Wolf Hall country life. Well, this much is certain: if I'd lived it, I'd be smaller and safer but I'd be no one I know.

FRUIT MOON

I

For me, it all began with a turn from the sink to find Katherine with her arms emphatically folded and a pointedness in her stance, even a petulance, which was something that, until then, I'd never seen from her. We'd been preserving apples that afternoon, and when she'd nipped from the kitchen to see my mother about our dwindling supply of cloves, I'd taken a bowl of dirty water outside to tip away into the sink. And then there I was, intending to get back to those apples but coming slap-bang up against her. She had news for me, apparently, but just as clear, to judge from the hard-folded arms and compressed lips, was that for some reason she was going to keep it from me until I asked for it.

It was easy enough to oblige. Squinting at her through the angled sunshine, I asked, 'What?'

Her chin tilted upwards, her head to one side. 'Edward's going to war,' deliberately sing-song, strained, high-pitched as if through gritted teeth.

I nearly dropped the bowl. '*What?*' Even though I didn't know what she meant, it hit me hard, as surely she would have known it would: that word, *war*. And, anyway, what war? There was no war! And Edward? Even if there was a war, why would Edward be going to it?

The same tone, her head tilting to the other side: 'He's off to conquer France.' As if, by doing so, he was defying her.

Point taken – she was dismayed and, understandably, beneath the bluster, afraid – but I needed to know what was going on; I needed her to stop the bizarre carry-on and explain what was actually happening.

No chance, though, because now she was exclaiming, 'Dust off the banner!' and it was caustic: the deliberately badly feigned jollity, the icy eyes.

Our Seymour family banner, which our father had earned in battle in France when I was three or four. By all accounts it'd been well earned, and it was beautiful, but still, like Edward it was suffering Katherine's derision. Then, just as suddenly, she seemed to lose patience with herself and dropped the indignation to tell me straight, despite keeping the fierce fold of arms and relating the explanation flatly to make quite clear that she didn't endorse it. A messenger, she said, had just arrived from the Duke of Suffolk, and Edward was required to go as a junior commander in an army to France. Some French duke was ready to move against his monarch, she said, and the other dukes were likely to rally behind him, and various countries had pledged their support; so this, now, would probably be the end of the French king. Our own king had a chance, at last, to reclaim France for England.

I was still trying to take it all in when she said they were aiming to sail on St Matthew's eve, in less than two weeks' time. So all the preparations and Edward's journey to Dover would have to be done by then. Flabbergasted, I backtracked to the beginning: 'Edward just told you all this?'

She nodded with grim satisfaction. 'Just now, in front of your mother and father.'

And I got it: that was what he'd done wrong, that was how

he'd upset her. And, actually, I felt it, too: the insensitivity of announcing to his new wife in front of his parents that he was off to battle. Not taking her to one side to break the news but treating her as if she were just anyone else, as if she were any one of us. He should've taken her to one side and held her; he should've known to do that. My perfect brother should've known very well to do that. What on earth was the matter with him?

Spotting that she'd snared my sympathy, she hauled it in on a deep breath that allowed her to relinquish the rigid stance, the belligerence, and give herself up to fear, let it come for her. Breaking away from me, she paced, circling, hugging herself, holding herself together, each breath shuddery and her eyes huge with unshed tears. Unnerved, I rushed to placate her, 'He'll be all right, he'll be fine,' but even as I was urging her to believe it, I didn't know if *I* did. It did stop her panic, though: she halted, drew herself up tall, gave me a look; a full, frank look but one that I failed to read, only feeling the force of it, and then was off, at a pace, back towards the house.

I followed, losing ground to her as each of her long-legged strides threw more distance back at me. Behind her, I banged through the door into the house and Bear, startled somewhere, hedged her bets with a bark.

Rattling into Hall, breathless, I almost ran into her, standing with my mother: the two of them standing side by side in what was for me a bewildering show of unity and stoicism. It was as if I'd imagined Katherine's distress only a moment ago in the garden.

My mother's benign moon face turned to me: 'Ah! Jane, this is Mr Wellbelove, the Duke of Suffolk's man,' and she gestured towards an unshaven, grimy man sitting at one of the tables. My mother meant me to offer a careful smile, but the man and I stared at each other. His mouth was full and rotating; he was being amply refreshed, but his eyes were those of a man who'd been riding all day long for several days. As was his smell. Nevertheless, Thomas was lounging beside him as if they made a team. Edward was nowhere to be seen: he'd already gone, I'd later learn, to round up his men.

My mother began telling me what I already knew from Katherine, finishing with, 'And isn't that such an honour?' Her smile permitted no dissent, but Katherine wouldn't be told. Close enough beside my mother to be invisible to her, my sister-in-law gave me a look that placed herself firmly in opposition.

Edward spent the five frantic days before his departure doing the duty of a knight's heir: calling upon the men in Wolf Hall's surrounding villages to join him in the king's army. Literally calling upon them: going from door to door to visit every family, hunkering down on earth floors to explain the situation to the best of his knowledge, offering reassurances where possible, promising assistance in the form of provisions and helping to plan how the man's work might be covered in his absence. He would have been only too aware of the magnitude of what he was asking of those families: not only that they hand over the head of household to go to war on foreign soil but that they do so at the start of the farming year when the heavy work needed to be done, the breaking up of the soil and the ploughing, to say nothing of the November slaughter and the late-autumn foraging for firewood, the endless wood-chopping.

When he returned home in the evenings, he didn't come into the parlour. We'd hear the closing of the main door and his footsteps across Hall, heading towards the kitchen; he was going to find himself some supper. No chess games for him, no farm gossip with Harry and his father, no lute-strumming with Thomas while we girls worked at our embroidery and Dottie and Margie were permitted the occasional, muted clapping game. He needed to eat, and he needed to get to bed.

That shutting of the door would raise our heads and there we all were, looking at one another but blankly, because what we were really doing was listening, dredging the sounds of the door and the footsteps for what we could find in them. Despair, or fear, or just resignation? Perhaps even exhilaration after a successful day, although that was less likely because, after all, this was Edward and he'd been mustering men for battle.

Listening to him making his way to the kitchen, I'd be wondering what he might find there and in what state – the chances of it still being warm, being appetising – and thinking how I might improve it, perhaps by making up some more sauce. Beside me, my mother was resisting her own urge to follow him into the kitchen and fuss around him, so I had to do the same. If Katherine hadn't been there, if this had been before their marriage, my mother would have got up and gone to him, I knew. But now, that was for his wife to do. So she didn't go. Nor, though, did Katherine.

Our snapping to attention there in the parlour every evening was also probably because we felt guilty to be resting up there, with our stomachs full. Actually, we too were working hard those days, from first light until last. We girls were working under my mother's direction because she knew exactly what was to be done; she'd done it all, twelve years before, for my father. Her primary concern was that her son, and his men as much as she could see to it, be protected from the wet and cold, and she began where it mattered most, sending for the cobbler, who spent a long day repairing and reinforcing Edward's boots along with those of anyone who could be persuaded to come up to Wolf Hall and hang around, or better still go back to work in stocking feet. That first day, the men of Wolf Hall were small-stepping and soft-treading, flinching and wincing their way over courtyard cobbles.

Meanwhile, she rummaged in chests and piles of laundry for hose that could be spared, advancing on me and Katherine time and again with numerous pairs looped over her forearm for patching and reinforcing. Despite the gravity of the situation, Katherine and I had to stifle giggles at the sight of her draped so extravagantly in men's hose. She, of course, was oblivious. Nor, for once, was she interested in the quality of our darning; on the contrary, she was actively dismissive of it, urging us to work with regard only for speed, which we found hard because it went against everything we'd ever learned. Nevertheless, despite the demanding pace of work and the household's air of solemnity, we couldn't quite resist holding up each and every pair of hose in order to speculate from the particular pattern of wear as to the identity of its owner.

With boots and hose under way, my mother turned her attention on the second day of preparations to the other extremities, despatching Harry to Salisbury to buy all the gloves that he could find. Under any other circumstances, Thomas would have insisted on going with him, but on this occasion he chose to stay home to help my father with the weaponry and armour, the horses and carts. He worked dishevelled among the men in the courtyard – no jerkin, cap discarded, shirt indecently unbuttoned and filthy where he'd wiped his armour-polishing hands down it with spectacular disregard for those who did the laundry – and then came into dinner reeking of whatever he'd been working into saddles and bridles or smearing down bowstrings. None of which could have been said of my father, of course, who remained as calm and collected as ever, despite, no doubt, working just as hard.

Once, when Thomas spotted Katherine and me taking a break at the day-room window, he hollered up to us, 'I'm off to the brook for a strip-off,' jubilant, as if scoring a victory, which in a way he was, over decorum, and flinging up both arms, perhaps purely an expansive gesture but perhaps suggestive of submitting to a removal of his shirt. Katherine turned to me, genuinely affronted and making no effort to hide it. 'He is so . . .' and she frowned, considering the best word, ' . . . *unnecessary*.'

I laughed, because it seemed to me, back in those days, that infuriating though Thomas was, if he could be said to have a glory, then that, surely, was it.

Closing the casement on him, she turned circumspect: 'Thomas wishes he was going, doesn't he? He wishes it was him who was going.'

The latter was more accurate, I suspected: he'd want to replace Edward rather than merely accompany him.

'He thinks he's better, doesn't he?' But there was no accusation in it: it was mere observation. 'A better—' and she peeked down from the window as if to assess him, to ascertain how he might indeed be better than Edward. A better rider? A better shot? 'Better with the men,' she decided.

I had to admit: 'Yes, I think he does.'

'And is he?' Dispassionate, her asking; a fair question.

Not one, though, to which I knew the answer. For all Edward's tireless efforts, it was possible – we both knew it – that Thomas was at least as favourably regarded by the men. Sitting down, retrieving her sewing, Katherine smiled, but humourlessly. 'He'd miss his mother, though.' It was intended as a simple put-down, but actually she was more right than she knew.

That day, I remember, the real baby of the family was busy gathering goose feathers for the fletcher, while his little sisters sat alongside us in the day room, cutting an old scarlet petticoat into strips so that they could stitch St George crosses onto jackets. Lil and Moll were turning any other scraps into band-ages. And on the third day, a bale of canvas was at our disposal, too, donated by the Dormers; and my mother – having drawn up a simple pattern – put Elizabeth to work cutting out and then stitching together basic canvas jackets. A few large pieces, a big needle, coarse thread and crude stitches: the ideal needlework for needle-shy Elizabeth, who spread her paraphernalia over the entire room and was tediously vocal on the subject of her new-found expertise.

For a rest from her as much as from our own stitching, Katherine and I went outside mid-morning, ostensibly to check on the troughs of crab apples intended for verjuice. Someone would need to give them a quick mashing, that was our excuse. There in the courtyard was Will Dormer, having delivered that bale of canvas then stayed around to help Thomas. Spotting us at the troughs, he approached with that loathsome strenuous non-chalance of his.

Katherine heaved a sigh of relief when greeting him, as if here at last came someone sympathetic to the various privations she was having to suffer. I was surprised: she'd been throwing herself into her work and of course I knew she was unhappy at Edward's impending departure, but it was news to me that she'd been find-ing the day such an endurance, let alone that Will Dormer was the one to whom she'd choose to unburden. And more surprises were in store. She and Will Dormer stood side by side to look over the scene of the Seymour household preparing to send its heir to war, and in their shared stance I detected opposition. Will Dormer blew into his cheeks to signify a certain scepticism and, on cue, Katherine folded her arms, drawing herself up. Judgement was being passed, I realised, and unfavourably.

Despite not grasping the nature of my family's alleged failing, I couldn't help but feel obliged to apologise for it – that was what seemed to be being called for, even as I baulked at it – and I was stung because never before had my sister-in-law so much as hinted that it mattered to her that I was a blood Seymour. Inwardly, I bristled, because we were allies, weren't we? Friends. Like sisters, but better. I was who I was; how could I help having been born a Seymour? There she was, though, dismissing me as just another one of them. And to impress Will Dormer.

And worse was to come. Will Dormer was showing her his hand. I couldn't see it, the angle was wrong, but her reaction was a sharp intake of breath, so I craned to discover that somehow, during whatever he'd been doing with Thomas, he'd suffered a cut to the left index finger; not dreadful, but fairly bloody. He was turning it over to Katherine for her opinion. She didn't take his hand but laid her fingertips on it to encourage him to tilt it further towards her and, after closer inspection, decided, 'You need that dressed,' at which he blew into his cheeks again. She insisted, 'No, really,' then laughed: 'Ol' Ma Seymour will have something for it,' and he, too, laughed, so that my mother became a joke between them. 'Or,' Katherine said, 'Jane'll do it,' and then she was off, just off and away with a self-important flourish to the turn and a skip in her step to show it as deliberate and, to her, gratifying, this abandoning of us in each other's company.

What on earth was she doing? Didn't she know that I couldn't stand him? She damn well did know; there was no way she couldn't know. What was she thinking, then? That Will and I needed to be shown what was good for us, and would end up grateful to her? Or perhaps she wasn't thinking at all, but simply enjoying that turn on her heel for what it was. Father James came suddenly to mind, poor old Father James and the bunny face, the cat's tongue. This was more than play, though, I knew; there was a cruelty to this; a small cruelty, maybe, and deep down, but it was there nonetheless. I appreciated that she was out of sorts, and I understood why, but I felt she really shouldn't be taking it out on me.

I could almost hear Will Dormer calculating how he might best be rid of me but, unfortunately, I couldn't do him the favour of following Katherine across the cobbles; she'd designated me to take care of a wound in full knowledge that it was something from which I couldn't possibly walk away. I'd have to go through the motions of examining it. He didn't look at me; looked at the finger instead, turning it this way and that but solely to benefit his own viewing. Then, just as I was about to offer, reluctantly, to clean it up, he pronounced, 'It's fine, thanks,' and strode off to rejoin the men. And so there I was, left alone, having to pretend even to myself that my humiliation hadn't happened and especially not at the hands of someone whom, until then, I'd completely trusted.

For the final two days before Edward's departure, my mother had us turn our attention to his stomach, working from her recipes to cook sustaining snacks which, she said, were packable and portable. Those were strange, difficult days. First came biscuits, the mixture for which was so dry and dense that it adhered to itself and to the bowls, spoons, rolling surfaces, cutters and, of course, our hands, thwarting us further by sticking to anything with which we tried to prise it from anything else. It had us in its clutches: clumps wedged between our fingers, and our palms caked. Eventually, patience depleted, Katherine stuck up a mixture-obliterated hand and demanded with considerable vehemence, 'Who would *ever* want to eat this?'

A fair point, in a way, but I felt obliged to defend my mother and anyway there was some truth in what I knew she would say: 'Well, if you had nothing else . . . '

Katherine allowed it, but only grudgingly: 'I suppose so.'

After the disastrous biscuits came fruit that was to be boiled to a pulp and left overnight in trays on the hearth to dry into leathery sheets that could then be sliced into strips, which meant that we suffered a long day of the slumping of pear flesh beneath the knife and the precipitous slide of the blade through apple flesh. Our hands which, the day before, had been coated were now exposed, our fingertips nicked and notched, the striations welling with juice.

Katherine said very little all afternoon, but I recall her once offering up, wistfully and apropos of nothing, that Edward would miss Harvest Festival, which struck me as an odd remark because he'd be missing so much else besides. Harvest Festival was just the one day and, as far as I knew, not even one to which he was particularly attached. Even if the expedition ended up being entirely uneventful, Edward's missing of Harvest Festival would be for him, I imagined, the very least of it. I found Katherine hard to fathom, during those two long days, and she unnerved me.

And daytimes were the least of it. While we'd been occupied trying to keep Edward warm and stave off the worst of his hunger, my mother had been making sure to be the one who would save his life, retreating to the still room to concoct salves and tinctures, syrups and ointments from poppy seeds, cloves, lavender and rosehips, spooning or decanting them into tiny stoppered or sealed pots where they'd be ready for the cleansing and soothing of wounds and illnesses. Come each evening, though, it was Katherine who was engaged on a special mission and it'd happened as she'd predicted: that very first evening, when the duke's messenger had retired early and Edward was in Great Bedwyn enlisting the village men, my mother had decided we should retrieve the family banner from storage.

Thomas had been first to the door, returning in no time to kneel on the floor, avid, like a boy with a puzzle, and unfurl it. Even before it was fully displayed, my mother noticed it had suffered a little from moth, her exclamation pitched between disapproval and disgust. Crouching down, her touch to the moth-pocked portion was as much soothing as exploratory. We all stayed back, respectfully suspended, waiting for her to pronounce remedy. Well, all of us except Thomas, who muttered an oath that had my mother slide him a reproving glance, *Watch your language*. When she was satisfied that she'd properly assessed the extent of the damage, she levered herself up with a heavy, steadying hand on her son's shoulder, and it was to Katherine whom she turned: 'A job for you, I think, Katherine, and your lovely silks.'

So, for the next four evenings, Katherine knelt at our feet with a girlish slope of her shoulders and one hand mole-like beneath the banner to raise the moth-eaten area as if coaxing it up for her ministrations. It was a strange view that I had of her on those evenings – the hollow at the base of her skull, over which lay the finest and most golden threads of her hair – but that wasn't what was disconcerting. Nor was it her readiness to set herself apart from us, refusing offers of help to lift the banner and place it across laps, insisting instead that it was easier to work down there on the floor when obviously it wasn't, but the subjugation in that pose and her wilfulness in adopting it.

2

All too soon came the eve of Edward's departure. For the five days since his summons I'd no more than glimpsed him, sometimes very early, in the outer courtyard, saddling up, and a couple of times very late, hauling himself up the stairs to his room; and once coming out of the still room with my mother, looking grave and baffled.

He didn't come home for his final evening, sending word that he was staying over at the Wroughtons'. He'd been caught up in last-minute business was the message, and he judged it prudent to accept their hospitality for the night. He'd leave there at dawn, we were told, and, all being well, would be with us an hour later, although we knew he'd have to move off quickly again to make up for lost time. It was a Friday, a day of fasting, so nothing elaborate had been planned for his send-off, but we Seymours weren't strict observers and my mother had been thinking creatively around the restrictions. When the news of his absence came, she did well to hide her disappointment but Dottie, who'd been so carried away with a sense of occasion as to have prepared floral displays for the table (daisies, grasses and rosehips), piped her protest at the unfortunate messenger: 'How *could* he do this? He has to say goodbye!'

My mother turned flustered. 'Dorothy! You heard the man! Your brother will be home, but tomorrow.'

Dottie, though, would have none of it – 'That is *too late*!' – and then Antony was competing with a wail of his own – 'I need to show him the shield I made!' – while Margie, never to be outdone, offered a disdainful 'You really do think he'd have made the effort ...'

Elizabeth's contribution of a bosom-exerting sigh was the one that my mother seized upon to rebuke. 'Elizabeth, please try to show a little more understanding ...'

Distracted by the clamour, I didn't immediately think to look to Katherine to convey my sympathy. She was being denied a last night to have her husband to herself. When I did glance over, I saw that although she met no one's eye, she looked entirely accepting, which I took to be admirably dignified. Thomas, though, did meet my eye, and his was a knowing look, but which I returned on a steely one of my own. If Edward said he was too busy to come home, I felt, then that was the truth of the matter, that was all there was to it and we didn't need Thomas's insinuation, whatever it was.

Katherine retired alone very early to her room that evening – no invitation for me to join her – and in the morning was ahead of everyone into chapel for prayers. Immaculately dressed, too, from pearl coif to lace cuffs and kid gloves; she could've been up for hours. Perhaps she had. Certainly she looked tired, whey-faced. She kept herself to herself; but then in chapel she never did. No one else appeared so contemplative: all of us distracted, instead, by listening for Edward's return.

After prayers, we all got on with our usual household tasks, but half-heartedly. Antony didn't help matters by haring back and forth between we girls in our room and his brothers down at the stables. He had to be spoken to, and more than once. The girls weren't overexcited, quite the contrary, but were no easier to manage: Margie, morose; Dottie, high-handed; Elizabeth, just plain nasty. Nothing much except squabbling was getting done. Even Katherine was neglectful with the broom and dusters although, dressed beautifully as she was, who could blame her?

Eventually, just before eight, word came that Edward had arrived in the outer courtyard but would come no further, was changing horses and heading off. We all dashed there from the house and if, when we emerged from the passageway, Edward's gaze searched the crowd specifically for his wife, I didn't notice. As for her, she didn't go to him, but hung back with the rest of us.

We'd pitched up in a rush only to find ourselves at a loss as to what to expect from him; there we all stood, stopped, assembled, self-conscious, as if awaiting inspection. Like his wife, he looked exhausted, although differently, darkly; a notch at the corner of each eye that could've been pressed there by a thumb. My breath was jammed against my heart to see him, just twenty-one, so very serious there beside his horse. Despite his effort to look glad to see us, we were, amid all those men eager for his attention, clearly a complication; this wasn't the time or place for emotional good-byes. Understandably, he was anxious to be off, to make the most of the first day's ride.

It wasn't until my father took it upon himself to usher Katherine forward that I thought of her, as did everyone else, there being a flurry as we Seymours drew back, mindful and contrite. Suddenly she was singled out and there was nothing for it but for her to go ahead and conduct her wifely farewell in public. Edward was dazzled, his shadowed eyes widening at her approach and emptying of his preoccupations; she filled his gaze – completely filled it, brimful. Her own head, though, was bowed. We watched the barest touch of her fingertips to the front of his jacket, perhaps no actual touch but – I couldn't quite see – just a gesture in that direction. For all its hesitancy, though, it had a weight behind it and held the sense of a reckoning.

He smiled ruefully as he said something, then laid a hand on her shoulder before lowering his lips, reverently, to her cheek. It was done so slowly as to be enacted upon her; she had to stand stock still to receive it. Me, too, to witness it. I couldn't get enough of it; such tenderness, as I saw it. Anyone less in thrall to my brother and his wife might've recognised that embrace, such as it was, not to be what a young husband going away indefinitely into mortal danger, should have been giving in parting from his bride.

With Edward's riding away through the gatehouse began the weeks and months of waiting for news of him, the longing for it but dread of it, the fear fired off by any courtyard commotion or unexpected dog bark or footfall. Each and every morning of those months, I woke to an unease that I couldn't fathom before it closed over me and claimed me: *Edward had gone to war.* Anything could happen, could've already happened, could now be happening, and he might never come back. Until then, I'd lived an uneventful life; this was my first experience of uncertainty of any magnitude. During my waking hours, the foreboding lurked as a pressure behind my eyes: easy enough to ignore as long as I was busy, but otherwise all too present. There was no mediating it, I knew; it would only be alleviated by his safe return.

But if it was bad for me, then how much worse was it for his new young wife? Yet she made no claim for special treatment, and we gave her none. There was no comfort to be had in the drastic circumstances of Edward's absence, so we didn't patronise her with the pretence of any, although I do now wonder at the wisdom of that. I tried to imagine how much worse his being away at war must be for her than for me, but however hard I tried, I didn't quite have the measure of it, because back then there was something that I failed to appreciate. With the passing of each month since the wedding – three and a half, by that time – there was, for my parents, an increasing likelihood that she'd announce her pregnancy.

Of course I knew it was a possibility, of course I did, but on the other hand, for me to have thought of my new sister-in-law, my new friend, as a mother was, somehow, back then, for me, a step too far. If any such news were to be broken, Edward couldn't be first to hear it, so, unbeknown to me, my mother was holding herself in a state of readiness for that particular honour. Katherine would've been only too well aware of it; she'd have known she was under my mother's daily scrutiny, however good-willed. And how she must've resented it. She had to endure the suffocating weight of an expectation which she and she alone, after Edward left, knew that she had no hope of satisfying.

Life went on, and busily, although that didn't make Edward's absence any easier on us. As soon as he'd gone, we needed to pre-pare for Harvest Festival, a Wolf Hall-hosted feast for every last neighbour and villager for miles around. When Edward left, it was less than a week away and, to make matters worse, Bax then succumbed to a fever, rallying only in time to roast the goose and lamb which, in his absence, Harry and Thomas had probably rather inexpertly slaughtered. Bax's sickness left Katherine and me to make the dozens of tarts, savoury and sweet: egg and cheese and Good King Henry; pear, plum, apple and bramble. Those were long days and I found I had to work hard in the kitchen to keep up with her. Her efficiency that week was alarm-ing: there was a ferocity to her scrubbing of surfaces and slamming down of trays.

I understood that she was unhappy and bewildered to have been thrown back on us, coming to Wolf Hall to be Edward's wife but in a matter of months being abandoned to we Seymours, but I'm not sure that understanding it in principle made it any easier to suffer in practice. Up close, bearing the brunt of it all day long for day after day, I'd worry that whatever I said or did inadvertently only served to infuriate her. For hours on end, she didn't look at me, and said little, and never with a smile. I was at her mercy, I felt, and was frantic to appease.

But then, occasionally, just as I was becoming accustomed to it, she'd shrug off her foul mood, literally, physically shrug it off, stopping there in the kitchen to draw down deep and rejuvenating breaths, and then there she was again, as she'd always been. She'd chatter away, or hum endearingly tunelessly, or offer answers to Antony's absurd questions and, misguidedly but touchingly, try to charm Margie. There she was, sparkle-eyed and impish-smiling, but the reappearances were all too brief and I learned not to trust to them, however much I wished I could.

Edward had never much been around the house, so his absence wasn't extraordinary even if the circumstances of it were, and although I was afraid for him and longed to have him safely back, I don't think I actually missed him. During that long, kitchen-bound week of slamming and sighing, it was Katherine I missed: the mischievous, capricious, irrepressible Katherine who, to my mind, had that summer become my friend. I pitied her the situation in which she found herself but, being fifteen, I probably pitied myself rather more.

Most of my family were having much more of Katherine's company, though, than usual: at the end of those busy days of preparation for Harvest Festival, she was sitting in the parlour for notably longer. She took no early nights, didn't excuse herself before anyone else did. Nothing so carefree. And if her protracted sitting there made me uneasy, even more unsettling was what she was doing with the time.

On the second evening of Edward's absence, she'd brought along a piece of linen marked with an elaborate pattern for embroidering and, when Dottie asked what it was, she said it was going to be a nightshirt for Edward. She didn't even look at Dottie when she said it, as if an answer were barely needed. Of course it was a nightshirt for Edward, was the implication of that resolutely down-turned gaze, because what else would she, a good wife, be doing with her evenings? The truth was that she'd never before sat sewing anything for Edward. To make matters worse, her brusqueness with Dottie had my mother stepping in – 'Oh, how lovely, Katherine' – only to have her approval left hanging, unacknowledged.

Every evening Katherine worked determinedly on that embroidery as if she had something to prove. Wifely was what she was, but, it seemed to me, belligerently so. Never before in three months of marriage had she struck such a pose; before then she'd probably have scorned it. Those uncomfortable evenings of banner-repair had been bad enough with Katherine down on the floor, head bowed, making a spectacle of herself, but this was worse because, I was quite sure, it held an element of provocation: she was daring us to expose the sham of it. I watched in vain for glimpses of her – the real her – beneath that mantle of wifeliness, but she never faltered and the evenings of smirking at Father James's snores seemed a lifetime ago.

Only Thomas dared to show his scepticism at her newfound respectability, for which she was furious with him. In passing, he'd exaggeratedly peek over her shoulder and say of the embroidery, 'Oh, *very* pretty,' or, 'Isn't Edward in for a *treat*?' or, 'Edward's going to *love* that!' Edward, in a field somewhere, at war: no one could've failed to detect the sarcasm nor appreciate how close it was to the bone, but to speak up and condemn it would have been to emphasise it. Ignoring it was safer. So my mother's frown of disapproval was the closest Thomas came to being reprimanded. As for Katherine, she didn't rise to it. In fact, she did the opposite: lowering herself over that embroidery, protective, and, as Thomas issued his ungenerous snipes, huffing sighs in which the venom was all too audible.

Her telling Dottie that the sewing was for Edward was the only time, to my knowledge, that she mentioned my absent brother in company during that difficult first week. Whenever we prayed for him, she did so alongside us, of course she did, but never contributed to any speculation as to his whereabouts nor joined in with the frequent expressions of concern for his comfort and safety. And it wasn't merely that she said nothing on those occasions; she made sure to meet no one's eye, and the wilfulness to her lack of participation was such that she might have had her hands clamped over her ears.

It was distressing, that first week of Edward's absence, to see her struggling, when a mere fortnight beforehand she'd been tripping around Wolf Hall with the lightest of steps and a leading smile. Wary and withdrawn, she was holding herself at a distance from everyone, adrift when surely she most needed us. And where did that leave me? Me, who'd been only too glad, until then, to throw my lot in with her. Well, like it or not, I was still a Seymour so, if anyone stood a chance of breaching the gap between my sister-in-law and everyone else at Wolf Hall, then it was me. But she didn't look to me, not once, and I was cowed by all that slamming and sighing; I was scared of saying something wrong and making everything worse. So my reticence joined hers and the silence between us became twice as deep.

But I hated to be failing her. Four or five difficult days after Edward had ridden away, we were together in the kitchen, making pastry, neither of us having spoken much except to complain about the inevitable difficulties of the task, when suddenly she ventured, 'D'you think he's all right?'

Well, if I were to know who 'he' was, then Edward would have had to be uppermost in my thoughts, and, actually, he was. The question being a test, though, because that was how it felt, put me on my guard, which might explain why I couldn't bring myself to answer. I should have just said, 'I don't know and I hope so,' which was what I was thinking and, although not much of a response, was probably all she expected. Then we could have wondered together at his welfare, which was, I suspect, all she wanted. We could have had a conversation about him, however tentative, however circumspect. But I wasn't quick enough and – it pains me to this day to remember – she was left looking into my pale eyes and seeing she'd get no help there. Before I knew it, she'd looked back down at her pastry, sparing us both, and the moment was gone, and irretrievable.

Anxious to do better, I held myself at the ready for another opportunity, which came the following morning, when we were back in the kitchen filling those pastry cases. Outside, a gust of wind caught an unattended bucket, dashing it across the cobbles. Startled, we exchanged a glance then a grimace in condemnation of the weather and whoever had been so careless as to leave an empty bucket to clatter around. Then, resuming the task in hand, nestling a spoonful of spiced apple into a pastry case, Katherine whispered to me, 'D'you think he's warm enough?' Her whispering gave it a sense of daring; not confrontational, but conspiratorial. She was inviting me to share her concern and this time I was quick: 'Don't know; hope so.' She said nothing back, but I had the clear sense that it had sufficed. His absence had been acknowledged between us, which, it seemed, was the most at the time that she could manage.

3

If I thought the tension was easing, though, what then happened between us on the eve of Harvest Festival showed me otherwise. My mother sent me into the garden, that evening, on one of the worst but most necessary of tasks: the clearing up of any dogs' mess. With so many guests coming, the job had to be thoroughly done, which meant, of course, that it was down to me. My mother handed me the bucket, but Katherine picked up the trowel. My sister-in-law would rather shovel dogs' mess, it seemed, than be left in her own company.

As we walked the paths with our gazes necessarily downwards, I summoned up the courage to try to convey that I appreciated how hard a week she'd had but, mumbling something about being sure that Edward would be home soon, I instantly regretted it, because no one could be sure, which was precisely the problem. It wasn't that, though, to which she took exception.

'Oh, he's be *glad* to be away.' It was a knife blade of a response, stopping me dead as she stomped on ahead. Whirling around on the path, she lobbed back, 'He won't *want* to come home,' and her eyes were hard, her throat sounding tight, closing like a fist.

There I stood, suspended, unable to make sense of it. She was upset, I told myself; this was coming from the strain of their separation. Instinct had me put down the bucket and start towards her, but she drew back into a fold of arms, a fierce hug of her own, and spoke fast to get it said before I could reach her, 'He doesn't love me, Jane, he says he does, but he doesn't,' and in it sounded clear warning that I shouldn't contradict her. Swiping furiously at a few tears, she stared me down. My heart was bashing at my breastbone, but I'd have to contradict her, because what she'd said was rubbish, madness.

'Katherine' – unfortunately it came out like a whine – 'he *does*.'

'And how would *you* know?'

For a heartbeat or two, I fully expected her to take back the viciousness with which it'd been said, to apologise for it and explain it away: *Oh, I'm sorry, Janey-jay, it's just that I'm so* . . . But no; just that burning stare.

'Katherine' – it felt ridiculous to be having to spell it out – 'he *had* to go—'

'*Jane*,' she countered, as if I were stupid not to know it, 'he was *glad* to go,' and stalked off back to the house.

It was as much as I could do to stand my ground there beside that stinking bucket, spared only the further humiliation of running after her. She was upset, I reminded myself again and again, but, still, I was cut to the core by that tone of hers. And to blame Edward for having gone! When he'd had no choice and was in some French field somewhere. I was struggling to feel sympathetic; she was truly testing my patience.

When eventually I did brave going back indoors, I wasn't alone again in her company for the rest of that day, so nothing more on the subject was said, which was just as well because by the following day it seemed to be well and truly behind us. So said her smiles and her verve. All her surliness had disappeared; she was a hive of activity that morning, getting Hall prepared, and had all of us enthused and organised, busy fetching table linen and bowls and jugs, even Elizabeth, whom she made efforts to win over by deference ('Here, or here, d'you think, Elizabeth?').

Later, when the musicians arrived – four of them – it was Katherine who welcomed them and saw to their refreshments, allowing my mother to stay longer in the kitchen with Bax. Then Harry's Barbara appeared and Katherine was off to greet her, and the pair stayed in each other's company for the rest of the afternoon. Side by side on a bench, surveying the various goings-on, they had an illuminated quality, those two who were Seymour-chosen. Both of them had their arms folded but Katherine's were lower slung, more relaxed, because Wolf Hall was already her territory, she was already a Seymour.

The previous day had been a bad day, I decided, that was all. A spectacularly bad day, and she'd said her worst.

After dinner, there was a lot of dancing, even for me: I was in a celebratory mood and danced with anyone who asked me, people I didn't even know. As for Katherine, she snatched Will Dormer's cap and plonked it on top of her own hood, refusing to relinquish it until he'd pledged a whole series of dances to her.

'Well, just look at Katherine,' Thomas muttered, sceptically, 'living a little.'

He was being unfair, I felt. She'd had a bad week, but, given the circumstances, wasn't that understandable? Thomas didn't know her as I knew her, I felt; he didn't know the best of her. She lived *a lot*, I wanted to tell him, but just not brashly, as he did. But I said nothing, because he was unreachable, deep in a sulk, his own plans to live a little having been quashed by my mother. In a rare wielding of authority over him, my mother had forbidden him to do as he usually did at the end of Harvest Festival: play football with the local lads, kicking and throwing the ball from village to village, the arrival at each inn being the scoring of a goal. She said that people living along the route found it an endurance; some had been pushed and shoved in previous years, and vegetable patches had been trampled.

'That is *not true*!' Thomas had protested, appealing, 'Pa?'

My father, though, had backed my mother, albeit with a resigned shrug of his eyebrows.

Thomas was incredulous: 'But you *always* let me!'

'But this year is different,' pronounced my mother, and then we'd all understood, or kind of understood: Edward wasn't here to salvage our good name, should it need salvaging; his being gone left us vulnerable.

At the end of the evening, my father did the farewells from the courtyard, and Harry rode off to escort Barbara home. Elizabeth made herself scarce while my mother ushered the children upstairs to bed. Lil and Moll immersed themselves in the scullery, and Katherine and I cleared tables in Hall, Thomas following us around to dismantle the trestles. When I'd yawned one time too many, Katherine told me to go to bed. 'Really,' she said, kindly, 'Just go. You're exhausted.' And with a glance at Thomas, she reassured me, 'We're fine here. You're not needed.'

Which was when it struck me: all day long she'd been trying to prove exactly that. *You're not needed.* Each and every cosy-up on the bench towards Barbara had put distance between us. Not that she hadn't made sure to welcome me whenever I'd ventured over – quite the contrary, she'd made a show of it, with a verbal flourish – 'Janey-jay!' – to accompany the physical one, the hand on my arm to settle me beside her – but only now did I understand why, all along, it'd had me feeling so uneasy. It was as if a show had had to be made, as if I were someone to whom she felt she should be polite. As if I were just anyone. With every solicitation of Elizabeth's opinion, and every coy wave in Will Dormer's direction, Katherine had been putting me in my place, as she saw it, hoping to show that I was no more to her than anyone else.

And there at the foot of the stairs, I realised why. The previous day in the garden she had, in her opinion, revealed too much of herself. But had I asked her to? Had I asked her to stand there yelling at me that my brother didn't love her? Not that I'd minded, I reminded myself, because anything my sister-in-law wanted to tell me, I was of course more than ready to hear. Because we were like sisters. Better than sisters. Climbing the stairs, I had to fight the urge to go back down there into Hall and say so, but I knew that if I did, she'd deny me. She'd laugh me off, probably with a rallying glance at Thomas: *What on earth's the matter with her?*

Getting into bed, I recalled how Antony, when he was small, used to cover his eyes when he wanted to make himself or someone else invisible. That was what Katherine had been doing all day long, only I didn't know which of us was supposed to disappear, nor why.

Katherine being difficult didn't diminish my feeling responsible for her; if anything, it only intensified it. Disappointed in her as I was when I bedded down that night, I was at least as impatient with myself because, I felt, I should know how to make the situation more bearable for her: me, her better-than-sister. Me, the ever-practical one. Me, alone, surely, of all of us in the household. Mere hours later came help, though, and from a most unlikely source.

In the morning, Katherine and I were in the scullery tackling the dishes that still needed washing (Marcus had a burn on his hand which had to be kept dry, Lil and Moll were embarking on the laundering of the tablecloths) when from the courtyard outside came Antony's bell-like voice. 'Daddy,' he enquired, pleasantly, as they clomped together across the cobbles, 'will Edward be killing people yet?'

My hope was that Katherine had somehow missed it, difficult though that would've been to do. Myself, I was careful to give no indication of having heard, despite being all ears. I was desperate to hear that Edward would see nothing of any battles, and desperate for that to be the truth. Trapped in my throat was a warning cry for my father: *Be careful what you say because we're here, just the other side of the wall.*

'Well, you know . . .' My father pitched high, as if musing and appreciative of Antony for bringing it to his attention when, in fact, I knew, he was playing for time, thinking how best to answer. 'If I remember correctly,' he began, 'it isn't often really like that.'

Beside me, Katherine was listening, easing up on the tray she was scrubbing, a handful of river sand sloughing from her cloth into the scummy water. I swear I felt her heartbeats along with my own and if throwing myself in front of her could have shielded her from whatever she was going to hear, I would have done it.

My father said, 'There really isn't very much of that, if my own experience is anything to go by.'

Scrubbing at the pot in my tub, I willed his each and every word to be the right one: no mention – *please* – of wounds, of terror. 'If Edward's experience is anything like mine—'

'Wait—' from Antony, possibly a bootlace come undone.

No – my heart contracting – *keep going, go away.*

'—there's an awful lot of riding around and' – my father half-laughed – 'an awful lot of moaning about food, by which I mean the lack of it. And, well, you know,' as if Antony did indeed know and they were merely sharing reminiscences, 'we were travelling with the entire Royal Chapel choir and six hundred archers, so there was a lot of parading.' He checked: 'Done?'

Go, please go, while Antony was still happy with talk of archers and choristers.

Antony's small sound of assent was followed by the striking of soles against cobbles; they were on their way again.

'And then, when we'd taken Thérouanne and were supposed to be resting up at Lille, we had a joust, but indoors, would you believe, in some grand house, the horses wearing felt shoes so as not to damage the black marble floor . . . '

And then they were too far across the courtyard for us to hear more, Antony spirited away on an anecdote.

Clutching the rim of my tub, I let my blood subside. Had my father known we were on the other side of the wall? He'd behaved as if he had, and I was full of gratitude. Not that Katherine would've known; I couldn't have her see that there'd ever been the slightest doubt in my mind that my father would have answered as he did. No question, for me, that Edward could ever be doing anything other than parading around to the accompaniment of the Royal Chapel choir. In my relief, I did even allow myself a momentary vision of Edward pristine on a soft-shoed steed. Katherine was similarly determined, it seemed, to give nothing away of her own relief, in that we didn't even exchange a glance.

Later that day, though, when she and I were setting tables in Hall and my father came through on his way to change for dinner, she dropped a handful of knives back onto her tray and sped into his path.

'Mr Seymour.' Startled, he nevertheless looked amused. Katherine, on the contrary, stood tall, shoulders squared, and spoke fast, seemingly wary of asking too much of him. 'I overheard you and Antony earlier. Is it true, what you said?'

Never before, to my knowledge, had Katherine directly addressed my father. No one much did. She'd evidently been at the ready, though, all morning. And polite though the question was, it was undeniably a challenge. My father looked keen to oblige her – that shine to his eyes – but baffled.

'You said,' she reminded him, 'that it's a lot of parading about.'

'Oh!' – contrite to have forgotten – 'but, well, yes, of course that's true,' and then perhaps a little surprised that she'd doubted him.

She backed down, 'Yes, sorry,' and then the pair of them were strolling the length of Hall side by side.

Careful to appear absorbed in my table-laying, my attention trailed them both.

'I should worry less,' Katherine said, anguished, 'shouldn't I.'

My father shot her a quizzical glance. 'Should you?'

How intriguing, to hear her talking so easily and openly to him; easier, perhaps, than I ever did. He didn't seem to find it strange, but, then, that was my father: taking people as he found them, holding them in his dark-shining eyes.

'I mean,' Katherine said, 'that I'm making a fuss.'

A fuss? My heart leapt, because was that what it was? The slamming around the kitchen, the frowning every evening over that embroidery, the insistence that Edward was glad to be away from her: was that all it was? Because 'a fuss', I could handle.

'I doubt Mrs Seymour made a fuss when you went . . .' But she waved the words away, reluctant either for his sake or her own to voice them. *To battle.*

Odd, too, for me to hear her compare herself and Edward to my parents. I tended to think of her as just a girl, like me, but here came a reminder that she was also Mrs Seymour Junior. Perhaps, if I half-closed my eyes and peered to one side of her, I felt, I'd be able to summon both versions at once.

My father dipped his head to hide a smile. 'Well, I don't know if she did or she didn't,' and he bounced it to me. 'Jane?'

I was picking up a hand-washing bowl and the water lunged for the rim; I'd been discovered eavesdropping. But how could I not have overheard? There were only the three of us in the room. I didn't know the answer, though; I'd been a toddler when he'd fought in France. Putting the bowl down, all I could do was shrug.

They were at the door and my father was about to go up to his room, but he stopped and turned to Katherine, serious, or as serious as he ever was. 'I think it's probably harder for you,' he said.

She was hanging on his every word. As I was too, I suppose.

'You're at the beginning of your married life. Margery would probably tell you she was too busy with the children when I was away, to be able to worry much about me.'

'The children.' That'd been me; I'd been one of them, keeping my mother's attention from her husband. To hear his gentle acceptance of it, I didn't quite know how I felt. Nor, actually, to hear him talk of children to his daughter-in-law, who didn't yet have her own – was that wise? But then, my father never said a wrong word to anyone; he might not say much, but he always knew exactly what to say.

Katherine took it, but sighed, heavily, doubtful. 'You're very kind.'

He dismissed that. 'You're less sure of yourselves at the beginning, that's all,' and then he was gone, into the oriel and onto the stairs.

'Less sure of yourselves': something of which he, himself, had sounded impressively sure; he'd made it sound entirely natural that my sister-in-law would doubt my brother's love for her. And he'd know, I told myself, with his quarter-of-a-century's experience of marriage, surely he'd know. And better still, she'd believed him. *Oh, my dear, sweet father*. I looked down to hide a smile, pleased and relieved that perhaps I wasn't alone after all.

4

A pity there was no such rapport between mother- and daughter-in-law. Nothing was wrong between them, but nothing was quite right either, and what happened during the following week, although no one's fault, didn't help matters.

Hard on the heels of Harvest Festival came Michaelmas, another goose for the chop and more baking for us to do, but at this very busy time Katherine took to her bed for several days with a headache. Shut-eyed and stirring only to throw up into a bowl, she once uttered a weary, resigned explanation of a kind: 'I get this sometimes.' Not before then, she hadn't. This was new for us; this was something about her that we hadn't known.

My mother ushered me along on her frequent visits to Katherine's room, where I had to watch her bustling around the bed, frowning with concern as she dabbed her daughter-in-law's temples with rosewater. The rasping of her voluminous gown in the deep hush and the trumpeting of floorboards at her every step had me squirm; I'd be willing her to leave, and I bet Katherine felt the same. When eventually my wish was granted, I'd stay behind to wash the bowl, refresh the damp cloth draped over Katherine's forehead, and hold up a cup of ale from which she'd take the odd sip. Occasionally, she'd open her eyes and look glassily in my direction.

Once, leaving the room, my mother indicated for me to follow her and, out on the staircase, whispered: 'Jane, is there anything I should know?' I was slow to catch on but the realisation, when it came, threw me: she was asking me if Katherine was pregnant. And it hadn't even crossed my mind. If Katherine was indeed pregnant, she'd been keeping it not just from my mother, but from me. Would she keep it from me? We spent – had spent – a lot of time talking but, admittedly, never about anything much. And a pregnancy would be really something. Apparently my mother felt it was something Katherine would confide in me, but I was less sure of that and I didn't appreciate my mother's scrutiny.

Standing in that irritatingly understanding gaze of my mother's, I could tell what she was thinking: that Katherine had some hold over me, but now here came my mother to the rescue. And how I resented it. She knew nothing, I felt, of Katherine and me. I myself barely did any more, so my mother certainly didn't. Her sympathetic gaze was saying that if I owned up, if I remembered to whom I owed allegiance, forgiveness would be mine. Well, frankly, she could keep it. She smelled of cloves and suddenly, overwhelmingly, I needed to be rid of her, and it wouldn't have taken much to push her down the stairs.

Turning hastily back to the door, I shrugged her off, 'I don't think so,' refusing even to give any indication that I'd grasped what it was that she'd been asking.

Katherine emerged from her sickbed peculiarly resolved to make a subtlety for Michaelmas eve. When she announced the intention at the dinner table, a certain briskness to her manner implied that we Seymours had been neglectful in having no such plans of our own and thus it fell to her, belatedly, to pick up the slack. This was odd, because if we were indeed remiss in our failure to make sugar sculptures, then we'd been so for the four months during which she'd been living with us and she'd never previously found fit to mention it.

We did at least know what subtleties were: the Dormers always had one at their feasts. They had a mould for the casting of boiled sugar into a generic figure which would then be equipped to suit the particular occasion (so, a wheel, perhaps made from stalks, for St Katherine). There was no such mould at Wolf Hall, though, which my mother had to tell Katherine, who then looked as if this were only to be expected and said she could sculpt instead in a mixture of sugar and ground almonds. That was all very well, but had she checked our supplies? We weren't due any more deliveries before Michaelmas. Not only would her subtlety-making deplete our supplies, but we were already stretched for time, particularly because she'd been ill. And Michaelmas was as demanding for as us Harvest Festival because, despite Edward's best efforts over some years, the villagers couldn't be dissuaded from the tradition of turning up with gifts; there might no longer be the procession that there'd been during my father's boyhood, but still people came to the gatehouse with flocks of ewes and barrels of fruit, and the very least we could do in return was provide a feast. For that, we needed roasts and pies, and plenty of them. Not a fancy sugar sculpture.

The children had no such qualms; they were delighted by the prospect, and intrigued: what would it be? What *could* it be, when she had just two days to work on it? Two days, moreover, of frantic pie-making.

Katherine maintained the intrigue. Whenever she found a moment in the kitchen to work on it, she stood with her back to us, and whenever she left, she took it away with her, wrapped in a cloth.

Then Michaelmas eve was upon us and in all the activity we forgot about the subtlety until, at dinner, Katherine slipped from the table to reappear, moments later, with something in her hands. Plonking it down in front of us – 'Here' – she stood back with a little laugh, dismissive of it.

Antony piped up, 'It's a candle!' and indeed, it was: a candle made of marzipan. 'Not a sword!'

We all froze, anxious as to how Katherine might take this, but, actually, she slid me a look just as she used to do – lips pressed down on a laugh but eyes flaring with it – which my heart lifted a little to see.

'It *is* a candle,' she teased him. 'It *isn't* a sword.'

'But' – strenuous indignation – 'St Michael has a sword!'

'Lots of people have swords,' she humoured him, 'but the Archangel fought the darkness, which is what's important about him.'

'It is,' Father James agreed, gladly.

'Yes, he fought the Devil!' Antony countered, a little happier now. 'He slashed his giant sword around, didn't he, and led God's army!'

'He judges souls,' said Thomas.

'He judges souls,' Katherine repeated, as if it were an item on a shopping list.

'Heals the sick,' added Father James with an appreciative nod in my mother's direction. She had the good grace to lower her eyes but my sister-in-law's gaze caught mine and I could see the mischief in it: *St Margery Seymour*.

'He was a good all-rounder,' said Thomas, and my mother beamed at him, blissfully unaware of the sarcasm. Good all-rounders were, in Thomas's view, deserving of scorn. Edward was a good all-rounder.

My father leaned dramatically towards Antony, wide-eyed to feign alarm. 'The Archangel has no face, did you know that? Or you hope he has no face; he only shows his face to those who are about to die.'

Antony was thrilled. 'Is that true?'

'As true as any of it,' muttered Thomas.

I cut in fast, instinctively, perhaps to cover for my brother, perhaps to protect my parents, perhaps both: 'It really does look like a candle.' It was artfully slumped, and a moderately successful attempt had been made to portray a beading of liquefied wax down its length.

'It does,' echoed Elizabeth, her own note of surprise rendering the observation less complimentary.

'It *does*,' said my father, with much more enthusiasm.

'Is this gold leaf?' My mother was peering at the flame with which the candle was crowned.

'Yes,' said Katherine, 'I had a bit.'

So, somewhere in her room there'd been gold leaf, just as there was lace and a jar of confits.

'And do we eat it?' My mother asked it over-brightly so that if Katherine took offence, she could laugh it off. No joke to my mother, though, really, I knew: there was a lot of costly food in that candle.

For Antony, there was no question – 'Yeeesss!' – its short-comings as a weapon more than compensated for by it being made of sugar and almonds.

Dottie, though, was scandalised. 'No! It's lovely! We should *keep* it.'

Smiling, Katherine shrugged, abdicating responsibility for the decision. All that fuss, but now, apparently, it didn't matter. Perhaps all that had mattered to her was the making of it.

My mother appeared unable quite to trust to that, though. She'd been the one to ask the question and when Katherine declined to answer, we all returned our attention to her, but she was prevaricating. She was afraid of upsetting Katherine, I saw, and my heart was in my mouth to see it: my mother, who never tiptoed around anyone but blundered through life thinking only of arrangements and obligations. There she was, fearfully mindful of Katherine. Not just me, then, I saw: not just me who of late had been cowed by Katherine. Not just me who was weary of having to tread so carefully around her.

'Anyway,' Dottie was keeping up her campaign, 'I don't think you could eat the gold.'

Father James said, cheerfully, 'I'm not sure that with *my* teeth I could eat *any* of it.'

Katherine cocked her head to consider her creation. 'I think you *can* eat the gold.'

'Isn't it very hard?' Margie didn't sound daunted but, on the contrary, ready to do battle. She only hadn't spoken before because she'd been subjecting it to a thorough examination.

'It might be,' Katherine hedged, 'a little.'

'A little very hard,' disparaged Thomas, elbows on the table and head in his hands, which would have been to risk a rebuke from my mother, had she been looking.

'You know,' my father sat back in his chair. 'I think it's up to you, Katherine; it has to be up to you,' and he looked pleased with himself, as well he might because he rarely spoke up at home, let alone decisively. He wasn't in the least wary of his daughter-in-law, I saw — but then, why would he be? He'd never had to endure her crashing around the kitchen. To him, she was just a girl who needed a little kindness; with her barely suppressed smile and those honeyed eyes, she was just a girl who'd been having a tough time. But he only knew the half of it.

He took the uncharacteristically definite step of bestowing the decision on her, and she liked it, graciously accepted it: rising to it and, moreover, taking pleasure in it. Tentatively, she suggested to him, 'Eat it?'

Amused that she still couldn't quite make the decision, he

folded his arms to show that he wouldn't be drawn – *As I said, up to you* – and, at that, she accepted defeat, tipping back her head in a soundless laugh before announcing her decision: 'Eat it.'

Antony whooped.

Dottie wailed: '*All* of it?'

Katherine swiped it from the table and wrenched off the flame. 'All except this,' she said, handing it to Dottie with a flourish, 'which you, Dotsy-pops, get to keep.' And so there she was, turned back – just like that – into everyone's favourite Seymour, and I almost believed it.

5

With October that year came winter, the gust-troubled month sinking whatever remained of summer, and even autumn, so that the memory of sunshine was as unlikely as a dream. Each morning I woke braced for the startling chill beyond my bed before spending the day recoiling from open doorways and mincing around courtyard puddles. At Mass, Father James was frequently drowned out by rain on the roof.

As long as Edward had survived the sea crossing, he'd be ashore and properly embarked on the campaign. Crawling from my bedclothes, I'd make myself think of him; how, perhaps, he'd had no shelter for the night. Dropping clean linen down over my shoulders and inhaling its comforting sour tang, I'd wonder if he'd depleted his own supply. Every evening, when we gathered close to the hearth, I'd hope he was near enough to a fireside. Bewitched by the interlacing of flames, I'd imagine they had news of him to unfold to me, that it was there if only I looked hard enough, whereas, of course, all they were doing was making pitilessly quick work of whatever wood we could spare.

The first Sunday in October was the Church Ale, to raise funds for St Mary's at Great Bedwyn, the first part of which was always hosted at Wolf Hall, and that year the weather decidedly put a dampener on it. It had to be held indoors, in Hall; no room for bowls or skittles and, even if anyone had felt like dancing, there wouldn't have been enough space between the various stalls. Foot-tapping was as far as it could go that year. The villagers arrived soaked from the walk or cart ride, some of their wares and handicrafts having suffered, too. The best we could do for them was greet them with hot, spiced, damson-syrup-swirled punch.

Ourselves, we weren't at our best; we all had colds and Katherine's was definitely the worst; she was muffled and reluctant all day, cringing at the frequent slams of the door. My mother would have been hoping, I knew, that Katherine's altar cloth would be finished, so that something could be made, that day, of its gifting to the church, but there'd been no sight of it since Edward had been called to France; it'd been displaced first by the preparations for his departure and then by the ongoing elaborate embroidering of the nightshirt. So all we Seymours had to show for ourselves at that Church Ale was our usual little stall of pincushions and herb bags.

Katherine stayed behind the table on duty with me for much of the afternoon, occasionally summoning the energy for a desultory wander among the other stalls and some obligatory purchasing (a little basket, some braided ribbon), and once venturing over to the lucky-dip stall, of which Margie was in charge, with my father's nominal assistance. I didn't doubt that Margie was running a tight ship, if a lucky dip can be such a thing. She and my father stood markedly to attention as Katherine approached, in cahoots, bolstering each other with elbow digs, *Here she comes*: the two most composed Seymours turned quite dizzy by the prospect of Katherine's patronage. They were acting honoured to have her custom, but underneath all that acting there was, I felt, some truth to it, and I was on tenterhooks that Katherine could find it in herself – cold-addled though she was – to respond in kind.

'Delve! Delve!' Margie was sprung to intervene if necessary, adamant that the dipping be properly done, refusing to settle for a less than fully committed rummage. My father stood by, faintly abashed, and he and Katherine exchanged an amused glance. Katherine did as Margie ordered but when her hand closed over an object, I noticed, it was at my father she smiled, liberated of all the sullenness with which she'd been standing beside me at our stall.

That cold October was bringing legions of mice into the house, and at last Mort came slinking from his summer torpor. We humans had few good reasons to be outside, yet, oddly, that was where Katherine more often was. Having finished whatever task was in hand, she'd stretch, sigh, say to me, 'I have to get out of this place, get some air.' She always made sure to ask if I'd join her but I rarely did because even if I'd felt up to braving the chill, I didn't have her freedom to come and go. Fetching and carrying for my mother, I'd glimpse my sister-in-law in the gardens, well wrapped in her cloak and usually in the company of my father and his dogs. Coming back indoors, she'd be all aglow: challenged by the cold – nose red-tipped, eyes tear-blurred, lips chapped – but unvanquished by it.

What, I began to wonder, did she and my father find to talk about out there? What was it that Katherine found so invigorating about his gentle company in the gardens? Eventually, I decided to see for myself, to go along with her when she next suggested.

It was a morning of rain recently having cleared and we were no further from the house than the flower garden when along came my father with the dogs. Or, more accurately, the dogs came along with my father, and the canine gang acknowledged us only in passing, led by their noses, but my father stopped.

Glancing after them, Katherine voiced a concern: 'Chopper's limping.'

'Well,' my father sighed, 'he's getting on, now, isn't he. His hips trouble him from time to time.'

It was good to have my father there with us in the garden and to hear his warm voice among the wind-racked, hissing lilacs, even if only discussing the dogs.

Sensing that he was the subject of discussion, Chopper circled back, self-conscious, for my father to reach down, with his own habitual stiff-jointed wince, and fuss him.

'He's done well, though. Haven't you, Chops? You've done very well.' Straightening up to send Chopper on his way, he said, 'And to think he used to go belting off and we'd not see him for days.'

That piqued Katherine's interest. 'Did he?'

'Oh, he did,' and my father sounded proud of him. 'He'd scarper, and we'd have to spend the day looking for him, wouldn't we, Jane.'

'Would we?' The memory that was vivid for him was lost to me.

'Ah, well, I suppose you'd have been small, back then.' His own recollection didn't stretch to my age, even approximately, at that stage. Sometimes, inevitably, I was just one of his children. 'No, we couldn't trust to him coming back of his own accord. Too many plans.' He said it admiringly. 'Plans that didn't include boring old Wolf Hall,' but his own glance at the house was appreciative.

He never stayed away from home unless it was absolutely necessary. Despite the distances he travelled for work, if there was the faintest possibility that he could come home for the night, he'd do it. 'I like my own bed,' he'd say, teasing us with a pause before adding, 'oh, and my own family.' Having ridden home, he'd sit at the fireside listening to us, his eyes closed, half-smiling, as other people listen to music. Easy to forget of him, after what later happened. He'd never lived anywhere but Wolf Hall and, it struck me, standing there in the garden, there'd come a day not so far in the future when it would be said that he'd lived his whole life there. He must have suspected by then that Edward and Thomas, ostensibly so much their father's sons, were full of plans that didn't include Wolf Hall; I wonder if he ever guessed that unSeymour-like, sandy-haired Harry would be the one to make it his home.

'Well, Chopper, my old lad,' he called mock-ruefully down the path, 'it comes to us all: the time when what's best about going away is getting back.'

'When I was a little girl,' Katherine said, 'I had a fear that I'd sleepwalk and then not be able to find my way home.'

I wondered, idly, if that was what our nocturnal flit to the brook had been for her, some kind of sleepwalk.

She added, 'I've never been one to want to go far from home.'

She'd had to do it, though, that two-day ride from her girlhood home to Wolf Hall. I sensed it strike my father as it struck me, but deferred to him to be the one to tackle it, which he did. 'Katherine,' he cleared his throat, 'would you perhaps like to visit your family while . . .'

While Edward's gone.

Her eyes found his. 'I think it's better that I'm here.'

Better how, I wondered: to show solidarity? Or better to receive news of him, if and when it came?

'Thank you, though,' she said, gravely, 'for asking.'

And then I was ashamed not to have thought, before then, to do so.

After a respectful pause, my father concluded, 'So, anyway, I didn't know: you're a sleepwalker.'

She laughed. 'No!' Then, 'Or not that I know of. If I am, I

always find my way back.' And a flourish of her hands: *Because —
see? — here I am, not lost.*

All three of us smiled at that, and my father took his leave,
rounding up the dogs.

Katherine and I took a different path. Raising her face to what
was left of the sun, she drew down a fortifying breath.

'Did you?' I probed. 'Did you really worry about that?'
Sleepwalking away, getting lost. Such a fear was so unlike the
preoccupations of my own younger self, in as far as I could
remember. I'd tended to worry about practicalities: whether I'd
done the tasks that I was supposed to have done, and done them
properly; and if not, whether I'd be uncovered and held to
account.

'I did used to think about it,' she said, which, I realised a
moment too late to object, wasn't quite the story with which she'd
delighted my father.

6

October dragged, that year, but at least it would be bringing the fair. Twice a year, Lady Day in the spring and St Luke's in the autumn, the fair would come to Great Bedwyn and we'd leave home after an early meal to spend the rest of the day there. The two-mile cart ride to the village was never less than tortuously slow, our fellow fair-goers crowding onto the lanes from manors and farms, and their children scampering alarmingly close to our wheels, made wild by the thrill of a coin in the hand. The crowds were drawn into Great Bedwyn as if on a lighted wick by the tang of roasting meats, but I'd be thinking of the Burbage baker's stall: spiced, fruited buns deep-seamed with cinnamon-rich sugar. First of all, though, as soon as we arrived, our little ones would have to be treated to comfits, their jaws hard at work and eyes low-lidded until they were sated and off elsewhere, leaving me encumbered with a handful of sweet-scented paper cones like strange lilies and the burden of having to remember, as accurately as they themselves would, whose was whose.

As for the men of our household, they always headed initially (and in some cases solely) for the ale tent, which even by lunchtime smelled of a day gone on too long. Just passing it was enough to make me feel faintly sick and sleepy. I could never understand the attraction: they had ale at home, so why waste precious fair time in there? At each and every fair, my mother warned Harry and Thomas to go easy on the ale, using a variety of euphemisms ('Don't overstretch yourselves,' 'Don't forget yourselves') and with varied levels of success. Never Edward, though, of course; Edward never needed warning.

All that was expressly forbidden to the rest of us was any consultation with a fortune-teller. According to my mother, fortune-telling was ungodly – no one should presume to know God's plans for us – and, in her opinion, the fair should lose its licence for its toleration of fortune-tellers. What, though, could've been done to stop them? They slipped through the crowds with their minders, careful not to seek custom but to let it come to them, which it did, in droves.

None of us ever needed warning to avoid the cock-fighting and dog-fighting, nor any ale-fuelled people-fighting, but Antony was entranced at each and every fair by the mock-jousters. He'd stand by their enclosure, commentating ceaselessly, probably just for his own satisfaction but, behind him with my hands on his shoulders to counter his inching too close to the fray, to protect those fine-sprung little bones in my keeping, I'd feel obliged to fake some enthusiasm and muster an occasional response ('Yes, Blue Knight's definitely the fiercest, isn't he?'). Antony should have been the one to have a life at court.

Those meaty-faced, sinewy players, brandishing their mock shields of toothy lions, blotchy leopards, peacocks more like scarecrows: each of them had had a previous life, the brute strength they brought to their displays having been wielded on ploughing or woodcutting or butchering back before they'd taken to the road. Watching over Antony's head, I'd find myself wondering who or what had made those men leave their towns or villages, and what or whom they'd left behind. Remembering them now has me wonder if they're still there, at least some of them, working the annual cycle of villages. Is 'Blue Knight' somewhere, even now, roaring to terrify and thrill a crowd of little boys? Avid fan though Antony was, it was me who contributed to the cap when it was handed around, although on principle I always extracted what both he and I knew to be an empty promise that he'd repay me later with whatever he had left at the end of the day.

Even as queen-in-waiting, I'm doubting that for me anything will ever equal the excitement of the Great Bedwyn fairs. Back then, my own particular fascination, and Dottie's, too, was for the acrobats and jugglers who'd be performing everywhere we turned. Dottie had an alarming propensity to get herself selected from the onlookers to act as foil: standing stock still and aghast while an impressive array of objects was lobbed around her head. I loved how the performers' ease and abandon was betrayed, if I looked hard enough, by a hard-focused eye, a sharp-bitten lip. For all their skill, every flip and every catch had a touch of luck at the heart of it, of course, and, just as soon as Dottie was out of peril, to my shame I'd never quite know if I was watching for those performers to catch or drop, land or fall. Margie, though, had no time for them, her admiration reserved for the toothpullers because there, she said, was real daring and they actually achieved something. Oh, Margie should be the one running this country, she'd be giving Cromwell a run for his money.

The fair was where we squandered our savings. Antony and the girls went for rag dolls, yo-yos, little drums, and Harry and Thomas would sift through trays of birds' hoods and bells. For me, the draw was the fabrics: stalls and stalls of them, more than we ever saw at Marlborough's market and better priced. My mother and I would relish a thorough exploration of what was on offer, usually with Elizabeth in tow, and even she, hardly the seamstress, would end up buying because she could never resist a haggle and at some point her bluff would be called.

All this was in the offing for Katherine at the St Luke's Day fair that October – knives whirling around Dottie's head, Elizabeth haplessly impoverishing herself – and as the day drew nearer my sister-in-law professed herself barely able to wait, busily concocting various plans for the two of us ('Why don't we . . .' 'Shall we . . .?'). But then, the very day before the trip, she broke the news that she wouldn't be coming.

The first I heard of it, I was hurrying along the screens passage, heading outside to give my cloak a brushing, when the door opened and in she came, hair damp-spangled and eyes sheened. Backing in to pull the door behind her, spinning free of her cloak, her breath heavy in her chill-clogged throat, she didn't detect me, and, turning, jumped to find me there. Perhaps that was why I rushed to explain myself, raising my cloak and the brush and, indeed, my eyebrows: 'Just getting ready for tomorrow.'

At that, all the light in her own face vanished and it was my turn to be brought up sharp. 'What?' She noticed that in one hand she still held a stick, one of the dogs', and, exasperated, busied herself re-opening the door and depositing it back outside. Speaking more to the stick and the door than to me, she said, 'Actually, I don't know if I'll be coming.'

What? I stood there, confounded. Because no one didn't come to the fair. Well, no one except my father, but he didn't really count and anyway someone had to stay with the dogs. And 'didn't know' if she'd be coming? What on earth did that mean? And why on earth *wouldn't* she come? Didn't she understand? Had I not managed to convey it? This would be one of our two biggest days of the year away from Wolf Hall; freedom for almost a whole day for the pair of us. She was forever saying that she needed to get out of this place: well, tomorrow was her big chance and, more to the point, there'd be sugar-drenched buns and back-flipping acrobats. Hadn't I told her that? But I had told her that, and I knew full well that she'd understood me.

So, what had changed? What was wrong? Was she ill again, building up to one of her headaches? She didn't look ill, though, not at all. But perhaps that was it, it struck me, perhaps that was it, because just look at her there, standing along the passageway from me, so brightly lit by her own blood: was she expecting a baby? Was that it? Could she not risk a jolting cart ride, an exhausting day away from home? Perhaps she'd had her suspicions but, with the journey looming, the prospect of the long day away from home, was having to face up to it and make a decision. Was that it?

A baby: my heart cleaved, half-soared, half-plummeted. A baby, boggle-eyed and floss-haired. A new Seymour. A new generation, no less. But, oh, the danger of it, too, for her: the mortal danger. I didn't know whether to laugh or cry, and feared I'd do both.

Not that it was a surprise, of course, I reminded myself: this I'd been fully anticipating. Hadn't I? Well, we all had, all of us at Wolf Hall. We'd been expecting exactly this, of course, from our newly-weds. Somehow, though (how?), I'd neglected to keep it in mind. Which had suited her fine, I realised. Because she'd never once mentioned babies to me. Never once. She'd needed at least someone at Wolf Hall not to be waiting on her pregnancy, and that someone, it seemed, had been me. I was easy company.

What did it matter, though? What did it matter if before now she hadn't confided in me – 'Janey-jay, listen, I'm a little late this month' – because here was the moment when she'd let me know and the silence on the subject of a baby would lay well and truly slain along the passage between us. What she was saying, though, was, 'I don't really need anything,' as if the trip to the fair were nothing but a shopping expedition.

No: no need for her to pretend to me. 'Katherine,' I asked, 'are you – you know – *all right*?'

Drawing her arms around herself as if it were in the passage-way rather than in the garden where she felt the cold, she said, 'I'm fine,' affecting astonishment, even, that I'd asked. And again, 'I'm fine,' but this time with a note of objection. Worse, she reiterated, 'It's just that I don't need anything.'

I swallowed my impatience – why did she have to make every-thing so difficult? – in favour of playing her at her own game. She wanted to talk shopping? Well, I could do that. 'You do,' I reminded her, 'need some ribbon.' Because that, we'd discussed; she couldn't deny it.

She shrugged. Someone else, it seemed, could choose it for her.

Well, I'd had enough, and changed tack to do my worst: 'If you don't come, my mother'll wonder,' and then there it was, just as I'd intended, a twitch of dread in Katherine's eyes. I wasn't particularly proud of having threatened her with my mother, the prospect of my mother's painfully exaggerated carefulness around her, and her bated breath, but she'd asked for it. And, anyway, it'd worked. Or so I assumed, but actually she simply resorted to defiance, 'Well, she has no cause to,' before sweeping past me down the passage, discussion over.

There I stood, ringing with what had been said but unable quite to hear it: what had just happened? Had we had a row? Why? What was it that was suddenly so important as to have her giving up a day with me at the fair? It never occurred to me ask who.

The next day there she was in the courtyard, seated in one of the carts, ready to leave with the rest of us as if there'd never been a problem. She hadn't explicitly denied she was expecting a baby, but she'd certainly implied as much and I was inclined to believe her; on that, I believed her. I was pretty sure, though, that there was something she was keeping from me.

Three cartloads of us were going to the fair, with Harry, Thomas and Mr Wallensis accompanying us on horseback. Thomas was already under orders – my mother's – to stay alongside us not solely on the journey there but also, crucially, on the way back, at dusk; and my father had cornered him, for once, to lay down the law, albeit in his typical manner, his dark eyes fursoft. They were too far across the courtyard for me to hear most of what was being said but I did catch, from my father, the word 'gadding', at which Thomas affected supreme boredom to imply that his father understood pitifully little of his life. This only served to goad our father, as much as he was ever goaded, and so he was persisting. Ralph, our stable lad, stood at a respectful distance with Thomas's increasingly jittery horse. The choice of horse was a battle already lost: Thomas hadn't been dissuaded from favouring Zephyr over a more reliable steed.

For once, everyone's sympathy was with Zephyr: we were desperate to be off. We'd worked hard to be able to get away early. We'd eaten at nine prompt, before we'd cleared up at top speed, forming a line from table to scullery onto which the low-angled autumnal sunshine had poured the colours of the stained-glass windows, firing a glint of determination in Margie's eyes and deepening Dottie's flush of exertion.

Our impressive teamwork had given Marcus a relatively easy morning of it and he was sitting opposite me in the cart with what was, for him, in his gentle way, something of an air of celebration. I always found myself self-conscious in close proximity to Marcus, which was ridiculous because no one at Wolf Hall was less assuming. Perhaps that was it, though: him so shy but me unable to help myself. It was his mouth that drew my eye, that extraordinarily, gloriously broad mouth of his. Squashed beside him was Moll, who'd donned her absolute best, as she did for every fair, which was never less than ill-advised, given the travelling and the muddiness of the fairground. Lil knew better, the only addition to her usual attire being a bandage on her finger, the result of some mishap in the kitchen.

Moll's cloak bore the spiral beaded brooch that my father had once given her for St Valentine's Day, having drawn her name that year from the barrel. She wore it on every remotely special occasion and never stopped telling us that, 'He has a good eye, does Mr Seymour,' although she must have known that my mother chose for him all the gifts that he professed to give. Moll bristled whenever she said it, as if we were bound to dispute it: as if she alone could appreciate his fabled 'eye'. For some years, it made for the only joke that Elizabeth and I ever shared: tipping our chins and hefting our non-existent bosoms as we recited it to each other, reducing it over time to a mere 'Good eye'. Whenever my mother overheard or even got wind of what we were up to, she'd tick us off, reminding us – rightly, of course, in retrospect – that Moll didn't have many treasures.

At last my father relinquished Thomas, perhaps satisfied that he had finally listened or perhaps just given up on him, and came over to say goodbye. Dottie heralded him, so it was to her that he headed and she clambered across both of us to the edge of the cart, the closer to get to him, desperate to know from him, 'Will you be all right here all alone?'

Royally all right, was my guess: he and the dogs with the luxury of the house to themselves for the whole day. Placing his hand over hers, he assured her he'd be fine, and when she asked what he'd like bringing back, he told her to save her money for herself. 'But thank you, sweetheart, for asking.'

'Nothing?' She was incredulous.

I'd bring him back a couple of those buns; I always did.

'I want for nothing,' he twinkled at her, 'I'm a lucky man.'

Then those merry eyes turned to his daughter-in-law. 'So, Katherine, ready for the delights of Great Bedwyn fair?'

She looked unsure. 'Ready as I'll ever be.'

His smile broadened. 'Well, Jane here, she's an old hand.'

And he was right about that, and I rather liked it; it went some way to soothe my smarting from her bid to ditch our trip. I knew a good thing, I told myself, even if she didn't. Our cart jolted into motion and my father stepped back to wave us off.

7

As it happened, Katherine needed no help to enjoy the fair: as soon as her feet touched the ground, off she dashed into the crowds, leaving Antony and me to run behind her. We caught up with her at the baker's stall, buying buns for us.

'Here,' she handed one to Antony, who dutifully proffered a coin, only for her to wave it away.

'Mama says,' he insisted, 'that if we want something, we should buy it ourselves.'

Katherine laughed. 'Well, Mama's wrong.'

Looking after Antony while my mother took the girls to choose themselves some fabrics was how Katherine and I earned time, later, to ourselves, and what I remember of our afternoon together among the tents and stalls is how brilliantly she haggled. Not combative and duplicitous like Elizabeth, she was full of cheek so good-natured that the traders, however wily or hard-hearted, couldn't resist her, couldn't go far enough for her; there was nothing that anyone wouldn't do for her. I remember, too, amid the hurly-burly, the considerable ease between the two of us, as thoroughgoing as the blood in our skin. Shouldering ourselves into the crowd around a trickster with his cards, or craning to survey a trader's wares, we could have been doing each other's breathing. I forgot my suspicion that she was keeping something from me.

Towards the end of the day, though, something happened to make me wonder. Not long before we were due to start the journey home, Katherine said, 'I'm bursting,' and, indicating a distant copse, 'I'll just pop over there.'

'Oh, no,' I said, 'not there,' because there, I knew, was best avoided.

When she turned to me for the explanation, though, I was stumped. I didn't know how to put it; nor even, quite, what it was that I'd be trying to put. What I knew about that copse was to avoid it: that was what mattered. Back in those days, if warned to avoid somewhere or something, I'd do so and not bother overly with the given reason; there was so much to avoid, in those days, and so many reasons, few of which ever stood up to scrutiny. Nevertheless, I tried to recall what I'd been told; it'd been Moll who'd said it: 'It's where people go.'

Katherine frowned, understandably baffled. 'People go?' and of course then I heard how inadequate an explanation it was, heard that it was no explanation at all.

People: 'Villagers.' Unable to recall Molly's exact words, I put it into my own, 'For romance,' which was pretty much how I understood it: lads and lasses spending time alone together, strolling arm in arm among the trees and looking into each other's eyes, perhaps exchanging kisses. 'For romance *and worse*,' I clarified, which I did suddenly recall was what Moll had said, and which I'd taken to be distinct from the kissing: gambling, probably, and fighting. The behaviour, like the consulting of fortune-tellers, of those who didn't know better.

But this only served to send Katherine off to see for herself what she shouldn't, and at a comical pace, skirts a-swish and elbows indignantly angled, to make fun of her own naked curiosity. Behind her went me, laughing at her audacity, at the absurdity of it, begging her to turn back even as I stumbled over hummocks of grass in the vain hope of acting as a restraining influence. She halted at the first trees, though, and I stopped calling, instead quickening my pace and risking my ankles on the rough ground to get to her, to be there, to see whatever it was that had her in its grip. As I drew level, she didn't acknowledge me, didn't relinquish whatever she held in her gaze, but reached for me, her hand clawing at my forearm, perhaps to pull me closer or perhaps to keep me at bay but in either case ineffective, because I stood where I wanted to stand, which was beside her.

Everywhere among the trees ahead of us were couples, each having claimed a tree trunk against which to recline. So many people in that copse, yet such stillness: a purposeful stillness, though, as if it were a dance of a kind. The silence, too, intent, rather than the mere absence of sound. There was nothing to hear among those trees but the doleful, fractured fluting of a wood-pigeon. The kissing in which those lads and lasses indulged was unlike any I'd ever seen or imagined: no polite pecking, but instead protracted and energetic, and savoured. Up on the wall at St Mary's Church was a painting of bodies entwined and falling into Hell, but the couples in the copse were nothing like those for-nicators, nothing like those helpless, pitiful figures tumbling towards flames with their buttocks bared.

Cloaks and caps were discarded among the trees, which was how I spotted Thomas: Thomas, capless; Thomas's dark hair. '*Thomas*,' I gasped, and Katherine's gaze snapped along mine to locate him. I was as much confounded by his abandoning the ale tent as his being ahead of us in the copse with a girl. A girl? Her hand was in that dark hair of his. 'That's *Lil*,' I breathed unnec-essarily, no mistaking the white of a bandage around one of the fingers.

Lil? Her unbandaged hand cupped his bottom, the fingers splayed for grip. Thomas was held hard to her but pressing harder still, rhythmically, as if his whole body were coaxing something up through hers. I stood there unable to believe what I was seeing. Actually, I didn't know what I was seeing.

Hadn't Thomas said something, that embarrassing time in the day room, about Lil being kissed in and out of her dress? Well, at least here she was in her dress, horribly rucked up though it was to expose spindly, shiny-stockinged legs. At least there was that. How did Thomas even know what to do, whatever it was that he was doing to her that had her clutching at him like that? Thomas: good for nothing except slouching around Wolf Hall and getting on everyone's nerves. Or so I'd thought. Thomas, a mere year older than me and as least as far away as me from marriage. Or so I'd thought. Not that he'd be marrying Lil, of course, and a sudden awful suspicion stole over me: was he forcing himself on her? Had he lured her there to take advantage of her? But to judge from that tight circling of the flat of her hand on his backside, she didn't look in the least taken advantage of — she looked born to it. And that, too, I would never have imagined: Lil?

Perhaps, I thought, that was the point of the painting on the wall at St Mary's: to show that you go about your daily business assuming you know what's going on when everywhere under your nose, should you look, there's this. I was stunned; I had no idea what it was that I was thinking or feeling, no idea even what I should be thinking, should be feeling. It was all new to me, all of it, every last bit — people among trees, the slow-kissing and the rucking-up of clothing by people who'd never be getting married to one another — but most startling to me of all was that I'd been such an innocent. Oh, I'd known I was hardly worldly wise, but until then I'd had no sense of the extent of my naivety, and the revelation brought me to an astounded stop.

Only momentarily, though, I told myself, because any time now I'd be turning away, recovering myself and moving off, leaving them all to it. That was the intention, but there I still was, gawping, as if I, too, were somehow bodily held, and even odder was the sensation that it was me who was being watched.

Katherine would come to my rescue, though, of that I was certain. She was a married lady and awful though it was that she had to see such behaviour from a Seymour, it'd be nothing, really, to her. She'd be able to make a good laugh of it and have us strolling away from the scene as if it were nothing, all in a day's fair-going. And then, halfway back across the common, beyond the hearing of the kissers, she'd look at me and raise her eyebrows and wrinkle her nose – *Thomas! Lil!* – and we'd be shrieking delightedly and derisively, getting the better of them.

When I did eventually look at her, her eyes fled mine. 'You know,' she said, clipped, as if I were the one at fault, 'that brother of yours really should watch himself,' but with her shame-hot cheeks and furtively averted eyes, it could have been she who'd been uncovered.

8

Not until the skirmish on All Souls a couple of weeks later did I discover the depth of the contempt that Katherine had developed for Thomas. All Souls was a serious undertaking at Wolf Hall: the one day of the year when, according to Father James, my two dead brothers came close enough to home to hear our prayers for them. My first-born brother, of whom I had no memory, and the last-born, whom I'd never seen alive. Every All Souls eve, our mother made the house wondrous and welcoming for her two lost boys: banks of beeswax candles in every room, and Hall ringing with the deft work of a hired trio of harpists. We Seymour children had grown up understanding that that there should be none of the silliness that, we'd been intrigued to glean from Moll, tended to happen in other households: a candle unexpectedly extinguished and, to shrieks of excitement, a hand lain on an unsuspecting arm.

That year, on All Souls, our new family member was, unfortunately, far from at her best: sharp-shouldered all morning, her eyes downcast and an incisor punishing her lower lip. It didn't bode well, but All Souls had to go without a hitch, so, nervously, I waylaid her in the oriel after dinner to ask what was wrong. She didn't hold back, her response a huge sigh and frank stare.

'Jane,' she levelled with me, 'is Edward coming here tonight?'

In her question was a note of challenge, as if I should be admitting to something. What, though? I had absolutely no idea what she was asking me. Edward, home? Had I missed something? Could I possibly have missed something? Panic skittered under my ribs. What on earth could it be that I'd somehow missed? Standing there willing her to say more, to offer some kind of explanation, I suffered a stare from her that was both reluctant and insistent: a refusal to let me off the hook.

But what hook?

'I don't know,' I had to say eventually, and, feeling profoundly stupid, I had to ask, 'Is he?'

'Well,' her stare-strained eyes reddened, 'If he's dead, then yes, he is, isn't he.'

And I got it, even as I sincerely wished I hadn't: a soul; Edward as a soul, already gone from the world and drifting around in purgatory.

But she couldn't say that! She couldn't even think it. I understood that she feared the worst, of course she did, but so did I and everyone else at Wolf Hall and none of us would dare think of him as dead because wherever he was and whatever was happening to him, he'd be trying his utmost to stay alive, and for her to think of him as one of the dead was the ultimate betrayal. It was a giving-up on him; it was, practically, as bad as wishing him dead. I had one immediate concern: my mother mustn't hear any of this, shouldn't even get wind of it; it'd be more than she could bear, more than she should have to bear.

I heard myself saying, 'Stop it, Katherine.'

But she pressed on. 'And I won't know, will I.' She was aghast, tremulous, transported by the drama of it. 'He could be here . . .'

She even glanced fearfully around the oriel, 'Watching me . . .' And suddenly her face was running – eyes, nose – and she swiped absently, approximately at it with her sleeve, which was shocking enough but not nearly so much as her thinking of her own husband pursuing her like a spectre.

Just then the Hall door opened, jolting her into self-awareness, and she turned abruptly to hide her face. It was Elizabeth who sauntered into the oriel: saving souls was one of the few tasks my sister considered worthy of her efforts, and she was making quite a show of carrying to chapel a big box of beeswax candles. The door hadn't properly closed behind her before it swung open again and in came Thomas, instantly several paces past her and up onto the stairs from where, glancing back down at that reverentially borne box, he teased, 'Sure you've enough there, Elizabeth?' She ignored him, but he called after her as she disappeared into the parlour, 'A lot of souls vying for God's attention tonight! Light the way, Elizabeth!' and then, raising his voice as if he himself were a soul pleading to God, 'Oh, down here, down here, please, please! Me, me!'

He shouldn't have said it, disrespectful of the dead as it was, but there was no malice in it and, anyway, Elizabeth's insufferable self-importance invited a needling. Thomas was only being Thomas, and even Elizabeth herself knew to make nothing of it.

Not Katherine, though, she flew after him, roaring up the stairs, 'Thomas!' So that the oriel's window-glass actually rattled. 'God listens to *everyone*.'

It was an absurd overreaction and Thomas did well not to be taken aback, managing instead to make light of it – 'Does he, now?' – which at least gave her the chance to adopt disdain, save face, walk away.

But she took it as further provocation: 'He's God!'

I knew I should do something – go and lay a reassuring hand on her shoulder, try to bring her to her senses – but in her self-righteous fury there across the oriel from me, she was unreachable. I had no sense of what she might do next, might say.

Too late, anyway, because, 'Who are you, Thomas Seymour,' and startling, it was, the disgust with which she yelled his name, 'to know *anything* of God?' With that, she whirled away, stamped back into Hall, leaving Thomas to take a step or two down the stairs in her wake, belatedly conciliatory. He appeared a little shaken but composed enough to give me that knowing look of his: *See?*

But I didn't – it was sheer madness to me – or I didn't think I did at the time. But actually, I had seen something: that Katherine was, to me, quite unknowable.

My father was the only Seymour she seemed to regard as being on her side, and thus he only ever saw the best of her. One dismal early-November afternoon she persuaded me to accompany her from the smoke-bitter day room for a breath of fresh air, and there in the herb garden was my father, engrossed in a lavender bush. He didn't look up as we approached, didn't offer us any proper greeting but remarked instead, in wonder and pity, 'It's still in flower.' Dutifully, we appreciated the solitary flower head, but actually I could only think of hurrying on: just once around the garden, Katherine had assured me. In the leaden, sodden air, even this briefest of pauses was proving hard for my feet. I was in mere soft-soled shoes; she hadn't given me time to go for my boots. Contracting my toes, claw-like, I shuffled on the path. My fingers, too, were beginning to sting, my hands red raw from all the salting we'd been doing, so I slotted them into my armpits.

Katherine, though, straightened from her inspection of the lavender to stand tall, drawing her cloak around herself and relishing a deep breath as she took in the garden, which was such a sorry sight: lanky, brittle stems blotchy with seed heads. Below ground, bulbs were sleeping and roots feeling their wet way down.

Her eyes gleamed. 'I do love this time of year.' *Despite everything*, her wistfulness suggested, *despite the decay*. She was unable to resist its peculiar charms, was the implication, glad to give into it.

I said nothing. Well, she hadn't been addressing me, anyway; to judge from the way she'd drawn herself up to say it, and the lofty, distant focus she'd adopted, she'd been declaring to an audience of which I was, at most, only half. Did she really love this time of year? Could anyone? Not the animals, that was for sure, because with Martinmas began the annual slaughter: everything to be hacked up, lathered in salt and stuffed into barrels to last us the winter. For the rest of the month, bellowing and squealing would be coming from the outbuildings, and the courtyards would stink of blood. The slaughtering unsettled the children: Dottie was febrile, which turned Margie stern, and Antony would at some stage get himself daubed with blood on his cheeks and forehead as a badge of dubious honour.

Katherine had never before mentioned any love of late autumn and I'd have said that summer was her season.

'There's no pretence, is there, in November,' she said, approvingly. 'It's not putting on a show.'

Unlike her: she did seem to be putting on a show, although not for me. My father was receptive and I had a sense that this kind of conversation, if that was what it could be called, was commonplace here in the gardens between the pair of them. Quite clearly, she felt my father was the only one of us who understood her. Quite possibly, it occurred to me, she was right.

'It is what it is.' Katherine flapped a hand at the desolate beds.

What it was, this time of year, was a wreck, which was a shame, seeing as how hard we'd worked on it. She shrugged: 'It is what it is' – fair enough – 'and no getting away from it. You have to face it. And I like that.'

I flexed my toes as hard as I could inside my shoes and rocked back and forth from my heels to the balls of my feet, not simply for warmth but to try to set us in motion. Once around the garden, she'd said, but she and my father continued to stand there breathing in the damp-reeking air as if it were doing them a favour. And now she gazed admiringly at the house. 'Mind you, I love being indoors, too, this time of year. Love settling down.' She hitched up her shoulders and dropped them hard, as if giving herself a consolatory hug.

I had to suppress a sigh. If she loved being indoors, then why were we out here? And for someone who loved being indoors, she'd been spending an awful lot of time lately in the desolate gardens. Edward would need to be home soon, I realised, before it became much colder, and the absence of him from all this chatter of the charms of autumn came to me like a breath on the back of my neck.

By this time, the dogs had become concerned by our lack of progress; George approached us, respectful but impatient, his eyes searching ours.

'Bear's in disgrace,' my father confided, his voice low to spare her the shame.

We both gasped. *'Bear?'*

'Bear.'

She did indeed seem to be skulking ahead of us on the path, keeping her distance.

'Got herself into the dry larder.'

A laugh escaped Katherine, her fingertips too late to her lips. 'Dogs! Why don't they *hide* what they've done?' She was incredulous. 'They're clever enough to *do* it – coming up with the plan, biding their time – but then don't think to cover their tracks! And there they are, when you come along, standing there with their spoils all scattered around them, just cringing . . . ' It genuinely appealed to her, this canine lack of guile, which in turn made me smile. 'Oh, *poor* Bear,' she breathed, heartfelt and fond.

'Yes, well, anyway,' my father said with his own smile, 'we're not talking to each other.'

Katherine raised one eyebrow, 'I'll say nothing more of it,' and turned her attention instead to the solitary flower that my father had found. 'You used to write poems for Mrs Seymour, didn't you, comparing her to flowers.'

My heart contracted, because it was me who'd told her. Not that it was a secret. Anything but: it was family lore and there was no reason that I shouldn't have told her, and every reason that I should've, now that she was a Seymour. But still, I felt implicated.

My father feigned surprise, 'Who told you that?' and looked pointedly from her to me and back again. Despite the note of protest in it, I could hear that he was proud, and rightly so. A family legend: his ardent wooing of his wife.

'Oh . . .' And Katherine was having fun now, emphatically avoiding looking at me.

There I was, in the middle of the pair of them, the subject of their indulgent attention. Well, there were worse places to be. I batted it back: 'She's family,' was what I offered my father in my defence.

Katherine seemed to find that funny, and gave a sceptical tilt of her head to elicit what he might say to it.

His own defence was offered with a flourish like a bow: 'I was young. Very. It was bad poetry. Very.'

'But she married you.'

'She forgave me, then married me.'

Untrue, of course; he was simply having fun. There'd been nothing for my mother to forgive. She'd loved him for it.

'Well,' Katherine offered her own verdict, airily, 'I think it was lovely of you.'

'No, really, you didn't see the poetry.'

I could tell he was pleased, though, which in turn pleased me. He was self-conscious, yes, put on the spot like this, but enjoying the opportunity to reflect fondly on the gauche, hopeful boy he'd once been. His conspiratorial glance came to me like a wink, as if the poetry-writing escapade was something we'd been in on together, although of course it'd happened long before I'd existed. Still, he was right, I suppose, in that I was family in a way that Katherine wasn't.

'Well, I'm quite sure it was lovely,' she said, 'but anyway it's not the poetry itself, is it, it's that you made the effort,' and her tone was cheery, but I had the faintest unnerving sense, even as I told myself not to be silly, that this was an implied criticism of Edward. No letter had yet come from him, as we were all too aware, although it was hard to imagine how, under the circumstances, one would reach us.

We were walking, at last, but too slowly. My father said, 'I only did it because my friend did it. Mr Skelton – you remember, Jane?'

I did, or at least I knew the name from various family stories: my father's friend, John Skelton.

He said, 'I was terribly impressed by his poetry-writing. Problem was,' an exasperated breath of a laugh, '*he* was good at it.'

Katherine said, 'Edward never wrote me poetry,' and so then there it was, as I'd feared, good-natured enough, yes, but still, she'd said it.

'You married him, though,' said my father.

She liked that. Drawing us in, she indicated that she had something to tell us. 'D'you know, I used to think he'd come for my sister. He'd leave my father's office – I'd find him around the house – and I'd assume he was looking for my sister.'

That I'd never heard before and, despite myself, I was suitably intrigued.

'I assumed that he just happened to bump into me on his way

to find Nancy, and was having to be polite to me.' She laughed at the absurdity of that feigned politeness. 'There he was, all serious and clever . . . ' She didn't say 'gorgeous', as once, to me, she had, ' . . . and *Nancy's* all serious and clever . . . '

A shortening of breath from my father, about to interrupt, pose a question or raise an objection, but she headed him off with the explanation, 'She never gets things wrong, never shows herself up.'

Whereas she did, she meant. And it was true, she did, and I remembered how it was what had drawn me to her. Well intentioned though she was, she was forever tripping herself up, couldn't help herself. She was at the mercy of herself and knew it, always ready to throw up her hands to it. Or that's how I saw it. In time, I'd learn that what had looked like openness was a mere lack of guile.

She said, 'They seemed to me to be the perfect match.'

'So,' my father said, 'he should've married Nancy?'

'Oh no, she's horrid.'

Startled, my father and I both laughed, which in turn startled her and she, too, laughed. 'Well, *I* think she is,' she half-apologised, or perhaps it was a refusal to apologise. 'Well, she *is*,' and her insistence had us laughing anew. Ahead, the dogs pranced around in their own way of laughing although at what, like children, they didn't know and didn't care.

'Anyway,' she said, 'I made my mind up to steal him from her.'

'*Did* you?' She had me, now. This, I felt, had the makings of a good story.

'But you didn't have to,' said my father. It wasn't a question and she didn't answer, just smiled with some satisfaction.

I wanted the story, though, enough to step in front of her and walk backwards, leading her on. 'How did you realise?' When had she realised that she didn't have to steal him, that he was already all hers?

'Oh—' she gazed distantly, less interested. 'It was one day when I said something like, "Nancy's in the garden," and he said, "Nancy?" Simple as that. I don't think he even knew who she was.'

No story, then, after all, but still we were laughing, all three of us, in celebration of her victory, her easy victory, so easy that it was in fact no victory at all because there'd been no battle.

'Well,' my father concluded, eventually, buoyantly, 'Edward never makes a wrong choice, does he, Jane?'

But Katherine thought that he had, or believed that *he* thought that he had. I glanced nervously at her but she said nothing, halting and reaching into the lavender bush to draw the fingertips of one hand the length of that brittle flower head: we were back where we'd started, I realised, we'd done our circuit of the garden.

She asked my father, 'You really don't write poetry any more? Nothing at all?'

'Good Lord, no.' Cheerfully dismissive, he turned to whistle for the dogs.

She drew down the scent from her fingertips as if it were something she'd hitherto been denied. 'Never tempted?'

'Young man's game.' He was gesturing for Bear to come to him, reaching to fuss her, making his peace with her.

'You're not old! You're half the age of *my* father.'

My father laughed at the exaggeration, which then had her insisting, playfully and ridiculously, 'You are!' before settling for, 'Well, you certainly *seem* to be.' With a passing pat of her own to Bear's head, she finished, 'You should try, you know, John. You should try writing a few poems. You might surprise yourself.'

WOLF MOON

I

The longed-for news of Edward's imminent return came on an afternoon that was, at first, like any other November afternoon. Most of us were sewing with my mother in the day room, my job being to perform long-overdue surgery on Antony's beloved night-time companion, the bedraggled Bibi. Katherine had taken the blacksmith up to the long gallery to see to a faulty hinge on the virginals' lid. Outside, the rain was one long sigh; inside, the fire was testy, spitting and smoking, my mother frowning at it from time to time as if to put it in its place, and Margie coughing. The only other sound was the rasp of thread drawn through fabric.

But just after three o'clock came a welter of boot steps on the stairs and the door banged open, giddying the wall-hangings, to deliver Thomas still in motion, already withdrawing but calling to us, 'Messenger!' He knew we'd know from his tone that the news was good, and from the lack of explanation that the news was of Edward.

'Dover!'

He slammed the door shut behind him in his haste to spread the word. A collective gasp rose around me as the hangings settled down like hands behind which passed a frantic whisper. *Edward was ashore in England and all but home.* My breath slipped its knot and unspooled.

'Thomas!' My mother was on her feet, hurrying to the door, ostensibly to object to so abrupt a departure but really because she couldn't take the news sitting down. She called after him again from the doorway, but he was long gone. Turning back to us, she voiced my own thought: 'Katherine.'

'I'll go.'

Not that I needed to say it: everyone knew I'd be the one to go. Off I ran, down the stairs and across the house, heading for the stairs up to the long gallery, brimful of the news, my breath bouncing against my ribs and my garters slipping down over my knees. Bax was loping along the screens passage but I hurtled past without sparing him a word. My steps hammered into that seemingly endless staircase leading to the long gallery, but I could see myself already at the top and hurling open that door. My sister-in-law had been held captive for a couple of months in a state of ignorance as to the whereabouts and welfare of her husband but, at last, I could release her with a single word: 'Dover.' I probably wouldn't even have to say it – she'd probably know as soon as she saw me, and, turning to me, she'd look exactly as she had in the beginning, when she'd first stepped over our threshold. We could start all over again, the stresses and strains of the previous two months behind us as if they'd never been. I hadn't acknowledged to myself, until belting up those stairs, how desperately I wanted that. Edward would be home and Katherine would be my friend again and all would be fine.

But at the top of the stairs the door opened to nothing, to no one; the long gallery empty, the virginals' lid demurely down and the hinge flush with it.

Where was she?

Back down the staircase in a rush of maddeningly little steps, my blood at a rolling boil; back along the screens passage, this time lobbing a fragment of apology at Bax. No sign of Katherine in Hall, either, or chapel or the parlour, nor the kitchen and larders, nor was there any response when I yelled for her outside the jakes. She could be anywhere, I despaired; this big old house was made of nooks and crannies. Why on earth hadn't she come straight back to the day room? Someone else, most likely Thomas, would have got to her first; she'd hear the news from someone else. Someone else, probably Thomas, would be the recipient of her profound gratitude while I lumbered around red-faced in wrinkled stockings.

As a last resort, I hauled myself up the stairs to her room, where, to my surprise, my knock elicited a faintly audible answer. I had barely enough strength left to push on the door. Inside, she was luminous beside the unshuttered window; and luminous, too, in one hand, was a letter which, presumably, she'd been reading in the diminishing daylight. A letter? As far as I was aware, she couldn't read well enough to be able to make much sense of a letter. Nonetheless, whatever was in her hand had absorbed her so that her focus on me was delayed, and I took that moment to try to catch my breath, scooping it back into my burning lungs from where much of it was ejected in a spasm of coughing.

She didn't remark on my disarray, didn't even seem to notice it, instead proffering what was in her hand – 'Look' – which I suppose I then did, my gaze going in that direction even if I took nothing in.

'Poems.' She was full of wonder. 'From your father. He's done it, he's had a go, and don't you think that's marvellous?'

My coughing was dragging me under; I tried to straighten up. I was half-laughing, too, by now, because if she thought it marvellous that my father had penned a poem or two, just wait until she heard what I was going to say.

'I can't read much of it, though.' She came to my side, pausing to ask, 'Are you all right?' but not long enough for me to reply, and, flourishing the missive, she asked me, 'See that word, there? What's that?'

It was as if one or other of us were dreaming and hard to wake; it was easiest just to answer, 'Autumn,' before, 'Ka—'

'And that one, there?'

'Michaelmas – *Katherine, Katherine* . . . ' And then, thank God, I did have her attention, or at least her eyes on mine. 'A messenger,' I managed, just.

All the life fled from her face and I realised my mistake.

'No!' Not bad news – anything but – and my coughing blasted into laughter. 'No! Edward's *back.*'

Such a sharp intake of breath that I might've slapped her.

No, not here, not yet. 'Ashore.'

Still, though, she didn't look reassured. 'Really?'

One hand, holding the poems, went to her heart and the other onto my wrist where the strength of her grip had my breathing falter. The grip was already dissolving into shakes, though, and I realised she was incapable of standing, and even as she was holding me down, I was going to have to hold her up. But in a trice she'd groped for the bed and got herself to it, let the edge of it take her weight. She asked again – 'Really?' – but just as blankly, as wide-eyed as before.

The news would have come as a shock, I realised – of course it would have, and how stupid of me to have imagined otherwise, to have burst into the room so very full of myself. Sitting down, half-sitting, warily, beside her, I noticed she was crying; saw it rather than heard it, because she was tight-lipped. The tears seemed wrenched from her eyes, making them a sore red. Sitting there shoulder to shoulder with her, I murmured some reassurances – 'Don't worry, he'll be back soon, he'll be fine' – as my own breathing settled, but she didn't look at me, her steadily leaking eyes fixed floorwards. I'd imagined we'd be there for a while as she regained her composure and gathered her nerve, but suddenly she stood, so abruptly that the rebounding mattress almost unseated me.

'Yes,' she said, clipped, if nasal, in dismissal of my reassurances. I had a dizzying sense of the two of us being somehow at cross purposes. She was done with the shaking and crying, but I wasn't so sure they were done with her. I anticipated some explaining away of the manner in which she'd received the news – just the shock – but no, not a bit of it. Instead, she crossed the room and, with her back to me, began tidying herself up, culminating in a harsh blowing of her nose before she was ahead of me through the door.

Downstairs, a tentatively celebratory gathering was under way in Hall, family and servants milling expectantly. Lil came in with a big bowl in each hand – almonds, dates – and Moll whipped the high table with a tablecloth. Antony made a beeline for Lil, intercepting her and hovering on tiptoe to see what was in the bowls, but every other face turned to us as we came through the doorway. My father had an arm across my mother's shoulders and Dottie was cantering around them, proposing various ambitious entertainments for Edward's homecoming.

It was Margie who took it upon herself to approach us, with a valedictory tipping of her nose into the air, to break the news: 'Edward's been knighted.'

'Really?' And so there I was, just as Katherine had been, minutes ago, up in her room – Really? Really? – but nothing like her because my grin was so wide that it almost hurt. Beside me, Katherine mustered an appropriate response but sounded dazed, which was how Thomas looked, too, over at the far end of Hall, not simply, I knew, because he was exhausted by his heroic dash around the house and courtyards but because, despite himself, he'd be finding it hard to hear of this important success of

Edward's. *Well, tough*, was all I could think, *Time to grow up, sunshine*.

Few people were quite bold enough to be looking one another square in the eye before Edward was definitely back on the safe side of the gatehouse, but my father was the exception. His eyes came for Katherine's and, standing there at her side, I too felt their draw, which was how I came to glimpse the smile he gave her: fleeting but somehow also long, and both joyful and gentle. 'See?' that smile seemed to say, as if he were holding her to something. 'See? He's coming home.'

I did see it, I definitely did, but back then I made nothing of it, and, really, why would I have? That smile of my father's, which said to his daughter-in-law, 'This is over now, and the rest of your life can begin.'

2

The final week of Edward's absence was the worst, in a way, because we were holding our breath and in the last few days it proved harder and harder to hold. In honour of their big brother's return, the children devised a pageant, which became disastrously overambitious and alarmingly paced, depicting a crazed ensemble of saints and growing daily more elaborate until even Mort and the dogs had parts. Every rehearsal degenerated into strife: Antony overzealous with his sword, which invited Margie's disapproval, which only inflamed him further; and Dottie was in the middle of the feuding pair, marshalling the dogs, panicking and pitching in to try to keep the peace. Myself, I had a lot less patience with them than I should have had.

Then, in the early hours of one morning that week, I woke to hear Katherine crying. Our rooms, on separate staircases, shared a wall. Only once before in my life had I ever heard such crying and on that occasion it had been through a closed door: my mother, when the baby John died. To call it despairing would be to dignify it. It was simply the kind of crying that just has to be done: it would go on and on and on until it was done. It would go on until it was done with her. Even if I got up and went to that room, there'd be no consoling her. So I lay awake in the dark while, on the other side of that wall, my sister-in-law gradually exhausted herself back into sleep. And then I lay awake a while longer, wondering. We were all going mad, it seemed to me, but in Katherine's case, not with joy. What on earth, I wondered, could have her, mere days from her husband's homecoming, so utterly desolate?

Edward had been likely to make it home on St Katherine's eve, but, in the end, he didn't. Mid-afternoon came the news that he was still about thirty miles away, which suddenly didn't seem to matter. With him back on home territory – my father even knew which inn he'd be stopping at – we felt able to relax enough to allow ourselves some cautious optimism. He'd be with us in his own sweet time and meanwhile we could enjoy the evening for ourselves. To everyone's relief, the children postponed their pageant. Our St Katherine's feast would go ahead, though, my mother decided. If it couldn't now mark Edward's return, it could instead be a celebration of our final night of waiting.

Katherine came later than any of us into Hall that evening and when at last she did appear, she took us all aback, her head bare and hair loose: the bride she'd never been, because she'd worn it coiled under a caul of gold thread and pearls for her wedding when she could have worn it down. She'd forgotten, was my first thought, she'd been distracted by her other elaborate preparations and had forgotten to fix her hair, cover her head. Encircling her waist were pearls that should have been looped around her neck and at her throat was a choker made from silk ribbon and a stunning brooch but, despite these efforts, my sister-in-law was only half-dressed.

Her first step into the room, though, showed me how wrong I was. That long-swinging hair was no mistake; she held her head high, the better to let it fall. A ripple of unease passed down the table but didn't touch me. As I saw it, she was leaving the past few miserable months behind, and in style.

We had musicians hired for that evening, and the food was particularly good: meat melting from the bone, an extraordinarily dense cherry sauce, and bread that was almost creamy. The fire burned with confidence for hours and its steady touch had the muscles of my back opening like flowers. When the dishes were being taken away and the handing around of the spiced wine had begun, Katherine called softly down the table: 'Antony? A dance?'

More accustomed to being told to sit still, my little brother leapt at the chance, my mother fretting in his wake over a kink in his collar. He and Katherine crossed to the small space bounded by the other tables and began a stately dance. For all that they made an incongruous pair, it was a proper undertaking, perfectly serious. I could see her murmuring prompts to him, 'Two steps, now, to the left. That's right.'

Margie stood up to make her proposal – 'Harry?' – and so they joined in.

Then Elizabeth sighed to Thomas, 'Come on, I need to practise,' and although he was going to decline – his hand tightening around his cup, ready to raise it, to object that he was too busy drinking – my mother caught and held his eye, *Do as your sister asks.* So, with a sigh even more fulsome than Elizabeth's, he capitulated.

'And look like you're enjoying it,' Elizabeth ordered, 'or you'll put me off,' to which he raised his hands in a show of surrender. Only Dottie and I were left at the table with our parents. My mother was concerned for Dottie but the response was a stern frown and a gesturing at a busy mouth: her priority was the cheese, which had just been brought to the table; she could never resist cheese. Placated, my mother leaned back in her chair and gave herself over to spectating.

My father stood, bowed to me – dear man – and extended a hand in invitation: 'Jane?'

Eventually, late, at my mother's request, the children were ushered off to bed by Lil and Moll, the rest of us drifting back to the table, where Harry entertained us with card tricks. Elizabeth retired after a while – she had her monthly, I knew – but everyone else remained at the table when all the precious beeswax had pooled and firelight alone painted the room in its colours. No one could quite give up on the evening. Perhaps, oddly, none of us could quite give up on the time when Edward had been away, of which, despite its difficulties, we had proved ourselves to be survivors. When we did all finally leave Hall, we had to salvage wicks for the purpose and, heading for our adjacent staircases, Katherine and I took a single one, which she carried. Neither of us spoke on our way across the house; we were both tired and anyway she'd not said much all evening, At the foot of my staircase, I was about to grope my way up as she held the candle aloft for me, but she said, 'Let's go up to the long gallery.'

She said it with no obvious enthusiasm, and I was baffled. 'What for?'

She shrugged. 'I love it up there.'

Well, she did, I knew, and – warm and well fed – I was feeling relatively well disposed towards her and didn't wish to deny her, on that night of all nights. More to the point, I didn't quite have the wherewithal to object; it'd be easiest to go along with it. Anyway, she was already turning away with our light.

The long gallery seemed to have been expecting us: when the door opened, there it was, composed, looking coolly and levelly back at us. The length of it drew us onwards but, much of it beyond the reach of our flame, also kept us in our place. A few steps in, Katherine paused and turned to me with a little laugh of delight, then, having placed the candle carefully on the floor, spread her arms just as she had on her very first day. Back then, she'd skipped into the morning sunshine but now she stood in the candle-glow and turned, slowly, relishing the space not by dashing into it but by wrapping it around herself. One of her extended hands reached for me, drew me to her, and then we were dancing or at least going through a few steps. No music, of course, but that didn't seem to matter. Dancing was the obvious use for so much space. Free of music, we were, not at its bidding, not having to fall in it with it but dancing instead as we chose, our shadow-selves looming and lumbering around us, undimmed by the dark.

We should have heard any approach from a distance but a mere scattering of footsteps immediately on the other side of the door alerted us to its opening and then there was Thomas, close-candlelit and deeper flushed from an evening of wine and his sprint up the stairs. My brother was in search of distraction and, all else having failed, we girls would do. Well, that did it, I decided: I was off to bed. In he sauntered, breathing hard, turning the light chaotic around him, delighted at his find – '*Thought* I saw shadows up here!' – and overly optimistic, as ever, of a welcome. 'What are you two up to?'

What were we up to? Nothing, really. And indeed Katherine said nothing, retreating into a fold of arms so that it was left to me to answer, 'Just dancing, a bit.'

I resented having to hear how silly it sounded. He seemed happy enough, though. 'Don't let me stop you,' and he put down his candle, about to hunker beside it, so keen to prolong the evening that he'd pay the price of polite interest in girls' dancing.

But Katherine and I stood there, the spell for us having been broken, which he must have realised because he was only halfway down before he reversed the descent, rising and beckoning for my hand. In order to get it over and done with, I allowed him to take me into a few dance steps.

'Head up, Jane,' he warned, which, despite everything, made

me smile, because it was a family joke, my graceless focusing on the floor, and then he turned, as that particular dance required, for the next partner.

Katherine hadn't been following us; she was surprised by his reaching for her, but she wasn't wrong-footed. If he was a good dancer, she was even better. No reminders needed for her to keep her head high, and Thomas, at the end of her arm, looked superfluous. Perhaps he knew it, because he broke off to ask, 'D'you know this one?' and embarked on a different, tricky sequence of steps, which he'd probably learned at the Dormers'.

Neither Katherine nor I responded.

Thomas prompted, 'Jane?'

'No,' I said, 'I don't.'

'It's not difficult,' he countered, as if I'd claimed otherwise. 'Want me to teach you?'

I said I was off to bed.

'Oh, come on!' I was, apparently, a spoilsport.

Well, so be it. 'Thomas, really, it's late,' and I retrieved the candle from the floor.

'Katherine, then?' he wheedled, 'Shall I show you?'

I opened the door, the light spilling ahead of me down the stairwell, while behind me Katherine sighed crossly. 'Oh, if you *must*.'

I halted, already a step down, because I was stealing away with her flame, which hadn't been my intention; I'd assumed she'd be following me. When I glanced around, she waved me off with the same impatience with which she'd just conceded to him.

'I'll take his,' she said.

And so I left them to it.

3

When Edward arrived home, it seemed that everything might well be fine; he seemed well, if even thinner in the face, which made his eyes look bigger and, for the first week or so, those eyes, free of their usual preoccupations, trailed we Seymours. And however much he hoped to hide his exhaustion, it was obvious in that benign, dazed expression with which he regarded us. Katherine stuck by his side so close as to take on something of it. She shored him up but there was none of that absurd wifely posturing in which she'd indulged when he was away; she seemed calmly accepting of her duty. And she was indeed built for diligence, I saw to my surprise; that long neck which had so often held her head high in jubilant defiance could bend just a little and then there she was, meek and mindful, and the steadiness of her gaze, which used to deliver long looks, was just as readily employed to serious effect.

In his first days back, Edward took time to reacquaint himself with life at Wolf Hall, happy enough to sit with his mother in the day room or to endure ridiculous exchanges with Antony. Everyone wanted his company. Well, everyone except Thomas, who took himself off to the Dormers', which was a relief to us all. Edward spent his time walking the dogs in the deadened gardens, and hanging around the stables, and once I came across him in the kitchen, chatting earnestly with Bax, who was treating him to samples as if he were a little boy. Katherine was there, too, ostensibly busy with her own task but, stealthy with her knife, she was listening to their every word. I tried to catch her eye, to exchange a smile: there I was in the doorway, stopped notably still, but she didn't look over at me, too protective of her husband even to risk the fondest mockery.

As he regained his weight and vigour during the following weeks, it seemed to me that his wife was losing hers. That taxing time of year, with the dietary restrictions of Advent compounded by the hardships of winter, meant that none of us was blooming, we all looked weary and wan, but Katherine was taking it worse than any of us. She went down with one of her headaches for three or four days, after which my mother secured a dietary dispensation in order to build her back up, and then a blind eye was turned so that the dispensation stayed in place until Christmas. She didn't take much advantage of it, though, claiming a poor appetite and every mealtime pushing the superior, much-envied food around her plate.

Then came Christmas at last, but on St Stephen's she succumbed to a second bout. My mother's view was that it was a bad time of year for those who were prone to headaches: stuck inside all day, every day in the fire-smoke, and then the fasting of Advent followed by the overindulgence of Christmas.

On New Year's Day, I walked in on my sister-in-law in the dry larder and saw, despite her frantic attempt to hide it, that she was crying. She'd turned fast but too late and she knew it.

'Yes?' She feigned scrutiny of a high shelf. 'What?'

I knew better than to take the hostility at face value. Excruciating though it was to have to stand there in the doorway with her desperate for me to go, I had to give her a chance to change her mind, to decide that she did, after all, need to confide in me. Only when the moment had well and truly passed with no sign of her relenting did I say what I'd come for – cinnamon – and then she handed me the jar without turning around. I was to leave her be and, it seemed, pretend to have seen nothing untoward, which surely made fools of us both.

Katherine stopped being my friend when Edward came home from France: that's the truth of it. Her first summer at Wolf Hall became just a summer, a May bride's first, frivolous summer before she properly settled down to the serious business of being the wife of the Seymour heir. So my father had been right, I thought, with his gentle, knowing smile: the rest of Katherine's life did start then. And from that time onwards, the two of us were simply sisters-in-law.

But was it that simple? Because why take it that bit further and try to revise the past, too? That was what she was doing: pretending it'd always been thus, ever since she'd first stepped over our threshold. Pretending she'd never been anything other than the perfect wife. It was obvious from the way she avoided my company and declined to meet my eye as if I didn't exist, the girl with whom she'd walked and danced in the dark, and the wifely Katherine was the only Katherine there'd ever been.

And something else. One night not long after the turn of the year, I'd left my bed because Dottie had a tickly cough; she was able to half-sleep through it but I had no such luck, and it was on my way to the kitchen for a spoonful of honey for her that I glimpsed Katherine. From the foot of my staircase, across a moon-silvered expanse of flagstones, I saw my sister-in-law at the oriel's unshuttered window. She was slotted onto the window seat, hugging her knees and facing into the night. She hadn't heard me, it seemed, but if I took a single step further, then she would. There was no sleepiness to her, illuminated as she was by the wolf moon. She was thinking hard, I sensed, thinking something through, the work of it as exacting as a physical labour. What was it that was keeping her so wide awake? In the hours of daylight, she hovered around Edward, yet in the dead of night, when she should have been dreaming beside him, there she was, at that window, animal-bright.

Having to resign myself to suffering Dottie's cough, I drew stealthily back up the stairs, but from that night onwards, I could never quite trust to Katherine being asleep. Lying in bed on the other side of the wall from her, I'd find myself half-listening for her tread, even for her breathing, even perhaps her thinking; I'd lie there wondering if she, too, was awake, and why.

That spring came, at last, almost a year after their wedding, the big news: Katherine was pregnant. It was Edward who actually announced it, in the parlour after supper one evening, but Katherine had looked to him to do it: he rose at her urging, unvoiced though it was. I'd glimpsed her sidelong glance at him, as pointed as a nudge in his ribs: *Go on*, that look had said, *do it*. He didn't, not immediately, batting it back with a scowl of his own so that she re-delivered it: *I said, Go on*. As if they were children owning up to something. Then he rose, self-conscious, clearing his throat to command our attention, and said he had some news, failing to specify good or bad. He pitched it over our heads: 'Katherine is expecting a baby.'

The squeals of delight seemed to startle him so that he, too, might have been hearing it for the first time. Perhaps that was when he allowed himself to believe it, and then he looked to his wife. She returned the look, but apprehensively. My mother spoke up, over all the congratulations, to ask when she was due. Second half of September, Katherine replied, not quite meeting her eye.

My heart was over-full beneath my breastbone. Sitting there in a room aglow with joyful faces, I beamed back at my brother and sister-in-law while trying to force that strenuous smile down inside me in order to feel it, because all I felt so far was that with a baby, Katherine would sail away from me into motherhood and leave me stranded in my Wolf Hall life. I hadn't expected to feel like that, I'd assumed I was beyond all that; she was no company for me by then, she was nothing to me bar a sister-in-law (*just one summer* – my mistake, I'd never had a sister-in-law before). But I'd been protecting myself, I realised to my disappointment and my shame. I knew I should have been across the parlour, as was Elizabeth – Elizabeth! – to give Katherine a hug; I should have been generous enough to be able to do that. The children were bouncing, literally bouncing, and Harry was laughing, and my parents almost crying. Thomas would be the odd one out, but I couldn't look at him for fear of seeing my ambivalence reflected there. I so badly didn't want to be like Thomas.

Oddly, Edward and Katherine appeared no more comfortable than I was. If the news had been of a business deal, Edward would've been graciously accepting the congratulations, but he looked flummoxed. As for Katherine, her gaze roved among us as if she'd been unsure of a good reception and still couldn't trust to it, and I wondered how she could ever have doubted it.

'Lent!' My mother turned, alarmed, wide-eyed, a hand pressed to her lips. We'd already endured three weeks of dietary restrictions, which Katherine – in her delicate condition – could have been excused, had she only spoken up. My mother crossed the room and crouched down to look, pained, into her daughter-in-law's face. 'Katherine, really, you should've *said*.'

It was Edward who spoke. 'But we didn't know, did we.'

He sounded irked. My mother ignored him and continued her appeal to Katherine. 'You'd have had an inkling and you should have said. I mean, I can understand' – a furtive glance around the room, *you might not yet have felt confident to tell everyone* – 'but you could have just had a little word.' *With me.*

'Honestly,' Katherine said, refusing to respond in kind, 'thank you, but I was fine.'

'But the *baby*—' My mother caught herself, unsure if she should've owned up so readily to her concern being not for Katherine, but for the baby.

Thus rebuked, Katherine did from then onwards make sure to eat more, but in all other respects she sought no concessions nor welcomed any. She worked as hard as ever around the house, actively taking on tasks and rebuffing offers of assistance. 'I'm not *ill*,' I heard her protest once to Dottie and Margie who, following my mother's example, were trying to deprive her of a broom. The small silence that followed was, I knew, the sound of the girls mulling this over; and presumably it satisfied them because they relented without further ado, and to my knowledge never again tried anything similar.

The one time I did see my sister-in-law accept help was, surprisingly, from Thomas. We were waddling across the inner courtyard, laden with laundry baskets, when he strode past us but then appeared to remember himself and turned back.

'Here.' He gestured grimly at Katherine's basket. 'Let me.'

She held it to her and I could almost hear her usual rebuff – I'm fine, thanks – before she said it. But then she didn't say it, changed her mind and heaved it into his arms. 'Thanks.' It was all she said and there was less than no gratitude in it. She didn't smile or even look at him, and nor did he at her.

My mother, though, persisted, forever snatching baskets from Katherine's hands and rushing to plump cushions behind her even as she was in the act of reclining on them. Quite unable to stop herself, she longed to make a fuss of her or, more accurately, of the baby she was carrying, and tried to hide her dismay at Katherine's pointedly robust self-reliance by affecting an indulgence of it: 'Oh, you young ladies these days . . .'

Edward, though, was made to answer for his wife's attitude.

One morning I was searching for Antony – he needed a hair-wash – and came across him at the stables with Edward, up on Edward's hunter. Standing by for my little brother to slide from the saddle into his big brother's arms, I spotted my mother advancing on us, looking concerned. 'Edward?'

I claimed Antony with a hand on his shoulder, the better to steer him indoors, while Ralph began leading Gawain back into his stable.

'Edward?' My mother pitched her enquiry past us and over the clatter of hooves on cobbles. 'Is Katherine all right?'

I faltered – had something happened? Antony slipped free of me, loping ahead. Katherine had seemed fine when I'd last seen her, mere moments before, combing Margie's hair for lice.

'It's just that—' Reaching him, she could lower her voice, into a sigh, 'Well, you know, it's that she just doesn't seem very happy to be pregnant.'

Oh, that, then, was all it was, Katherine's ongoing all-too-obvious impatience with the plumped cushions.

'Is it because she's worried, d'you think? Because of course I can understand that, but she should rest assured that there's no one better than Mrs Gilhooley.'

Mrs Gilhooley, the midwife.

'Yes,' said Edward, notably uncomfortable at being waylaid on the subject and perhaps especially near the stables, that most masculine of territories. 'I'll tell her.'

Antony stopped short. 'Oh!'

'*Antony.*' I'd had enough – fetching him had taken long enough already – and, besides, I didn't want to seem to be eavesdropping, which was exactly what I was doing.

'My stick!' he wailed, to which I folded my arms emphatically: *Quickly, then.*

He scampered back across the courtyard and I made a show of watching him, of being in the courtyard on legitimate business.

'And,' my mother asked Edward, 'there's nothing else wrong?'

But Edward had never had a pregnant wife before: how could he know how happy his wife should be, or at least seem to be? I sensed him pondering the extent of his wife's failing in this respect, and the extent to which he could be held at fault for it.

'She's fine,' he said, making it sound like the last word on the matter.

That was a mistake; Edward was losing his touch. My mother hadn't picked her way across the cobbles to be dismissed so easily; she wasn't going to say, 'I'm sure you're right,' or 'I'm glad to hear it,' and then just turn on her heel.

'Come *on*,' I called to Antony, even though he was doing just that and at a fair lick.

My mother said nothing, so Edward had to say something more. 'You're right,' he said, 'she probably is worried.'

My mother allowed it with a sage nod, but didn't shift. It didn't suffice.

Antony reached me with an extravagant skip.

'Right,' I said. 'Come on.' At last we could get going. 'Hair-wash. Now.'

'Can I do it myself?'

'*If* you do it properly,' which he never did.

Behind us, I heard Edward claiming, 'Katherine really isn't one for show, that's all.' But that was worse: the implication that my mother had failed to grasp something so fundamental about her own daughter-in-law. And, anyway, that use of the word 'show', as if all she was after was mere show.

So, on the whole, it wasn't going too well. Not only had my mother been brushed off by her difficult daughter-in-law, but also by her beloved eldest son. And as time went on, it didn't get any better. Quite often I'd glimpse Edward snapping-to and changing direction on a staircase or in a passageway to avoid my mother, and never before from him had I seen the likes of such disloyalty.

Nevertheless, my mother didn't let up. She refused to be denied any opportunity to celebrate her daughter-in-law's condition, however stony the reception, to which end she'd rope in any of us who happened to be around; even the dogs would do. Katherine would walk into a room and her mother-in-law would enthuse to everyone and no one in particular, 'Well, goodness, I think Katherine's showing already, don't you?' No response required, which was just as well in the case of the dogs but suited the children, too. They'd look up, unfocused, from whatever they were doing, momentarily disoriented, as if having half-heard something from afar and of no concern to them, like a hunting horn.

It got to me, though; I could see that Katherine hated it and I didn't know where to look. Elizabeth would roll her eyes, but then she rolled her eyes at anything and everything that my mother or indeed anyone said, although sometimes she'd rouse herself to offer a pearl of wisdom such as, 'At least you can gorge yourself silly when you're pregnant, because you'll end up enormous anyway.'

In that particular instance, my mother secured a sulky retraction. 'No, not *her*,' Elizabeth tutted, 'I didn't mean *her*, *she* won't look hideous, but lots of ladies *do*.'

All these comments Katherine endured with a tight little smile that didn't reach her eyes.

Come the end of every day, in the privacy of their own room, my father would probably be the one to bear the brunt of my mother's frustration with Katherine ('Why doesn't she ...' 'You'd think she'd ...'): that was my guess, because he had the look, I felt, of a man having to be careful what he said to his wife.

Visitors proved a rather better bet for my mother. Somehow it was legitimate for Lady Wroughton and Mrs Dormer and

Barbara's mother to be vocal on the subject of Katherine's rapidly altering physical state ('Oh, that's a good-sized bump, Katherine; you're carrying high, aren't you?'). It was permissible for them to enquire after her health – her legs and ankles, her back and ribs, her appetite and digestion and bowels, her sleep – and, unbidden, they offered excitable accounts of their own experiences ('Oh, I had the most terrible . . . '). They asked after her plans, too: names, birth attendants, nurse and wet-nurse. She answered politely but evasively.

'Oh, she's *shy*,' Mrs Dormer sympathised once, when she'd left the room, although it wasn't quite clear with whom she was sympathising.

I didn't think Katherine was shy. Nor did I think that apprehension, natural though it would have been, was what was keeping her quiet. I couldn't imagine the reason for it. All I knew was that she never made reference to her pregnancy nor mentioned the baby unless prompted, and then barely. And she wouldn't front-lace: the time for it came, as Moll resisted no opportunity to herald ('We do need to be letting it all hang out, now, Lady K!') but somehow Katherine always slipped her clutches and it never got done, was endlessly deferred, and there she was, every day, the fabric of her gown stretched ever tighter.

I watched my sister-in-law retreating behind that everexpanding belly and sometimes, just sometimes, felt I should be trying to reach her, felt I should, if only for old times' sake, be extending the hand of friendship. And then, for want of knowing how else to do it, I'd mimic those visiting ladies, who'd received the best response from her. I'd say something like, 'Boy or girl, d'you reckon?'

But she wouldn't be drawn. 'We'll find out soon enough, won't we.'

Even if I was direct – 'Can you feel the baby move?' – she didn't really answer, not really.

'Sometimes.'

I wondered if she was like that with Edward, too. So thoroughgoing was her nonchalance that perhaps it extended to their most intimate moments, or what should've been their most intimate moments: the pair of them in bed in their nightshirts and no mention of what was between them.

But then, Edward was so often away that summer, the second summer of his marriage; he'd been granted a royal appointment, a first step but a big one, albeit in the household of the royal bastard son. The little boy had become the Duke of Richmond and Edward had become his Master of the Horse, overseeing the stables, which provoked Thomas to take the drastic and reckless step of riding alone to Francis Bryan's, having left us a note, to beg him to try to secure something similar on his behalf. Generously, Francis took Thomas in.

Harry had moved to our other house, at Elvetham, to prepare it for him and Barbara after their forthcoming September wedding, and so my father was having to cover both his and Edward's usual Wolf Hall work. All of which meant that we were largely a household of girls and ladies that second summer of Katherine's, stitching our way through the days. There was so much to prepare for the baby. Even Elizabeth helped, although she kept to sewing on buttons and attaching lace borders. Dottie and Margie made their first grown-up pieces, and the rather stuttering stitches had a charm of their own. We could have used what was in store – ten babies' worth of clothes and linen – but the unspoken sentiment was that this baby should, wherever possible, have new. A new generation, a new start. And, anyway, no one was in any rush to unpack what had been put away when the baby John had died.

Katherine took up the altar cloth again, which we'd all but forgotten. Once, when she'd left the room, Dottie whispered, 'Why isn't Katherine sewing for the baby?'

'Oh—' My mother didn't look up, 'Some ladies are superstitious, which is perfectly understandable.'

Dottie didn't get it. 'Superstitious?'

I cringed as Elizabeth launched in: 'Tempting fate. The baby might die.'

'Oh!' Dottie was horrified, her sewing limp in her hands.

My mother stared pursed-lipped at Elizabeth, who challenged, 'Well? It's true, isn't it?'

It was to Dottie whom my mother addressed her reply. 'It *is* true,' she allowed, gently. 'For some ladies, it's too much to hope for, which is why it's up to us to do it for them.'

And indeed there we were, day after day, our white stitches laid down in white cloth like little bones, barely visible but detectable to the touch, while the expectant mother worked on a border of pomegranates, the ripe, split fruits in a ruby thread so rich that it was almost granular, and each one a slow-setting sun, collapsing in on itself.

4

Johnny's birth a couple of weeks early, at the end of August, upstaging Harry and Barbara's wedding, wasn't all that was unexpected. Katherine was more surprised than anyone by the delight she took in her baby from the very start. She was bowled over by how lovely he already was.

My mother let me into the room sooner than she should have, and some of the cleaning up was still to be done. The sheets had been changed but the bloodied ones were still piled by the door, and Lil and my mother were scrubbing floorboards so that I had to step around them and their bucket. I'll never forget coming into that room, how good a moment it was. Propped up in bed, Katherine was drastically pale but when she smiled at me, that smile went everywhere, even tweaking her ears, and she had dimples. I could have sworn she hadn't had dimples before.

Not yet properly swaddled, merely linen-wrapped, the baby lay beside her in the bed.

I hung back, uncomfortable at being privileged over those who were still cleaning, but Katherine spoke to me across the room: 'He *knows* me.' She was amazed and thrilled. 'See?' She gestured to his tiny face, 'If I speak, he starts looking for me. See?'

Laughter hummed in her words. 'He doesn't do it for anyone else, only me; he knows it's me.' And then she was talking to him rather than to me, a fingertip to his button nose, 'Don't you, eh, hmmm? Don't you? You know it's me.'

I ventured a little closer to see that indeed he did: those dark eyes, so dense as to seem lightless, even sightless, were searching strenuously for the source of his mother's voice. He was not to be deflected; his life might have depended on it. His expression-less little face had a stern, unforgiving air.

'Oh, he's beautiful,' I breathed. He was deliciously, comically weak-chinned, as I now remembered all newborns to be, and there was that glorious full nub of top lip. 'Who does he look like?' I wondered aloud.

'Like himself,' Katherine said, which felt, to me, like a rebuke. Somehow, I'd already managed to say the wrong thing.

'Oh, it's too early to tell,' my mother called cheerfully from the floor.

Katherine gave a little laugh. 'I tell you, Janey, I don't know how I'm ever going to go through *that* again,' but she sounded pleased with herself and quite sure that she would indeed be going through it again.

I didn't know what to say; I couldn't begin to imagine what she'd been through. It had been more a call to the other ladies in the room, though, because on cue they all clucked and exclaimed: 'Oh, but you forget,' and, 'It'll be so much quicker next time.'

'Too quick,' said Mrs Dormer, 'the second one hurts worse,' and then they were off, all of them, competitively reminiscing on their own labours. Lady-talk. Katherine left them to it, turning her smile to her baby boy and running her fingertip appreciatively over his delicate skull.

She had to miss Harry and Barbara's wedding, was still in childbed at the time, not yet churched, but she didn't seem to mind. Nothing appeared to bother her any more. She was so happy after Johnny was born. In his presence, she shone, her eyes unnaturally bright, and through those eyes she was seeing the world anew because she was seeing it for him: 'Look at the goat, Johnny! He's a funny old thing, isn't he! What's he up to, over there?' And Johnny did look, right from the earliest days: ever willing, genuinely fascinated and studious. Katherine had him with her all the time that Mrs Crumpsie, his wet-nurse, didn't have him, and even when she did, Katherine didn't leave but stood over them both, chatting away.

My mother and Katherine began to work as a pair, their wariness of each other vanished, as if it had never been. They consulted each other and collaborated on feeds, sleeps, clothing and outings. When talking directly to Johnny himself, my mother's manner differed from Katherine's; there was none of Katherine's coaxing, no buttering up. My mother was efficient on Johnny's behalf, as if they were in accord as to what was needed. 'We have to get you cleaned up, don't we? We'd enjoy a stroll down to the brook, wouldn't we?' He trusted her absolutely, utterly content to lie there and see what she could do for him; and, as far as I was aware, she never failed him.

Edward was all fingers and thumbs with his little boy but enjoyed making something of his uncharacteristic incompetence and of deferring to his wife: 'Oops, Katherine, he's—'

In response, she'd adopt a certain weariness: 'Oh for goodness sake, Edward, he's only . . .'

Unlike Edward, my father had the benefit of extensive experience and would pitch in, heading for his grandson as he came into the room, scooping him up: 'How's my little man today, eh? Learned much about this big, bad world of ours?'

And Johnny would regard him admiringly: his grandfather, source of all wisdom.

But it was Dottie whom he seemed to regard as his companion. When he'd learned to smile, he smiled most often for her, and understandably, because the two of them got up to adventures. She was forever negotiating to take him from his mother – 'Back in a tick, I promise, I absolutely promise' – and lugged him around in his carry-basket, rustling up wonders for him: a snail, a feather.

Neither Margie nor Antony participated in any of this: for them, at least in the early days, after the thrill of his arrival, he was less interesting than the dogs. Elizabeth, too: sometimes she even seemed to have forgotten that he'd been born. And me? Well, I did try, I really did try, but could never get him to come to me. I only had to look into his crib for him to burst into tears, and then there was Katherine bustling over to save him from me, to whisk him away, 'Oh, come on, fusspot.'

When he was just under a year old, Katherine told us that she was pregnant again, and during her second pregnancy, she was happy; and then the birth went well and everything looked set to be wonderful. It was all so nearly wonderful.

5

Ned was born on St Thomas à Becket's day, two Christmases after the one his mother had lost to a headache when Edward was newly home from France. Two sons in two years, and it was impossible by then to imagine a time before they'd existed. Edward was away at court for Ned's birth, unfortunately, and then twice more during his first six or seven weeks. Returning to Wolf Hall in late February, he found himself riding through snow, but luckily the frost nails had stayed in the horse's shoes since the last trip. His wife was already asleep when he arrived but the rest of us had stayed up, and then we kept him up when, it occurs to me now, he must've been longing for his bed. As ever, we were keen for news, and, as ever, he obliged, telling us how the princess Mary, who was Dottie's age, had been at court.

He'd brought us back a little something, as he always did: this time, a book-sized wooden box of six oranges. We knew of oranges but, until then, had never actually seen one. Elizabeth took one from the box to examine it, to sniff it, then passed it on.

'Eat them,' Edward encouraged no one in particular, perhaps slightly impatient with us. 'They *are*,' he emphasised, ' for eating.'

'But then they'll be gone!' protested Dottie.

'But then I'll bring you some more.' He beckoned for the unboxed orange to be handed to him. 'Share one, then, just the one; share this one.'

He punctured it with his thumbnail and the air was suddenly alight with its scent. In his hands, it shrugged off its peculiar skin, the woolly pith exposed in its flecks, strands and patches. He prised the segments apart and handed them around. What a contrast, I found, between that startlingly searing scent and the insubstantial squelch inside the tough sheath.

The following morning, despite his exhaustion, or perhaps even because of it, Edward woke early, too early. Inadequately rested and somewhat at a loss, he guessed I'd be up and came to find me to ask me to do some minor repairs to his clothes. A button was missing from one jacket, a hook and eye from another, and the lining of a doublet was coming away. It was down to me to take care of his laundry while Katherine and my mother were busy with the new baby.

There we were in the day room, him showing me what needed doing, when Katherine walked in carrying Ned. Until then, she and Edward hadn't yet seen each other; Katherine had spent the night in the nursery on a mattress alongside the boys because they both had bad colds. She, too, looked exhausted although, as ever, differently from Edward: he was darkened, shadowed and stubbled, whereas she was blanched, which gave her a startled look.

'Oh!' She was ill-prepared for the reunion, partially dressed as she was and with Ned whimpering and snotting on her shoulder. She demanded of Edward, 'Did you get that chamlet?' Presumably she'd asked him to pick up some fabric for her en route. It was as if she'd last encountered him mere minutes before, not a week and a half ago.

Edward looked hopefully at his infant son, expecting Katherine to lift him away from her shoulder, to turn him and reveal his little face to us, but she didn't and he was left looking at the baby's back. Katherine held their son to her like a shield.

'Edward?' The mention of the chamlet had Edward looking blank: his wife might've spoken in a foreign language, or worse, he might not quite recall who she was.

Then, 'Oh . . . ' and the heel of his hand to his forehead; he'd forgotten. Katherine tutted, turned, and went back through the doorway with Ned boggle-eyed over her shoulder.

Edward stood looking after her, stunned. Me, too: I bet no one treated him like that at court. But that was how it had often been, lately, at home between the pair of them.

'Actually,' Edward said, as if resuming a conversation which we hadn't been having, 'I think I'm going to take Katherine along with me next time, to court.' He spoke with a forced brightness. 'I think it's time to be doing that, now I have a room there.'

I doubted that'd improve relations between the pair of them. 'Have you mentioned it to her?' Katherine had always been dismissive of court life, never shown the least interest in it, often rubbished it. In her view, it was all show. Her life, by then, was very much at Wolf Hall.

There was a notable pause before he admitted, 'Not yet.'

Well, I didn't envy him having to broach it. 'Perhaps wait 'til she's in a better mood.'

He gave an exasperated sigh, as if to wonder when on earth that would be. 'She'll just have to get used to the idea.'

I doubted she'd see it that way.

He was worried, though, it was obvious. 'It'll only be occasional. It doesn't look good for her to keep staying away. She needs to make an effort. Philippa can show her the ropes.' Francis Bryan's wife, Philippa Spice. 'And anyway,' he sounded piqued, 'you'd think she'd jump at the chance.'

He looked to me to confirm it: that if it were me, I'd love to go.

Would I? I honestly didn't know; I'd never considered it, I

really hadn't. Court wasn't for the likes of me, I'd always felt, and never would be, and I was probably happy with that.

'She'd have to leave the boys,' I ventured. That, I felt, was the main problem.

'For *a week*,' he protested, pacing to the window and staring moodily into the courtyard, 'a week or so at a time, that's all. And only occasionally. And anyway,' he whipped back around to me, sour-faced, 'it'd do her good.'

I didn't like the sound of that; the punitive note to it.

'Them, too, actually. And they're—' He flapped a hand, impatient, dismissive, 'Growing.'

Growing all the time, he meant: needing their mother less.

But they were tiny. He didn't understand.

'And,' he said, 'they've got our mother.'

Well, true, she would find it no hardship to have the boys to herself from time to time.

But this wasn't a matter of arrangements, about who could care for the boys and for how long. No, Edward and Katherine inhabited two different worlds and Katherine was in no hurry to partake of her husband's.

'It's just that . . .' I cleared my throat. 'Well, she's such a country girl, isn't she?' Which was one way to put it.

He said nothing, which I took to be affirmation; he was only too aware of the gulf between them.

Suddenly I felt so very tired and wanted Katherine to come back through that door and fix whatever was wrong between them, or try to; it shouldn't be left to me.

He changed the subject: 'Are you sure you have time to do this today?' his dark eyes on mine were concerned.

I assured him that I did.

'Well, I appreciate it,' he said, 'I really do.'

In turn, I appreciated him saying so. Had we been different people, I might have laid a hand on his arm.

He sighed hugely in a kind of summing-up. 'You know, Francis and I should probably be talking to the Dormers about you.'

I didn't follow.

'Good family, but Will's a third son. Won't be easy to marry off.'

'No,' I said. I wasn't agreeing, I didn't mean that Will wouldn't be easy to marry off; I meant, *Stop*. My stomach had dropped to my shoes.

Edward regarded me kindly. 'There's no shame in having a good word put in for you.'

How would you know? 'Not Will,' I managed.

But he laughed softly. 'Will's all right.'

All right? As if all right was all right. And, anyway, actually, he wasn't; he wasn't even all right.

'Jane—'

I cut him off. 'I'd rather stay here.'

'Here?' He was incredulous.

'Yes,' I said, with much more certainty than I felt.

Did he really hold life at Wolf Hall in so little regard? Your family is here, I wanted to remind him. Your children.

He didn't appreciate what he had, I felt. And his wife: she could have the best of both worlds, trips to court and a life at home, but still she acted hard done by. *Well, try being married off to someone loathsome.* I gathered up Edward's garments. I wouldn't hear a word more; I was going back to bed, I'd do his repairs there.

At the door, I let loose a parting shot: 'Katherine might just find herself a bit out of place at court.' He assumed it'd be plain sailing, but I wasn't so sure; he was forgetting that his wife wasn't wholly conventional.

He rolled his eyes, but mine was a serious point and I pressed ahead with it. 'I mean,' I cast around for an example, 'she can't even read, really, can she?'

This he dismissed with a weary sigh.

'She *can't*, Edward.' Did he really not know? Did he really not know what kind of girl he'd married? But, then, how would he? He was almost never home. He hardly knew her. 'Our father once wrote her some poems,' I told him, 'and she had to ask me to read them to her.'

He just scoffed. 'Our father? Poems?' Which further annoyed me because this was beside the point.

'He *did*, when you were in France. She couldn't even read words like "autumn".'

He looked amused, and shrugged. This was a fight that he was refusing to have. He asked, 'Can you do those this morning?'

'Probably,' I said, before I shut the door on him.

It sparked something for him, though, my mention of those poems, although I didn't know it at the time; it was only later, from Katherine, that I'd learn what happened.

At first, Edward was intrigued by what I'd said, because his father? Writing Katherine poems? His father and Katherine had nothing to do with each other. Our father had nothing much to do with any of us, really, except Edward himself, and even then the conversations were pretty much limited to work. And Katherine had never mentioned any poems. And, Edward wondered, why wouldn't she have? He might have considered asking her, but feared she'd jump down his throat; he was too tired for that.

At night, too weary to sleep without her beside him – again, she was with the boys – he pondered those poems and decided to have a look for them, just a little look. If they had ever existed, he doubted Katherine would have burned them. Who, given poems, would go so far as to burn them? So he got up and opened her oak chest; he didn't know what she kept in there but he knew it was where she kept whatever she had.

There were some clothes that he recalled having liked her wearing, in which he hadn't seen her for a while, and her wedding dress, which he hardly dared touch, and, deeper down, cloths, bleached and rolled, that he suspected she used monthly. At the very bottom, he found a small bundle, linen-wrapped and ribbon-tied. He untied it, unwrapped it, and there was no mistaking his father's handwriting. Four poems, instantly recognisable as standard courtly fare, comparing the subject to flowers. As far as Edward knew, his wife was no fan of poetry. She laughed at courtly conventions. Didn't she? Yet those poems had an air of being treasured, he felt, despite or perhaps because of being kept at the bottom of that chest. He wished she'd mentioned them. It seemed odd that she hadn't. He pondered how little he knew of the life she led at Wolf Hall while he was away.

He couldn't re-tie that ribbon exactly as she had; tying ribbon was no skill of his. If she ever came looking for that little bundle, he knew, she wouldn't be fooled.

He probably didn't intend to raise the subject with his wife, but the next night, when she was back in the bed with him, he found himself saying, 'You never told me that my father wrote you poems,' hearing how he sounded pleasantly surprised, chummy, chatty.

But she would have none of it. 'What?' She was probably already half asleep.

'Jane said. Said my father wrote you some poems when I was in France.'

She murmured, 'I told him to.'

Of all the responses he might've expected, that wasn't one of them. 'You *told* him to?'

'Yes.' *And?* But then she did explain, or kind of: 'He's good at it, but he never does it any more, which seems a shame.'

There was no answer to that. A moment later, he asked, 'And were they any good?'

She sighed, pointedly: she was desperate to get to sleep. 'How would *I* know? What do *I* know about poetry?'

And that was that.

Except that he added, 'It's just that you never said.'

To which she mumbled, 'You were away, remember?'

Some minutes later: 'Those poems—'

'What, Edward, *what*?' She'd been on the brink of sleep.

He made himself ask it. 'Did you keep them?'

'No!' Irritated by the suggestion. 'Why would I?'

Perhaps she'd forgotten that she'd kept them: that was what Edward decided to think. It was feasible. It'd be easily done, buried away as they were, even if, at the time, she'd wrapped them with such care. It was a long time ago that she'd wrapped them up: two years. That was what Edward told himself. But he had an inkling of what he'd find if he looked for them again and when he did so, the following day, he was right: they were gone.

Two days, he gave her, two whole days in which to say it: Oh, those poems? Remember? Those poems of your father's? Well, guess what – turns out I did still have them.

And after those two days, he raised it with her: 'Those poems of my father's . . .'

'Will you *stop* going on about them.' They were both in bed again; she turned her back on him.

He was taken aback by her vehemence, and, anyway, 'I am *not* "going on about them".'

Nothing from her.

'Katherine, really, honestly, I'm not "going on" . . . It's just that, well, I suppose I'm wondering if it was . . . quite right for my father to be writing you poems. That's all.'

No response.

'I mean,' he didn't like to have to say it, 'courtly poems written to his daughter-in-law . . . how does that look?'

She turned on him. 'Who's looking?'

A fair question, but a mistake because the answer – loud and clear in the silence – was that *he* was. He retreated to, 'I just don't know if he should be writing you poems.'

'He isn't,' she retorted, which only made matters worse: the implication that it'd been a discrete period of time, the time when Edward had been away.

Edward sighed pointedly. 'Well, all right, but perhaps just don't encourage him.'

And then – why on earth did she do it? – she glared at him and said, 'He didn't need any encouragement.'

He would have counselled himself against reading too much into what she'd said in haste and when goaded, but it stayed with him, and the following night, in bed, under cover of darkness, he dared to ask her, because he felt he should: 'He didn't . . . *bother* you, did he, my father? That time when I was in France.'

He wouldn't quite have been able to imagine it – his father bothering her – but what did he know, really, he would have asked himself, of what went on at Wolf Hall when he was away?

She threw it back at him, hotly, 'Edward, your father is a lovely, lovely man.'

He lay there contemplating it, then said to the ceiling, 'I'm sorry that I've never written you poems,' but despite it being said in all sincerity, there was inevitably a tetchiness to it.

Katherine sat up – snapped up – to object, 'I don't want poems, Edward.'

He said, gently, as a reminder, 'I'm working very hard you know, Katherine.'

She said nothing, because she did know. She hadn't needed telling. Everyone knew; no one could fail to know how hard he worked. It was his answer to everything.

Then he made it worse by adding what she knew he'd add: 'And I'm doing it for you.'

She was glad he'd said it, though, because now she could shout it down. 'No, you are *not*.'

He tried to insist, 'It's for us.'

'No, it is *not*!'

She really was shouting, and I remember hearing it through the wall: I heard shouting. No one ever shouted at Edward.

I hadn't discerned the actual words but later I'd learn that she'd shouted, 'I don't care about any of that! Don't you understand? I don't want any of that! You, bowing and scraping to make your way at court. What I want is . . . '

Words failed her.

'Poems,' he countered scornfully. He, too, was up; he couldn't take this lying down.

She fumed, 'What I want, Edward,' and she didn't want to have to say it, but there was no avoiding it, 'is to be *loved*,' spitting out the word to deride it between the two of them as an outlandish expectation.

He said nothing, just lay back down in the bed. He could have said – should have said – 'You are,' but he didn't.

6

The first I knew of any of it, bar there having been some shouting, was when I was taking advantage of a rare dry February afternoon to get a few rugs beaten. It was the one task for which I never had any trouble garnering assistance from the junior members of the household, so long as I restricted myself to holding one end while they argued over whose turn it was to be left holding the other and whose to be free to indulge in the flogging. Chopper was bothering us, agitated, barking at each thwack, whether in excitement or alarm, I didn't know. Perhaps both.

So there I was, coughing on the dust, reverberating with the blows, refereeing the children and shouting at Chopper to pipe down, when Katherine came across the courtyard to me and, in the midst of the mayhem, turned her back to the little ones to ensure us some privacy. Quietly, below the whooping and beating and barking, she asked me, 'Why did you tell Edward that your father wrote me some poems?'

For a beat, my heart seized, because for her to know that I'd told him, he must have told her, and because the two of them clearly weren't on good terms, I doubted he'd done so in celebration of her muse-like quality. My guess was that he'd somehow used it against her, although I couldn't see how.

There'd been no complaint in her question, though, no accusation; it was just a question. She was here for an answer. But what *was* the answer? I couldn't exactly remember why I'd said it, but, to my sudden shame, I did recall the spirit in which I'd delivered it, and it hadn't been generous. What I recollected of the encounter was how cross I'd been with Edward for having the temerity to try to marry me off when he himself, in my view, had married the wrong girl. Cross at him, too, for having made that marital mistake; cross, perhaps, even with Katherine for being the wrong girl. I'd been tired was what came to mind and, yet again, as it felt to me, trapped in the middle of some altercation of theirs.

I didn't answer, but deflected: 'Shouldn't I have?'

She gave a weary flex of her eyebrows. 'Well, he doesn't seem terribly pleased.'

I checked, 'Edward?' because she could've meant my father. My father, surely, was the one with face to lose; my father, revisiting his gauche boyhood self.

She nodded: Edward.

I was genuinely puzzled. 'But what's it got to do with him?' Why would Edward be bothered?

Turning to go, she agreed with a widening of her eyes and a shrug: *Search me.*

A day later, my mother asked me to nip up to Katherine and Edward's room to fetch Katherine's little box of silks; she had an idea of a shade of green she'd like to use on some sleeves, but nothing in her own box came close and Katherine had invited her to look in hers. But Katherine had forgotten to bring the box downstairs, and then, apparently, while Johnny and Ned were napping, she was busy in the long gallery, undertaking what my mother suddenly seemed to regard as the most crucial of tasks, the supervision of the girls' virginals practice. So it was me who had to drop everything and go in search of those silks. As it happened, all I had to drop that morning was one of those little hammers with which, all Lent long, we pummelled strips of stockfish in an attempt to make it faintly palatable. However much of that disgusting dried fish we pulped, there was always dismayingly more in the barrel, so, despite resenting being at my mother's beck and call, I was happy enough to down tools.

I was still a few steps short of their door when I heard Edward: not on his way to the barber in Burbage, as my mother had told me, but in the room and sounding relatively cheerful. 'Next time,' he was saying, 'I'll be bringing Francis's tailor back with me, to make you something really special, because we're off to Greenwich for Lady Day.'

The final few words were flourished to bestow what was presumably intended as a fabulous surprise on his wife. Which it was for me, too: Greenwich Palace, and for Lady Day, not simply one of the biggest feasts of the year but, when it fell during Lent, dietary restrictions would be abandoned for that one day. And at Greenwich, I imagined, that would be done in some considerable style.

Katherine's response was, 'Mr Marychurch at Marlborough is fine for me, Edward, thank you,' but with a striking lack of gratitude. 'He knows exactly how to cut for me, and I'm not going to take my business away from him just because you've decided I should look like a stuffed partridge.'

I cringed, physically, my backbone bumped onto the stone wall, to hear this from her. It had been a peace offering, he'd been making a gift to her (and what a gift! A court-worthy new dress and the Lady Day feast in a palace) but she'd hurled it back at him. Had she really needed to be nasty? Couldn't she have put on a brave face and pretended to be pleased, or at least to be considering it? But then, she was spoiling for a fight – 'stuffed partridge' – and Edward, I knew, would be wise to leave it, step away, walk out of the room. If he did, though, he'd come across me stuck on the stairs.

'I'm going nowhere for Lady Day,' Katherine continued. 'I'm not leaving Ned; he won't even be three months, and that's too young.'

Incredibly, and admirably, Edward persisted, with increased good cheer: 'But Ned'll be fine! He's a big, healthy boy, he's fine with Mrs Pluckrose' – his wet-nurse – 'and, anyway, my mother's here.'

Katherine wouldn't budge. 'You go.'

It was me who needed to be going, I told myself, I should be off this staircase and away; I couldn't risk one of them huffing out of that room to find me here. How, though? How to get back down the steps without giving myself away? True, I'd managed to get up – oblivious, too, all a-scamper . . . but, still, I didn't fancy my chances. *Just go*, I urged myself, *Just do it*: six, eight steps and I'd be safe. But I stood there, unable to trust to my luck.

'Katherine,' Edward's voice was lowered, pleading, 'It's taken me a lot of work to get us a room——'

'Well, go and stay in it, then.'

'—— and until now,' his voice even softer, a stab at intimacy, 'there's always been the . . . ' He seemed to have to consider how to word it, ' . . . the boys.' *The pregnancies* was probably what he'd avoided saying, although I didn't know why he'd wanted to avoid it. His wife had been pregnant for much of the previous year and a half, and travel for her would've been ill-advised. 'And now, I think, it might do us some good to get away together.'

'What would do us some good, Edward, is to *live* away somewhere.'

I was rigid on those stairs, my back to the wall, barely daring to breathe. I'd had no idea this was a bone of contention, but it'd had the ring of being well rehearsed. I'd assumed that Katherine was settled at Wolf Hall, now that the boys were born; happy, even.

'Yes.' Admirable patience from Edward, if rather strained. 'And you know that I'm working on that.'

Was he? How? Harry and Barbara had moved into Elvetham now they were married; there was no other Seymour house. He'd have to buy one, or build one.

'No, Edward, you're working on a bigger room for yourself at court.' And then she wailed, 'Barbara and Harry have their own home!'

He echoed it, 'But you didn't want to live at Elvetham!'

So they'd discussed it then. Well, Katherine had been right to decide against it; Elvetham was bleak and I pitied Barbara.

'Katherine, I just don't understand you! Anyone else would jump at the chance to go to court for Lady Day.'

'Yes, but I'm not anyone else, am I!' She'd lobbed it back, twice as loud. 'That's why you married me, remember? That's what you said: I was *different*,' the word spoken with contempt. His word, chosen especially for her, and there she was, ridiculing it.

This I desperately didn't want to hear. This was between the two of them in a way that wasn't true of decisions as to where to spend Lady Day or even where to set up home, which were, fundamentally, mere practicalities. This went to the very heart of the pair of them: it was about what had made them the couple that they were, or had been. It was about what had drawn them to each other and sealed them together. Katherine was different and he loved her for it; that had been the deal, was the implication. But he'd reneged on it, was her accusation.

'Can you remember that, Edward?' She gave a hoot of humourless laughter, scorning the boy he'd been. 'But then you got me home and decided better of it.'

'Stop this,' he said. 'Will you just *stop* it.'

And I recalled, suddenly, dizzyingly, how different Katherine had indeed been in the beginning, that light in her eyes and the lightness in her step, and there on the stairs I felt for all of us. Why hadn't she gone back, when Edward returned from France, to how she'd once been? Why hadn't that happened?

'If it's "anyone else" that you want, you should've married my sister.'

'Katherine, listen. Listen—' He might've grabbed her wrist, her forearm, he might've been tussling with her. 'Please just listen to me.'

She was trying to make a break for it, and sweat bloomed on me. *Run*, I told myself, *Just do it, make a dash for it.*

'You are a wonderful wife.' But he sounded exhausted, going through the motions. 'You're all a husband could wish for, and I'm very sorry if somehow I give you the impression that I feel otherwise, but all I am asking is that you do something, occasionally, for the good of this family.'

'You have no idea,' she was outraged, 'how much I put into this family. You're off, swanning around, but I'm stuck here with your bloody mother!'

That was unfair; my mother would have been upset to hear it. Yes, she was irritating, but she was good with Katherine's babies. And was Katherine going to say something about me, as well? *Your bloody sister, Jane; your bloody useless stupid lump of a sister.* I began sidling down the stairs. *Run, just run.*

Edward sighed emphatically. 'You get on well enough with my father, though, don't you?'

There was a pause, then, 'Oh, Edward, will you stop it.'

'No, *you* stop it.' Pathetic, childlike, in sheer frustration.

'I *have*!' Katherine screamed, suddenly, at him. 'I have. Don't you understand that? Can't you understand it? I have. We have. We did stop.'

If I didn't quite know what it was that she'd just said, nor did I stop to wonder. I didn't have time because the row was over and she was going to come charging through that door. I had less than a heartbeat left in which to disappear, that was all I could think. And there was only silence, the terrible silence of that room, in which to do it. I could have slipped down in all the tumult but – stupid, stupid – I'd left it too late. Nevertheless, I had to do it and panic took me down: a slew of panicky, fluttery paces, my breathing as loud, to me, as my footfalls.

At the bottom of their stairs, I drew back into the adjacent stairwell – my own – as Katherine thumped down and then across the oriel, towards Hall. Then came the crash of the Hall door.

My legs were shaking and my chest hurt; I dropped to sit on a step and heard Edward. He was slower, in no rush to go anywhere. I listened for him to cross the oriel, then heard nothing more: he'd slipped into the parlour, I presumed, probably on his way through into chapel.

I emerged to discover that I'd misjudged; he hadn't left the oriel, but was sitting on the window seat. We were facing each other, and my breath reversed, bounding back into my chest but I could hardly step back into the stairwell; I was going to have to brazen it out and walk past him. He'd know I'd have heard the shouting: even if I'd been up in my room rather than on the staircase, I'd have heard the shouting, if not the exact words, then the commotion. At least he wasn't looking at me, at least there was that; his head was bowed. Careful to walk casually, I was in fact with each and every step anticipating his glance, rehearsing in my mind the rueful smile that I'd give before looking rapidly away again. But he didn't look up. He knew I was there but he didn't look up at me, didn't acknowledge me, and in turn I obliged him by keeping my eyes averted. And, actually, I'd already seen more than enough. I'd seen my brother bereft of hope, which was something I'd never seen nor even imagined possible.

7

Was it, I wondered, about those poems? But why on earth would Edward be bothered by poems? Katherine had said he hadn't been 'terribly pleased' to hear of them, but lately, I knew, neither of them had been terribly pleased with each other in general.

All that day, I tried to recall exactly what I'd heard: 'You get on well enough with my father, though, don't you?' It had been his response to Katherine's dismissal of our mother as 'your bloody mother', though, which – surely – made it fair enough, because that had been uncalled-for, harsh. Edward probably felt that his wife could do with being a bit more like his mother. Less like his father – following the dogs around the gardens in all weathers, pontificating on poetry – and more like his mother. Katherine was diligent enough at first glance but my brother knew, as did I, that her heart didn't lie in wifeliness, which was probably worrying him now that he needed to be showing off his wife at court.

He was elsewhere for the rest of that day, and must have gone to the barber at some point because at supper he was clean-shaven. After supper, he didn't join us in the parlour but for some reason went to the stables in search, he said, of Mr Wallensis. Katherine had looked tired all day, and had been busy with the boys, but when I offered to go to the chandlery for a couple more candles – I could see my father was having difficulty in reading his paperwork – she rose to accompany me, which set me on my guard. What did she want with me? As soon as we were on the other side of the door, her sigh confirmed it: she had something to say. I felt conspicuous, had to remind myself that she had no idea I'd overheard her and Edward arguing: I knew nothing, I reminded myself.

'I do wish you hadn't told Edward about those poems,' she said.

So did I.

She didn't seem to want to apportion blame, though; on the contrary, she'd said it with a faint, forced jauntiness, as if what I'd done couldn't have been helped.

Unfortunately, she was wrong about that: I'd said it in unkindness, not that she knew it and I hoped she never would. But I'd had no idea that it would cause such trouble (and why, I wondered, had it?) and I was glad of the opportunity to apologise. 'I'm really sorry, Katherine.'

We walked in step through Hall. 'Oh, well,' she said with another sigh, but this time taking stock and accepting it, 'he knows now.'

He certainly does.

I did contemplate raising it, asking her why the poems were so contentious between the pair of them, but then we'd turned together into the screens passage and, coming to the door to the kitchen courtyard, she halted so that I had to do the same. Looking me in the eye, she said, 'I did love him, you know.' She wanted it said; she needed it understood. 'I really did love him,' and there was defiance in the tilt of her chin, in case I tried to take issue with it.

No chance of that. I nodded, feeling uncomfortable, because it had been a long time since she'd talked to me intimately. That tone of hers came as an echo from a time that had passed and – I realised with a pang – even if I could go back there, I doubted I would.

She dropped my gaze to look away at nothing, the floor, walls, ceiling. '*Do*,' she corrected herself, '*do* love him; still do. Of course I do. You don't stop loving someone just because ...'

No, of course not. I folded my arms to hold on to my own warmth; I wanted to be fetching those candles and hurrying back to the parlour. It'd been a long day; it was February, it was Lent, I was exhausted. I didn't want to be here in this draughty passageway, subjected to this; I wasn't going to be drawn in. For a time, I'd been ashamed of putting myself so readily at Katherine's mercy in that first year she'd lived with us, but by then I knew the reason was that I'd been fifteen to her twenty-one, and, realistically, where else than at her mercy could I have been?

But that time was well and truly gone. I turned to the door and braced myself for the chill. Behind me, she was saying, 'And he loved me. I do know that.'

The door opened to owl conversation: a pair side by side somewhere up on the roof, their rusty-hinge screeches solicitously paced.

'But nothing happened.' She took the door from me to hold it open so that I could have some light from the bracket in the passageway. 'But, well, you know that.'

I didn't know what she was talking about, nor was I particularly bothered. The sky was sheathed in stars. Katherine shivered extravagantly.

'And I did try, with Edward.' She turned indignant. 'I really tried, and there was nothing I wanted more than for us to be happy.'

Four or five quick steps across the courtyard and I reached the chandlery door, pushed on it, reached inside, felt for a shelf, a box, a handful of candles.

'But he never wanted me.'

From the corner of my eye, I detected her shrug: *He never wanted me*, simple as that. And I wondered: could he have loved her yet somehow not wanted her? Because he had loved her, I was sure of it. I didn't know; I didn't pretend to know the ways of those who were married.

And then she said, evenly, as if she herself were in awe of it, 'When Edward came home from France and I had to walk away from your father and go back to being Edward's wife, it was like being buried alive.'

Buried alive? That did pull me up sharp, but when I turned, the light from the doorway behind her made her darker than dark; her face was invisible to me. *Walked away from my father, going back to being Edward's wife*: yes, I remembered it, I felt sure I did; I remembered my father ushering Katherine forward, across the outer courtyard, under everyone's gaze; remembered her touch to Edward's jacket and his small kiss to her cheek. Katherine sighed. 'He said to me, "You're Edward's wife,"' an odd little skip in the phrase as if she didn't quite believe it, as if it were a joke or a curiosity and she needed to hear it, to listen to it, to consider it.

8

Edward didn't come into the parlour that evening, nor, that night, did he go to his room, their room – instead sleeping in the room that was now often solely Antony's but which had been Edward's, too, before he'd married. Thomas wasn't there: knowing Edward was due home, he'd yet again contrived to stay at the Dormers', this time for several days either side of the Dormers' forthcoming St Valentine's celebration. Antony would have been unaware of his surprise roommate because he was asleep. And Edward was gone before first light. That, then, was why he'd been to see Mr Wallensis the previous evening: to arrange an early departure. No one knew where he was headed. 'Business,' he'd told Mr Wallensis, 'four or five days.' If it had been business, my father would have known, but he, it seemed, was as mystified as the rest of us.

Something was up – badly up – and the unspoken suspicion in the household was that it was to do with Katherine. No one else had overheard any row, as far as I knew, but everyone was well aware that relations between the pair of them were strained and never more so that in the previous couple of days. She ceded nothing, though, keeping busy around the house, toting her boys on her hips. She said no more to me on the subject of Edward, for which I was grateful. All we could do, any of us, was await Edward's return and hope that the situation, whatever it was, would blow over.

Late on the fifth evening, after the children had gone to bed, and Father James too, with a cold, Edward came striding in on us in the parlour with, it seemed, an announcement at the ready. My mother's breathless exclamation – 'Edward!' – was ignored as he positioned himself at the fireplace to command our attention. He looked nervous, though, his Adam's apple jittery, and at a disadvantage in that he was unshaven and, inevitably, travel-grimy. His nervousness made me nervous; I laid aside my stitching, steadied myself for whatever was coming. His gaze moved around us, his audience, but alighted on no one in particular; he wouldn't be deflected.

Composing himself by linking his hands behind his back, he began, 'I'm sorry to have to tell you this—' And evidently he was, because then he faltered, exhaling a pent-up breath which was itself shaky. For all the formality, he was distressed, and my heart contracted to see it of him as much as in anticipation of what we might be about to hear.

He drew himself up to start again. 'I'm sorry, but my marriage—'

He stopped, unable to go on. Whatever he was trying to say, he'd obviously rehearsed it and had taken a run at it, but still couldn't do it, couldn't say it. What was he doing, standing there and trying to tell us about his marriage? We all knew the marriage was troubled, but that, surely, was personal, for him and Katherine alone.

He looked at the floor in utter defeat and uttered, simply, but loudly and clearly, the allegation that would change everything for all of us: 'Johnny's not my son.'

No one breathed; it had no impact for a moment because we

were waiting for it to make sense, for him to say something more so that it'd make sense, because as it stood it certainly didn't. Perhaps he'd spoken in code, I thought wildly. Perhaps what he'd said, the actual words he'd used, had a completely unrelated meaning; he'd said, 'Johnny's not my son,' but to convey something entirely different, which everyone else in the room except me understood.

But then I got it, or I told myself I did: he was ill. Yes, that must be it: he'd come back home delirious. Because sometimes people said strange things, had strange ideas, when they had a fever, didn't they? And how on earth was he managing to stand there, my poor sick brother, on his own two feet, in front of that fire? I felt a rush of love or pity, a rush of feeling for him, for probably the last ever time. I wanted to be up there, taking hold of him, helping him, wanted to be doing something, because poor Edward, poor, poor Edward, Edward of all people to be showing himself up in such a manner. If it were anyone else up there in trouble, he'd be the first to their aid.

And then, thank God, my mother was coming to the rescue. 'Edward—' And saying it just right, gently, with that characteristic comforting rustle of her gown as she sat forward. I knew what she was going to say next: *You're very tired . . .*

But he didn't let her, he talked over her. 'I've been to see Katherine's father—'

That was where he'd been?

'No.' And this was Katherine, belatedly, and, actually, I'd forgotten about her. Edward's claim had been so bizarre as to have no more consequence, to my mind, for her than for any of us.

But she was putting a stop to it. 'Stop it.'

None of my mother's reticence, and of course not, I told myself, no, of course not, because this was what needed to be done. She was still sitting on her stool, but forward, lurched, close to falling, her lips grey and eyes stark. We'd all turned to her, even the dogs. Whatever was happening, it was happening between Edward and Katherine now, and the rest of us were spectators.

Edward, though, ignored his wife, even taking strength from his pretence that she wasn't there, becoming more businesslike, brisk. 'And he's unwilling to take her back, so I've had to—'

'*Edward!*' Katherine sprang up, outraged.

'—make other arrangements.'

She advanced on him: to do what, I couldn't imagine, but in any case I tensed hard, my chest tight. My father rose, shadowed by Bear, to intervene, but doing it slowly to play it down, making something of wincing at his stiffness and, in a reasonable tone, he said, 'Edward—'

Edward whirled to him. 'Don't you dare say a word.' Swift, low, vicious, the lapse in composure was quite obscene.

Beside me, Elizabeth drew her breath through her teeth as if suffering a wounding; as for me, I couldn't breathe at all.

My mother was horrified – '*Edward!*' – all caution gone.

Katherine demanded of Edward, 'What are you *doing*? Have you gone *mad*?' and her own breathing was ragged, as if she'd been running.

Badly shaken, my father had stopped in his tracks, but my mother drew herself up and stepped into the breach, suddenly impressive. 'Edward,' she spoke quietly but with considerable resonance, 'I don't know what's going on between the two of you but you *do not* bring it in front of us like this.'

My mother was going to save the day: whatever it was that was wrong, I told myself, it was about to be over. My mother could do it. I'd never seen Edward in such a state but she had: she'd seen him when he was a little boy, gripped by unreasonable notions.

He answered her with a firm, cool, 'This is family business.'

'No,' she was just as assertive, 'it isn't. This, whatever it is, is for the two of you to—'

He turned emphatically to address Elizabeth and me, unable to talk to his mother because she refused to hear it, and refusing to speak to his father or to Katherine. It was to Elizabeth and me that he said, 'Of course, I don't know about Ned—'

My father caught Katherine by the wrist, a good catch, lightning quick, almost an act of violence in itself in its speed and surety; he stopped the blow, arrested her hand before it smacked into Edward's face.

'Jesus,' Elizabeth was moved to murmur, sounding almost appreciative and, appalling though it was, it had indeed been something to see.

Katherine raged at him, 'How can you say such a terrible, terrible thing?'

Until then, I hadn't really taken it in, but she was right: what he'd claimed was the very worst accusation he could possibly make, damning both her and the boys, utterly damning them.

My father still had hold of Katherine's arm, foreshortening her lunge at Edward.

'You are *sick*!' she yelled at her husband.

'I am?' It had broken the spell for him; he could no longer resist responding to her, and was almost gleeful. '*I* am?'

Mum turned to Elizabeth and me, and said, calmly, 'Girls—' *Go.*

'No.' Edward was just as resolute. 'They need to hear this. This is family—'

'No one needs to hear this. Girls . . .' And she gestured towards the door.

But when I attempted to move, I couldn't; my legs turned heavy, refused me. And Elizabeth actually sat back, arms folded, unbudgeable.

212

My father had recovered himself sufficiently to try again. 'Edward—'

'But . . . ' Edward was thus goaded into continuing. 'Ned, I'm afraid, is by the by, because—'

Katherine spun around and spoke to us all. 'Don't listen to him.'

She was still frantic, but something of Edward's brisk, undemonstrative tone had come into her own; she'd decided to play him at his own game. For me to oblige her, though, to refuse to listen to Edward, was impossible. What he'd said couldn't be ignored: why would he have made such a dreadful accusation? I'd never imagined that my brother could be vindictive, but was that what I was witnessing?

Then he asked her, 'You'd really have gone on with this lie?' And suddenly all the antagonism was gone; it was a genuine question, anguished. 'You'd have kept this up? All our lives?' His eyes searched hers. 'You'd have done that to this family?' Sheer disbelief, and real sadness. Whatever it was that he was claiming of Katherine, I saw, he did truly believe it; he hadn't made that accusation for effect. He believed it, but, of course, he'd got the wrong idea somewhere along the line. How, though? Edward never got wrong ideas. He certainly never got wrong ideas and then voiced them so horrendously publicly.

We were all listening for Katherine's answer, all we Seymours, spellbound. She said, evenly, 'I don't know what you're talking about,' but it struck me as unconvincing; she was having to make an effort to hold steady. I wanted to believe her, but couldn't, quite: I could see she was testing him, testing the water. The two of them stared at each other for a long moment and I had the sense that he was giving her the chance to admit to something. She didn't take him up on it, instead repeating, 'I don't know what you're talking about.'

He looked to the rest of us with a regretful sigh and I realised he was going to tell us, and I both very much wanted to know and very much didn't. Edward appeared resigned to us having to know and to his having to be the one to tell us.

He said, 'Katherine had a love affair' – derisive – 'while I was in France, of which, I'm sorry to say, Johnny is the result.'

Well, I knew instantly that he was wrong, and the relief was wonderful. There'd been no love affair, I knew, while he was away: I remembered only too well that awful time. How could I forget? I could swear there'd been no love affair. Katherine had pined hard for him and it was me more than anyone who'd had to weather it, slap bang up against her foul moods. She'd been no woman in love back then, I was certain of it, and this notion of Edward's would have been laughable if it hadn't just caused such an altercation. Katherine, too: she closed her eyes and exhaled, her own sense of relief obvious. And my parents: shaking their heads, knowing that there'd somehow been a huge misunderstanding. For just a moment longer, we still had hope.

Katherine said, 'That is absurd, Edward.'

But that was when he came up with what he had on her: '"It did stop."' He was quoting, and I recognised the words. '"We did stop." Your words, Katherine,' he reminded her, triumphantly, 'your exact words.'

I remembered them being said, but hadn't understood their relevance at the time and still didn't. As for Katherine, her eyes widened at their impact; she was surprised. An incisor crept briefly onto her lower lip. 'That had nothing to do with Johnny.'

What didn't?

She'd said it softly, trying to make it for Edward alone. 'And it was over before—'

What was?

My mother turned abruptly towards Elizabeth and me; she got that far but then words failed her.

'But not *long enough* before.' Edward's mouth was a line and he stared his wife down.

She more than matched him, though, stepping up to him, gaining ground on him, her own eyes narrowed. 'And for you even to *think* it.' The words reeked of disgust.

I couldn't make sense of any of it; my heart was hammering.

'What "love affair"?' Elizabeth piped up, sceptical. 'What "love affair"?'

My sister-in-law and brother looked at her as if they'd both forgotten she was there. Moments ago, Edward had made something of addressing her but now all he could manage for her was a mere, 'It doesn't matter what love affair,' before turning back to his wife and appealing to her as if the rest of us weren't there and agog. 'You *know*, you *know* that Johnny—'

'Oh, but I think it *does* matter.' Elizabeth was cheerfully incredulous.

And all strength to her, I felt: for once, I was impressed by my sister, even awed by her.

'It doesn't matter,' Edward seethed, pointedly refusing to look at her. 'It's over, I'm satisfied of that, and – I can tell you – it'd benefit no one here to have the subject aired. What matters is the practical problem that we're left with, which is that Johnny isn't my son.'

But that was ridiculous, and my father put his head in his hands, my mother put a hand on his arm. So obviously baffled, they simply didn't know where to start.

But Katherine did. 'What?' She rained scorn on him, 'so, for two years he is your son, he can be your son, there's no problem with that darling little boy being your son, and then all of a sudden he can't be?'

She threw up her hands, despairing of him.

'But I didn't know, then, did I?' This near-howl of frustration from Edward brought the other two dogs to their feet, so that all of them were a-skitter. 'I didn't know! All this time,' he marvelled, 'all this time, I've been thinking, "How come?" How come Johnny arrives at the end of August and he's such a big, healthy baby? How can that happen? It's a kind of miracle, isn't it?' And he widened his eyes, to parody his naivety. 'Oh, weren't we lucky! Weren't we blessed! Because there really could be no other explanation, could there?'

He was shouting: Edward, whom I'd never known to raise his voice, and my own blood clamoured inside my head. 'Because what other explanation could there be? Perhaps I was stupid but, you know, Katherine, it never once occurred to me that I couldn't leave you alone for a couple of months with my own father.'

Her intake of breath was sharp enough to hurt her.

Our father? For a moment, I was even more lost.

But my father wasn't: 'Edward!'

Nor my mother: 'Edward!'

'Papa?' Elizabeth sang it out: it was madder than she'd hoped, and she gave it less than no credence.

And somewhere in all that, and to my horror, I got it.

Katherine recovered herself to roar, 'How dare you make such a vile insinuation! Your father behaved impeccably and honourably and for you to think otherwise—'

'My father,' Edward was yelling back at her, but jabbing an accusatory finger in his father's direction, 'had an *affair* with *my wife*! Just how is that "honourable"?'

I wasn't sure I was still properly alive, breathing, on my cushion, in the parlour. Was this actually happening? Was it possible for such a thing as Edward had said to be said and for us all to hear it and the following moment to come rolling along as normal, as if nothing much had occurred? Well, if time itself hadn't stopped, my mother had, her hands to her face and her eyes fixed wide on Edward.

My father was within a whirl of distressed dogs, reaching for them to calm them, but he spoke up to put Edward right: 'Edward, this is absolutely—'

'Stop saying "affair",' Katherine cut across, furiously contemptuous. 'It wasn't like that.'

'Son—'

Edward turned his back on our father, reserving his ire for Katherine. 'Oh, sorry, what *was* it like? I'm afraid I'm not up on the finer distinctions.'

This was about the poems, surely, I realised; incredible though it was, this had to be about the poems. But how could it be about the poems? Poems! What on earth was the matter with Edward? I stood up, if spectacularly shakily. It was me who'd told him about the poems: in that sense, this, whatever it was, was my doing, so somehow I had to try to undo it. They were just poems: I'd even seen them.

Edward was busy warning his mother against his wife. 'Here it comes: the denial. More lies.'

'Oh, but I'm not denying it,' Katherine countered, hotly.

That, he hadn't expected. Nor, of course, had any of us. I stopped, only half-standing. My mother's hands moved to her mouth.

My father was at the door, ushering the dogs into the oriel. 'Katherine—' He sounded exasperated.

She didn't acknowledge him. 'Why would I deny it?' she asked Edward, defiant. 'Yes, he wrote me some poems.'

Poems, yes – *you tell him* – and my panic subsided just a little, so that I began to sit back down.

'I don't lie.' She began to circle him, as if inspecting him. 'I'm not the one around here who lies. My feelings for your father were genuine, Edward, and I won't deny them, I'm not ashamed of them. But that's not something you can understand, is it? Genuine feelings.'

Now what was she saying? I had a horrible suspicion that, stuck halfway between sitting and standing, I was making a sound, a kind of keening, but couldn't quite hear over the thumping of my heart. What I did know, for certain, was that Katherine had to stop speaking. She'd said enough.

Not in her opinion, though, she hadn't. 'You think love's something to be ashamed of? Oh, but yes, you *do* think that, don't you. But,' her face veering to his, 'nothing happened.'

I'd heard that from her before – in the kitchen courtyard, just a few nights before – but only now did it dawn on me what she meant. *For you even to think such a thing*, yet there we all were, poor us, thinking it, because she was insisting that we think it. I sat down. My father's opening of the door for the dogs was doing nothing to alleviate the unbearable heat of the room, and vomit reared to scorch the back of my throat.

Haughtily, Katherine refuted the accusation with her insistence, 'I am your wife, Edward.' Then, 'Why don't you ask your father? Ask him if anything actually happened,' and she gestured across the parlour at our father, which meant that she did, at last, look at him, but there was nothing in the look, it was neutral, practical, devoid of anything unsaid.

My father didn't return the look, instead addressing Edward, 'You have this wrong, Edward, completely wrong,' but in that same instant it occurred to Katherine that this wouldn't suffice, because her father-in-law was hardly a disinterested party.

She'd need someone else to back her up, and that was how she came to nominate me: 'Ask *her*.'

Me?

'She'll tell you.'

Edward frowned. This was mere diversion, as far as he was concerned, but my mother slid her stunned stare to me and Elizabeth sat forward, fascinated. And Katherine: her coppery eyes were wide and clear in mine, as if to hold me to something.

'She'll tell you.' It was Edward to whom she spoke but me to whom she looked, unwavering, hopeful.

Closing the door to return to us, my father began again, 'Nothing of the kind,' but faltered at the silence around which the rest of us were stuck: me on one side and everyone else on the other. I was going to have to bridge that silence, even if I wouldn't be telling them anyone anything they didn't already know.

I said, 'Nothing happened,' although in barely more than a whisper because I hated to be saying it at all: it simply didn't need saying, it was absurd to be saying it; it was no more than a prompt to Edward.

'Edward,' – *please, stop this* – 'nothing happened.' There I was, imploring him, my brother of whom I didn't recall ever before having asked anything.

'And she'd know,' Katherine insisted of me, shrill, self-righteous. I wished she'd shut up, because everyone knew. No one, not even inexplicably aggrieved Edward, would actually think that my father . . .

'Oh?' Edward took a step towards me, suddenly interested, as if sensing sport, 'You'd know, would you?'

No actual question nor proper challenge, but a mere mock-humouring to belittle me in front of the others. I knew very well not to rise to it, not to take it personally: it was his wife with whom he had this argument and I just happened to be caught, momentarily, in the middle, yet again.

'You,' – *pitifully dull Jane* – 'you'd know what Katherine, here, was up to, would you?'

I couldn't look at those fierce dark eyes.

My father insisted, 'This is offensive, Edward,' taking him by the shoulder only to be vigorously shaken off. Edward was busy relishing that in all this mess and muddle, here was something on which everyone could agree: that it was presumptuous of me –

me, of all of them – to think I could know anything of how exactly Katherine had conducted herself during that time. Suddenly, as he saw it, there was a good chance he wasn't alone in looking to have been made a fool of.

Still unable to raise my eyes to his, I appealed, 'Edward . . .'

My father told him, 'Think of your mother.'

But no, not now that he had a victory in his sights. 'You, Jane, yes, you would know, wouldn't you?'

Katherine was remonstrating with him, 'Of course she'd know!'

But he ignored her to narrow in on me: 'Because, oh, well, you knew everything that she got up to, didn't you?' Meaning that I didn't. 'You knew, for instance, all about those "genuine feelings" of hers for our father.'

And so there I was, exposed as ignorant of something which, by anyone's standards, was really quite something not to have known. I so badly needed Edward to stop, I wanted so badly to disappear, I was shaking so hard that I feared I was going to fall into pieces, and it was to escape his eyes that I looked to Katherine's, which I should never have done. Because how extraordinary they were, bright and beautiful and unblinking in mine. Her very breath, too: held there, it pressed hard against my own heart.

Three years before, when she'd crossed our threshold, I'd been the invisible Seymour, not one of the glorious boys, nor blowsy Elizabeth, nor one of the charming children, but nonetheless those eyes of hers had come for me and swept me up and for a summer we hadn't looked back. For that summer, we'd spent our days together, stitching and weeding, pastry-making and fruit-picking, and at the end of those days we'd retired to her room to lounge around in the fading light and talk about anything and everything and nothing. And once I'd followed her into the darkness, down to the brook. Once to the deep-shadowed gallery, to dance with her in silence. And in that time she'd spared me nothing: not her dread and loneliness when Edward was away, nor her despair that when he was home he didn't love her as he should. And yet he had the temerity to stand there and tell me that I hadn't known her. Well, it was he who didn't know her, and didn't love her, and look how it'd ended up. She'd told me that my father was handsome and lovely and that she didn't want to go to the St Luke's fair because – the realisation hit me even if, at the time, it'd passed me by – he was staying at home. She'd taken me along on her strolls with my father, sometimes before I could even fetch my boots, and, in front of me, she'd asked him to write poems and then, when he'd done so, she'd shown me them. And when I'd broken the news to her that Edward was due home, she'd sat down next to me and cried. 'Buried alive' was what she'd said of how she'd felt when he returned. She'd said those very words to me.

Sitting there under Edward's outraged gaze, I was convinced: his wife had hidden nothing from me; I might not always have been sharp enough to see what was there in front of me, but she'd hidden nothing from me.

'Yes,' I said to Edward, looking him hard in the eye as I said it. 'Yes, I did know,' and then, when I didn't immediately retract or make a move to qualify it and he made a move to laugh it off, I reminded him, 'I knew about the poems, didn't I? It was me who told you about the poems.'

'Jane!' That was my mother, aghast, and I couldn't look at her.

'But, but, *but* . . .' Elizabeth was addressing Edward, but so insistently that we all turned to her and she sat back, pleased. 'You'd been back nine months, hadn't you? You came back on St Katherine's, remember? So what's the problem? It's nine months, end of November to end of August.' End of August, when Johnny had been born. 'So of course he is yours.'

In the heat of the moment, I didn't know at first what she was claiming; I doubt anyone did.

She was counting on her fingers in demonstration: 'End of December, January, February . . .'

I raced ahead and she was right, *she was right!* Why had none of us thought to question it?

But Edward had lowered his face into his hands and was rubbing disconsolately at his eyes. Katherine was staring at the floor.

Even Elizabeth couldn't fail to detect their awkwardness. 'What?' Her smile faded. Why wasn't this good news? 'It's nine months,' she reasserted: incontestable fact.

There was a considerable pause, reluctant on the part of Edward and Katherine but puzzled on everyone else's, before Edward responded.

'Yes, but Katherine and I . . .' He floundered and almost looked to his wife for help. 'Katherine and I didn't . . .' There was a too-visible swallow, a kind of guttural flinch. 'Enjoy relations for some time after that.'

Oh.

Did we just hear that?

Katherine moved very slightly towards him and I thought she'd lay a hand on his arm but, instead, she spoke softly to him: 'You tried, though, you always tried, and what'll have happened is—'

'Really,' he countered, witheringly, 'I think I'd know.'

She moved back, silenced.

Well, that, I really, truly didn't believe we'd heard, and I might've checked with someone, just a glance, had I dared to meet the eye of anyone in that room.

Edward snapped to. 'So, you see?' and he spread his hands, *There you have it.* 'That's why, when I find a sheaf of love poems and my wife cheerfully admits to me' – he flourished a gesture in her direction, *Here she is, you all heard her* – 'that she did indeed fall in love with my father while I was fighting in France, and then nine months later we have Johnny ... well, that's why I can't believe that "nothing happened".'

Katherine shrugged, sulkily, belligerently but at a loss. *Well, I'm telling you, it's the truth.*

My father had once again been standing back but now he roused himself, 'Edward, no, no—'

But Edward again cut him dead, spoke over him: 'And so, the boys will stay with us – they're Seymours, after all – but you, Katherine, will go to the nuns at Wilton; they're expecting you the day after tomorrow.'

Then he was away, past his father, to the door. Katherine, too, though, a step behind him, to catch it before it closed, to haul it wide open and then slam it behind them both.

9

No door had ever been slammed at Wolf Hall that I remembered, but that one slammed on those of us in the parlour with the brutality and finality of a trap door: *You stay here*. And so the four of us, my mother and father, Elizabeth and me, were flung back on each other, but everything in me rebelled against that particular fate and before I knew it I was across the room and yanking at the door; and then there I was, pitched up in the oriel among the anxious, eddying dogs.

Katherine had followed Edward up the stairs and, somewhere above me, was railing at him, her words indistinct but the tone unmistakeably livid. What she had to say to him felt, oddly, like no particular concern of mine, merely disconcerting at most, like the scrabblings of mice at night in the eaves. I had something that I had to do: that was all I could think. I had to be doing something.

Checking my way was clear, ordering the dogs to stay, I sped across Hall to the courtyard door, which, opening, spilled Mort around my feet and, as I stepped over him to exchange places, I understood why: the cold of the courtyard came as a physical blow. I might have screamed if my breath hadn't already been snatched away. Nevertheless, I set myself against it, beginning a soft-soled slithering over ice-sheened cobbles. The darkness, too, bore down on me – there was no more than a scratch of new moon, unnerving in its clean execution – so that I had to feel my way with my feet from pool to pool of bracket-light so faint as to be from a bygone age.

Soon, despite the clanging coldness in my nose, I was breathing a haze of horse scent incongruously reminiscent of a balmy summer's evening: I was close to the stables. *Keep going, nearly there.* Emerging from the passageway between the inner and outer courtyards, I looked and listened hard but detected no one; I was too late, everyone gone fireside. While we'd been screaming and yelling in the house, they'd finished up their day's work and gone, leaving the stables the province solely of their legitimate inhabitants. From somewhere came hollow-ringing hoof scuff like the clearing of a throat, from somewhere else a noseful of horse breath as unselfconscious as a baby's sneeze, and everywhere was an almost palpable dense-eyed dreaminess. There they were, the horses, and many more of them than I needed but, lacking men to saddle them, they were no use to me.

Then, though, in a far corner, darkness stirred as water would around a body: Mr Wallensis, judging from his bulk and his being last to leave.

'Mr Wallensis?' I spoke up to alert him, to allay any fear on his part as I appeared in the gloom like a wraith, although I doubted he'd know the voice as mine and, anyway, it didn't seem to soften the blow for him of having been observed – however briefly and barely – when unaware. He froze. Me, too: I felt a pang for springing on him in the last moments of his long, cold working day.

Just get on with it, Jane: 'Mr Wallensis, we have to fetch Thomas.' But instantly realising my mistake and rushing to reassure him, 'No – no, no – no one's . . .' *Ill, dying, died*, and there was a heartbeat's dizziness because even if I'd wanted to explain what was going on back at the house, how would I? How would anyone ever explain it? 'But we need Thomas here, we need him tomorrow, as early as possible. Someone needs to go at first light and get him . . .'

My words, like my shivers, were running everywhere, and even in that meagre light I saw Mr Wallensis frown and glance behind me for a source of authority, and I didn't blame him – he didn't do it to defy me, to thwart me. There I was, one of the girls from the house, turning up at the stables at an ungodly hour on a bitter night, underdressed, wind-stung, nose dripping, and babbling about needing my brother, and my errant brother at that.

Mr Wallensis would be thinking that I'd squabbled with the family and wanted Thomas to side with me. He barely knew who I was. One of the girls from the house. What he certainly would know was that fetching Thomas from the Dormers was no business of mine; any such order would come from my father or Edward or, at a push, from my mother. But what he couldn't possibly know, yet, was that it was beyond the three of them, at that time, to do very much at all.

So, yes, I understood his reluctance but I couldn't have it, couldn't allow him to stand there, turned solid-faced from the cold, blocking me from the means of reaching Thomas. My tone, still ringing in my ears, had been solicitous, but there'd be no more of that. 'Get Thomas here, please,' I said, 'as soon as possible tomorrow.'

Still sceptical, nevertheless he moved himself to ask, 'And Mister Harry?'

If Thomas, then Harry, too: that was what he was thinking. Or, indeed, Harry, surely, over Thomas.

'No. Leave Harry.' Because not only was Harry a day further away and his wife about to give birth but, I knew, he'd be no help. Harry is an appeaser. Harry has always hated discord whereas Thomas thrives on it. Thomas was the one – the only one of us –

who'd stand up to Edward to shout him down. Never cowed, he'd know his mind and he'd speak it. I was banking on his self-interest, too: with his ambitions, he, least of all of us, could afford a family scandal. Edward wouldn't listen to what Thomas actually had to say – I wasn't so naïve as to think that – but the mere fact of opposition might just stall him long enough, I hoped, for him to come to his senses.

I began making my way back to the house, but now that I'd done what I'd had to do, exhaustion came for me, making my heart bird-feeble at my ribs and my limbs nothing but shivers. Making me nothing: nothing and going nowhere, prey for the wind as it rushed across the miles. And on the other side of a roaring stretch of miles was Thomas at the Dormers', standing tall, candleflame-gilded and smiling, rock-steady in a confidence in his own splendid future. He might have been made of an entirely different substance from me: something fine and plush, which would brush up as good as new. There he was, in the Dormers' bright Hall, while the rest of us were in the depths of the forest, done for.

Ahead of me in the darkness, our own old house seemed to be listing, breaking up, and sucking us down. I couldn't make myself go back in there because I didn't know what I'd find. Anything, absolutely anything, might be being said in there. No, I'd stay outside in the cold, lie down and let the wind pick my bones clean. Or Thomas would take me away: he'd return tomorrow and find me, then turn around and take me with him. Thomas would always have somewhere to go. Or I could even do it myself, and do it now: return to Mr Wallensis and insist he take me somewhere, anywhere. Where, though? To Harry? Harry would take me in. Barbara was nice enough, and there was a baby due. I could be useful if only Barbara would let me. That was one possibility.

Or tomorrow I could simply start walking and leave it until later to worry about where. Plenty of people lived their lives on the road, I reminded myself. What mattered – all that mattered – was that I didn't ever go back in to Wolf Hall. I could never again look at anyone who'd been in that room. What had happened in there? Some awful misunderstanding, that was what, a dreadful, incomprehensible misunderstanding; something to do with dates, the details of which were beyond me but which Thomas, I was sure, would instantly grasp and dismiss. He'd be able to explain it to me; he could explain it away, because whatever his faults, no one was ever able to pull the wool over Thomas's eyes. If he'd been there in the parlour, if only he'd bothered to be there, for once, then little of it, I imagined, would have been said. He would have shouted Edward down, even laughed at his absurd claims – and oh, what I would have given, for once, to hear that laugh. But instead what I'd heard was Edward, our shining light, our golden boy, making a sickening allegation, by way of the most excruciating admission of his own inadequacy, against his wife, his father, and his baby sons. He'd retract, of course, I was sure of it, and probably even before Thomas arrived, but so much damage had already been done.

Damage: I knew even by then that what would never be explained away for me was Edward's cruelty. I reeled across that courtyard with him burned on to the back of my eyes: him standing there and stating his case, delivering his verdict. He'd called us together – we'd gathered in good faith – before meting it out to us, sparing no one, not even my mother. Particularly not my mother. Then he'd passed sentence on his wife: made witnesses of us all while he'd handed down his sentence. What exactly had he meant, 'the nuns at Wilton'? For a period of penance? For how long? Could he really order his wife to a nunnery? I'd never even heard of anything similar, or not in our own lifetime. I wanted so badly to think of it as madness on Edward's behalf, but I knew he'd not been mad. Was it just a threat? A sharp reminder to an allegedly adulterous wife of what she could have expected to suffer if she didn't have the luxury of a forward-thinking husband? Because Edward was no man to concern himself with nunneries; I was surprised he'd even known where to find one.

But I didn't doubt that he had. He didn't make empty gestures; he dealt in practicalities, and dealt brilliantly with them. I didn't doubt he had actually been, as he'd claimed, to Katherine's father and to the Mother Superior at Wilton. Which meant they'd know at least something of his allegation. And there could well be others, too. Self-reliant and well informed though Edward was, he couldn't have gone that far without legal advice or spiritual guidance. So there would almost certainly be others who knew.

Those were my preoccupations as I crossed back across that courtyard: practical concerns. I was nothing if not my brother's sister. Rage, too, bubbling under – in that sense, too, I was my brother's sister. Because all Katherine had done was turn it into an opportunity to say her own little piece, to indulge in some utter nonsense that had made matters immeasurably worse. I was refusing to think about what she'd said, adamant not to dignify it. For her to have imagined such a thing of my father! How little she knew him. How little she knew any of us, to think that she could stand there and say what she'd said and claim it as a kind of triumph. That was madness, and, in a way, I felt sorry for her, pitied her for her delusions. Edward was right in one respect, I felt: it would be better if Katherine were gone. It would have been even better, though, if she'd never come to Wolf Hall. My brother should never have married her. But he had, and there were the boys, and it was the boys who mattered, I reminded myself. We had to think of the boys.

And my father: then I turned my ire on my father, because what had he been doing, pandering to his daughter-in-law? Yes, he'd only done as she'd suggested – write poems – but he'd carried her suggestion away with him and made time for it and tended it. Where had he made time for it? In his office? When we'd assumed he was working? We'd have been sitting in the parlour feeling sorry for him for having to work late, but he'd have been sitting there in his office thinking of Katherine. How long did it take him to write those four poems? Several evenings? Several whole evenings spent secretly on his daughter-in-law.

'You're Edward's wife,' that's what she'd told me that he'd said to her. Well, if that was true, then a certain conversation had been had between the two of them, but not one, it seemed, that my father had then gone on to make known to anyone else. I understood why he'd kept it to himself – he liked to keep everyone happy – but still, what I would have given on that cold night to get hold of him and shake him.

But that was nothing to what I would've done to my sister-in-law if I could have; I despised and despaired of her. And yet there I was in that freezing courtyard, crying and telling myself that those tears were tears of fury, but they weren't and I knew it. The thought of Katherine had got me by the throat and nearly had me howl because her heart beat brighter and sang at a higher pitch than anyone else's, and if that heart could have been held in my hand then I'd have done it: I'd have taken it up and carried it to safety. I'd still have done that for her, after everything that had happened and everything I now knew. And so it was me I despised for my weakness, it was me of whom I despaired.

And what, actually, had I done? Back there in the parlour, what had I done? I'd spoken up because Edward had been talking rubbish and I'd been in a position to counter it: that's what I told myself. Then, when he'd then tried to discredit me, I'd had to defend myself. But standing there by the door, ready to go inside because there was nowhere else for me to go, I had to face that what I'd said in the parlour had suggested I'd known Katherine had considered herself in love with my father, and I'd been happy enough to go along with it.

10

In the morning, I woke more slowly than my sisters, rose reluctantly and was late to prayers. Edward was last of all of us and – having stayed at the back – first to leave. Katherine, by contrast, had positioned herself right at the front. My parents weren't there, but sometimes for morning prayers they kept to the closet adjoining their bedroom, although on this occasion there was no light visible up there.

After prayers, I arrived in Hall to find the children at the table with bread and preserves and ale, but the fire unlit and the air itself stiff with cold. Red-nosed, they hadn't thought so far as to equip themselves with extra layers.

'Why isn't—?' Exhausted, and exasperated beyond words, I could only gesture at the hollow fireplace.

Margie spoke through a mouthful, 'Moll's run off her feet.' Inexpressive, to emphasise that the words were Moll's own.

'Her *trotters*,' said Antony.

I hadn't the energy to tick him off.

'Lil's gone with Mama,' Dottie explained.

'Where?'

'Elvetham.' She said it unsuspectingly: indeed, excitedly. There was a baby expected and, as far as Dottie was concerned, her mother had had to leave a little earlier than anticipated. She didn't seem to consider it odd that she'd gone with no word or note of goodbye.

Thrown, I fell back on pretending the same enthusiasm. 'Oh, really?'

Elizabeth, I noticed, didn't catch my eye: nothing unusual in that, but I wondered if she too had found our mother's sudden departure to be ominous. Our mother had abandoned us, was my suspicion: she'd got up and gone, and, once she was there, with the baby due in a couple of weeks' time, she wouldn't come all the way back home again before the birth. She'd be away, now, for weeks on end. She'd packed while we'd slept. I dreaded to think what might have been said between her and our father. Or, perhaps worse, what hadn't been said.

Mr Wallensis had suffered a second surprise visitor to his stables within hours. I wondered what he was thinking. Had he told her that Thomas was returning? If so, what had she made of it? Not enough, it seemed, to detain her.

'Did we get a messenger, though?' Dottie's question was for anyone and everyone. She was puzzled. 'We didn't, did we?'

No one seemed quite to want to admit it, but the general murmur suggested that there'd been no sight or sound of any messenger.

'She'll have just had a feeling,' I lied. 'Or maybe she decided that we're likely to get snow.' So she'd need to be travelling ahead. 'Where's Papa?'

Elizabeth raised her head but still didn't quite meet my eye; she said something but hardly moved her lips, so I failed to catch it.

'What?'

This did get me a direct look, but of contempt. 'Gone after her,' pronounced more distinctly but no louder: for me, not them, to hear. Elizabeth's gaze sat uncomfortably in mine and my heart shifted beneath my ribs. We'd been abandoned: in the midst of this impossible situation, we'd been abandoned.

'Perhaps she forgot something,' chirped Dottie, who evidently had heard.

'Yes, probably,' I made myself say.

Antony sang out, 'So, now we're like orphans!'

'Stop it,' I snapped, which shocked even myself.

Startled, he rushed to explain himself, 'We can do as we like,' but the bravado was gone and he sounded unconvinced, even desolate, and I felt bad for him, even more so when Margie drove it home: 'With *Moll* in charge?'

I nodded at the Moll-neglected fireplace. 'We need this lit. Go into the parlour for now. Take your—' I indicated their trenchers and tankards.

The banging and scraping of implement-laden children on the move was such a distraction that I didn't notice my sister-in-law come in, but suddenly there she was and the sight of her filled me with dread. In her all too obvious desperation, she was far more than I could manage. She looked awful: at least as bad as when she had one of her headaches. Unlike when she had a headache, though, she was on her feet, and she had Johnny hoisted onto a hip. Her dejection suggested that nothing between her and Edward had been resolved, and I felt the dash of a hope that I hadn't known I'd been holding.

My first thought was that the children shouldn't see her like this: neither Dottie nor Margie were fools, they'd know something was up. Luckily, though, Dottie had eyes only for Johnny, who was – despite an extravagant snot-silvering – the very picture of composure in comparison to his mother. At Dottie's delighted exclamation, he squirmed to be relinquished and then bustled off to join her. I absorbed myself in chivvying the procession of parentless children – Take this, Don't forget that, Be careful, Come back for that, Hold the door – and gave Katherine the barest explanation – 'It's too cold in here' – with the aim of sending her, too, on her way. I suspected, though, that she'd not been bringing Johnny to Dottie; she'd come for me. Well, hard luck, because I was off to find Moll. I could have lit the fire myself but she made a fuss if anyone else did it – she claimed to have a method – and Moll-fuss that morning would have been intolerable.

Once the children had gone, Katherine trailed after me across Hall as I'd feared she would, but I resolved to do nothing for her; I'd already done more than enough. My attempt to leave her behind was scuppered by her longer strides, but I acted as if I were well ahead nevertheless and didn't deign to look at her, instead speaking ahead to the door. 'My mother's gone to Elvetham.' She might as well know it.

'Elvetham?' Taken aback, she lost a little ground. 'Why? What did she say?'

'She didn't.' I was into the screens passage before her, and then to the door that led to the kitchen area. 'Left before we were up. And my father's followed her.'

Behind me in the passageway, there was a catch of sole on flagstone, an abrupt halt. I'd known it'd be a blow, and I'd intended it as such: he'd gone to my mother, and she'd get no help from him. I shouldered the kitchen door but there was no Moll inside nor even anyone to ask; and reaching around Katherine, I tried the various other doors – larders, buttery – to no avail.

'Any idea' – I kept it brisk – 'where Edward is?' Determinedly practical, as if no different from wondering as to Moll's whereabouts.

'He was in Antony's room, last night.' She sounded baleful, although surely that was the very least of her troubles. And it wasn't what I'd asked; I could have guessed that for myself.

Where on earth was Moll? What was she playing at?

'You spoken to him?' Lunging into the kitchen courtyard, I yelled Moll's name only for it to fall flat, and it was that from which I rebounded into my sister-in-law's gaze.

She seized the opportunity: 'Jane.' *Listen.* 'He has a letter.' She was entrusting me with something; I didn't want it, but she pressed it on me: 'I've seen it, read it.' The smallest of apologetic winces, a correction to mean that she'd read as much as she'd been able to read. 'He showed me.'

I didn't want to know. 'What?' *Get on with it, keep it practical.* 'What is it?'

Something committed to paper, that was what, and I didn't like the sound of that.

'Written by my father, signed, witnessed—'

'What *is* it?'

She swallowed a throatful of tears. 'Forty pounds a year, every year, to the nunnery for my keep.'

It was almost admiration that I felt for my brother, because he really didn't do anything by halves, did he; he didn't merely ride around the country disgracing his wife, but secured redress from one of the injured parties – because her own family stood to be at least as damaged as ours – and in perpetuity, and in writing.

'It's nothing,' I said.

'But I've *seen*—'

'But that's what he *does*!' Did she really not know? Edward would have been covering all eventualities; second nature for him. He'd get it on paper. He'd be properly prepared. Just in case. It didn't mean he'd end up using it. There was everything still to play for, and Katherine needed to realise that, she needed to get on with it; not mope around, trailing me down passageways and trying to lay this at my feet. I didn't understand what had gone on – dates, babies – but if there was anything to understand, she'd know what had happened; I didn't. Whatever had happened, she wouldn't be going to a nunnery – that simply couldn't happen to our family – but she was the one who had to ensure that it didn't.

But, 'I don't know,' she was speaking at least as forcefully as I had, 'how to stop him,' and her eyes, in mine, refused to let me go. 'I don't know what more to say to him. I *don't know*, Jane.'

And there she was, giving up on herself and giving herself over to me, a certain grandeur to the gesture.

I had no idea what to do.

But then I remembered that I did, I did know, and I'd already done it. 'I've sent for Thomas.'

'Thomas?' Genuine disbelief from Katherine, before the objection: 'Not Thomas.'

'*Yes*, Thomas.' She was in no position to dictate, as I saw it. She didn't like Thomas, but, frankly, she could lump it.

She drew back, affronted. 'This has nothing to do with Thomas.'

I would've retorted that it had everything to do with all of us, but the Hall door was opening behind us and then there was Moll, affecting boredom: 'You yelled?'

Thomas was home much sooner than I'd anticipated; I was still helping Moll clear up the parlour when somehow, even before there was actually anything to hear of it, I detected his arrival. So far, so good. Mr Wallensis must have done exactly as I'd asked and sent someone for him at first light, if not earlier, and Thomas must have left the Dormers immediately, then and there, neglecting morning prayers – not that he'd have regarded that as a hardship. Never had I been so glad to see my brother, despite having to face telling him what was happening. I ran into the courtyard as he was sliding from the saddle, and in turn, he was heading for me before his feet had properly reached the ground.

'Jane?'

I turned for him to follow but he lunged, grabbed me — *No, here, now* — and was clearly in no mood for prevarication, so I drew him into the archway connecting the courtyards; it'd have to do, it offered a little privacy.

'It's Edward,' I said, unnerved by my own voice, its frailty. Thomas's eyes widened, barely perceptibly, as if he were turning from a light, but otherwise nothing: he didn't know what to think so he'd think nothing for the time being and I was going to have to tell him what was happening. *Why was this falling to me?* 'He's saying Johnny isn't his.'

But still no reaction, nothing, just the stare, as if he hadn't heard me; he had, though, because we could hardly have been standing closer to each other. And so — the horror of it — I was going to have to do it, to press on into the very worst of it.

'He says,' and I truly wondered what I was about to hear myself saying, 'that Johnny is our father's.'

Thomas would laugh, surely, because what I'd just said was absurd, and if I were him, arriving home to hear it, that was what I'd probably do; what I definitely wouldn't do was believe it. For a heartbeat there was nothing from him, before something, an utterance that I took to be, 'What?'

So I had to say it again, had to look him in the eye and make it clear: 'Our father's.'

He went to take issue with this — a frown, a contraction of the lips — but the resolve melted into incredulity: 'Pa's?' Only a whisper, but all too audible in the confines of that small, low archway and I flinched, checked to either side for eaves-droppers.

Our father's: I intended to confirm it for him but my throat had closed up and I could only nod, just the once, and then there was the slam of tears into the back of my nose and I had to hold my breath or I'd be begging, 'Please, Thomas, make this all right, please just make it all right . . . ' Someone began crossing the outer courtyard; the pair of us held each other to silence until the footfalls faded.

Then I said, 'He wrote poems for her,' as if that could possibly be an adequate explanation for the news that I'd just broken, and indeed there was no sign that Thomas understood. How I wished I weren't crying. 'She says she was in love with him.'

At this, he did react, and predictably: an exhalation, exasperated and dismissive.

'That's what she *says*!' There was no time for quibbling.

He winced, making much of being prepared to indulge me: *Now then, Jane, let's go right back to the beginning . . .*

'When Edward was in France,' I said, 'the time when he was in France,' and somehow that did it, that did have him listening. 'Our father was kind to her,' I gabbled, 'and they used to talk, they used to walk in the gardens together and—' But I could hear how ridiculous it sounded and Thomas was shaking his head.

'Edward found them, the poems, and she'd kept them hidden and—' *Don't you see?* But there was something crucial I hadn't so far said: 'Nothing happened, though.' And I repeated it, emphasised it, 'Nothing happened,' hoping it'd be enough, that he'd understand. 'But the problem is, Edward says it *did*.' My voice was high, fracturing. 'He's saying it *must've*. Because Johnny can't be his: that's what he says. Because the dates are wrong.'

'The dates aren't wrong,' Thomas said.

'But they are, because—' I couldn't say it.

He frowned. 'Because what?'

I didn't know how to say it.

'Because *what*?'

I took a breath, took a run at it: 'Because Edward *couldn't*.'

When Thomas realised I had no more to add, he almost laughed: 'What?'

'At that time,' I clarified, 'he couldn't.'

'And' – utter disbelief – 'he told you this, did he?'

'He told all of us. He had to.'

And it did get through: the impact had him take a backwards step, then he paced a circle to steady himself.

Surreptitiously, I wiped my nose on my hand.

'Right,' he said, taking stock. 'Jesus,' and he sounded defeated.

'But,' I rushed to offer some hope, 'Katherine says they did try.'

He didn't respond.

'So d'you think—?'

'How the fuck do I know?'

Somehow I stood my ground.

'*Jesus*,' he despaired, loudly.

I didn't dare breathe.

'Jesus.' A flail of his arm, gesturing beyond the archway. 'How the fuck do *I* know what people here ...'

Please, Thomas, please: I'd never heard him speak like that. He wasn't reacting as I'd expected, but he was my only hope. He was going to have to calm down and turn practical. I tried to rein him in: 'Our parents are—'

'And what's *he* saying?' The question was fired at me. 'Pa – what's he saying?'

'Well' – *do you really have to ask?* – 'he's saying no.' *Of course*, and I repeated with equal force: 'No!' Because did my brother really not understand? 'Nothing happened.'

Hadn't he heard me the first time? What on earth was he thinking? How could he even think it? 'She says she was in love with him, and he—'

'Oh stop it,' and this was vicious. 'Love,' he derided. Then,

239

pacing again, almost stamping up and down that passageway. 'Christ! Why did Edward ever marry her? Stupid bastard. Couldn't he *see*? She's a complete disaster.'

Perhaps, but what was done was done and we needed to keep to the matter in hand.

'And our saintly father,' a bitter hoot, 'falling for her charms? Well, Christ, who's next? Father James?'

That was enough. I understood that he was angry but if he went on like this, he was no better than Edward.

'She didn't—'

'You don't know what she did!'

It boomed inside the arch but I drowned it with my own roar, 'Of course I do!'

He turned his back on me and kicked the wall hard, twice. Then, 'Where's Ma?' he asked over his shoulder.

'Gone.' I could barely bring myself to speak to him. 'To Elvetham. Pa, too, after her.'

He turned around to face me, suddenly enlivened. 'Yes, and you know what? That's what I'm going to do, I'm going to get back in the saddle and ride away and leave them all to it. Leave this family to destroy itself. Leave Edward and his fucked-up wife to—'

'Thomas!' My heart was wild in my throat. 'You have to talk to Edward.'

'Nope,' and he was off, striding into the courtyard, towards the house. 'His wife, his mess, he can deal with it.'

I dashed behind him. 'But he says she's going to Wilton.'

'Best place for her.'

His loathing took my breath away. 'But the boys!'

He turned around without breaking his stride. 'You think they need a mother like her?'

Now I was enraged. 'Stop it, Thomas!'

'Listen,' he bellowed back at me, 'she had one job to do, and that was be his wife, but she didn't do it.'

'He didn't love her!' It was, I knew, a pathetic excuse – her excuse, my sister-in-law's, and no excuse at all, but it was all I had and I was desperate.

Thomas halted, then came towards me. 'That's because he's Edward,' he said, as if explaining to an idiot. 'Edward doesn't love anyone. And she'll have known that; you can't miss that about Edward. But she was still keen enough to be his wife.'

He was right, I knew, but still it shocked me: the bleakness of the marriage and the depths of Thomas's contempt for them both. But practicalities, practicalities . . .

'Please.' I slipped past him so that it was me, now, who was walking backwards, trying to head him off from the house, 'Forget her, this isn't about her. You know he can't do this to the family, you know he has to be stopped, and he'll listen to you.'

'Listen to *me*?' That he pretended to find hilarious. 'Where've you been for the past eighteen years?' Then, resolute, 'No, this is nothing to do with me.'

'It is,' I insisted, 'It is.' But he wouldn't meet my eye and we were already halfway to the main door. 'Because how's it going to look for you at court?'

He paused long enough to answer. 'Not half as bad as for Edward, but he'll be well aware of that and he's still happy enough to risk it. There's nothing I can tell him that he doesn't already know.'

But this was madness, because surely the point was, 'You know our father's not responsible.'

'I do not know that.' And he was away again across the cobbles.

But, 'You do, Thomas.' What was the matter with him? What was he playing at? I was yelling, now, and didn't care who heard me. Cowardice from Thomas was something that I hadn't expected to encounter and it was all I could do to insist: 'You do, you absolutely do know that, and you have to make Edward see it, or' – *did he, himself, really not grasp?* – 'we're all lost.'

The response was a slam of the door; and so there I was, stranded, even my own breath running from me, and, tipping my head back to try to reel it in, I glimpsed a figure withdrawing from an upstairs window. Edward: somehow, I knew it; that shadow had an Edward-bearing to it. In my dismay and desolation, I couldn't think back over what exactly he might have overheard and what he might've made of it, and whether it might matter.

11

I resisted dashing after Thomas, infuriate me though it did to let him get away; he'd see sense, I was certain, when he'd warmed through and eaten something. Badgering him would only further rile him. Anyway, I couldn't face being back in the house, behind those dark-eyed windows and that gnarled, burly door with people I couldn't even pretend to understand, so I stayed in the open air, the courtyard, walking around and trying to calm down, gather my thoughts. After several circuits, though, those four walls, the insensible sky and the crushing cold had me feeling just as trapped, so I decided to go to my room. Not for long, I told myself, just long enough for Thomas to get himself together.

But pushing on the Hall door, I saw my mistake because there in the middle of Hall was Edward and, beyond him, by the far door to the stairs, his wife. The two of them glanced at me – Edward over his shoulder – yet there was nothing in either look; they were on the brink of something and my appearing in the doorway was neither here nor there. I could have – should have – retreated, so why didn't I? I don't know, just a sense that it would be disingenuous, because I'd seen what I'd seen and there was no pretending otherwise, and perhaps also the faintest suspicion that whatever was about to happen should be witnessed. So, despite considerable trepidation, I closed the door behind me and took my place, although not for long, I didn't think, because Edward was in no mood to be waylaid.

Whether Katherine had come across him in Hall by chance or had been looking for him, I couldn't tell, nor could I tell if words had already been exchanged. She'd come in from the oriel and presumably from the stairs, and something of the momentum of descent was retained in her stillness: she was ready for business. Dressed for it, too, unlike earlier: everything was impressively in order with the exception of her girdle, the waist-encircling length of pearls and enamel flowers having swivelled round – Johnny, the likely culprit – to hang down the back of her gown like a tail. Oblivious to it, which under other circumstances would have been endearing, she held her head high and announced to Edward, 'I won't go, you know.' And instantly I was dazzled, because of course: it could be as simple as that. She'd refuse to go. Because what could my brother do? Drag her kicking and screaming to a nunnery? Well, no one at Wolf Hall behaved like that, and least of all Edward.

She came walking towards him and so audacious was that saunter of hers that she could have been balancing along the rail of the minstrels' gallery. She had a strategy, beautiful and compelling in its simplicity, and she had perfect confidence in it. *Like a queen* came to mind as I watched her, although in those days I knew nothing of queens. Beyond reproach, then, perhaps. Inviolable. She stopped at a respectful distance from him to enquire, gently, as if from concern, 'So, what will you do?'

My first twinge of alarm: *No, don't push it, Katherine.*

'What will you do, Edward?' Faultless, that impression of concern for him, yet all too clear was the barb in it. 'Will you take hold of me?' And she surrendered her arms to him: offered them up, outstretched, into the space between the pair of them as if together they might like to consider that particular course of action.

I couldn't see Edward's face, for which I was grateful and frustrated in equal measure. Firelight snapped along the golden thread of Katherine's sleeves.

Stop this, Katherine, before it's too late. Yet I was willing her onwards, too.

'Is that what you'll do?' Again, that unnerving politeness. 'Is that how you'll wrench me from our little boys and through that door?'

A wink of the pearls on her hood at its doorwards tilt.

From Edward, nothing.

As my own heartbeat came stealing up on me, Thomas emerged guilelessly from the screens passage; he'd been to the kitchen and, unknowingly, was blundering in on this. I didn't dare look at him; I'd recognised his tread just as it had stopped dead. I was conscious of willing him, too, although as to what, exactly, I didn't know: *Do something. Stop this. Turn and run.*

Neither Katherine nor Edward acknowledged him. Katherine sighed in mock-sympathy for her husband's predicament. 'So, will you manhandle me? Or will someone have to do it for you?' She was in danger but she knew it and defied it; her fury and daring were lethal but she was exulting in them. She could do anything, it seemed to me, and I couldn't take my eyes from her. 'Surely you have a plan, Edward; you always have a plan. And you do have to get me through that door, or' – stupidly, I thought she'd veered to kiss him – 'I stay.'

Threat delivered, she withdrew into a triumphant fold of arms.

Did she mean it, did she really mean it? Would she stay? Yes, she did mean it; her very life depended on it.

'Not as my wife you don't.' Edward had taken up her tone, to all intents and purposes contemplative and reasonable, his circling of her just as deliberately casual. 'And if you're not my wife' — a shrug, *interesting question* — 'then who are you?'

I longed to look to Thomas for some kind of support but didn't dare, for fear that taking my eyes off the situation would risk its escalation. As if the weight of my gaze could hold it in check. Edward flung an arm to indicate the high table, a flourish that under any other circumstances would be an invitation: 'Where's your place?'

That same tone, mimicking his wife's, as if the question genuinely interested them both. 'When my parents come back, will you be sitting up there alongside them?'

Katherine's lips tightened as if this were a cheap jibe to be endured, but Edward was right and she knew it. That table, stripped of its linen, stood there sleek and gleaming in readiness for we Seymours. It was impossible to imagine Katherine sitting up there among us as if nothing had happened.

'No?' Edward feigned mild disappointment. 'Oh, well, I suppose you could sit down there somewhere' — the arm in the direction of Thomas and me — 'in the company of ...' *take your pick* '... Marcus or Ralph, perhaps. Or Lil.'

He stepped into his own circle, closing in on her. 'But I don't know who'll serve you.' Stopping, he addressed the side of her head, or more specifically one of her ears. 'I don't know who'll lay a place for you and bring you a trencher. Because which servant in this household would defy me?'

He was right — no one. No one would dare, and never before nor since have I been as afraid of my brother as I was then: his complete confidence in his own power.

'But,' and he was on his way again, pacing, 'you're not one to let a little awkwardness bother you, are you? You could always go along to the kitchen and help yourself. Because you're happy enough to do that, aren't you: go around Wolf Hall helping yourself.'

I didn't quite know what he meant, but more puzzling was how she managed to stand there and take the nastiness of that tone. Myself, I was shaking close to collapse; I felt so feeble, I felt I should know what to do and hated that Edward should have me like this.

'Because if something's there for the taking,' the shrug done this time with his mouth. 'Take it.'

Her composure snapped, and she whirled to him: 'I am the mother of your sons!'

He stepped back, expansive, as if to consider. 'But that's the problem, isn't it.' And back to the pacing. 'After what's gone on, I can't be sure. And a husband needs to be sure of his wife, doesn't he, when it comes to heirs.'

His sidelong scrutiny suggested that her physical form alone might offer the required assurance. 'Absolutely sure. No grounds for doubt. None. Which is why the penalty for a wife's adultery is so harsh' – hands up, seeking permission to qualify – 'should a husband pursue it. But me? Well, I could go to the king with this, of course, but in my opinion,' *my humble opinion*, as if his reasonableness were a mere foible, 'the penalty is barbaric.'

I didn't want to know, I really didn't want to know, I didn't understand any of it; all I wanted was for this to stop. A glance at Thomas revealed him to be as horrified and helpless as I was.

'You could go to the kitchen,' Edward resumed, as if none of that had just been said, 'because if I were to discover you there, thieving, I could hardly set the dogs on you, could I. Because they know you.' He spoke softly. 'It'd confuse them. Which would be cruel.'

Outraged, her eyes reddened, and Thomas spoke up: 'Edward—'

'Or you could hope that someone would take food up to your room for you. Jane might, if she felt she could get away with it.' He didn't look at me. 'Or Thomas. So, you'd have food in your stomach, perhaps, but what about clothes on your back? You're a good seamstress.' He took her off guard with a touch to her sleeve, the lightest of touches, yet disconcertingly lingering. 'So you could do a lot of patching.'

It was at least as much for his own sake as Katherine's that I was praying for him to stop, but I knew by then that none of us would be emerging unscathed.

'You could darn and mend for years and years, I suppose, but eventually' – he swooped, struck her gown hard with the back of his hand – 'it'd fall into nothing.'

Her panicked recoil had Thomas take a corresponding step forward. 'Edward.'

His reluctance was audible but all eyes turned to him and Edward's in particular were expectant.

It took him a moment but then he managed, 'This isn't right.'

Edward laughed, he actually laughed. 'Isn't *right*?' He seemed delighted. 'You know what, Thomas? You're going to have to spare me your wisdom on right and wrong.'

Thomas closed his eyes, emphatically, wearily, and said so quietly that he could've been speaking to himself, 'Don't be so fucking stupid.'

Then his hands were at his face and Edward was cradling one of his own. He'd hit Thomas and there'd been a scream – from Katherine or me, I didn't know, but something like a scream, an intake of breath, a scream in reverse. Thomas lowered his hands to look disinterestedly at the blood on his fingers, some of which was dripping to the floor. There they were on the tiles: those bright droplets, a startling spatter. Edward turned on his heel and banged through the door to the stairs. Thomas's gaze moved to me and he said, almost conversationally, 'Stop crying.'

I didn't know I was, and didn't know how to stop; jammed a fist at my mouth.

Katherine was standing stock still as if it were she who'd been punched, but then suddenly she was away through the same door as Edward, although not, this time, it was clear, to follow him.

'Stop crying, Jane,' Thomas said again, almost kindly, before he, too, turned and left.

12

Not knowing what to do with myself nor where else to go, I retreated to chapel, the only place I could be reasonably sure of no one coming across me. Everywhere else at Wolf Hall was somebody's or held something that someone would soon be wanting or needing, but we Seymours didn't go to chapel outside the hours of prayer and Father James was tutoring Antony in the long gallery.

I don't know how long I sat there like an animal in hiding in a hole – perhaps half an hour – before I became aware of something that came into focus as Ned crying upstairs. I was used to Ned crying, but never like that, never at length; he was an easily placated baby.

Eventually, his distress drew me towards him, took me tip-toeing from chapel and upstairs to the foot of his parents' staircase. If he was up there in their room, I reasoned, then presumably he was with one of them, but then why the incessant, frantic crying? My scalp prickled with unease. Listening hard into the clamour, I detected no adult voices. Whoever was up there with him was alone.

Gingerly climbing the stairs, I discovered Edward sitting

hunched on the top step with his back to the door. I stopped dead and we stared at each other, equally startled. He was crying and, even more incredibly, making no attempt to hide it. He sniffed fulsomely. 'She has Johnny in there, too, I think.'

I didn't grasp it, and he had to explain, 'She's bolted the door.'

I glanced over his head at the closed door as if it'd confirm its resistance. *Practicalities*: I had to establish what, exactly, was happening. 'What's she saying?'

He shrugged, desolate: nothing.

There was no time for that. 'But you know she's in there?'

'The door's bolted,' he reiterated.

Of course, that door could only be secured from the inside, there was no lock, only a bolt that was beyond Johnny's reach.

The noise from Ned was intolerable; we had to stop it. I blasted it with, 'Katherine?' and shot Edward an accusatory, 'Is she all right?' If I didn't know precisely what I meant, in a way I did and so would he. But how could Katherine possibly be all right in there with that noise? What was happening?

He didn't reply, merely warned me, 'She won't answer.'

Not to you, maybe. Stepping over him – what on earth did he think he was doing slumped there? – I hammered on the door, 'Katherine?' And to Edward, again, 'Is she all right?'

She'd better be, because if not, then neither were the boys. Certainly Ned had worked himself into a state, but Johnny's silence, if he was there, was perhaps even more alarming. The commotion at the door only served to intensify Ned's fury, now joined by a baleful wailing from Johnny, the very sound of dismay and disappointment, as if he'd been badly let down and I didn't like that, I really didn't like that. What on earth could it be that had him crying like that? But at least we knew for certain that he was in there. Why still nothing, though, from his mother? Her two little boys crying their hearts out, and nothing from her.

'Katherine!' An order, *Open the door.*

And then I was having to yell soothing words at the top of my voice: 'It's all right, Johnny, sweetheart, we're here, we're here, now, and is Mummy there with you? Can you ask her to open the door for us?'

I asked Edward, 'What about the window?' because I couldn't think: in which direction did the room face, and did we have a long enough ladder? She'd shutter it, though, if she really did want to keep us out; if she hadn't already done so, she'd do it when she heard someone coming. And, anyway, what use to us, really, was a window? Heavily leaded, with its tiny casement opening, although for the briefest moment I felt I had the strength to smash it, lead and all.

Edward didn't dignify the question with an answer; all he said was, 'You'll have to get her out,' and it was a statement of fact.

And he was right, I knew he was right. So I gave it a last go, gave it everything I had: 'Katherine! Open this door!'

Then, to Edward, 'It'll have to come off its hinges, go and get someone.' The blacksmith, the locksmith, our steward, anyone.

His look was one of disbelief – *involve someone else?* – which in turn dismayed me because surely that was nothing to what was in store if he persisted with his wife's public disgracing.

'NOW!'

And he did it: scrambled to his feet and belted down the stairs.

For several heartbeats, I did nothing at all, didn't think, didn't breathe, and then it just happened: the bolt growled and the door opened. Katherine was as pallid as if she'd just endured a blood-let. Stepping aside to admit me, she then bolted the door in my wake. The room was fetid. We stood face to face, but Ned's roars might have been an insect trapped inside my ear and I couldn't think what it was that only moments ago I'd been desperate to say.

Both boys were on the bed, Johnny amid a scattering of his mother's jewellery – *Look, Johnny! Mummy's treasure!* – with which he was playing as if ordered at knife-point, and the baby propped on a pillow, presumably in the vain hope that a concession to a single physical comfort would compensate for the neglect of other, more pressing needs.

With an air of defeat, Katherine said, 'He wants feeding,' as if I couldn't hear it for myself.

Yes, and changing, too.

I made a move for him. 'I'll take him to Mrs Pluckrose.'

'No.' Her hand on my arm; her eyes, on mine, stark. 'The boys stay here.'

I was to fetch Mrs Pluckrose here? But, 'He needs changing, too.'

She glanced at him, and blustered, 'Well . . .' *We can do that here.*

Well, yes, we could, but, Jesus, 'It'll be quicker to take him to Mrs Pluckrose,' who was equipped.

Her eyes were knuckle-hard and the words, although whispered, were drawn tight: 'The boys stay with me.'

But this was wasting time; I quite simply had to get him to Mrs Pluckrose. 'Edward'll be back,' I warned her: back at her door, and all of us back where we'd started.

Her flinch was confined to the surface of her eyes, releasing a couple of tears. Tethered to her distress, Johnny looked up, the fragile composure of his own face falling into a howl. I swooped on Ned, who didn't see me coming; he was beside himself, everything heavenwards — face, limbs — and his tiny tongue like a clapper in a roaring bell.

The day room was where I headed. I had no idea where Mrs Pluckrose was but Dottie was bound to be in the day room and she was a safe pair of hands. As it happened, she was already in the doorway, alerted by Ned's shrieking and at the ready to receive him, and behind her was Margie, whom I told to go and find Edward, intercept him, insist that he keep away from his room for a while. I didn't doubt she could do it.

Back in his parents' room, Johnny was in possession of his mother's wallet of silks, and was gravely garlanding himself. Having opened the door for me, Katherine returned to him, sitting on the side of the bed, supervisory. He turned his big, serious eyes to me and I dredged up a smile that he didn't return but acknowledged with a bashful deflection of his gaze. The strewing of the silks on the bed had me realise that the cushions were gone, and then I spotted them: they were in Katherine's oak chest; the chest was open, packed.

My heart sprang on guard. 'Where are you going?'

She didn't answer the question, instead saying resolutely, 'The boys are coming with me,' and holding me hard in her gaze to keep me at bay, to warn me off: she'd permit no challenge.

But, 'Where?'

Still no answer; a slight softening, though, a relenting, an appeal for me to listen to her silence and understand it.

'Where, Katherine?' But I did hear the lack of an answer for what it was: 'The nunnery?' and for one glorious moment I almost laughed, because it was absurd.

It was ridiculous, some new silliness of hers: this packing up of belongings was no more than pique. She was calling Edward's bluff, hoping to shame him; she was playing the martyr. Something like that: something equally self-pitying and pointless. And, 'No,' because I'd had enough, more than enough: it seemed to me that I'd suffered years of such wilfulness from her. I snatched the cushions and dumped them back onto the bed, thinking just in time to make a kind of presentation of them to Johnny, 'Here, sweetie, these are for you, to go with your jewels.'

Not that he seemed alarmed, watching me just as his mother did, steady and regretful, in his case with a string of pearls draped over one hand like a rosary. Edward mustn't catch wind of this, I knew, because what would he make of it? It was as good as an admission of guilt, couldn't she see that? Margie would do her best to detain Edward but, formidable though she was in opposition, he'd be up at his door soon enough, and he shouldn't know what his wife had been doing. As far as he knew, she was fighting him all the way. And she was: that was exactly what she was going to do. She'd stop this nonsense and she'd resolve whatever the problem was between them. I couldn't do it for her; I'd backed her up when she'd asked, but I could only do so much. She herself was going to do it, and she was going to do it then and there, for her boys and for our family. On her own account, she could do as she damn well liked – I really didn't care, at that point, if I never saw her again – but no way was she taking the rest of us down with her.

'Unpack the chest,' I told her, but what, I wondered, was the matter with her? Why that look? As if she were letting me say my piece; sitting it out, taking it honourably, like a shamed dog. 'You did nothing wrong,' I had to remind her. 'Nothing actually happened.'

'Jane,' – breaking it to me – 'I do have to go. The boys'll come with me, but I do have to go. I can't stay here.'

What was wrong with her? This was so typical of her, I could have slapped her. 'They were *poems*, Katherine.'

A slow, sorrowful, slap-worthy shake of her head, her face rigid in mortification. 'I do have to go,' her eyes brimful of appeal: *Don't ask, please don't ask, just accept it, just understand.*

What bizarre, self-glorifying notion had she concocted for herself?

'Stop this,' I endeavoured to kept my voice low, as if a hoarse, desperate whisper might be less alarming for Johnny. 'Stop it.'

She was intent on embracing her fate as she saw it, the fate of the wrongdoer, but she needed to be thinking of someone other than herself for a change. Anyone else, and she could do a lot worse than start with my father. My father had done nothing wrong: I didn't know much, in life, but I definitely did know that.

255

If she capitulated over the nunnery, how would that look for him? He'd had some kind words for his daughter-in-law, that was all, because he was a kind man, too kind; she'd been unhappy and he'd taken her under his wing, and if she'd dreamt of more, of a special place in his heart, then so what? Edward wouldn't like her for it, but he could hardly make the case for a nunnery. It was *she* who was failing to understand: no one cared about her dreams.

'No,' I insisted of her, because for once, just for once, she was going to behave properly, with consideration for other people, and I turned to the chest, 'We're putting everything back where it belongs.' But suddenly, decisively, she rose, and somehow, in a step or two, she'd swept me with her to the window and there we stood, side by side, which was when she told me.

13

Think back two years, she said, to St Katherine's eve, the eve
of Edward's return from France. When everyone else went
to bed, she said, we went up to the long gallery: did I remember?
I did.

And along came Thomas, offering to teach us a new dance.

Yes, I remembered: I'd opted for bed, but she'd taken him up
on it and I'd left the two of them there in the light of a single taper.

She'd felt she wouldn't be able to sleep, she said, so she decided
she might as well put the time to good use. Better than lying alone
for hours in the dark. Thomas then did as he'd promised, demon-
strating the steps for her and directing her attempts to copy them,
despite the evening's wine taking its toll on him: 'No, uh-uh' –
he'd raise a hand to call her to a halt – 'you've got to go to the . . .
the . . . '

'Left?' Sleepless though she was, she was nevertheless weary.
'To the left, here, Thomas? Is that it?'

'Left! – yep, that's the one. But perhaps not quite so . . . so . . . '

'So what, Thomas?'

He could only laugh at his helplessness in the face of her
exasperation: 'Just . . . '

'Just what, Thomas? Lighter? Faster? What?'

All he could do, in the end, was show her – like this – and so there he was, taking those steps again with the considerable, enviable ease which came from evenings of practice in the Dormer household.

She scrutinised those steps and their sequence, holding the recollection firmly in mind when she moved to reproduce them but somehow they eluded her, tripped her up: she found that she couldn't do that dance, or only imperfectly, approximately. She couldn't even see where the problem was, couldn't quite account for the shortfall between intention and execution. She'd recognised those moves of Thomas's exactly for what they were, she was sure of it, she'd understood them and known what it was that she had to do but then, when she came to make them, they didn't quite happen. And worse, Thomas was witness to it: sneery seventeen-year-old Thomas, of all people. But suddenly, just as inexplicably, it was there, that dance, it was right there at her feet – the steps, their sequence – and she could repeat it time and time again until the mystery was how she'd ever got it wrong. Now she couldn't have got it wrong if she'd tried.

Thomas watched, standing back enough to sit down, eventually, on a stool, and then, when he was satisfied, rising to join her. There they were, the two of them, perhaps not so much partnering each other as dancing the two parts of the same dance at the same time.

By then, I'd been gone quite a while and it seemed to Katherine that it was done, the dance learned, practised, committed to memory, and she should no longer be putting off going to bed. So, with perfunctory thanks to Thomas, she swiped the taper from the chest on which it'd been placed, but moved too quickly and the flame veered in its wake, throwing off smoke as it drowned.

They both groaned, defeated, because how could they possibly find their way from the long gallery and down the stairs in darkness so dense that it seemed hard even to breathe? There was nothing for it but for them to edge their way along, the flat of a hand offered up to the tapestry-lined wall, while their eyes adapted. Thomas offered to lead the way.

'Whatever you do,' Katherine whispered ahead to him, 'don't yank down any of Margery's tapestries.'

The prospect struck them both as hilarious. The disloyalty was delicious. In daylight, those treasured tapestries presided over the gallery, but now, abandoned to the night, they hung there at their mercy, practically inviting desecration. If something did go wrong, no one would know who'd done it.

Thomas breathed a regretful, 'Oh God,' and whispered back at her, 'I'm pissed and I'm going to be horrible tomorrow.'

Tomorrow, when Edward the hero would return and all Seymours should be on best behaviour. That, too, struck her as funny: Edward wasn't even home yet but already his homecoming was a disaster. She put Thomas straight: 'It's all right for you, he's not expecting anything of you.'

She'd intended it lightly, but the misery of it hit her square in the chest and Thomas was taken aback by the depth of her sigh: stopping in his tracks and turning to her, although of course he'd see nothing. Unaware that he'd halted, she bumped into him, her free hand up to his chest to recoup her balance and re-establish some space. She felt bad for him, too, all of a sudden: Edward was a hard act to follow. She knew only too well how it was to be forever falling short. In that sense, she and Thomas were allies.

And although Thomas's hadn't been the chest against which she'd been longing to rest in all that time when Edward had been away, there it was, right in front of her, and so, fleetingly, she laid her head on it, to take what she needed. No one would know, not even Thomas, really, drunk as he was. Gingerly, he placed a hand on her back – a brotherly gesture – and, held there like that, she faced her dread of Edward's return: didn't fight it, didn't have to pretend. There'd been so much pretence for her of late, that it was giddying to be able to give up on it, however momentarily.

Thomas's breath was warm on the top of her head and there was his chin, too, the jut of it, a resistance that was somehow pleasurable. She hadn't reckoned on how difficult it would be to pull back from the warmth of him. She'd not been held by a man for a long time and perhaps never unambivalently. Thomas had no qualms, she could tell, but she sensed he'd been taken unawares and it was surprisingly satisfying to have rendered him at a bit of a loss.

She drew away from him and duly he dropped his hand. But there had been that unexpected connection between the two of them, to which she wanted to give her blessing before it disappeared, so she craned to bestow on him the lightest of kisses, not unlike those with which in later years she'd grace her sons' heads before leaving them to sleep. He reeled a little but not enough to take his lips from hers: he was a seventeen-year-old boy after all, and a drunken one at that. She detected a mindfulness to his lack of response: he was being careful, she realised, he was having to be careful. And hadn't that been her dream? To be kissed by someone who couldn't stop himself. Not Thomas, of course, but her lips stayed on his, nevertheless, to keep there the potential of such a kiss. Thomas, too, she felt: his lips were on hers even though, had it been physically possible, he'd have been looking pointedly in a different direction.

Then she made to move away but didn't, quite. Which made it a brush of her lips across his. Which made it a kind of kiss. Still, no one would know, probably not even the pair of them themselves because the chances were, come the morning, they'd have no memory of it. And anyway, this was only Thomas, he was just a boy and this was nothing, this was what he did with servant girls. How different, though, from Edward's cold mouth, how different from the way Edward kissed her, and it was definitely kissing that was happening, now, and actually it'd been happening anyway – the lips on lips, the brushing of lips over lips – so why pretend otherwise? No more pretence, not tonight. Because this was her chance – her one chance and her last – to press her mouth hard and open to someone else's and she was discovering that, for her, it couldn't be too hard. Nor for Thomas, it seemed, she didn't have to worry about Thomas; he was giving as good as he was getting.

There was that ache, too, underneath her – that deep-down, insistent ache of which Edward, merely by his presence, had made her feel ashamed – and Thomas shouldn't have known it was there, yet he seemed to be playing with it with every touch of his tongue on hers. He was also turning her around, reaching behind her with one hand for the wall, checking for an absence of tapestry so that he could press her back and pin her there, the better to kiss her. Those tapestries! Despite the kissing, she smiled and then so did he. She sank back but then his weight knocked the breath from her and her shoulder blades crashed into the panelling and she surfaced from her reverie, which was when it all should have stopped.

But instead she whispered to him, 'Let's go to my room.' It was a practical solution to the problem of that linen fold digging into her backbone, and that was all it was; that was as far as she was thinking. She just needed a little more of him, just a little more time with him. There was no plan. Nothing would happen. What could happen? He was her husband's little brother; she was his big brother's wife. He was drunk and her mother had warned her that her husband would be no use if he were drunk, and indeed, at Lammas, when Edward had had too much wine, hadn't those been Thomas's own words? 'He'll be no use to you.' Well, now it was Thomas himself who'd be no use; she could kiss him all night long if she liked and she'd be perfectly safe.

Thomas said nothing. He must have wondered if he'd heard her right but didn't dare question his luck. He was seventeen and drunk. He allowed her to guide him. She gloved his hand with hers and groped with the other for the door, her stealth in opening it striking the two of them as comical, as did the oblivion of everyone beyond the staircase: a household of Edward-types earnestly asleep and the two of them on the stairs in league against them.

How different life would've been, it occurred to her, if she'd married Thomas. There'd have been a lot of this, she'd bet: sneaking off together, giggly, to bed. A lot of bed, a lot of early retiring and late rising, and perhaps even moments mid-morning as the chapel bell was calling her to Mass, the thought of which, alongside the impossibility of it, whipped her heart from its beat.

Descending that staircase with Thomas on her heels, she marvelled: she'd be having this living, breathing boy to herself on her bed for a while, and he wanted it at least as much as she did, and what a revelation that was. And whoever would've guessed? The two of them, who'd always been so badly at odds.

When they reached her room, he drew his fingers through her hair so that she too felt the life in it. Edward had never touched her hair; she'd always combed it through before bed then tidied it away again into a single plait. Thomas breathed against her neck as if relieved of a burden, and her own inhalation of his warm, secret saltiness slid beneath her breastbone to knock her, almost, off her feet. He drew back from her and nudged her around to face away from him so that he could unlace her gown, and of course, of course, because the gown was bulky and she couldn't lay comfortably in it on the bed. He worked slowly, no doubt because he was less than sober, but it was clear that he knew what he was doing, that he was practised at it, which came as no surprise to her; the surprise was the thrill it gave her. She noted the barely perceptible tightening of each lace as he made enough slack to free it; and soon all the fabric was being lifted away from her, across the room, with a sound like overhead wing-rustle. He draped it over a chest, and there, looking lovely, it might never have had anything to do with her: she looked at it and it seemed to look back at her, and it was as if she and it denied all knowledge of each other.

She stood in the softness of her kirtle but Thomas was loosening that, too, tackling its side-lacing so that she had to raise her arm for him. She'd never before been undressed by a man. She didn't even undress herself so much as change clothes, donning one garment before emerging from the other so that briefly she'd be wearing both and never none: it was how she'd been taught and it was how she changed into her nightdress whenever she came to bed for Edward. But here was Thomas with his fingers threaded into her lacing. And if he could do it, then why shouldn't she? She twisted to get to work on him, popping buttons through buttonholes, and when she slid his jacket from his shoulders, he took it from her and dropped it on top of her gown. He was down to his doublet and hose, but she – when he'd removed her kirtle – was in smock and stockings. Well, if her, then him, too, she decided: his doublet should come off, although it'd take some doing, thoroughly laced as it was to the hose. She worked her way around his waist, unpicking every one of those ties until the doublet could be shed and he was left in shirt and hose that was held up by nothing now but his hips.

Time at last for the bed: she went to open the hangings but his hand came to her arm to halt her and, when she turned to answer that touch with a glance, he drew her smock up and over her, the linen buffeting her head and white-blinding her. Now she was naked except for her stockings and she'd never been naked that

263

she remembered in front of anyone, not even herself. Unnatural, was how it felt, which perhaps he understood because quickly he cloaked her with himself, and she clung to him, Don't go, don't move. Over his shoulder, she spied her smock on the floor: it hadn't made it as far as the chest.

He parted the hangings behind her and then the pair of them were on the bed, but instantly he drew back again, this time to take off her stockings. She could only watch with a kind of incomprehension as they came rolling away from her, first one and then the other: relinquishing her, those much-darned woollens, to leave her across the bed in the lantern-light as she'd never before seen herself.

She refused to be alone in this, so, when he tried to settle back down, she tugged at his shirt, prompting him to strip himself of it, and then she eased his hose down until he obliged her by wriggling and kicking himself free so that he, too, was naked. She'd never even imagined two bare bodies together, she, diligent embroiderer of peach-hued Adam and Eve. Nor could she have anticipated the heat of his skin on hers and how he seemed to be melted over her so that nothing of her stayed untouched. She was aware he was hard but she knew she was safe because he was drunk and even if he hadn't been, he would never dare, because in a few hours his brother would be coming through that door downstairs. And indeed he didn't dare, but just kissed her: long, luxuriated-in kisses to her mouth, and others, lighter, elsewhere. She, too: her own lips relished the rolling of bones inside his skin and the confidence of muscle.

But by now her ache had become not quite bearable and she longed to know – she'd been longing to know ever since she'd married – how it would feel to have a man inside her and to have him stay there, not slip away as Edward did. Edward retreated from her, every time, sighing and bitterly disappointed, leaving her adrift. Would that happen with Thomas? Thomas, who'd unvested her of every last stitch, then dressed her up in kisses? She doubted it.

She shifted him so that he was beneath her. No one would know; neither of them would tell a soul because both their lives would depend on it. Not that he'd even remember, probably, in the morning. She pressed down onto him.

'Katherine.' It was the first thing he'd said since the long gallery: her name sounded in warning, as if he'd suddenly woken to what was happening.

She stopped his mouth with the flat of her hand, but he turned his head to escape it and urged her – 'Katherine' – to her senses.

Her answer was to press harder, but this time with her hips: a flex that eased him inside her. To that, he didn't respond, didn't even breathe, not at first; but then, when at last he did, the breath came as a kind of laugh, a mix of incredulity and admiration in it and something like resignation, but perhaps closer to despair. And he countered that pressure of hers – if warily at first – with his own. What he didn't do was shrink from her. It was startling how perfect a fit they were, the two of them, and in sheer grati-tude she kissed him; and then she divined that perfect fit with the next push down onto him, and then another, and with each one it was a little more pleasurable, if that were even possible. And no one had ever told her it would feel this good but then, perhaps no one knew, perhaps only they knew, only the two of them. It was impossible that it could be still more pleasurable, yet it was, time and time again; it was, confounding her over and over again, and she had to find just how pleasurable it could possibly be, and that, in the end, was all that mattered.

HEYDAY

I

As soon as Katherine had gone to Wilton, Edward took me to the queen to lead the quietest and most respectable of lives, and if I'd been able to feel anything for him, I might have felt sorry, because, so very clever as he was, he could never have foreseen what was about to happen. At any other time in the history of England, his plan would have worked a treat – my life would have been among the quietest, the most respectable – but, as bad luck would have it, I walked right back into the middle of the tricky business of a man setting aside his wife. And this time, not just any man, nor just any wife.

Walked? *Crept*: I crept into court, a decade ago, to disappear in the ranks of those many maids of honour. What should have been a cause for celebration – the first Seymour girl in the household of a queen – was, under the circumstances, a kind of exile. And if my own family wouldn't have me, then no other family would. I was at court because I had nowhere else to go; I was in the service of the queen as a last resort. The best I could hope for was rehabilitation: salvaging some respectability for myself and my family, perhaps, if I kept my head down.

We thirty maids of honour and almost as many ladies-in-waiting were in the service of a queen who, it seemed to me, appeared to be attending *us*. There she was, Queen Catherine, in her gorgeously canopied chair, presiding benignly, as if mindful to do her very best by us. It looked to me that if for some reason we all left her, she'd happily pack up and go to her little daughter in Ludlow. She was anything but the imposing figure of my imaginings, that Spanish daughter of king-crusader and warrior-queen, that victor of Flodden. Short and stout, she wore her finery dutifully, her huge, jewel-heavy crucifix staring us down, lunging whenever she reached to the floor for her sewing basket.

Fortyish, she was a good handful of years younger than my mother, but my mother – even hard-worked and careworn as she was – had a vitality that this pale and pouchy queen lacked. Not that the queen didn't work hard in her own way, the work she chose for herself being worship: she was relentless in her routine, rising after a few hours of sleep to be at her altar at midnight, and back there again to start each day at five. All that kneeling had taken its toll, I saw, in that she always rose with a wince, needing the arm of one of her ladies.

After Mass every morning, she wrote to her daughter, the eleven-year-old princess. I should've been writing to Dottie and Margie, but what would I have said? There was too much to say, it seemed to me, and nothing to say: that was how it felt to me. Most days, the queen received a letter in return, which she read avidly, commenting fulsomely in Spanish to her closest attendant and I'd listen, captivated, even though I didn't understand a word. My mother didn't write to me, nor me to her, and I couldn't imagine how that would ever change.

Afternoons the queen devoted to needlework, her basket of silks at her feet like a faithful little dog, and it was disconcerting, initially, to glance up and see her baring her teeth before I realised she was snapping a thread. She always had to pass the needle, beseechingly, to someone else for threading, and within a day or two of my arrival, probably to have me feeling welcome, she was reaching over several heads with her gentle smile to pass it to me.

I was glad of something to do for her. My father and Edward had served the king by going into battle for him, but how was I to serve the queen? I'd come into her household knowing how to sweep floors and polish plate, wash and dry and fold linen, feed pigs and hens, harvest vegetables and bottle fruit, roll pastry, make candles, lay tables, amuse babies and mind children – but a maid of honour did none of that.

And hadn't I dreamt of an end to daily drudgery? I was scared, though, of inadvertently neglecting some vital duty and thereby showing myself up, although, of course, everyone would've known at least something of what had just happened in the Seymour household (*Isn't she the sister of—? Didn't—?*)

Thankfully, there were practicalities to concern me: where to be and when, and when to kneel and to rise, when to stand in attendance or settle on a cushion; and which essentials were due to me – food, firewood, clean laundry, candles – and when and from where to fetch them. I even took a few days to be able to find the way undirected to my own room (which staircase? Which floor, which door?) and at least as long to distinguish among the three Annes with whom I shared the bed.

What did come easily, every day, was dinner. The aroma from the queen's private kitchen would deepen all morning and when, at last, the meal was carried up the stairs and served, I definitely did have something to do: eat, eat, eat, and all the more so when I learned how frequently and strictly the queen observed fast days. Within weeks, I was letting out my kirtle, and I've had to do so at intervals ever since.

During those difficult first days at court, I marvelled at the queen, at how very much worse it must have been for her, at sixteen, to have travelled so far from home to so foreign a land. Within months, it had all been over for her: she'd been widowed and shut up in that old house on the Strand in the clothes she stood up in, reduced to foraging for berries in its tangle of riverside garden while her father refused to have her back – because the deal was done – and her father-in-law refused to pay for her upkeep.

It had been seven long years before her young brother-in-law had come along: the new king, but a mere boy, eighteen to her twenty-three. He'd known his own heart and mind, though, and he'd come as soon as he could. It was the first decision of his reign, to go against the advice of his councillors, who were looking elsewhere for a match, to marry his neglected, impoverished sister-in-law. He could have had anyone, but he chose her. The big-hearted boy-king rescuing the ragged princess: no wonder the queen could never quite believe, to the end of her days, that her husband would ever do anything but right by her.

Each morning, I'd watch the Annes dress excitedly and speed down the staircase from our room then billow across the courtyard. Why hurry, I wondered, just to sit sewing for hours on end with no distraction save the thud of one's own blood inside one's ears. Those panelled rooms of the queen's could have been sunk into the ground for all that was evident of the outside world. At some point in each day, though, something did happen, in that the king came to visit his wife. The considerable ceremony in his wake always looked faltering and fussy because he'd duck in through the doorway ahead of the attendants, as if giving them the slip. Close behind him would be a chosen few, one of whom, often, was Edward, and another my cousin Francis, sporting an eye-patch after having been blinded in one eye while jousting.

Then, somehow, it was as if we girls and ladies were interrupting *them*, those gentlemen: they acted cheerfully put-upon, making much of a good-natured reining in of exuberance, which we, in turn, it seemed, were supposed to regard indulgently, *Oh you bad boys.* Fantastically dressed, they were, those few favoured gentlemen: I'd never seen anything like it and had to remind myself not to gawp. Every fabric was embellished and embossed, and I couldn't help but imagine an army of tailors and embroiderers behind the door, eyesight burning down like candles.

Those gentlemen might draw the gaze, but the king shone: he was everywhere in a room like light, underneath every reverently lowered eyelid. Half the height again of his companions, he was dressed in white, gold, blood red and venous purple. He himself was a palace, a living, breathing, cavorting palace; there were whole rooms of him, it seemed to me, rooms furnished with treasures and towering one upon the other from the shoes upwards, those shoes soled with Spanish leather, stitched in thread-thin gold, buckled by clustered rubies.

He'd sling himself into his chair beside the queen's. She was bulkier than him but neater, sitting composed with her hands linked in her lap; she could have been his well-meaning aunt, fond and indulgent but a little shy of him. Often they played cards. He'd leap up and fetch a table before it could be fetched for him and they'd rearrange themselves at it, calling for a couple of companions: perhaps Lady Maria, with an uncharacteristic gleam in her eye and coins jingling in the purse which, cheekily, she held aloft; and once in my first week, Edward, stepping dutifully from the crowd when it was his name that was called.

When I first glimpsed Edward in the king's entourage, I was struck by how young he looked. Among those joust-solid men of the king's, he was so lean as perhaps to have been considered delicate. I knew, though, that he was all the stronger for it. Watchful, his dark eyes were brighter than any others; when they looked for me, I took mine away.

One afternoon towards the end of my first week, a black-haired girl came walking into the queen's room as if she owned it: a tilt to her chin and a swing to her narrow hips. No, actually, she was no girl: girl-sized and girl-shaped, but my second stolen glance revealed her as the wrong side of twenty-five. We maids and ladies were sitting there stuffed into our clothes to show them to the best advantage, but she looked about to shrug hers off. Our pretty colours – rose, apricot, sage – tried hard to please, but she wore black and was strewn with jewels. She flew in amid us, as clever and cocky as a crow. Half the roomful of maids and ladies returned their attention pointedly to their cards, their needlework, their lapdogs, and half turned to welcome her. She approached the queen but stopped short and bobbed curso-rily: a mockery of a curtsey. I flushed as if it'd been me who'd been flung this disrespect. Who – what – was this woman? She turned her back on the queen and joined a huddle of ladies who were keen to ingratiate themselves with her. As if she were someone.

The queen continued her stitching, but now looked stranded up there on her chair. I wanted to help her but didn't know quite what was wrong and, anyway, it wasn't my place. Following her lead, I resumed my needlework but a lapse of concentration sent the needle into my finger, the shock of which – rather than pain – drew tears to my eyes. Steadying my breathing, I puzzled over who that woman was, why she hadn't shown proper deference to the queen and why the queen had turned a blind eye.

Minutes later, the king arrived. All smiles as usual, he greeted the queen with his customary kiss but, rather than sitting with her, strode across the room to the black-haired woman who was rising, laughing delightedly, to receive him. They, too, kissed, and were instantly in conversation about a forthcoming party. Was this his sister Mary, perhaps? But he and his sister, I'd heard, shared the Tudor colouring. And anyway, my instinct told me that this woman, for all her mock-curtseying and king-kissing, was one of us, here to serve the queen. Why, then, was she kiss-ing the queen's husband and – with such ease and familiarity –

making plans with him? I couldn't believe she was his mistress because I'd once overheard praise of the king's impeccable discretion and there was nothing discreet about this. I shouldn't be witnessing it, that I did know. How, though, could I avoid it? An averted gaze was no more than that; they'd still be here, the pair of them, in the middle of the queen's room, laughing and making their arrangements. Whether we liked it or not, we were all spectators; and the queen, up there on her chair, more so than any of us.

The king didn't stay long and the woman left with him: there was mention of a stroll, the gardens, a lovely evening. Without a word, a handful of our company accompanied her, as if accustomed to doing so. Those of us who remained sank into silence, no chatter, not a sweet nothing to a lapdog, not even the slapping down of a card, which persisted until, some minutes later, the queen seemed to notice it.

'Music, please,' she requested smilingly of her musicians, and, as they first drew their bows across their strings, we all sighed with satisfaction, as if that was exactly what we'd wanted, as if that was all that'd been missing.

The following day, I learned who the black-haired woman was. Until then, no one had breathed a word. My fellow maids of honour probably assumed that my brother kept me informed; little would they know that he barely spoke to me and certainly not about love affairs.

Francis was the one who took it upon himself to tell me, sidling up to me so that I was on the side of his good eye and making polite enquiries about my time so far at court. I had an uneasy sense that there was more to come, and suddenly he lowered his voice to say, 'So, now you've seen Anne Boleyn.' He'd sounded amused. I wanted to resist, to refuse to be drawn in, but found myself staring fearfully into his one eye with my unvoiced questions: *Who is she? What's happening?*

The eye slid away when he whispered, 'Won't be his mistress; wants to be his wife.' I was trying to make sense of this – the king already had a wife – when he added, approvingly, 'She's ambitious.' Then, bowing minimally to take his leave of me, he advised, 'Keep in with her.'

Oh, but I couldn't have kept in with Anne Boleyn if I'd tried; it didn't take me long to learn that. As far as she was concerned, I was one of the many maids and ladies who didn't exist. I didn't read books, discuss ideas, have opinions, didn't make witty conversation or, indeed, any conversation. Didn't dress in anything my mother wouldn't have chosen for me. Something else I learned, though, was that I couldn't care less. Because although I'd known everything there was to know about what I wasn't, Anne Boleyn's saunter into the queen's room, that day, had shown me, at long last and to my considerable relief, what I *was*, which was the opposite, in every imaginable way, of her.

2

And so, coming to court, I'd walked in on the king leaving his queen. Literally: when the queen noticed a pearl hanging loose on her gown one afternoon, it was me to whom she turned – her trusty new needle-threader – for the quick repair of the offending stitch, which was why I was on my knees at her feet when the king arrived. He came unannounced and unexpected; as far as we all knew, he was still away at Beaulieu, hunting. Even with my back to the door and my face in the queen's skirts, I knew it was him because in his presence everything transforms – even silence, which somehow rings differently. Then there was the ker-fuffle of silks as ladies rushed to bended knee and the queen was foisted from her chair. I dropped the needle, left it dangling, to turn and perform my own genuflection, but the queen's hand was on my head to hold me still and there was nothing I could do. There I was between the pair of them but with my back to the king, which, for all I knew, was treason.

The queen must have sensed from first glance that he'd come with no kiss for her; he'd be coming no closer, so she kept me there as if I could be the reason. He usually made a show of affection but this time there were no niceties. He spoke her name softly, to warn of serious business, and said, 'We should—' *Go somewhere more private.* But her hand on my head was heavier — we were going nowhere — and he accepted it. What he had to tell her would be public soon enough and she'd be distressed to hear it, but could be trusted to be dignified. And, anyway, who was I? No one. Whoever I was, down there between the two of them, I was of no consequence.

'Catkin,' his voice was low for only her, and me, to hear, 'I am so very, very sorry to have to tell you this . . .'

And so there I was, listening for the second time in as many months to a man telling his wife that she was, as he saw it, not in fact his wife.

Differently, though, this time; told differently, with no accusations, no recriminations. A mistake, was how the king ruefully put it, there'd quite likely been a mistake; someone, somewhere along the line, had quite possibly made a regrettable, reprehensible mistake whereby the king had been given poor advice all those years ago, as to the legitimacy of marriage to his brother's widow. In front of me, that pearl-glorious gown was so still that there might have been no one in it, but actually she was letting every grain of sound settle on her so that she could weigh it up: she'd have needed to know exactly what she was being told. And duly he talked on, getting it done. Their lack of a son, he said, which was the immense sorrow of their lives, was probably God's punishment.

She spoke up. 'The Pope—'

'Was wrong, quite probably.' The dispensation of all those years ago, he said, should probably never have been granted. 'Forgive me,' he murmured, 'my best girl,' because he'd acted in good faith, he assured her, and from his deep and abiding love. But she'd been his brother's, first, and no man — according to the Bible, he said — should take his brother's wife. The queen's hand, on my head, steadied me. The king told her there was to be an

investigation to settle the matter and if they were both exoner-
ated, as he sincerely hoped, then he'd marry her all over again
and with more pomp and ceremony than she could imagine.

I wouldn't have known that she was crying had he not then
implored her to desist as if it were the crying itself that was hurt-
ing her. And I only realised that her tears weren't for herself
when she whispered to him, 'My poor darling, that this woman
makes you do this.' Which was when I realised, too, that unlike
her I had, until then, been taken in.

Which I shouldn't have been, given what had only recently
happened back at Wolf Hall; I should have been wise to lies.
Three years before, my sister-in-law had come across our threshold like a fall of light and there we'd stood, we stymied
Seymours, never having seen the like; and for a while, for a
summer, that was who Katherine had been to me: the girl incapable of hiding anything. But I'd learned that I couldn't have
been more wrong. Not that I blamed her, or not by the time that
I was kneeling there before the queen, because, I knew, Katherine
had been unable to help herself: she'd been, more accurately, the
girl who couldn't help herself. It was me, I felt, who should have
seen what was coming. I should have been the one to know.

'You have to tell them,' was what I'd said to her when at last
she'd told me the whole truth, up in her desolate room on that
dreadful February day. *Now*, I meant.

Incredibly, she shook her head, an anguished, tight little refusal.

But it wasn't her choice to make: it wasn't *her* truth, for her to
dispense as she wished; it was *the* truth. And the truth is what gets
told in the end: that's what the truth is. It's what finishes all the
lies. I should have said, 'Listen to the word, Katherine: hear it rip
through the air and come to a thud of a stop; just the one, single
note; you don't mess it about or meet it halfway.'

Her sigh was shaky. 'Everyone knows your father had nothing
to do with it.'

'But—'

'*Jane,*' she turned impatient, too tired for this, 'he knows. Edward: he does know.' She was round-eyed, unyielding. 'He knows. You saw him—'

Hit Thomas.

She relinquished me and turned back to the window. 'He knows.' Flatly, accepting.

I was confounded, unable to think how to make her see sense.

And, anyway, she got in first, coming back at me with the challenge, 'Oh, so, what? You want me to go ahead and announce it? Do you? You want me to do that?'

I burst out, 'You have to tell the truth about my father!'

But she seemed bored, as if I were merely being tiresome: 'Everyone knows the truth about your father,' and she batted away the anticipated objection. 'They do, Jane, you kno*w* they do. No one's doubting your father.'

And, actually, wasn't that exactly what I'd thought, all along? Wasn't that what I'd told myself? That no one could possibly believe it of my father.

'But if I tell them what I just told you,' she spoke emphatically slowly, to make clear that she'd already thought it through, 'then they'll know the truth about Thomas, too.' She held me hard in her gaze, letting it sink in. 'And that'd ruin Thomas.'

'Yes, but—'

But what?

'It'd ruin him,' she repeated, 'and you know it.'

I did know it, I supposed; I wished I didn't, but I did.

'He's family, so you'll close ranks.' *Blood Seymours.* 'And he'll stay, but Edward'll make sure nothing ever happens for him, he'll make dead sure of that, you know he will, and it'll become all too obvious, and what with me gone . . .' *Everyone will guess, and it'll ruin him.* 'If I tell the truth, then that'll be the only difference, that'll be all we gain.'

The last word was said lightly, to disparage it. She returned to the winter-blank window. 'He was a boy, Jane.'

Thomas, a year older than me and so alarmingly well versed in the ways of the world.

'Pretty much still is,' she said. 'A boy. It wasn't his fault.'

Hers, then: her fault, and she'd be the one to pay for it. This wasn't quite right, I suspected, but I couldn't see my way through it.

She turned back to me and feigned reasonableness: 'I can't stop you, of course. If you feel you should go ahead and explain.'

It was Thomas, Edward. Listen, everyone, it was actually Thomas.

What, then, though? Were we really to leave the truth half-told and muddled with supposition? Were we all permitted to know what didn't happen – Edward didn't father her son, nor did my father – but not what did? Was she really, honestly suggesting that that was how we leave it?

She was, and, incredible though it is to me now, we did.

3

Queen Catherine faced the truth of her own situation with sadness but no alarm nor rancour, and I was very taken with her refusal to allow the king's lie. Here, I felt, was someone to stick by: if I were to throw my lot in with the queen, I'd be safe. And to be safe, back then, after what had just happened at Wolf Hall, was what mattered.

Weeks went by, became months, and still the queen showed no sign of being unduly troubled. The situation would pass, was probably what she was thinking: the king was in the grip of something, but have faith and show patience and it would pass. Which seemed to me, back then, as good a plan as any. And anyway, right was on her side. Her first marriage, to the brother, had been no marriage – *nothing happened* – and the king knew it. Everyone knew it.

In the meantime, though, Anne Boleyn was allocated her own rooms. In a palace where the rest of us slept three or four to a bed, the king granted that woman a riverside apartment on the floor below and staffed it fit for a queen. Still, it meant that we didn't have to see her any more; at least there was that. Nor did we see any more of quite a few of the queen's ladies, who no longer continued up on to our top flight of stairs. Their voices did, though: we'd be sitting sewing to the incantation of the queen's songbirds and up through the floorboards would come peals and gales of laughter. Once, from the stairs, I glimpsed Thomas and Francis leaving that apartment looking very pleased with themselves.

Edward didn't like her: he told me so as we stood together one day outside the queen's rooms and, below, Anne Boleyn's door was shut too freely, bouncing our gazes into one another's.

'I don't like her any more than you do,' he muttered, 'but I think I know which way the wind's blowing.' He'd come to the queen's apartment requesting to see me – a first – and I'd stepped from under the avid eyes of maids of honour who were unsure if he was a catch: so good-looking and doing so very well for himself, but there was the matter of the repudiated wife and dis-inherited baby sons. He warned me, 'You don't want to get left up here.'

I hadn't asked for his opinion on which way the wind was blowing, and being left with the queen was exactly what I did want. So I said nothing, but that was hardly unusual for me where he was concerned. In any case, he hadn't come to discuss the queen's situation, but to bring me bad news from home, which was, in nearly a year, my only news from home. Margie and Antony had died, he said. The previous day. All I could think at first, standing there, was that he was being cruel; cruel, as I knew he could be. Because how would he even know? Although when, eventually, I did look at him, he seemed weary enough to have ridden all the way there and back.

'It was the Sweat,' he said. Antony first, he told me, and then, later that same day, Margie. I asked him, 'Are you sure?' just in case he'd back down: *Oh, well, actually, Jane, now that you men-tion it* . . .

'Everyone else seems well,' he allowed, and then, unnecessarily, but perhaps glad to be able to account for them, he elucidated. 'Our parents, Liz and Dottie, the little ones.'

The little ones: the boys, Katherine's boys. Something else to know then, and it struck me like a pebble in a wave: there they were at Wolf Hall, and not with Katherine. She'd left vowing that she'd have them follow her. At the time, her departure had been a relief to me, exhausted and confused as I was, but the boys, those little boys. I'd wanted to believe they'd be joining her.

Was she alive? No word of her in almost a year. And news, now, only, of the Sweat. In a nunnery, the Sweat would shift over a row of beds during a single day, like a shaft of sunlight.

I checked with Edward, 'Is there anything else?'

He shook his head.

'Thank you,' I remembered to say, as I turned back to the queen's door, 'for telling me.'

I'd not seen Margie and Antony for almost a year by then, but together they'd made a tune at the back of my mind which had always been playing; if I hadn't been able to make it out note by note, I'd been confident that when the time came, I'd pick it straight back up again. And I'd kept memories of them on me like charms: the golden down that bridged Antony's eyebrows; the garish splash of a vein across his right collarbone; his hair's sleep-scent, and that scent's day-long devil-may-care persistence. Margie's definite parting of her lips before she spoke, sounding a missed beat with which she'd draw our attention; and the dropped stitch in her left eyebrow; the surprising inelegance of her crooked second toes. Did Katherine do that with her own boys, to keep them with her? Gather them to her, bit by bit? I imagined she did. But now Edward had told me that never again in this life would I see Margie and Antony: never see Antony hurl himself through a doorway, taking on trust an unequivocal welcome; never see Margie poking at embers as if they were personally failing her. I knew it, for certain. Katherine, though, she might not even know if her boys were alive or dead.

All those years, at Wolf Hall, of *careful, careful, careful*. Fires to keep away from, carts to keep from under, wells to keep out of, and then along came the Sweat one summer afternoon. My mother would have had a long day of it and in the evening she'd have had to wash down her little girl and boy and lay them out. I remembered drying Antony, once, after his bath; he'd been submitting grudgingly, affecting a slightly sulky rebound from each rub of the cloth when, looking down on my head – which he didn't often get to do – he asked with genuine interest, 'Who will look after me when I'm old?'

I'd been quick to answer, 'Your children,' but I'd had to stare at the floor to compose myself, because it was too much to think of him left to those future children, who would probably only ever know him as wearied and beset. *This* was Antony, I'd felt: this, here, was Antony, boy-brilliant, and all the other, later Antonys would be the ghosts.

Antony would be nineteen now, and a better brother to me, I don't doubt, than Edward and Thomas. And Margie? I like to think there'd have been no Queen Anne, that so-called queen, if Margie had been around. If Margie, rather than me, had come to court, she'd have put that woman straight and seen her off. It's something I remind myself to do: look at the people here through Margie's eyes. She'd have no time for them. And it's when I'm free of all of them – crossing a courtyard, perhaps, alone at the end of the day – that, sometimes, I sense a little of Antony, like a wink of the air itself.

After Edward told me about Margie and Antony, I went back into the queen's apartment to stay because there was no going back: Wolf Hall as I'd left it was no longer there. Where I belonged, from then on, as I saw it, was with the queen. I'd be safe with her; there was nowhere safer. And, hedging his bets,

Edward left me be. So, there I stayed, and Masses were said and meals served, and I didn't look up but threaded silk into silk, stitch by stitch, inch by inch, day by day for another year.

In all that time when we maids and ladies lived up there in that apartment like nuns, our only visitor was the king, who came as often as he ever had and was as affectionate to the queen as he'd ever been. Keen to be seen to do right, I suppose. Keen to keep in her favour in the hope, perhaps, that she'd give in, give him what he wanted, step aside. The queen received him on every occasion like the old friend that he was, but never missed a chance to state how – as he well knew, she said, and as God was her witness – she'd known no husband but him. Those were the only times in more than a year when I felt something like a smile, because it was good to witness him so discomforted. That mighty man was no match for her.

And if, below, that door was flung to and fro in its frame at all hours, it was just noise and, like everything, one day would stop.

To think it easier for a king than a common man to set aside his wife is to forget that a king's wife is a queen. The queen was entitled to have her case heard by the Pope in Rome. First, though, at the king's request, a representative of the Pope was despatched to London, although he took his time coming.

'Rock and a hard place,' sympathised Thomas, whose first proper job had been to accompany Francis to deliver the king's petition to Rome. We were passing each other on the stairs and having to make conversation. 'Devil and the deep blue sea.'

'Better to travel than to arrive,' Francis Bryan laughed, the eye-patch crinkling. 'Life on the road: soft beds and hard harlots.'

If the Pope's man took enough time, Thomas had implied, the situation might resolve itself one way or the other before he arrived. But if everyone else understood the Italian cardinal's reluctance, the queen never seemed to suspect it; she was full of concern for his various travails. When eventually he did reach London, he took straight to bed with a protracted bout of gout.

Once he'd arrived, though, we queen's ladies, too, were to head for London. The case was to be heard in Blackfriars Priory, and both king and queen would lodge separately for the duration in adjacent Bridewell Palace. I was to leave the Greenwich rooms that had for two years been my home, to become a city-dweller. And it was no weather for city-dwelling. The Italian cardinal had brought the heat with him: it'd stuck to him and he'd dragged it into England, where he crawled into bed and it, too, lay down and began to stink. Opening windows only let it in, although open them we did, of course, in desperation. It was heavy work to move the queen's household: clothes and jewels to be packed, linen and hangings and cushions and carpets, plate and utensils, mirrors and candles, the queen's own altar, trestles and beds, clocks, harps and lutes and virginals, the songbirds and the monkey, parchment and ink, soap, grain and wine and cheese, preserves and honey, spices and remedies. It needed to be done because although that old palace in London on the bank of the sludge called the Fleet was ready to receive us, it was entirely empty.

But empty of Anne Boleyn, too: at least there was that. She was to make herself scarce because the Pope's man was in England and there could be no hint of impropriety. He'd come to examine the validity or otherwise of the royal marriage; there was to be no mention of any mistress. Not that he'd be fooled, because no one in Christendom could fail to know of that woman. But, anyway, she was to go back home to Hever, and one day the absence of door-slams made itself felt in the queen's rooms like the sudden cessation of a pain.

In the days before our departure, heat lay like filth on the floors and walls and windows of our Greenwich rooms. When men came to dismantle furniture and heave boxes, the smell of their sweat was so dense and persistent as to make a physical presence of its own, like a malevolent spirit. For we maids and ladies, there was stacking and rolling and folding to do; we whose laps were usually blanketed with needlework were up, instead, and busy. The flush to the queen's cheeks came not just from exertion, though, but from the thrill of her time finally having come. She was to be heard, soon, at last, and what was the truth but that which should be spoken loud and clear?

And so eventually there we were, one morning, stepping aboard the barge, each maid or lady pressing the barge a little lower in the water. The air glittered with midges and the sun shone through the red silk canopy to give us all a bloodied look. Almost three years before, my brother had sent me to the queen to sit and sew and say my prayers, but now I was on my way into battle, and gladly.

At Bridewell, there was no possibility of open windows. The Fleet, which should've been running into the Thames, had died in the heat and lay putrid alongside the palace. Reassembling the household was done in airless rooms; we did most of it at night, like thieves in reverse. During the daytime, the closed windows failed against London's bells, a church on every corner, so that my bones rang with them, and those windows were useless, too, against the noise of the crowds, which I took to be another feature of city life until one of the ladies said, 'Isn't it heartening?' and I realised the clamour was for the queen. I dared a peek and there they were, down in the lanes: hundreds or perhaps thousands of Londoners waving up at us, cheering us on.

And then I thought of my sister-in-law. I couldn't help but recall her up in her room on that last day; of the two of us together at her window, the house cavernous and cold behind us and everywhere beyond us the bleak Savernake Forest. It was unbelievable that it should ever have happened. It shouldn't have happened. I should never have stood by and let it happen, I should never have let Edward send her away. But I hadn't known what to do, hadn't known what else to do, hadn't even known what to think. It'd seemed easiest, at the time, for her to go. And she, herself, had been convinced that she should go, and so were Edward and Thomas, and against the three of them – older and worldly – who, back in those days, was I?

In the case of the queen, though, I knew, it'd be different; thank God it'd be different. Couldn't be more different. London watching – holding a vigil, no less, outside our windows – and no shred of doubt, in this case, as to who was in the right. The queen took to honouring the crowd with her presence, braving open windows and leaning from them as if the air outside were rose-scented, until she received a letter from the king: 'Stop the smiling,' it said, 'you're an incitement to riot.'

Which is treason, it didn't have to say, *and you know the penalty for that.*

Close to a month went by before the Italian cardinal was back on his feet but then, one morning, there he was at our Bridewell door, alongside our own English cardinal, requesting an audience. I doubt it was his idea, he hung back. But, then, none of it was his idea: he'd still have been in bed, if it were up to him, he'd still have been in Rome. The queen never refused a visitor, even when that visitor was Cardinal Wolsey, the king's right-hand man, so she welcomed them both but made a particular fuss of the Italian.

'You must take us as you find us, I'm afraid,' she said, not afraid in the least. We'd been sewing and she had a skein of thread looped over her shoulders. *Business as usual*, said her smile, *I'm sure you understand.*

Cardinal Wolsey himself was built of threads stitched tight in elaborate embroidery, and he was draped in furs and gold chains and medallions; all he lacked was a crown. He was clearly uncomfortable, the hum of sweat all too apparent beneath the incense of which he reeked. He began in Latin.

'In English, please,' smiled the queen. *If you have something to say, we'd all like to hear it.* The Italian cardinal didn't quite hide his smirk. Our cardinal gave us a nervous glance – *incitement to riot* – before continuing: if he and his esteemed colleague might be permitted to offer a suggestion, he said, as to how the whole vexatious matter might be resolved, then perhaps the queen, godly as she was renowned through all Christendom to be, would welcome the opportunity to take up the veil?

A nunnery: they wanted to make a nun of her.

Had they been speaking to Edward?

She smiled her lovely, gentle smile. 'Yes,' she said, 'I'd love that,' and a roomful of ladies whirled to attention, bewildered. 'But,' she blew a sigh, 'God made me the king's wife,' and drew the length of thread from around her neck. 'Now, thank you, your Eminences, for your concern, but will that be all? Because if you'll excuse me' – she flourished the thread – 'I have wifely work to do.'

Oh, I never doubted her; how could I ever have doubted her? There was wrong in the world but she was the one to right it. And two days later came her chance, came the summons and she left for Blackfriars on the arm of gawky Griffin Richards, her Receiver General, allowing none of us to follow because she wanted us waiting on her return.

We all made a dash for the window that gave the best view of the bridge, and there they were, the pair of them edging into that haze of stomach-churning stench: a voluminously crimson-clad queen and a lad fast outgrowing his livery, a sleeve riding high as he waved his free arm at the cloud of flies. They took it at his pace; no doubt he considered it hers, but he was the one picking his way across that bridge with exaggerated care and she, patiently and respectfully, walked even slower than usual for him.

They were inside Blackfriars for no time at all, but word travelled faster and London was already proclaiming her victorious when they came back into view on the far side of that bridge. It was she who was waving now, and not at the flies. The jubilation of the crowd had us press forward at the window and I forgot myself and opened it; no one stopped me, no one said a word or, if they did, I wasn't listening and they didn't really mind.

We didn't know it then but we'd soon learn that she'd declined to take her place on the throne that the king had had built for her in that hall, opposite his own. She'd refused to address the court. Instead, she'd crossed the room to her husband to ask him for justice. She'd knelt and he'd tried to raise her, but she'd shaken him off. She'd never done him wrong, she said. She'd always done right by him, and there was no need for this trial because he was the only one to know the truth of their wedding night and he knew it very well. There he stood, told, and when she requested permission to take her case to Rome, what could he do but grant it?

Getting herself to her feet, she'd glanced around for Griffin – 'Come, Griffin' – and then, with the lightest touch to her helper's cheek as if mindful of fever, said, 'Let's leave them to it.' She'd walked away, leaving the court to weeks of witnesses wrangling over the state of long-ago royal bed linen – *did they, didn't they?* – before Cardinal Campeggio called for an Italian-sized summer break, from which he returned only to refer the case to Rome. The king was stumped and the world well and truly righted.

Or so everyone thought, but, incredibly, Anne Boleyn continued to make herself queen. A confidence trick: there she was, one day, as Lady Anne, well on her way with a bogus coat of arms and liveried servants, and every evening, it was she, now, who presided over the royal entertainments. The real queen kept to her rooms. Sometimes from a staircase window I'd see Anne Boleyn struggling across a courtyard in layers of cloth of gold and ermine, encrusted with jewellery so bulky that it could only have been king-gifted. For all the high-held head, she was scrawny in her too-long sleeves; she was getting on in years. She could dress herself up as queen as much as she liked and sit herself in the queen's chair but she couldn't *be* queen so long as the real one was still living in the queen's apartment. Nevertheless, dissenters were disappearing from the king's household, either going quietly – granted leave – or otherwise. When the queen's favourite bishop narrowly survived a poisoning, his cook was boiled alive for the offence on the order of the king, but no one believed that poor man was to blame. We ladies began locking and bolting every last door at night.

And still Edward left me there. He'd have made the calculation that to remove me would be to draw attention to my having been there so long. Safer to lose me, to leave me lost. After all, it wasn't that I was so much to lose.

4

When the end finally came, it couldn't have been more different from how anyone had imagined. By mid-morning, that July day at Windsor, the queen's advisors were much in evidence in her rooms and, even by their standards, looking worried. Something was up; something new. The queen sat taller than usual to hear from them, braced; and we maids and ladies sat tight, waiting to be informed but careful to give the appearance to the contrary. Something of it percolated down, reached me as a whisper from a fellow maid: the king and his entire household had gone, moved on, disappeared, leaving no word for the queen.

Well, I knew not to believe it. It would have been physically impossible for the king's vast household, hundreds of men with all their various effects, to have sneaked from the very same building in which we'd been sitting sewing, and particularly on a day so fine that our windows were wide open. There they were, those windows, across the room from me, framing a sky of high-rolling cloud; if I were to move nearer, they'd offer up the queen's private rose garden. That was all, though, admittedly: the garden was the view from our room in its entirety; no courtyards, gatehouses, landing stages or thoroughfares.

But even if it were possible – at a push, a considerable push, with considerable preparation – the king would never have done it; he'd never have just left her. Would he? After everything? After all those hearings and petitions and enquiries? None of which, in his view, had achieved anything. Was this, then, how he'd do it?

I stood up, and all eyes in the room came with me: me, standing in the presence of the sitting queen. Barely standing, though: shaking. The queen, concerned, halted her consultation with Lord Mountjoy to say my name, or what passed for my name whenever she, unable quite to sound a 'J', tried to say it. Unbearable though it was to be standing there under all that baffled scrutiny, it'd be worse not to know what was happening outside our room. I glanced around them in disbelief: sitting ducks, lame ducks, did they really not want to know the truth of what was being done to us?

I fled the room – let them think I was sick – for the courtyard, and there at the foot of the staircase it stared back at me: doors oak-dark and windows brilliant with cloud-glaze. No sign or sound of life except the squabbling of house martins in a nest somewhere above me. More than mere absence, the desertion of that courtyard was something accomplished, and its accomplishment was being flourished for me: *See?*

Done.

Gone.

The closed doors and windows were lips tightened and eyes widened in a parody of denial: barefaced, a denial that anyone had ever been here or would ever return. I crossed the courtyard to Hall, only to find the door locked; I hadn't even known that a Hall door *could* be locked; Hall was for anyone and everyone, day and night, whenever the king or queen was in residence.

So, this was how he'd done it: the king was gone, and the queen – this Hall-locking made clear – was no longer the queen.

Chapel, too, was barred, I discovered. How thoroughgoing, then, this locking-up, how pitiless. The queen could worship in her own private closet, but what of the rest of us? As for our more basic, immediate needs, standing there in that fresh air, I didn't have to investigate the kitchens to know that nothing that morning was being cooked. The queen's private kitchen would have to cater for us, for all of us in her household, down to the stable lads, although it was hard to imagine how supplies would stretch and two cooks would cope.

Which was it, I wondered, as I turned back to those walls of windows like shields: were we locked in, or out?

At the gatehouse, I surprised a solitary porter and a dozy dog, which didn't growl so much as clear its throat.

'This is a lady,' the porter reprimanded the dog; then, to me, no less sharply, 'Where did you come from?'

The queen's rooms, I told him.

'No,' he shook his head, 'they've all gone. Early this morning. Just the cleaners left behind.'

I hadn't the heart to break it to him that only he and his dog stood between the queen of England and the big bad world.

Having received a month's notice, the queen began planning a move to a house in Hertfordshire from where she'd concern herself in particular with the plight of her disinherited daughter. She'd have to reduce her household and, at last, word arrived from Edward, as I knew it would, for me to pack up and be ready for him. There was no choice: there was nowhere else for me to go. I'd been away for seven years only to be back where I'd started. When Edward and Thomas came for me, Edward said that he was getting married to Anne Stanhope – one of Anne Boleyn's ladies – and I'd live with them at Elvetham, which Harry and Barbara had vacated in favour of Wolf Hall. I said nothing but, when he rode ahead, I asked Thomas, 'Anne Stanhope?'

Thomas whispered back, 'Says jump, and he jumps.' It amused him, faintly, fleetingly, to have said it, but then he looked away because he knew what I'd been asking, what I couldn't bring myself ask, and either he couldn't or wouldn't answer.

What happened to Katherine?

Because Edward already had a wife, and a wife only stops being a wife if she becomes, instead, a bride of Christ, or if she dies.

Thomas, what's happened to Katherine?

If I'd asked, I'd have had to hear the answer. My throat throbbed with the unvoiced question, and Thomas, awkward, spurred his horse onwards to join his brother.

Edward was carver at the feast to celebrate the coronation of the new so-called queen and a month later was once again at a top table, but this time at his wedding. Then I lived with him and 'Stan' for two years: two years during which came their first two babies to keep me busy. There I was, the spinster sister, and so it had ended for me, as I'd long suspected it would.

5

How, then, did it come to this? How, two years later, could it possibly have come to this? Me, turning queen: me, a May bride, a May queen. I know what people see, or think they see: a Seymour-sister, cleverly Edward-manoeuvred into place. Clever Edward, to realise what it was that he had, shut away at home. Because look at me: no ambition nor zeal, no attraction for other men nor any allegiances bar a muted, long-standing loyalty to the first, recently deceased queen, which now stands in my favour. No interest in any future beyond that of the king's (and just look at these childbearing hips), nor any past of my own.

For anyone remembering anything of the Seymour scandal — if they ever knew much, and are able, a decade later, to recall it — it was a long time ago and far away, and anyway it concerned the old man, whom no one ever sees, and a girl who seems no longer to exist. And in any case, what would the dull Seymour-sister have had to do with it? Just fifteen when the brother married and seventeen when the marriage ended. Everyone thinks I'd have known nothing of what happened and probably only ever knew that long-ago May bride from a distance.

I might be dull but I'm discreet, too, and diligent and dependable – everything that the pretend-queen never was – which makes me perfect, makes me the sensible choice: it makes perfect sense to be making me queen. I can't be bettered. I'd say Edward can't believe his luck, but Edward doesn't believe in luck.

What he believes in is hard work, but this was no work of his, he had nothing to do with this. It's something else he never saw coming. I don't do this to oblige Edward; I do it to honour the old queen. It's for her that I'll usurp her usurper so utterly that no trace remains of that woman. If I didn't do right in the past, if I didn't know how to do right, I'm certainly going to do it now.

And cannon-fire, two miles downriver on this glorious May morning, will get me started. One brutal blast and *the queen is dead, long live the queen.* Will she, herself, hear anything of the split of her own nape under the sword blade? Not that I pity her, but still: the cracking in two of the bony stem of her, the pouring of her blood to the ground. Perhaps I should have been brave enough to ask the king: 'Couldn't she just . . . ?' Perhaps she could have just gone away. Because surely a nunnery would have done.

I'm listening hard for that cannon-blast because I can't have it springing on me when I'm half-stripped and splashing at the washbowl, or spooning preserve onto a piece of bread. Imagine failing to distinguish, quite, between the execution and the growl of a lady-in-waiting's stomach. And I can't *ask*, can I: can't look around those in-waiting eyes and ask, 'Was that . . . ?'

I envy those nearer the Tower, inside the city walls: the explosion barging in on their haggling and their water-lugging, their lute-tuning and floor-brushing. It'll have them glancing skywards even though they'll know that's not where the noise came from, but leave them in no doubt that the deed is done.

I want to be alone when it gets to me; if anyone were here with me, I wouldn't know where to look. I'm keeping to my bed in shutter-darkness. The ladies – my ladies – are across the stairwell in the day room and they think I'm dozing, but the truth is I'm wide awake and lain wide open to what's coming: on top of the bedclothes to take the boom inside my bones and have my body buckle. What I've told the ladies is that I'm ill but not so ill as to need a physician. Just some sleep, I said, just for a little longer. *Go away, all of you.* They didn't like it, of course, because, as queen-in-waiting, I should never be alone, even asleep. My snub-nosed sister-in-law came swishing into the room, tried to cajole me with a falsely cheerful 'This is silly,' but I raised myself on the pillows and said – the first time I've ever said it – 'Do I have to order you?'

Will I hear the cannons? Will that blast really flash two miles along the river to rattle all the little lead teeth of my window and kick its way through the shutters and bed-hangings? If I don't hear them, I'll have to be told; some man of the king's will stalk into this house with the news like a cat with a kill.

As soon as those cannons have sounded, I have a job to do: be queen as if the last one never existed. Give me a job to do and I'll do it, and I'm nothing if not thorough. And in this case it'll be my pleasure. Give me time and no one will so much as remember the name Anne Boleyn. Just give me enough time.

Or I could make a run for it. This – now, here – is my chance to escape, the last ever time in my life that I'll be alone. I should just do it, shouldn't I: dash down the stairs to the river, the landing stage. Plain Jane, washerwoman-hefty, late twenties but with the tread of a woman twenty years heavier, so ordinary that no one would spare me a glance.

But where would I go? To Katherine, is what I've found myself thinking. Well, there's a thought. What would she make of this? She'd never have imagined it for me: this, last of all, and for me, last of all the girls in England, if she ever imagined anything for me, which she almost certainly didn't. If I could go to Katherine, we could disappear together. She's been so good at disappearing. She could show me how it's done.

I've been careful not often to think of her in the decade since she went, and I've had help with that, no Seymour ever again mentioning her in my hearing. Not only did she have to be gone but, like the pretend-queen kneeling now for the swordsman, she was never even to have been. When she left Wolf Hall, the Seymours turned their backs on her and they've kept up that turning, the relentless grind of which has made her nothing beneath it.

6

If mine was no happy ending when I was finally came away from Queen Catherine's household, the king's was much worse. At least there was that. The pretend-queen's household was releasing my new sister-in-law from duties for two weeks of every four and from the beginning she was coming home full of the decline of that new royal so-called marriage. Then, last year, she came with news that almost rendered her speechless: so desperate was the king for a break that he'd be travelling wife-free for the summer and Wolf Hall was on his itinerary. Edward's many years of hard work were to pay off; the Seymours were to be rehabilitated. We were, at last, officially beyond the scandal.

To Wolf Hall, then, for me, after almost a decade's absence, because we Seymours were to be reassembled in the king's gaze as one big, happy family. During my two years in Edward's household, I'd had news of the family – my parents' health, Harry and Barbara's five children, Elizabeth's four, Dottie's two – which I'd been glad to hear, but still I'd found every reason to remain at Elvetham and no one, I noted, had ever objected. Now, though, I was being expected to swallow bad blood and return to a Wolf Hall clean-swept of ghosts. Moreover, I'd have to get to my knees for a king who'd I'd witnessed, at length, ridding himself of his queen.

Come the day of departure, I feigned fever, although it stuck in my throat to do Edward the favour, to hand him the excuse to keep me hidden, the dowdy spinster sister who was complicit in the misdemeanours of his first wife. I failed to reckon on Stan, though, who always gets what she wants and for this biggest of occasions she definitely wanted a united front. She sat pertly on the edge of my bed to pledge herself to my rescue: 'I'll get you there, missy, one way or another. I nursed my poor old mother to her dying day and there's nothing I don't know about levering a big prone lump into her finest clothes.' And I didn't doubt she'd do it: there she was, eyeing my bedcovers and thinking of hoists.

If only to deny her the opportunity to demonstrate those well-honed hoist-wielding capabilities, I did get up – careful, though, to dress then in my oldest, plainest clothes, to look like the nursemaid that, in her household, I practically was. And that was how I came to arrive, a couple of days later, at Wolf Hall's gatehouse, to be put to shame by servants spruce in royal livery. Those same servants were chaotic, though, in their unloading of a delivery of dozens of boxes of oranges, which let me give Stan the slip, and I went to the garden to let my stomach settle and my head clear after those two long days on the road.

The shade of the arbour was bee-drone drowsy and I must have closed my eyes because next I knew, I was being nosed by a dog, and behind the dog was someone dressed in velvet that was closer in kind to liquid or flame and linen so fine that I'd only ever seen the like in the queen's lap, like a fall of spider-silk. Well, I knew better than to raise my eyes any further. To one side of that velvet and linen, though, was Edward, at whom of course it was permissible to look, and I saw it cross his mind to have a stab at denying me, disowning me, pretending I didn't exist: *Moving swiftly on, Your Highness . . .*

The king, though, was already exclaiming.

'My sister Jane,' Edward announced, hurriedly dutiful, 'just arrived.' *By the looks of it.*

I was scrambling to my feet so that I could drop down, but the king tired of it before I'd properly begun and stopped me, catching me absently but deftly by the elbow. I kept my eyes down; his shoes were pearl-fastened, fur-lined.

'Jane.'

It was no more than a repetition but, because he'd spoken my name, I had to look up at him. And had I not been off guard and half-asleep, I'd have managed to hide my shock, but he saw me see him for what he was. Which was nothing, really. All gone, the self-belief that had once made him who he was. He could barely look me in the eye: he, the king, could barely look me, Jane Seymour, in the eye. What I saw was a man who'd made a monumental mistake and knew it, a mistake for which so many people had died, and all for the sake of a woman. What he saw, though, when he looked at me, was that there's nothing I don't know about men who've made mistakes over a woman. There's nothing I don't know about shame. There was nothing he needed to hide from me.

And it really was as simple as that, I think: that's why I'm here – that's why it's me who's here – upriver of that woman and the swordsman.

No block for her, no axe: she'll die with her head up. She was a mistake of the king's but the king never makes a mistake, so she'll be struck out with such speed that no one sees it happen and then the blood will slide in a single wipe from so sharp a blade. For not even three years did England have a pretend-queen. Blink and you've missed it.

*

Thirteen Mays ago, Katherine Filliol stepped across our threshold and for just under three years she was my brother's wife. When she went, something of her lodged in my heart. Sometimes I've thought of it as jewel-like and sometimes malign, but now I see that it has simply been biding its time. Because from tomorrow, there'll be no one who can stop me going to find her, if, in the end, I decide that's what I want to do.

All that is known of Katherine Filliol (Filioll/Fillol) from the historical record is that by the time her father's will was written in 1527, her marriage to Edward Seymour had broken down. Her father left her forty pounds per annum for as long as she remained in an 'honest house of Relegion of wymen'. Neither she nor Edward were left anything else, although Edward disputed the will and had its terms set aside in 1530, whereby he then inherited various manors and lands. In 1534/5, he married Anne Stanhope, and in 1540 had Parliament grant that his second son by Katherine – Edward – should succeed him only if there were no male heirs by Anne or any subsequent wife. There was no mention of the first son, John.

Edward had ten children with Anne Stanhope, nine of whom survived infancy. Edward's second wife was evidently a forceful character, alienating more than a few of his colleagues over the years.

There is no record of what happened to Katherine. The widely believed story that she was repudiated by Edward because she had had an affair with his father comes from a marginal note in Vincent's Baronage, which was added well after the lifetime of the protagonists: *'repudiata quia pater ejus post nuptias eam cognovit'*.

Jane Seymour was betrothed to Henry VIII on 20 May 1536, the day after Anne Boleyn's execution, and married him ten days later. During their marriage, she was instrumental in the rehabilitation of Henry's eldest, estranged daughter, Mary; and in October 1537, she gave birth to a son, Edward, but then died a week and a half later. She was the only one of Henry VIII's consorts to receive a queen's funeral. On All Saints' Day, her embalmed body was borne through black-draped Hampton Court to the chapel, from whence it was moved in a great procession twelve days later to Windsor Castle for burial in St George's Chapel, in the tomb that Henry intended for himself. Their son became king – Edward VI – at the age of nine.

Jane's brothers Edward and Thomas went on to make glittering careers for themselves at court, albeit in very different ways, but both ended up on the block. During the remainder of Henry VIII's reign, Edward had distinguished himself as a soldier and member of the Privy Council, and although the king's will stipulated that a council should rule collectively for the boy-king, Edward was, within days of the new king's accession, elected by that council to be Lord Protector of the Realm. He created himself Duke of Somerset.

As for Thomas, he married the late king's widow – Katherine Parr, dowager queen of England – in 1547 with what was widely viewed as unseemly haste, and then, the following year, when she was pregnant, caused a scandal by his over-familiarity with her fourteen-year-old stepdaughter, Princess Elizabeth. At the time, thanks to Katherine Parr's good sense, disaster was averted, but after she had died in childbirth Thomas was soon back in trouble on this and many other counts, not least his conspicuous efforts to curry favour with the young king at the expense of his brother. Despite his considerable charm (Sir Nicholas Throckmorton, a contemporary, said of him that he was 'fierce in courage, courtly in fashion, in personage stately, in voice magnificent, but somewhat empty of matter'), many councillors tired of his antics and in January 1549 he was arrested, whereupon he refused to answer the thirty-three charges of treason and demanded an open trial.

Keen to avoid that, the council moved against him with a Bill of Attainder, which Edward found impossible to sign at its first presentation. Edward was placed in an extremely difficult position by his brother's arrest, not just in the sense of the personal conflict that he undoubtedly felt, but in the eyes of the world. If he moved against Thomas, he would be guilty of murdering his own brother, but if he didn't, he'd be guilty of favouring a traitor. He would have been painfully aware that some councillors would be glad to see him so compromised and, indeed, it was this faction that ensured that the two brothers didn't meet again after Thomas's arrest, fearing that Edward would be swayed by a personal plea.

In the end, Edward did sign. Thomas was executed in March, refusing to make the usual confessional speech on the scaffold but instead using the opportunity to try to smuggle via his servant two letters for the princesses, warning them that his brother was aiming to estrange their brother from them. When told of his death, Princess Elizabeth is reputed to have said, 'This day died a man of much wit and little judgement.'

During Edward Seymour's time as *de facto* ruler of England (1547–9), far-reaching reforms occurred on religious and social fronts, earning him a great deal of affection among common people, particularly in London, but the period was marred by considerable unrest elsewhere and costly war, as well as his own ostentatious profiteering. Eventually the council, under the increasing influence of John Dudley, moved against him. He was arrested and stripped of the protectorate, but later released and to some extent rehabilitated before being re-arrested and condemned on twenty-nine counts (commonly regarded as trumped-up) of treason. He was executed in 1552.

Of the rest of Jane's family: her brother Henry married again after the death of his first wife, Barbara, and had children either by Barbara or the subsequent wife, before living into old age. Jane's sister Elizabeth's second husband (of three) was Gregory Cromwell, son of Thomas Cromwell, with whom she had several children, and her sister Dorothy also married and had children; both Seymour sisters are believed to have lived into their fifties. Jane's father, Sir John, lived to see her become queen, but died later that year; his wife outlived him by many years.

Jane's own son, Edward VI, in whose short reign much of the Reformation was effected, died aged fifteen in 1553, and was succeeded (after the Lady Jane Grey debacle) by his much older half-sister, Mary ('Bloody Mary'), who then initiated the Counter-Reformation.

After Edward Seymour's execution, his wife, Anne Stanhope, married the household's steward and lived a long life. It is recorded that Katherine Filliol's two sons were with Edward Seymour in the Tower before his execution. The elder, John, died there a few months later, but the younger, Edward, went on to become High Sheriff of Devon and to live to a good age. After the failure of the line with the death of the 7th Duke of Somerset in 1750, the line of descendancy reverted so that it is from Katherine Filliol's son that the current Duke of Somerset (the 19th) is descended.

Acknowledgements

It's very good indeed to be at Little, Brown and to be able to continue working with my editor, Clare Smith: many thanks to those who made the move possible for me, principally my agent, Antony Topping, and Clare herself, and David Shelley, each of whom, in his or her own way, saw me expertly and patiently through what was a difficult time for me.

And then, as if that wasn't enough, Antony and Clare had to tackle the book itself: Antony, first, incisively, and then Clare, at length but always with her characteristic wisdom and grace. Thank you, you two, and you know I mean it.

Thanks, too, for being so welcoming and for doing sterling work on my behalf, to Richard Beswick, Susan de Soissons, Stephen Dumughn, Charlie King, Hollie Smyth, Duncan Spilling, Victoria Pepe and Zoe Gullen.

And thanks as ever to Jo Adams and Carol Painter for the generous, cheerful lend on numerous occasions of Birdcombe Cottage. I was about to say that a lot of this book was written there, but actually, upon reflection, it occurs to me that I spent most of my time there, over the past couple of years, staring at the walls. Lovely walls, though.